CONFRONTING THE DAMNED

"We still do not know for certain during the scan what happened," said one of the specialists. "This species is manifestly not primitive."

"But they fight among themselves," argued one of his colleagues, "which for a species that has achieved their level of technological sophistication is unprecedented."

"There is also the Human itself." All eyes turned to T'var. "It cooperates with the scan and any other examination. It speaks only of peace and friendship and insists that is the ultimate goal of its people."

"I am not interested in why or how as much as I am in whether it can be used against the Amplitur," Caldaq said.

"NO!"

Startled, Caldaq looked down to the medical pallet at the scientist who had mentally interfaced with the Human. She leaned back against the backrest and repeated more quietly, "No. This species as an ally we do not want. Anything to do with them we do not want!"

By Alan Dean Foster
Published by Ballantine Books:

THE BLACK HOLE
CACHALOT
DARK STAR
THE METROGNOME AND OTHER STORIES
MIDWORLD
NOR CRYSTAL TEARS
SENTENCED TO PRISM
SPLINTER OF THE MIND'S EYE
STAR TREK® LOGS ONE—TEN
VOYAGE TO THE CITY OF THE DEAD
. . . WHO NEEDS ENEMIES?
WITH FRIENDS LIKE THESE . . .

The Icerigger Trilogy:
    ICERIGGER
    MISSION TO MOULOKIN
    THE DELUGE DRIVERS

The Adventures of Flinx of the Commonwealth:
    FOR LOVE OF MOTHER-NOT
    THE TAR-AIYM KRANG
    ORPHAN STAR
    THE END OF THE MATTER
    BLOODHYPE
    FLINX IN FLUX

The Damned
    Book One: A CALL TO ARMS
    Book Two: THE FALSE MIRROR

A
CALL TO
ARMS

Book One of The Damned

Alan Dean Foster

A Del Rey Book
BALLANTINE BOOKS • NEW YORK

A Del Rey Book
Published by Ballantine Books

Library of Congress Catalog Card Number: 90-42423

ISBN 0-345-37574-2

Manufactured in the United States of America

First Hardcover Edition: April 1991
First Mass Market Edition: April 1992

Cover Art by Barclay Shaw

For Robert and Melody Bryan:
May all your cats purr,
And carry you wherever you wish to go.

One-who-Decides lay back on the sickle and relaxed, the curved command lounge suspended high above the floor at the end of its powerful, flexible armature. At a touch it would drift higher or lower, left or right so that the Amplitur could inspect, interview, check on, or give advice to those under its command. It could do the same by means of the communications hook clamped snugly across its head, but it believed strongly in the personal touch.

It lay comfortably on the supportive cushion, straddling it with four short, stumpy legs. This arrangement allowed free movement of the two tentacles that protruded from either side of the head. Each ended in four manipulating digits that rippled and flexed lazily as though conducting an unseen orchestra in a silent waltz.

The globular gold-flecked eyes scanned the vast chamber, the slitted pupils expanding and contracting as they focused on specific sectors, seeking positions where efficiency could be improved. When making such suggestions One-who-Decides spoke always encouragingly, never with the brusqueness that characterized other races. The Amplitur had never been harsh. Once, they had been hesitant, but that was all before the Purpose. Before maturity.

Hard to believe there had been a time before the Purpose. One-who-Decides knew it was so because of history. The very idea was alien, an unbelievable fragment of another time and universe. It was realization of the Purpose that had matured and forever altered the Amplitur.

Now it was changing the galaxy.

Prior to realizing the Purpose, the Amplitur had been content to refine their modest civilization: excelling at certain arts, mastering intricacies peculiar to their species, wishing only to be left in peace to develop at their own pace, desiring only to be themselves. Then had come realization of the Purpose.

One-who-Decides gently nudged a control and the sickle swung left and down toward Navigation. How could the Amplitur have existed prior to the Purpose? Baffling!

Early evolution had been entirely instinct-driven. Amplitur lying quietly in the warm waters of the homeworld, barely able to hunch about on muddy shorelines on as yet undeveloped legs as their sensitive tentacles probed the mud for crustaceans and edible bivalves. Amplitur in which intelligence was still a flickering spark, reproducing through mindless budding, creating offshoots of themselves as they converted vegetable matter and animal protein into energy by means of clever intestines and horny mouthparts.

That much it could comprehend. What was difficult to imagine was the Amplitur civilization that had existed prior to the Purpose. It was there for any to examine: in the histories, in the ruins and records of past triumphs, in the steady march of the unique Amplitur technology.

All meant nothing: technology, art, even life itself was meaningless without the Purpose to give form and substance.

Merely pondering it was enough to bestow strength and confidence on the uncertain. One-who-Decides was honored to be an Amplitur in its service.

Crew and ship hummed softly beneath the hovering sickle and its questing passenger. Technicians chatted in their multitudinous languages, exchanging gestures and humor. The latter was a concept the Amplitur struggled hard to understand. That they could comprehend that which they did not themselves possess was a tribute to their perseverance.

Not that it mattered. What mattered was that they all served the Purpose. It was the hallmark of civilization.

Of course, there had been one or two species blind to the Purpose. History told of them as remorselessly as it spoke of advancement. Races who could not be convinced or biologically altered or otherwise persuaded of the truth. The relentlessly hostile and unremittingly insane. Nothing for them but the most reluctant elimination lest they stall the expansion of truth.

This the Amplitur regretted most of all. Not so much because they found the obliteration of an entire species inherently wrong, but because once gone a people could never be integrated into the Purpose. It was a step they had been forced to take only twice in thousands of years. Memory of those isolated catastrophes served to prod the Amplitur and their allies to ever greater efforts.

One-who-Decides was determined that it would never preside over such a failure. Those ancient Deciders had done what was necessary, but the stigma of failure still clung to their bud-lines.

The Amplitur had come far since those times. Many new peoples had joined with them to advance the Purpose, and general knowledge and science had expanded accordingly. Other races contributed mightily to expansion, providing new ways of thinking, new approaches to old problems, each adding its own special abilities to the service of the Purpose.

In this the Amplitur viewed themselves as no better than any other race. All were equal beneath the Purpose. As its discoverers, however, they knew that certain responsibilities accrued to them. These they had not sought and would gladly have surrendered, if a new species capable of assuming the burden had appeared. In the absence of such, the Amplitur continued to serve.

Someone had to make decisions, One-who-Decides knew.

Other peoples contributed in different ways. The Crigolit were fine soldiers who bore the brunt of fighting when that could not be avoided. The Segunians were skillful manufacturers. Multitudes of active T'returi fed many more peoples than themselves. The Molitar, physiologically similar to the Amplitur, supplied brute force and an overawing appearance whenever that was deemed useful. Sometimes an impressive demonstration was enough to convince the recalcitrant to alter their ways.

It was also cost-effective. Combat was wasteful and time-consuming. A life lost in battle was a mind lost to the Purpose.

No reason for such solemnity, One-who-Decides thought. All was going well. Not long ago another intelligence had been brought into the Purpose. Physically powerful but technologically primitive, the Ashregan had resisted only briefly in the face of a technology so far in advance of theirs that they could barely begin to comprehend it. When contacted they were less developed than the Crigolit, more so than the Molitar, and as helpful as any.

Unlike some other peoples, they had wisely chosen not to fight when fighting would have been futile. They had demonstrated unexpected maturity by immediately opening themselves to the beauty and wonder of the Purpose.

That was the inevitable decision of any truly civilized people, One-who-Decides knew as the sickle swung from Navigation toward Internal Engineering. Seeing their commander approach, the staff at that position busied themselves. Their reaction pleased it.

The Commander could not have smiled had it wished to, for its mouthparts were not well designed for expression. Light flashed off its mottled orange skin, the gold and silver streaks which identified individual Amplitur highlighting its torso and head.

The entire wall opposite Engineering was transparent: a concession to aesthetics. Screens and long-range detectors were much more useful for locating objects outside the vessel. The transparency was a testament to Amplitur-allied manufacturing techniques. Within certain physical limits they had achieved perfection, of which the wall was one demonstration.

One-who-Decides studied the streaking stars, the staff responsible for safely convoying a craft full of living organisms between them, and abruptly nudged a control. The sickle shot upward. Many Amplitur were afraid of heights, but not One-who-Decides. It was a thing which could be conquered. One responsible for the safety of many ships could not be dominated by psychological weakness.

It had been driven out through introspection and sheer determination, the kind of determination which had raised One-who-Decides to commander. Modest gratification for much hard work.

It was only a matter of having confidence in the supportive technology, in the padded sickle and the woven fiber armature and the motors that enabled it to move freely above the command center. Not everyone could do it, One-who-Decides knew. Slitted eyes regarded the efficient bustle below the hovering perch.

A dozen different races worked side by side in the Command room while others executed vital functions elsewhere on the ship. None felt superior to its neighbor. Tiny Acaria assisted massive Molitar. Spindly Segunians made way graciously for fluid Ashregan. All were united by the Purpose. All save perhaps a few degenerate individuals, for there were individual exceptions in every species. The crew was a tight unit, their thoughts and actions devoted to a single end.

That was all the Purpose was. An end. There was nothing exotic about it, nothing even a simpleminded Vandir could fail to understand. The Purpose was integration: utter and complete physical, cultural, and mental integration.

When a race reached a certain level of technological and sociological sophistication, it either self-destructed or began a long slide leading to complete cultural degeneration. Voices of promise that might have contributed to a great multiracial civilization vanished in mindless orgies of barbaric self-indulgence or atomic immolation. They were forever lost to the Purpose.

When that happened the Amplitur sorrowed, and their allies in the Purpose sorrowed with them. On such occasions something distinct and unique went out of the cosmos, never to be shared or enjoyed by others.

Once, the Amplitur had actually intervened in a desperate attempt to save a psychotic race from itself, so great was its promise. Such had been the fury, the blind hopelessness, and the depth of self-loathing to which that people had sunk that not even the Amplitur with their peculiar abilities had been able to forestall the cataclysm. In spite of all that could be done, the species perished, destroying itself utterly and rendering its exquisite planet uninhabitable.

One-who-Decides raised the front part of its body, aware that the eight tips of its tentacles had been clenched almost painfully during its thoughts. This was an improper time for such musings. There was work of Purpose to be done.

Sometimes logic and reason were not enough. On such occasions it was necessary to employ primitive but graphic methods to demonstrate new realities to the unenlightened. The Amplitur always regretted this, but not as much as they would have regretted abandoning an intelligent race to the inevitability of self-destruction. As a people, the Amplitur had dedicated their very existence to the prevention of such disasters. As long as they had the will and the strength to help, no species would fail to realize its full potential.

For this sacrifice the Amplitur did not expect even gratitude. Their sole reward lay in the knowledge that by their work they were furthering the Purpose. Merely to *be* Amplitur meant to be ready to sacrifice oneself.

From time to time members of other races and even the occasional Amplitur would question it all. What was the Purpose? What might be its end?

With unfailing logic it was pointed out that the Purpose was the end unto itself. When the work was done, when all had been unified, something greater would manifest itself. For now it was enough to do the work, secure in the knowledge that it was the right work to do. Reason was a wonderful thing, One-who-Decides knew.

But when would an end be made to it all? When every intelligent being in the galaxy had been integrated into the service of the Purpose, it was declared with the certitude of obviousness. And, if Amplitur science eventually succeeded in finding a way of crossing the intergalactic gulfs, when any intelligences there had also been brought into the Purpose.

One-who-Decides could not concern itself overmuch with such weighty matters. There were decisions of much more immediate import to make. Everything that happened aboard ship eventually devolved upon the Commander. It was a responsibility to be accepted with honor.

The heavy body shifted irritably on the cushion. Soon would come the time of reproduction, which could not be allowed until the present effort on behalf of the Purpose had been satisfactorily concluded. Once there had been a time when such biological functions had been dictated by simple hormonal balances. Only in the time of civilization had the Amplitur learned how to adjust their body's endocrine system . . . and those of others.

One-who-Decides could not allow decision-making ability to be impaired by the exigencies of reproduction. A tentacle tip made a note to report for testing. If necessary, a pill could be taken.

Golden eyes studied the vast arc of the transparent wall, pondering the expanse of space outside the ship. Much beauty was to be found in the cascade of stars and worlds, in the iridescent wash of nebulae so like the changing gold and silver patterns that highlighted Amplitur skin. Underspace shifting diffused the shapes beyond, reducing great suns to ethereal blurs of color which only added to their loveliness. Only in the full light of the Purpose could such magnificence be truly appreciated.

One-who-Decides did not have eyes capable of making sense of what they saw. Only advanced instrumentation could do that. With a gentle exhalation the Commander turned back to the sickle's control panel.

This expedition was to be regretted.

The majority of new races readily accepted the logic of the Purpose and embraced it fully upon first encounter with Amplitur envoys. Sometimes the Amplitur's presence was not even required and allied peoples could make the presentation themselves, for the delight of the newly persuaded often exceeded that of their instructors. There were even instances when the enthusiasm of allied races had to be restrained lest they give the wrong impression to those very people they were trying to convince.

Yet there remained those times when reason and logic were not enough. On such occasions a display of the nobility of Purpose was usually sufficient to convert the recalcitrant. A small force of, say, thirty warships suddenly materializing from Underspace in orbit around an indecisive world was often enough to persuade the locals to take the requisite next step up the ladder of galactic civilization so that they, too, might bask in its glory.

Only rarely had it been necessary to use actual force. Like now. Such work the Amplitur found emotionally draining, but they could not in good conscience delegate it wholly to their friends. Their destiny compelled them to participate in such action against their own wishes.

The power arm hummed in response to a command and the sickle plunged its passenger floorward, until it hung a short distance above the highly reflective surface. A passing Ashregan officer blinked and turned in response to the gentle mental touch from One-who-Decides.

"Ship status, engineer?" One-who-Decides was not ignorant of the condition of the vessel, but it would not do for its subordinates to think that their commander spent all its time high above the floor, dreaming upon the sickle.

The Ashregan responded. An efficient species, physically strong but not particularly intelligent or imaginative. One-who-Decides thought of them as catchalls, as nonspecialists who could be relied upon to do a little of everything efficiently but nothing especially well. They made good supervisors, good integrators.

The Commander listened to the report and accepted the slight bow which passed for a sign of respect among the Ashregan peoples before dismissing the officer with a slight mental push that was simultaneously reassuring and rewarding. The ability to do that was the other thing which distinguished the Amplitur from all other intelligences. Even from the Korath, who for sheer intellectual capacity exceeded their Amplitur mentors.

Only the Amplitur possessed projective minds. Only they could convey through thinking alone their wishes, desires, and the pure beauty of the Purpose. All other races were receivers, sensitive to varying degree to Amplitur projections. Those who were naturally deficient could be biologically altered to make them more receptive, and their newfound receptivity passed on to succeeding generations. The Amplitur were deft bioengineers, and the altered races did not object to the procedure. Why should they, when it strengthened their bonds within the Purpose? Furthermore, the Amplitur could only project. They could not truly "read" the minds of their allies. There was no question of invasion of privacy, a basic need which the Amplitur themselves understood.

Talented though they were, the Amplitur had yet to find a way to alter the mind of another being to make it projective. The burden of projection therefore remained heavily and solely their province.

Perhaps that was why the Amplitur had been the race chosen to reveal the Purpose to an ignorant universe, thought One-who-Decides. Other peoples had been given strong legs and muscles to drive them. The invertebrate Amplitur had been compensated for their physical deficiencies with the ability to project. Thanks to their peculiar ability, feelings and actions could be communicated among peoples of antagonistic evolutionary backgrounds, with the Amplitur acting as relays for the demands of the Purpose. There was no loneliness within the Purpose. All worked together to advance it. Perhaps in time another species would achieve projection, or Amplitur scientists would devise a way to modify another mind to project as well as receive. That would be a grand day for all.

And presently one entirely hypothetical, mused One-who-

Decides. Enough to be content with the ample work still to be done.

It might not be necessary to use weapons. The Amplitur could project much besides orders and good feelings. Uncertainty, discomfort, and as a last resort and then only to advance the Purpose, pain. If applied selectively to ruling members of a hesitant species, this was sometimes enough to mute their resistance. When it was not, an individual or two might perish. That was still preferable to an armed assault on the surface of an inhabited world.

That was not going to happen here, One-who-Decides thought firmly. War was the last resort of the incompetent. The proper thing to do was not to place oneself in a position where such an outrage was required. The very thought of it sent a subcutaneous ripple down the mottled torso.

Sometimes the Commander wondered what it would be like to have a skeleton instead of a flexible internal webwork of ligaments and tendons. Bones were an evolutionary throwback, of course, restrictive and confining. They compelled the species to concentrate on physical development to the concurrent neglect of the mind. All the higher intelligences were invertebrates, with only a few exceptions, like the Ashregan and Crigolit.

Amplitur bioengineers had managed to free individual Ashregan from their skeletons. But the results, while functional, were considered aesthetically unpleasing to the species involved. So there was very little work done in that area anymore. The Ashregan and their biological relations were doomed to haul their calcified innards around with them to the end of time. Still, they were accepted as equals within the Purpose, even if the biologists did tend to regard them as evolutionary freaks. They were to be admired, thought One-who-Decides, for having developed intelligence in spite of such a handicap.

That was the true beauty of the Purpose, that it excluded no one. An Ashregan could stand side by side with a Molitar, while an Amplitur mediated between them.

That was what really mattered, the Commander knew. The meeting of minds, the unity of understanding and Purpose. That was what bound together such a diverse assemblage of peoples. Not insignificances like physical differentiation.

The work ahead filled One-who-Decides with trepidation as worst-case scenarios were anticipated. Nevertheless, it would be pursued with vigor and dedication in the knowledge that the end result would be an important expansion of the Purpose and the greater mystery for which it stood.

Just because they were fighting the Sspari did not mean the commander had to like it, even though it was the work for which it had been trained.

Fighting was a disagreeable business, smelling strongly of uncivilization, as did the need to maintain enormous stocks of war material and the fleets to transport it. One could not even take joy in victory, since achieving it would require the death of large numbers of the enemy . . . all intelligent minds lost to the Purpose. The only satisfaction lay in knowing that the surviving Sspari would be fully integrated into the delights of the Purpose. And because those Sspari who would perish would never know that pleasure, One-who-Decides regretted their forthcoming deaths even more than those that might occur among its own kind.

There seemed no other way. All avenues of persuasion had been tried. Though a diminutive and physically unimposing race, the Sspari were possessed of a stubbornness and inability to see reason out of all proportion to their size.

All of which meant nothing, One-who-Decides knew. It was intelligence which mattered. That the Sspari had, though not to any great or unusual degree. Enough, however, to warrant their inclusion in the Purpose, as soon as they could be taught not to resist their own destiny.

Even the traditional show of force had failed to convince, serving only to warn them of what was to come and allowing them time to prepare. The Amplitur knew that might be the result, but they tried it anyway. The peoples of the Purpose did not attack without first trying persuasion. They were integrators, not conquerors.

Next had come the traditional attempt at subverting the government, through innuendo and bribery carried out by allies who physically resembled the Sspari. The morality of such methods was often questioned, but the Amplitur would do anything to avoid war, that obscene offense against reason.

Unfortunately, the government of the Sspari had not fallen.

The resultant conflict had raged for years, with the Sspari occasionally making advances. Though they fought with a tenacity which was as determined as it was foolish, the overwhelming strength and diversity of the Peoples was slowly pushing them back to their homeworld. When the Amplitur gained ground, they rarely surrendered it back no matter what the cost, while the Sspari could be induced to make orderly retreats.

How could they stand against the peoples, who fought from a position of moral as well as physical and intellectual strength? Racial or planetary sovereignty counted for nothing when ranged against the Purpose. Furthermore, the Amplitur possessed the patience of the ages, and the confidence that victory was inevitable. The only variable was time.

One-who-Decides did not understand how the Sspari could fail to see this. Could they not see that full integration was inevitable? That was the destiny of all intelligences, save those two whose extermination had been regretfully required. That would not happen to the Sspari, the Commander vowed. And when the war was over, only a minimum of genetic reengineering would be necessary to insure their eternal happiness.

It was terrible, though, that intelligent beings on both sides had to die to bring that about.

The instrument arc that clung to the Commander's forebody above the eyes provided a steady flow of information about the ongoing battle. Had the flagship been positioned a few more planetary diameters in, it might have been possible to see the small flashes of light which signified the presence of warships dropping troop shuttles to the surface of the Sspari homeworld. Ships of the Purpose would phase out of normal space to be confronted by the Sspari defense forces, there would follow a brief exchange of immensely powerful weaponry, and then one ship or the other would retreat back into Underspace.

The idea of combat in Underspace, at supralight speeds, was naturally absurd. You could hardly do battle when your presumed target outpaced both weapons and tracking devices. So combat took place in orbit around contested worlds, when ships materialized back into real space. If damaged, one could retreat back into Underspace and safety, so long as there was power to do so. Such encounters were a matter of guesswork and seconds.

Real combat took place on the ground, where heavy weapons could not be used lest they fatally damage the very environment an attacker was seeking to control. The trick was to remain safely in real space long enough to land or reinforce troops. It was this that the Sspari were striving so strenuously to prevent. Let the attacking ground forces gain control of the Sspari centers of communication and technology, and there would no longer be reason to fight. The Amplitur had found they could leave the business of policing any postcataclysm fanatics to the local people themselves, once their allegiance to the Purpose had been secured.

One had to admit that for such an unprepossessing folk, the Sspari had fought long and hard. All for nothing. The fleet of the Peoples had reached the Sspari home system. The Sspari had tried to stop them near an impressive three-ringed gas giant, where the fleet had phased out of Underspace. Now they had been pushed back to their homeworld.

The Commander observed it through the towering transparent wall. A lovely world, all brown and green. Soon the command staff would be able to view it in person.

One-who-Decides was honored to direct this final assault force. Mottled orange hide rippled fluidly. It was always an emotional moment when a new species was brought to the Purpose.

At first there would be sadness among the Sspari for those who had perished. But the Amplitur were the kindliest of victors. They required no reparations, desired no vengeance. They wished only that which they had sought from the beginning of the unfortunate conflict: understanding.

Peace would be struck, whereupon the Sspari would find themselves living exactly as they had prior to the war, with the exception that instead of wasting their time striving for individual racial achievement they would now be contributing to the much vaster and more satisfying ends of the Purpose. This often produced an outburst of rage among the population, when they realized that their leaders had led them into battle and sacrifice for nothing.

The Amplitur and their allies would do their best to prevent such a bloodbath from occurring. For now, though, there was a final battle to be won. The information arriving from the ships darting in and out of real space indicated that it should not take much longer.

So it came as something of a shock when Suern of the Korath and Co'oi of the Crigolit swung up in front of the Commander on a sickle of their own.

It was Co'oi who reported through the translator that hung

against her thorax that the landing forces were being attacked in strength by an unknown, hitherto unsuspected group of vessels. One-who-Decides did not panic. That was not in the nature of the Amplitur.

The information arc allowed rapid communication with Amplitur on other ships. There were twelve in all: only twelve among thousands of other peoples, scattered throughout the fleet. Twelve to make final decisions and give advice. They were along more to offer moral support than strategy, since it had been assumed that the Korath and their allies were more than capable of putting an end to the Sspari resistance.

They were also present to aid in dealing with any unexpected developments, of which this certainly seemed to be one.

"I thought the location and number of all surviving Sspari warships down to the last were well known to us?"

"So was thought it," said Co'oi of the Crigolit, antennae twitching uncontrollably.

"Calm yourself," said One-who-Decides, issuing in addition to the words a projection of soothing reassurance. The Crigolit relaxed visibly.

"Explain the apparent contradiction."

"The attacking vessels are other than Sspari." The Korath's voice was almost inaudible. "The fleet has been forced to cancel the planned landing to deal with the new threat."

"How many attacking vessels?" asked One-who-Decides.

"Uncertain still." The Crigolit paused as she listened to the reports competing for time on her headset. "Real-space conflict time is an approximation at best, but the number large is."

"Capabilities?"

"Some weapons new, not yet analyzed. Explosive plasma. Dangerous and difficult to avoid."

"Artificial intelligence guided?"

The Crigolit was hesitant. "Cannot yet be stated with any certitude."

The Commander shifted on the cushion, wishing for the legs of a Molitar. "Change to defensive mode. Break off the proposed landing and contemplate an englobement."

Suern of the Korath spoke up. "Might that not be premature, Commander? The Sspari will gain hope from it. I would rather deal with a dozen unexpected warships than give an enemy new hope."

"I would rather be thought hesitant than reckless. My first concern must be for our own. We can phase to Underspace only a limited number of times. I would not like to be caught in real space, unable to phase out, with an overpowering force waiting for us." One-who-Decides conveyed a mental imperative to the Korath, who blinked. "If this is a clever ploy of the Sspari we will find out soon enough. If not, wisdom dictates caution. We will worry about the psychological effects on the Sspari later. Presently we must do battle with what we can see."

The Crigolit acknowledged with a wave of both antennae while the Korath spread its upper limbs.

One-who-Decides nudged a control and the sickle rose on its flexible arm, shifting to battle control on the far side of the room. Events bode ill. Whence this unexpected assault, these unanticipated reinforcements of a lost cause? Ships of unknown type, new weapons: everything pointed to a space-traversing race other than Ssparian. But the Peoples had been pushing back the Sspari for more than a hundred years. From the moment conflict had been joined to the present day they had no known allies.

Flashing, brightly lit battle predictors gave One-who-Decides more information than had its subordinates. There lay the Sspari, trying to cover the space between their homeworld and the fleet. There the fleet itself was arrayed, ships phasing in and out of Underspace according to traditional tactics. And scattered among them were bright pinpoints of red, vessels of unknown origin trying to time their emergence into real space properly to engage the ships of the Purpose. Injuries were being suffered. Damage was heavy.

One-who-Decides sorrowed for the losses on both sides. It was not afraid for itself. No Amplitur who had served the Purpose for a lifetime feared mere physical dissolution, except insofar as that might inhibit or slow the advance of the Purpose.

There were decisions to be made, and One-who-Decides proposed them. Its good sense and confidence lent strength to worried officers and technicians. Simultaneously it stayed in contact with its fellow Amplitur throughout the fleet. One-who-Listens and Tall-straight-Walker had assumed personal command of the defense.

It was soul-rending to see a glowing dot—bright green in the case of the Peoples' forces, yellow for the Sspari, intense red for the unknowns—vanish from a screen, indication that it had been impacted by a plasma ball or thermonuclear device or some other terrible weapon which caused the loss of hundreds, perhaps thousands of lives. Lights dancing on a screen were feeble indicators of the issues at stake.

So simple and silent, the vanishing of a light. With it perished offspring, families, clanmates, friends; hopes and dreams and fears. Not to mention the setback to the Purpose.

It was foolish and wasteful. The Amplitur passionately hated both.

There was little time for sleep all the rest of that day and the greater part of the following. As the Amplitur required less than many, One-who-Decides was still alert when the critical moment came.

According to the predictors, circumstances had degenerated to the point where a small group of hostiles might successfully interdict any landing without sufficient support from the fleet. This allowed the Sspari to divert vessels from planetary defense to attack.

Even as this was realized, one of the strange alien vessels materialized into normal space concurrent with the flagship. There was a brief exchange of firepower before the flagship could retire once more to Underspace. Damage had been sustained though hull integration had been maintained.

But the Korath had planned well. Inspired by temporary success, the Sspari had diverted too much of their effort to attack. Materializing from Underspace on the far side of the planet, ships of the Peoples managed to put substantial landing forces down on the surface before the defenders could react.

Upon learning this, the remaining Sspari vessels broke away in a desperate attempt to deal with the landing. Their new allies, realizing that the battle they had come to aid was lost, retreated permanently to Underspace.

Essentially the contest for Sspari was over. Ground combat, the real fighting, might take another hundred years, but Sspari resistance had been broken. Final victory was something the Crigolit, Ashregan, and other combative races would achieve. The Amplitur could go home.

Now was time to consider reproduction as well as the identity of those whose appearance had nearly turned triumph into defeat. Whoever they were, they had fought extremely well. Had they arrived earlier, the commander might now be contemplating disaster.

It was clear the unknowns were technologically advanced. More dangerously, they understood the components of warfare and were capable of employing them. Most races could not, being psychologically unsuited to the manipulation of the patently mad. Only extensive bioengineering had made the allies of the Amplitur combat-capable. What sort of methods did these unknown assailants use? It was imperative to learn more about them. One-who-Decides issued directives to that effect.

Not all the enemy had succeeded in avoiding or fleeing destruction. One severely damaged vessel was discovered drifting motionless in orbit, unable to move, unable to seek sanctuary in Underspace.

It was a great stroke of luck. The brief but intense moments of spatial combat between ships only infrequently produced survivors. This was due to the types of weapons used and the unforgiving nature of space itself, whose harsh conditions usually finished what complex weapons had begun.

A Segunian-commanded warship had located such a vessel. Whether its internal life-support systems had survived intact and functioning remained to be determined, but One-who-Decides was hopeful.

Time and careful handling eased the captured vessel alongside the much larger flagship. Its shape was different from those used by the Peoples, but not incomprehensibly so. It was possible to divine function from observation.

Its drive was inoperative, but external inspection showed no evidence of implosion. Its builders were skilled.

Analysis revealed that the light which emerged from unbroken ports filled a normal chunk of the spectrum, suggesting that the crew possessed good vision within familiar parameters. The presence of oxygen and nitrogen in common proportions was noted.

Short of confrontation there was little means of judging physical shape, size, or capability. That was shortly to be remedied by a boarding party. They would go in prepared to deal with resistance but admonished above all else to secure live specimens.

Limited resistance there was, stubborn and frustrating. It was overcome by the introduction of a mild soporific into the ship's ventilation system. A short while later it proved possible to extract the survivors one by one, like so many seeds from a pod. It developed that the appearance of the Sspari's unexpected allies was to be but the first of many surprises.

Instead of finding representatives of one race as was normal, the boarders encountered individuals representing several different species. That much was self-evident even to nonspecialists, who were used to dealing with races whose types could include miniature workers, multiple sexes, or androgynous types like the Amplitur themselves.

That was not the case on board the captured vessel. Its crew was clearly composed of members of half a dozen different species, all working in apparent harmony and cooperation.

It was a discovery fraught with promise as much as threat. For while it meant that the Amplitur and their allies might now have half a dozen new races to battle, it also introduced as many to be integrated into the Purpose.

The Amplitur were overjoyed. For the first time they had encountered a federation of races other than their own. Here was a group of intelligences which had learned to cooperate among themselves without the Purpose to guide them. There was much to be learned from this discovery.

Not all the ships which had come to aid the Sspari had been destroyed. A number had escaped to warn their fellows. That was to be regretted, since it would have been useful to maintain surprise. The Amplitur were not long on regret. It was a waste of protein. They would cope as they had always coped.

The diversity of the captured vessel's crew was impressive. There were even non-oxynitro-breathers aboard: two methane-suckers and one which extracted oxygen from water. Nor were the captives awed by the force they had encountered. They believed that their own federation rivaled in strength that of the Peoples of the Purpose. The delight of the Amplitur was magnified tenfold.

It called itself the Weave. When joined to what the Amplitur had laboriously constructed, it would effectively double in size the Peoples of the Purpose.

A revelation of great import, which the Amplitur recognized with a conference on board the flagship of the expeditionary force. A few high officers among the allied races spoke out against the meeting, lest the Sspari launch a last, desperate attack and catch all the Amplitur vulnerable on a single ship.

The possibility did not trouble the Amplitur. Given such an unlikely happenstance, a Molitar or Korath could take over and finish the resultant battle effectively. The Amplitur regretted the dependence which their allies occasionally displayed. Did they not realize that within the Purpose, all peoples were equal?

Fast-blue-Breeder had requested the meeting. The moment needed to be commemorated.

As they gathered aboard the flagship there was much intertwining of tentacles tips and soft husking of mouthparts. Despite the stress of the expedition and attendant combat, two of the Amplitur were reproducing. Following a fifteen-month gestation period, the large buds blossoming from their backs would be carefully removed and placed in nursery environments to mature as new individuals.

Until that time the budding infants would depend on nutrients supplied by their parenting bodies. Though immobile, they were capable of learning, both through observation and the instruction offered via intimate telepathic communion with their parent.

In a cleared recreation chamber the commander of the captured vessel was brought before the gathering. The locale had been selected to reassure, not to impress.

In addition to the Amplitur a number of Crigolit technicians were present, together with some Segunian go-betweens. A single Molitar guarded the doorway, its bulk effectively obscuring it.

The twelve Amplitur rested in a semicircle as the tall, thin alien faced them. He favored one of two legs, obviously injured. Within the fleet which had attempted to aid the Sspari he ranked somewhere in the middle. Not the equivalent of One-who-Decides, but higher than a technician.

The thin frame was covered with fur and the short snout filled with sharp teeth. It was vertebrate and male, which was not as surprising as the fact that all the races of the captured ship were vertebrates.

Preliminary research suggested that the organization to which these diverse species belonged, their "Weave," was as contentious as it was powerful. Arguments and even actual combat between members was endemic.

The Amplitur understood. To be united within the Purpose was very different from being tenuously tied together by feeble treaties and imperfect alliances. The latter bespoke an organization strong only militarily. Offered the beauty and inevitability of the Purpose, the fractious peoples who comprised the Weave would eventually put aside their disagreements and arms to join together with the more mature intelligences of the Purpose.

None of the languages utilized aboard the captured vessel were especially complex, including that of the ship's commander. Mechanical translation was feasible. The Amplitur, of course, had no need of it.

The alien regarded his captors, straining to isolate shapes in the dim reddish light. One of the observers noted his difficulty and ventured a solicitous projection. "Is the illumination too weak for you?"

The alien officer stumbled and clutched reflexively at his head. "Who said that?"

When no reply was forthcoming he took several long strides forward. His long muscular arms and sharp teeth could have inflicted considerable damage on the slow, soft body of an Amplitur, were it not for the gentle restraining field that stopped him. He felt of it hesitantly before backing away.

"Can he see us?" one of the other Amplitur thought generally.

"We have been assured," Fast-blue-Breeder opined, "that his vision is competent within the accepted spectrum, which is to say that it is efficient and like that of the majority of our allies in being shifted further toward the ultraviolet than our own. Nonetheless . . ." At Fast-blue-Breeder's direction, brighter light filled the room.

The alien regarded the twelve silent Amplitur. Tentacles and their manipulative digits wove silent, indecipherable patterns in the air. His mind simmered with uncertainty.

Fast-blue-Breeder raised one tentacle and spread the four digits by way of greeting.

"We mean you no harm."

"You show otherwise," the alien responded.

"You attacked us. We responded as necessary. We are told that your name is Prinac and that you are the ranking surviving officer of the vessel now under our control."

"What are you going to do with us?" the alien asked sharply. Its black nose and ears were in constant motion.

"Brusque and impolite." The thought occurred to all the Amplitur simultaneously. "Indicative of a primitive species not long a-venturing."

"You will not be harmed," said Soon-dark-Concerning, a half-mature bud bobbing gently on its back, silent and observing. "You are going to be brought into the Purpose."

"What is this 'Purpose'?" the alien inquired. "That is all we have heard about since you took us, this 'Purpose' thing."

One of the other Amplitur explained.

"And what if we do not want to join your Purpose, like the Sspari who requested our help?"

"There is no choice for an intelligent race. Were we not here speaking with you now, there would still be no choice. Eventually the Purpose would find you. It is what it is."

"Maybe it's not what it is for us," countered Prinac. "What then?"

"You will be persuaded." The Amplitur wondered why this was so, that so many races were slow to see the beauty and wonder of the Purpose.

The alien commander adopted a typical bipedal defensive posture: legs bent, hands extended. A primitive display, thought One-who-Decides, for all that it was backed by apparent intelligence.

"My people can be very hard to 'persuade.' As can our Weave allies."

"You are not truly united," said one of the other Amplitur. "You argue among yourselves, but rarely resort to combat."

"We are not by nature inclined to combat," Prinac shot back, "violence being the hallmark of the uncivilized."

"On this we are agreed," thought Fast-blue-Breeder communally.

"But we will fight if necessary to avoid being conquered by anything like you."

"We do not 'conquer.'" There was exasperation in the thoughts of the Amplitur who replied. "Within the Purpose all are equal. So shall you be with us."

"From what I have seen and heard," the alien responded, relaxing a little, "you Amplitur seem to be a little more equal than any of your friends."

"We were the first to realize the Purpose, the first to understand its implications." One-who-Decides gestured imploringly. "You must realize that nothing you can say, no objection you can raise, is new to us. It has all been said and raised by dozens of races before you.

"If we were the conquerors you speak of, how is it that in this vast force which has defeated the objections of the Sspari and driven your own allies into thoughtfulness we number only twelve?"

It made the alien hesitate. Double lids blinked.

"That is the truth? This is all of you in the whole fleet?"

"We always tell the truth," said Fast-blue-Breeder. "When one struggles to serve and understand the Purpose, there is no rationale for prevarication. It is wasteful."

"We possess no extraordinary physical strength or fighting ability," said another of the twelve. "The soldiers aboard this one vessel could overpower us easily any time they wished."

"Why don't they?" asked Prinac stiffly.

"Understanding the Purpose, they have no wish to."

"Well, I do not understand, and I do not want to, nor does any of my crew."

"Understanding takes time. In a universe as vast as ours, revelation is in short supply. It is anyway a better thing when understanding arrives through study and thoughtfulness rather than coercion. Then one *truly* understands."

The alien hesitated. "You have said that you are not going to harm us. What *are* you going to do with us?"

To the Weave commander it appeared as if those confronting him had suddenly gone comatose. In reality they were conferencing. Nor was it the first time they had done so. His eyes widened in realization, the slit pupils expanding horizontally.

"Telepathy is a fantasy, direct mind-to-mind communication a dream. It violates the laws of conservation of energy as we understand them. But you can do it, can't you? You really can?"

"It is a survival trait unique to us," One-who-Decides explained gently. "In its early days our world was an extremely primitive and hostile place. Despite this ability we do not feel that it makes us any better than any other people. Only different."

For the first time, the alien commander projected fear. "Can you read my mind?"

"No," said one of the Amplitur quickly. "And remember that we always speak the truth."

"If you cannot read another mind, how do you . . . ?"

"We project. That is the gift. Anyone can receive. That ability lies dormant in most developed minds. With none to project to you, you do not even realize it is present.

"If you observe carefully you will see that none of us has been moving our mouthparts, though we are quite capable of communicating by means of modulated sound waves, as you do. We have been projecting to you from the moment you appeared before us. Having never been projected to before, you naturally assumed that we were communicating with you by means of sound waves. That has not been the case.

"As you will also note, there is nothing in the least detrimental or harmful about the process."

"That does not answer my question. What are you going to do with us?"

"I think," replied One-who-Decides, the matter having been already agreed upon, "that we will assist you in repairing your ship."

"What's that?" Prinac blinked again.

"We will help you to fix your vessel to the best of our ability. Since the mathematics are unvarying, the means for traveling through Underspace are universally similar. Only materials and design differ.

"We intend to allow you and your crew to return to your home. Though we had no quarrel with you, your people attacked our ships and killed many. You will serve as messengers, apprising your people of our existence and intent. Hold nothing back, tell everything. We will supply you with additional information and statistics where your own observation is inadequate.

"I sense your fear. You will not be interrogated or mind-altered or otherwise persuaded against your individual will to do any of this. Should you choose to do so, you may say nothing, or invent your own tales. We cannot prevent that. You will simply be provided with information. It will be your choice as intelligent beings to disseminate or conceal this information as you see fit. Surely you cannot fear ideas!

"Nothing will be concealed within your ship or implanted upon your physical person, although we could easily do both."

Long-burdened-Walker moved slightly forward and demonstrated.

The Weave officer suddenly bent double, his hands clasping the sides of his head as he dropped to his knees. It lasted only for an instant but took longer for him to recover. When he rose shakily, his hands were trembling and his tongue was hanging out of the side of his mouth.

"What—what was that? What did you *do*?"

"There are many means of communication." One-who-Decides projected compassionately. "Are you still in pain? Do you require the attention of a physician?"

"No," said Prinac weakly. "No, I will be all right." His expression, such as it was, had changed radically. "Which of you did that?"

"It does not matter." One-who-Decides gestured with a tentacle. "Any of us are capable of such communication."

Prinac took a deep shuddering breath. "I begin to understand how twelve of you can control a force of this size."

One-who-Decides was appalled at the implication. "We do not do so through that type of communication."

"You do not have to. It is enough for those serving you to know that you *can*. This is how you keep everyone in line."

"No one is 'kept in line.' We are all servants of the Purpose together." One-who-Decides strove to be patient in the face of such ignorance. "You will come to realize this, and then you will be ashamed of your thoughts.

"You may choose to resist with force. You know that you would not be the first to do so. It results only in unnecessary suffering on both sides, since in the end all are contentedly integrated into the Purpose. When that day comes you will no longer fight and argue among yourselves, understanding as you will the true meaning of existence. Archaic concepts such as interspecies conflict over simple physical differences or mental outlook will disappear."

"We might beat you, you know. You have no idea how strong the Weave is. And you will not learn more from me, my crew, or our ship's storage facilities. Because no one knows how big the Weave is, exactly. I do not think you have ever faced anything like it."

"It matters not. Without a singleness of purpose to unite, there can be no true strength. You live lives of aimlessness and wasted existence and can therefore pose no real threat to us. The Purpose is not the Amplitur, nor is it our allies. It exists exclusive of us, outside and beyond us, the real reason for everything that is. You cannot defeat that.''

''That is to be seen,'' replied Prinac even as he sounded less confident of his own power and philosophy.

It might take a little longer, One-who-Decides mused. It was often such to varying degrees with primitive peoples. Gentle persuasion and reassurance almost always worked, though it was true they had never before encountered an organization like this Weave. But what an astoundingly grand opportunity it presented!

Elation flowed between the twelve. Not one, not six, but an unknown number of new intelligences to bring to the Purpose. This was one of the seminal moments of history, and it was a privilege simply to be present.

He felt a great love and affection for this Prinac; representative of an alien species, commander of a hostile warship. The projection rolled out from all and they could see that the Weave officer was affected by it.

''You are mad'' was his response when the wave had subsided. ''I do not love you. I do not love your Purpose. I do not love anything about you. Your intentions I find repulsive and your persons unpleasant. I especially do not like the way you treat your slave peoples.''

''Slave peoples? What is a slave?'' inquired another of the Amplitur.

Prinac explained.

There was some uncertainty among the twelve. ''This concept is foreign to us. We do not understand what you mean.''

''I will try to clarify.''

Still the Amplitur failed to understand.

''There is no slavery, as you call this thing, within the Purpose. How can there be, with all intelligences being equal?''

''But you are not equal. You Amplitur are in control, whether by virtue of the fact that this 'Purpose' is your creation or through your ability to project telepathically. You control and the rest are subject to you. They do not try to rebel because they are afraid.''

''You display ignorance, which is understandable.'' One-who-Decides spoke, resorting to words for the aesthetic effect.

"You there! Scomatt, third officer of the Crigolit. I am One-who-Decides. Are you afraid of me?"

"Of course not," said the Crigolit. "We work within and for the Purpose, and furthermore, we are friends."

The fleet commander projected satisfaction, which the alien, too, could not fail to feel. "You over there, Aswen of the Segunia. Do you fear me?"

The response was the same from all, even from the huge Molitar who guarded the door and could have crushed every Amplitur in the room before mere weaponry could have reduced it to a pile of disorganized jelly.

Fast-blue-Breeder regarded the prisoner. "We do not understand what you accuse us of."

"Because you are blind to it."

"Are you so certain that it is we who are blind? We offer you cooperation, understanding, empathy, and openness within the Purpose and you respond with fear of domination. Why do you think your vision so much more acute than ours? Why should it not be the other way around?"

"All I can say is that my own people will never be part of your Purpose, no matter what you do. You can hurt me up here," and he tapped the side of his angular skull, "even kill me, but it will not matter."

"We intend no such thing." The Amplitur were shocked at the notion. "We do not wish to kill anyone."

"Tell that to those who crewed the ships you destroyed."

"They attacked us," One-who-Decides reminded the alien. "I say again that we had no quarrel with you and your kind."

"The Sspari came to the Weave. They explained what was happening. Many within the Weave were reluctant to send help because they did not want to get involved, but others saw rightly that you would find us eventually. Better to find out what we might be up against as soon as possible than to wait for you to surprise us." The alien's thoughts were awash with obvious pride. "That is what the Weave is about."

"It sounds not so very different from the Purpose," observed another of the Amplitur. "Save that you argue among yourselves to no end."

"We value our independence," Prinac told them. "Something your 'allies' seem to have forgotten."

"All are free to act as they wish," said One-who-Decides,

"within the Purpose. Daily life differs on all worlds, among all races. Neither we nor anyone else interferes with another race's culture or art or traditions. Within that context we all strive toward a greater common goal, one which renders all friends. Not masters and slaves, as you describe it."

"This is not for my people, nor I think for any others within the Weave."

"Do you not see," said a tired Amplitur, "that the very discussion we are now having has occurred many times in the past, and that the end is always the same?"

"Perhaps this time it will be different."

"No, it will not be different." One-who-Decides moved forward on short, stumpy legs. "It may happen quickly or it may take much time, but no other outcome is possible. The Purpose is the Purpose. So it has been for thousands of years. This will not change."

"And in spite of everything I have said, you are still going to help fix my ship and let me go?"

"Have I not said that we speak always the truth? The message must be conveyed. It is horrid that many had to die to allow that. Fortunately many of your ships escaped to safety."

"Yes, I imagine that surprised you." The alien did not try to conceal his satisfaction.

"It did not surprise us, and it pleases us. We regret the loss of any individual intelligence in a universe of millions of worlds inhabited by perhaps thousands of intelligences. The death of even one diminishes the Purpose."

"You really are a strange bunch," Prinac commented, scratching his long upper lip. "If you were not fanatics you might even be likable."

"Fanaticism and dedication are terms whose parameters could be argued endlessly. We believe we are dedicated. We already like you; for your forthrightness, your honesty, and your bravery."

"Don't like me. I prefer it that way."

"On this thing we must insist." One-who-Decides gestured with a tentacle, the manipulative digits lining up to point. "Go back to your vessel, to your own people and to your allies. Tell them of what you have seen. You will be supplied with all the information your storage facilities can accept. What you do with it is your concern.

"We ask only that you do not censor. Let others judge as freely as we let you judge. Reveal or destroy, but do not modify.

"We will not be able to monitor your actions or affect them in any way. The range of our ability to project is short."

"How can I be sure of that? How do I know you are not telling me that when you could actually influence me or my crew over a considerable distance?"

"If we meant you harm, intended to try and 'control' you," Fast-blue-Breeder pointed out, "why would we tell you otherwise? Why not simply do it?"

"I do not know." Prinac let out a short, whistling breath. "I am not a philosopher; only an officer on a small ship."

"Then do not take decisions of great import upon yourself. Let others observe, analyze, decide. Think for yourself. In this be," and there was something akin to mild amusement in the Amplitur's projection, "independent."

"I admit I do not understand you people." Prinac started to back away from the twelve, in the direction of the single doorway. No one moved to stop him. "All I can say is that we will never be a cog in your Purpose."

One-who-Decides directed the Molitar to move aside. " 'Never' is a term we understand, I think, far better than you."

Chichuntu was a sublimely beautiful world, elegant and refined as its inhabitants. The Wais were ornithorps: tall, quiet, manicured of manner and appearance, rarely flustered, and always comfortable no matter what their surroundings.

They possessed the kind of self-control, Caldaq thought, that had always eluded the Massood. Their uniforms were never dirty and they walked as if dancing. Polite they were in conversation, and formally correct without being unctuously so. Wais society was perhaps the most complex in the entire Weave. Every movement, every gesture and inflection contained multiple levels of meaning and implication, usually comprehensible only to another Wais. Compared to their own language and culture, those of the other races were simple, almost childlike. They were also natural mimics. The combination made them unsurpassed linguists.

Because of this, Wais worlds were often chosen to serve as regional command bases despite the formalized protests of the inhabitants. It was pointed out that because the Wais were so polite and correct, their presence and indeed their society itself had a meliorating effect on the more contentious members of the Weave, where everyone lived in fear of giving casual offense to his neighbor.

It was hard, however, to become upset during a discussion moderated by a Wais, to shout imprecations and insults to a Wais translator knowing that it would automatically moderate both accusation and response. Oftentimes shame and embarrassment prevented trouble before it could happen.

A regional command center seemed out of place on a world

like Chichuntu. On Massoodai, for example, it would have been sited far away from any metropolitan area, or buried deep within granite mountains. The Wais had insisted on placing it within the boundaries of a major city park, and had proceeded to beautify it with fountains and landscaping.

Indeed, this whole world was one vast park, Caldaq mused. It was not to his liking. Too many hedges, too many closely planted trees. He would have preferred open plains, where trees clustered in small, defined places or grew respectable distances from one another. Where a Massood could move traditionally, as his ancestors had traveled, fully utilizing his long legs, covering distances with great strides. Not in pursuit of trade or quarry, but something more honorable.

To run long, leap far, jump high: that was what the Massood did best. It was because of that tradition, because sport held importance within Massood culture, that they had turned out to be one of the few Weave races suited to combat. It was a task they had assumed reluctantly, as would any intelligent species.

But someone had to do the actual fighting. The S'van and the Hivistahm and the Lepar and even the Wais contributed much in the way of support, but when it came to combat they were not of much use.

Besides the Massood, only the Chirinaldo made decent soldiers, and those dizzy heliox-breathers were poor companions on a blasted battlefield.

He adjusted his dress vest and shorts, smoothing out the short gray fur that peered from beneath the hems. The irises of his eyes were a lighter gray, the vertical pupils almost black. At the same time he tried to relax. That was something of a contradiction in terms. A Massood could not really relax. Immaterial on the battlefield, it often kept them from promotion to command positions, where the presence of a calmer S'van was more reassuring.

Therefore it was doubly significant that Caldaq, being not only Massood but young, had been given captaincy of a ship.

The honor was not unprecedented, but it was uncommon. Awareness of this only contributed to his nervousness. The trimmed whiskers at the end of his muzzle twitched maniacally.

Curling one upper lip, he dug with a neatly trimmed claw at a bit of food that had lodged between two molars. Extracting the fragment, he examined it idly, glanced around to make sure no one was watching him. Ancestors forbid a Wais should catch him spitting on their groomed grounds. He derived a perverse pleasure from doing so.

What did Command want with him? His thoughts were a jumble of hopes and suspicions.

He made a last check of his person, which would have seemed immaculate to any but a Wais, ran a claw tip over his teeth one more time, and paused briefly to sniff the air ahead. It smelled of green growing things and flowers. There were flowers everywhere on this world. It confused his sense of smell.

Regional Command was located in an unprepossessing structure surrounded by a decorative lake. Once long ago he had accompanied his parents to such a place. They had been soldiers as well, though none had risen so high. He was acutely mindful of his responsibilities.

His parents hadn't wished to be fighters any more than he had, but since the Massood were just about the only Weave species which did not go into shock on the battlefield they had little choice. At least there was no lack of backup and support from those many races they helped to defend. The Massood did not have to manufacture any tools, grow their own food. Everything was done for them by those Weave peoples incapable of participating in combat.

The black tuft normally present at the tip of each ear was missing from his left one. He flicked it repeatedly with a finger, a nervous habit. It was a genetic shortcoming often remarked upon by females. It marked him as distinctive, though not necessarily attractive.

Inside, he followed the readout display which floated in front of his eyes, guiding him.

What do they want with me? he wondered. On the whole, I'd rather be running.

He was a fine runner, too. Not as good a jumper, which was surprising considering his height. His most pronounced talents, however, were not visible, such as his ability to pause and consider before leaping into battle.

The Amplitur, now, could simply bioengineer such desirable characteristics into their client races. Since the Weave could not, it was forced to make use of existing biological diversity among its citizens, diversity which sometimes threatened to tear the fragile coalition apart. Internal dissension was commonplace. Only the threat posed by the hated Amplitur held it together.

Massood edginess could contribute to this dissension when concentrated in the confined compartments of a ship. A nervous captain wasn't considered the most suitable to command a warship crewed by members of very different, highly argumentative races. Only Caldaq's ability to control his natural instincts had enabled him to achieve that exalted position at such a youthful age.

Other Massood frequently asked how he'd managed it. He tried to explain that it was a matter of thinking differently, of controlling one's feelings as much as one's metabolism. Easier to speak of it than put it into practice, they replied.

He was several floors above the lake when the automatic door admitted him to his destination, after first running a thorough check on his identity. The Amplitur were not above reengineering similar physical types within their dominion to resemble members of Weave species and then sending them forth to instigate trouble on specific worlds.

For example, one of the Amplitur client peoples closely resembled the Hivistahm, and they caused considerable trouble every time their agents were slipped onto a Hivistahm-populated world. It was left to the locals to root out the infiltrators, which they did with varying degrees of success.

He didn't much care for the Hivistahm. They were scaly green complainers, always dreaming of home, their fine-boned fingers capable of engineering and tech work beyond the ability of the most skilled Massood. Somber, homesick, and serious, they were not the best of company on a long voyage. But their dedication and talents made them invaluable to the war effort.

Caldaq was grateful that there were no client races of the Amplitur who resembled the Massood.

Brun was waiting for him. Like many S'van, he occupied an executive position, having risen far faster in the command hierarchy than was possible for any Massood. Caldaq was not jealous of this. It was the way things were.

Like the Massood the S'van were mammalian. There the similarities ended. The S'van were short vegetarians, not as sophisticated as the Wais but more so than the Massood. Their squat, hirsute bodies were clad in practical clothing devoid of adornment. They were given to boisterous love songs and highly emotional renditions of complex poetry.

Though not the linguists that the Wais were, they were comfortable among strangers, from the fighting Massood to the simple and often incomprehensible Lepar. Their nonthreatening appearance was a major reason why they were able to get along so well with representatives of many different species.

Mentally they were lightning-quick, invariably making the right decisions at difficult moments. Not just for themselves, but for everyone else. It was only natural that they should rise to positions of importance.

If someone was smarter than you, it was a fact to be accepted, not an opinion to be argued. You could object, take command yourself, and die nobly, or let a S'van make the right battlefield decision and live. War was not a sport. Caldaq was content to take orders from hairy, good-natured S'van, as were the rest of the Massood.

It was different with other races. Because of its very nature a Wais giving orders could be insufferable. That inbred attitude of superiority rapidly grew tiring. But the S'van entertained no such illusions, cultural or otherwise. They were regular people. Just smarter than everyone else. If one irritated you, you could pick it up and toss it out the nearest window. Metaphorically speaking, of course. In many ways it was the S'van and not the Wais who held the Weave together.

Brun was typical of his kind. Much older on the relational scale than Caldaq and half his height. Stocky, tailless, with a blunt flat face displaying rounded grinding teeth. Tightly curled black hair spilled over his head like oil from a fountain, trimmed to expose the eyes, nostrils and mouth. The impenetrable beard, like a creeping jungle, had to be cut back every three days.

Though his salutation was cheery as ever, Caldaq thought he detected an uncharacteristic undercurrent of concern. Save for him and his host the office was empty. This was flattering but it also made Caldaq wary. He was being singled out for something. Whether good or bad he did not yet know.

For all that Brun was so much shorter he didn't seem so. Perhaps it was the air of confidence which accrued to many S'van. Perhaps it was the fact that he was a regional commander.

"Problems?" Caldaq spoke fairly good S'van. Like its originators it was deceptively simple. The language was capable of vast elaboration.

"What do you think?"

Caldaq considered. "It is rumored that the Amplitur and Crigolit are massing with the T'returi for a major assault in the vicinity of the Jiidge worlds."

"Then you know as much as anyone else." Brun's voice was liquid and perfect. He paced away from the Massood—not out of fear or dislike but so he wouldn't have to crane his neck as much to see the captain's gaze.

The commander led him through a door and into a refulgent starfield. Stepping into a projection room was exactly like emerging from the hull of a ship into deep space. Except the stars were not real but rather exquisite simulations which could be expanded or contracted like the field itself at an operator's whim.

As they walked through the projection the room automatically sensed where their feet would fall and provided the necessary transitory support. It would supply steps or downramps as required.

Each point of light could be enlarged to show an entire system. Caldaq recognized many of them. After all, the display encompassed only a small part of the galaxy. It was difficult enough to try and memorize the relative positions of the worlds of the Weave, the Amplitur, and those in the immediate vicinity without trying to deal with the incomprehensible vastness beyond.

Other dots when expanded would reveal themselves to be ships, or whole fleets. Within the projection a complete corner of the galaxy was represented, with its inhabited worlds, suns, nebulae, and baffling instruments of warfare. He noted combat activity in the Protan Sector. With Brun's permission he voiced a request to the machine. That portion of the projection obediently expanded to show individual vessels orbiting a world. Everything he was witnessing in miniature was happening in real time, parsecs distant. It gave one pause.

Not the projection itself. That was simply a superb example of Hivistahm-O'o'yan workmanship based on S'van design and a probable Turlog overview.

No, what was truly awesome was the idea of trying to conduct war on a galactic scale, moving ships and personnel through hundreds of parsecs of real space. To keep the conflict lumbering along required every iota of scientific and technological skill both the Weave and the Amplitur could muster.

What wore you down, Caldaq mused, was not the Amplitur's skill in combat or their ability to make the best use of their allies. It was their patience, the sense of inevitability they strove to project. No matter how many defeats you inflicted on them, no matter the extent of their losses, they never entertained thoughts of surrender.

Hundreds of years ago it had been accepted that they would have to be utterly destroyed in order to end the war. A daunting project when one considered the fact that the location of the Amplitur homeworld was unknown. The Weave hadn't the slightest idea how far back in the starfield it lay, or even in what direction. There were times when the task seemed hopeless.

The alternative was terrifyingly simple. You didn't have to fight the Amplitur. All you had to do was join them in their Purpose, become one more component of whatever structure it was they were dedicated to building.

Trouble was, they held all the controls. If you gave in, as one or two species had, there was no going back. No chance to reconsider. In all the hundreds of years it had been fighting, the Weave had yet to encounter a single race that had been allowed the privilege of changing its mind. The Amplitur were careful. There could be recalcitrant people, but not recalcitrant genes. Give in to the Amplitur, give in to their Purpose, and you acknowledged their right to mess with your DNA.

Now that was truly frightening.

Caldaq ordered the expanded scene to return to scale. World and orbiting vessels vanished, subsumed once more by the immensity of their surroundings.

Brun led him on. There was no up or down inside the projection, no back or forward save as it related to your own perception. Many became uneasy inside the projection and had to be led out. It made the Wais uncomfortable. A huge, powerful Chirinaldo with its love of bright illumination would have found it intolerable. Caldaq thought the darkness and simulated stars relaxing.

"You are anxious to fight." Brun had climbed a couple of invisible steps and turned, now eye to eye with his companion.

Caldaq could have matched his ascent, but that would have been impolite.

"No one with half a brain is anxious to fight. Better to say I am impatient to participate. It is what I have been trained to do."

"And in an exemplary manner, too. I've studied your record. There are those who think you show exceptional potential. Based on personal acquaintance, I naturally dispute that."

A joke, Caldaq knew. His whiskers quivered and his nose twitched, as did the tips of his fingers. The S'van were always joking. They could joke about extinction, or the end of entropy. The Massood had their own sense of humor. It was only that the S'van's was so much more . . . expansive than anyone else's. That, and the fact that one never knew for certain exactly what they meant. They were so quick.

"Relax. I didn't call you in here to make fun of you." Brun stared into the depths of the projection, eyes gleaming between beard and forelocks.

"Your rapid ascension and an overview of your work suggest that you might be suited to a special mission."

They were going to give him a ship, Caldaq thought. Because of his "special temperament," as it was so delicately phrased in his records. He would not be the first Massood so honored, but it would mark him as unique because of his age. Members of his lineage would be proud.

The S'van was watching him, his teeth clicking softly. Another sign of amusement. That was one thing about the S'van. Whenever their intellectual superiority started to grate, they would inevitably inject an interracially comprehensible obscenity or something else to lighten the atmosphere. Caldaq sometimes wondered if they did this because they were inherently jovial or because they were nervous about the reactions their superior intelligence might stimulate among less mentally endowed peoples.

"The ship's name is . . . well, I don't know the Massood analog, actually, nor even the S'van. She's Hivistahm-built, of course. All the newest technology. Fully multispecies serviceable to accommodate just about anybody in the Weave. Not big enough internally to suit the Chirinaldo, but then what is?

"Not your usual warship. Been specifically modified and equipped for extended Underspace travel."

"A sabotage mission?" Caldaq fought to control his excitement, was betrayed by the quivering of his extremities and the dilation of his pupils. This was a chance to make a name for himself and his lineage.

"Where am I being sent? And what of my mission and crew?"

"You're to be assigned quite a mix. Fellow Massood among them, of course. Not all have been preassigned. It was felt you should have leeway to engage specific officers you might want to work with in the event that . . ."

"Gratefulness for that." It was the Massood manner to say what one wished to when one wanted to. Used to dealing with Caldaq's kind, the S'van took no umbrage at the interruption.

"You may have anyone you wish, provided they can be spared from their present positions. You'll have a full complement of Hivistahm techs with the usual O'o'yan companions, a top-notch Lepar work crew, and at least a couple of Chirinaldo. A Wais or two."

Caldaq winced. "Must I?"

Brun cocked his head slightly to one side. "What would you do if your mechanical translators failed?"

"Manage with gestures, if necessary." Caldaq's upper lip curled in amusement, showing sharp teeth.

"Sorry, Captain. You'll have to take them. Also a few S'van." Brun added the last offhandedly. The S'van strove always to maintain a low profile. "And I think you will have a Turlog."

Caldaq was surprised at that. The vessel they were assigning him to must be larger, its mission more important, than he had hitherto expected.

There were not many Turlog, not even on their homeworld. They differed substantially from every other race in the Weave. Indeed, it was whispered they had more in common in many ways with the Amplitur than with species like the Massood or Lepar. But they had no love for the Amplitur, or their Purpose.

They weren't antisocial so much as solitary by nature. Though hermaphroditic, they laid eggs and did not bud like the enemy. Any species which evolved without the need for intersexual contact had no need to seek or develop the companionship of its own kind.

It was a shame there were not more of them, because they had the unique ability to concentrate on two and occasionally three separate subjects at the same time. This made them especially valuable in combat situations, when strategy and tactics were being implemented.

While not throwing themselves wholeheartedly into the war, they had recognized the danger posed by the Amplitur and had joined the Weave specifically for the purpose of combating them. They were long-lived and slow to reproduce. To have a mature individual assigned to one's vessel was viewed in some quarters as the best of all possible good-luck charms.

"Where exactly," Caldaq asked with Massood directness, "am I going with this ship?"

"I'll show you."

Brun led him through the starry void until Caldaq sensed they had crossed all the way to the opposite wall of the projection chamber. In any event, the star systems which now surrounded them like paralyzed glowbugs were unknown to him. They stood on the edge of the unfamiliar.

He heard a tapping sound. "You're going here." Caldaq saw that the Commander was rapping on the black wall.

"I do not understand."

"You're going out. Out into the rim."

"But there's nothing there. That region is unexplored, unstudied."

"Actually, I think there's a bathroom there."

As far as Caldaq was concerned, this time the S'van humor fell flat. Brun sensed as much and continued in a more serious vein.

"You are going hunting, but not for Amplitur, or Crigolit, or any others. You are to search for potential allies."

Caldaq's mind whirled. He knew that on the rare occasions when a warship could be spared from combat it might be sent out to try and expand the Weave, though most new allies arrived in the form of spacefaring peoples who encountered the Weave in the course of their own travels. It was much the same with the Amplitur.

But while such far-ranging expeditions sometimes encountered life, it was rarely intelligent and hardly ever useful. To the best of his knowledge, only two species capable of contributing even minimal support to the war effort had been so contacted since the conflict had begun.

In other words, such journeys were a vast waste of time.

It was not what he wanted to do. It was not what he had been trained for. His family lineage bespoke a different destiny.

He tried to hide his feelings, but his lips drew back to show teeth. It was not so dark that the S'van failed to notice.

"You're upset. Don't be. This work is important."

"Be that as it may, it is work the O'o'yan or Hivistahm or even the Lepar might do. Well, perhaps not the Lepar. But others. Why the Massood?"

"Any expedition into the unknown must prepare for every conceivable contingency. We know neither the boundaries nor extent of the Amplitur's influence. There is always the chance they may have allies in sectors we do not suspect. That is a possibility that must be contemplated."

"Let someone else contemplate them!"

Brun remained calm. It was useless to try dressing down a Massood for insubordination. "You expected a front-line vessel, perhaps a landing command."

"I am expected," Caldaq replied carefully, "to fulfill certain expectations."

The commander sighed. "I am familiar with the Massood and their hierarchy of familial obligations. Believe me, you will be more than fulfilling them by carrying out this command.

"You were selected because of your unique temperament, your ability to control yourself in moments of crisis. It is because of this, if I may be permitted to stretch a point, Turlog-like capability that you have risen to the position you now hold. Certainly an experienced S'van or Hivistahm captain could lead such a mission, but it was felt that there would be advantages to having a Massood in command."

Caldaq hesitated. "Then you expect to encounter trouble out there."

Brun's teeth clacked softly. "We don't know *what* to expect out there. If we knew what to expect, we wouldn't have to send a vessel to go look."

"Communications?"

"There's all sorts of electromagnetic babble, just like there is everywhere else, but whether it's spewed by pulsars or unknown astrophysical phenomena or something else we've no way of telling at such a distance. The galaxy, my young Massood, is vast: the portion occupied by the Weave and the Peoples of the

Purpose, very small. Again, if we knew these things, we would not have to send you to find them out for us.''

Though still displeased, Caldaq was calming down. After all, what more did he have a right to expect? Command of a landing force on a critical contested world? True, he had participated in half a dozen combat situations, but to fight and to command were very different matters.

What more natural than that they should test someone promoted beyond his years with captaincy of a vessel to be sent into a potentially threatening but noncombat situation? The experience would be good for him. The S'van was right. The S'van, affectionately curse them, were always right.

They were offering him an advanced ship with an experienced, diverse crew. Specialists aplenty. He would not have to order S'van, for example, to fix a broken condensate, or use Lepar in a fight. There would be a Turlog to help design tactics and Chirinaldo to manage large weapons systems. He'd never worked with either species before, but anyone commanding a large-scale operation would have to do so.

It was one thing to give orders to fellow Massood, something very much different to do so to a Chirinaldo. Experience.

They parted in the manner of S'van and Massood, Caldaq having acquiesced to the directive.

But he was still unhappy.

★ IV ★

Caldaq considered resigning as he waited to board the shuttle which would convey him to his command, five planetary diameters out. It would be a dramatic gesture, a statement of confidence and independence. He also knew with great certainty that it would not be accepted. The only consequence would be an invidious notation on his record. Nor would it go down well with his family elders.

It might return him to combat, yes: frozen in rank and with reduced respect among his peers. The Massood appreciated the bold, but not the foolishly wasteful.

Still, he had half determined to go through with it when he encountered his assigned Second-in-Command in the embarkation lounge. She was not what he expected.

Older, but still stoically beautiful. Combat had hardened her grace. While nothing more might be added there was little that age could take away. Her attractiveness was firmly set in the mortar of experience. Despite the difference in their ages, it was impossible not to regard her as a mating partner.

Only the slight alterations and cuts necessitated by her gender differentiated her uniform from his. Their eyes met evenly. Variations in size among the Massood were insignificant among mature adults.

Her name was Soliwik and she was a river of good advice and reassurance. Listening to her, talking with her there in the embarkation lounge helped to calm him in a way the suave Brun could never have managed largely because she was, like him, Massood. She displayed none of the jealousy that might have been expected from one assigned to serve a junior male promoted beyond her, nor was she averse to discussing the situation with him.

"I have been told you possess an unusual temperament."

His foreshortened ear flicked nervously. "They say that I possess self-control. More than the average Massood. They like the way I make decisions." He picked comfortingly at his teeth, employing several ritual motions. It appeared to other races that the Massood never seemed to know what to do with their hands and long, triple-jointed fingers. Tooth-picking and mouth-cleaning were elaborate social arts among the Weave's best soldiers.

"That is what they tell me, anyway. Myself, I do not feel very much in control."

"It will pass. You are uncomfortable with the task that has been assigned to you, unable to decline and afraid you may fail. I have seen your records and studied your lineage. You will not fail."

He jerked around to stare at her, ignoring the murmur of alien tongues, the strange sights and smells that filled the embarkation lounge. The abruptness of the movement was normal for a Massood, in whose vocabulary the word tentative did not exist.

"We have only just met. What makes you so confident of me?" In Massood society it was impolite to offer unsolicited evaluations of another's personality, much less to make behavioral predictions.

Soliwik did not back down. "Because I have observed how individuals react in such situations. I have seen enough to make judgments. You will be too busy settling disputes among your crew to have time to worry about why you are doing what you are doing and whether or not you should be doing something else." The front half of her upper lip curled.

"I have had the same expedition briefing. We are to reconnoiter a large, remote, unexplored section of sky. Who is to say we may not see some combat there? This mission is not a punishment or expression of no confidence in your abilities. I think it is very much the opposite. You must approach it as such while keeping your teeth clean and sharp."

He considered her words carefully. "Do you believe there will be hostilities?"

"One may believe anything of such a region. Who is to say

what peculiarities may be encountered out where the spaces between the stars are so vast?''

''What you say is truth.'' Slowly, expectation was beginning to replace his initial angry disappointment.

''Simply returning with ship and crew intact will be sufficient to advance both our careers and reputations. I know that you have been trained to fight, as have I. This offers a better opportunity than assigned combat.''

''How can that be, if no fighting is involved?''

''First because in combat the chances for failure are magnified, and second because in large-scale engagements the actions of a single vessel rarely count for much. In this we will be on our own. If we fail, there will be none to witness it, and if we succeed in any aspect, the glory will be entirely ours.

''We both seek challenge. The Massood have always done such. Here is an opportunity that can be as unique as we make it, even if there is no bloodletting involved.'' She hissed slightly. ''I understand that you have contemplated resigning.''

His eyes blazed. ''Who told you that?''

''Departure is not time to begin a feud. Enough to know that I know. Is it true?''

He gestured by way of acknowledgment. ''I had so considered.''

''You could not resign. The Massood do not resign without good reason. Personal displeasure at an assignment is not sufficient reason.''

''Don't lecture me,'' he replied irritably.

''Consider our prime objective,'' she said, blithely ignoring his request. ''The Weave is home to few fighting peoples. There are only ourselves, the lugubrious Chirinaldo, and exceptional individuals among such as the Hivistahm and S'van. Sheer numbers limit our ability to confront the Amplitur. Trained fighters are too valuable to be allowed to resign.''

''My mate favors this journey,'' he murmured. ''She longs for cubs.''

''Conception is not permitted on a warship.'' Soliwik spoke coolly. ''Birthing is for stable surfaces.''

''She knows, but hopes for time upon return.''

His Second-to-be gestured understandingly. ''I would think that would be readily granted if we achieve the least of our objectives. What does she besides fight?''

"She is a tech upgrade specialist. There will be plenty for her to do."

"I look forward to greeting her."

"I, too, long for cubs." The confession surprised Caldaq. It was a subject he tried to avoid. Distractions could be detrimental to his performance. But there was unexpected pleasure in the confession.

"I had a litter myself, some twelve years ago." Soliwik's whiskers curled upward. "All three grown now. There was a fourth who did not survive post-littering. One is a high jumper of some note, though these days there is little time for her to practice the true arts." She pointed at his legs. "You look something of a jumper yourself."

"Runner," he said, correcting her. "Better to be a jumper on a ship. Facilities for running are never what one hopes for."

"I sympathize. I am also a jumper, but for distance, not height."

"So is Jaruselka. Perhaps the two of you could jump together."

Mate-jealousy was uncommon among the Massood. Knowing that Soliwik had already littered would help promote friendship between the two females. Strong bonds were formed quickly and easily between individuals of both genders, an early evolutional and not societal development. Mutual reassurance on a personal level was vital to personal growth. "Verbal grooming," a S'van researcher had dubbed it. Instead of picking lice from each other's short gray pelts as their ancestors had done they now extracted neuroses from one another's souls.

A shame they could not share a litter, he thought as the shuttle rose orbitward, giving him ample opportunity to study the long legs of his second as she braced herself in the seat next to his. His own limbs were giving him plenty of trouble. Save for the Chirinaldo, the Massood were taller than any other Weave species. They had a difficult time with the general-use seats found on most vessels.

When they returned from this voyage he would have to give serious attention to littering. The delights of domesticity were in short supply among the Massood, vital as they were to combating the advance of the Amplitur. Being of equal size and musculature, the females fought alongside the males. Perhaps even more importantly, both genders possessed similar temperaments.

Jaruselka greeted them in the lock, reserving an especially hearty greeting for Soliwik and putting her immediately at ease. They embarked upon typical Massood conversation, frenetic and full of specialized female terms. Caldaq felt pleased rather than excluded.

The next day his Second showed them the ship, which was unusually spacious. So were their personal facilities. It was better than he'd imagined, even though he'd expected something of the sort since the ship had been specially modified for extended cruising. Everything was new and contemporary, as Brun had promised.

As Soliwik made the introductions, Caldaq took particular care to try and memorize the names or identification vowels of as many of the crew they encountered as possible.

Most prominently there were the members of the Massood combat group, some of whom he was able to identify from family suffixes. Others were strangers to him. It was difficult not to linger among them, enjoying the relaxed conversation and swapping stories.

As soon as possible, he made contact with his Chirinaldo fire-control team. A mated pair, they were pleasant and ponderous, their high, squeaky voices incongruous as ever. They were much too nice to be in control of the ship's awesome defensive weaponry, a Chirinaldo specialty. Communicating through standard electronic translators, they spoke cheerily of their ability to obliterate other vessels and the hundreds of sentients aboard the instant he should deem it necessary.

Because of their size their movements were restricted to limited areas of the ship. Their perspective on life and death was intriguing. Conversation with a Chirinaldo was always full of unexpected surprises and revelations. In the rare event of combat between vessels, their talents would be invaluable. They could command multiple weapons with unmatched skill.

Their counterparts among the Amplitur's allies were the Molitar, who were even bigger and stronger but not, it was joked among the Weave, nearly as bright.

Dainty O'o'yan bustled past, monitoring instrumentation and readouts, their slim bodies and hands working as fast as those of a Massood but with far greater dexterity. They were friendly and even attractive, harmless in stature and appearance, but a little strange. Some of their low-level conversation was difficult even for a Wais to understand, and they preferred to associate almost exclusively with the larger, more sophisticated Hivistahm, whom they closely resembled.

When encountered, the ultrapolite Wais greeted him exquisitely. Of all the crew thus far encountered only they moved about the ship in perfect contentment. Like everyone else, Caldaq knew the apocryphal tales of battered worlds from which survivors emerged filthy and tattered . . . except for the Wais, who drifted through war and peace alike attended by invisible, undetectable cleaning facilities.

They spoke perfect Massood, of course, though he personally found their intonation too proper. It was a relief to leave them and encounter some of the Hivistahm.

Theirs was the biggest contingent on board, and it was they who were largely responsible for the day-to-day operation of the ship. Though a good deal shorter than the Massood, they were considerably taller than the average O'o'yan or S'van.

Soliwik had left them for a few moments. Now she returned to inform them that their departure from orbit was imminent . . . contingent upon his consent, of course. He indicated that she should proceed, confident that with S'van in charge of navigation and Hivistahm engineers overseeing the Drive everything would go well. He returned to his conversation.

With their slightly bulging slitted eyes and bright green skins the Hivistahm were physically colorful. Their appearance belied their somber personalities. They had long, narrow snouts, much longer than those of the Massood but full of equally sharp if narrower teeth. Slim arms and stronger legs were good for running but not jumping. Hard, scaly skin gleamed iridescently where not hidden by thin, superstrong attire. Pleated pockets overflowed with tools and devices designed to perform arcane tasks. A typical Hivistahm tech would spend most of its time grumbling. Not complaining but simply muttering under its breath, worrying and dreaming of home as it perfectly executed this or that delicate task.

Superb technicians, they never balked at taking orders from others. Not even from the S'van, whose attitude they found far too frivolous for their liking. Of all the races that comprised the Weave, the Hivistahm were perhaps the most dedicated to defeating the Amplitur, more so even than the Massood. They shared a racial dread of being integrated into the mysterious Purpose that went beyond actual understanding of what it would entail.

Among the Weave it was said that a warship crewed by S'van and Massood might achieve more in battle, might execute the more brilliant maneuver or achieve the greater result, but that one largely run by Hivistahm would always return home.

And then there were the Lepar. As usual, the only amphibious intelligences in the Weave were difficult to locate, working as they did in the cramped, less attractive sections of the ship where energy and heat and water and air blended into the technological brew that kept everything running.

They found several, including the officer in charge, lazing in a water bubble, keeping themselves moist. To Caldaq they looked competent enough. He didn't particularly like the Lepar, nor did he know anyone who did. Their presence was useful because they could tolerate extremes of temperature and oxygen deprivation that would kill a Massood or Hivistahm or S'van. In an emergency their work might prove vital.

Their build was stocky without being graceful, wide blunt faces flanked by external feathery gills. Eyes were tiny and black and their skin was slimy and of a dark unpleasant cast. They were as ugly, he thought, as they were necessary.

They greeted him in badly broken Massood, a valiant but ultimately futile attempt to eschew the use of translators. The Lepar were always trying to do what they could not. Speak other languages with the fluency of the Wais, run a ship as efficiently as a Hivistahm, even fight like the Massood. In the end they could only do the little they could.

Their intense, small-eyed stares caused him to turn away in embarrassment at their condition. They wore little clothing, a necessity given their natural bodily slime and half-aquatic existence. Among the known intelligences, only the Lepar possessed long tails, a source of some amusement and many jokes among the other evolved species.

Caldaq reminded himself that regardless of his personal feelings, as captain he could not even appear to look down on members of another Weave race. After all, the Lepar did much of the most dangerous work on board, and all of the dirtiest, and they carried out their unenviable duties quietly and without complaint. Unlike the Hivistahm, for example. Their contribution was as important as that of any other species.

Turning back to face them, he found himself wondering not for the first time what thoughts they debated in their highly guttural, unelegant language. Wondering what might lie behind those tiny, dull black eyes.

He excused himself as soon as possible, which appeared to suit them fine. They showed no especial need to be loved or even liked by the other races. All they wanted was to be left alone to do their jobs. This worked out well, since it was also what everyone else on the ship wanted for them.

Actually, out of the entire crew the presence of a Massood combat group was probably the least necessary, since in the event of hostilities the ship's long-range weaponry as directed by the Chirinaldo should be more than sufficient to handle any awkwardness. But he was glad of their presence if only for the company of his own kind.

Soliwik commanded them, and was in fact only Caldaq's second where matters of combat were concerned. The actual running of the ship was managed by two S'van.

This did not trouble either officer. There might have been friction between a Massood and Hivistahm, or Massood and O'o'yan, but not between Massood and S'van. It was almost impossible to get mad at a S'van. Arguments were easily defused by a casual joke, an offhanded comment. The S'van had raised compensatory humor to a high art, and an infectious one at that.

Caldaq wondered if it was an ingrained skill or one the species had developed to insure its survival. For despite their brilliance and their successes at colonization of new worlds they could have easily been destroyed by, say, the Massood or even the Hivistahm.

Such thoughts reminded him of Soliwik's remark, that he was going to be too busy settling arguments among the crew to worry about personal matters.

The ship, at least, would give him no problems. It was a technological wonder, incorporating all the latest developments in Weave science. Since it had not been designed as a true warship, there was a great deal more room to devote to activities of a pleasurable nature.

A good deal of effort, for example, had gone into providing the Hivistahm with the cool, dark, humid living environment they favored, while not, as was sometimes the case, forcing the S'van to share it with them. And while there was always room for smaller species like the O'o'yan, the Massood often found their quarters cramped and constricted because of space limitations. Not on this vessel.

It made it easier to keep them on a combat footing. That was necessary because while they did not expect to run into the Amplitur or any of their allies, they likewise had no idea what else they *might* run into. So while there was no reason to anticipate combat, neither was there on board a total absence of tension.

He soon discovered that there was much to keep him occupied, especially once they had entered Underspace. Even so, he found time to socialize with his fellow Massood. He and Jaruselka had time to themselves apart from their duties, and he was delighted to see that his mate and Soliwik had formed an instant friendship. It was particularly comforting on a long voyage for an unlittered female to have the companionship of an elder who had given birth.

It took a great deal of pressure off him.

★ V ★

There were frequent discussions of routines and objectives, with a Wais always present to clarify and explain nuances that might escape the electronic translators. One thing that did not have to be debated was course. Destinations had been determined by the astronomers of the Weave long before the ship had been readied for departure. Isolating suns likely to have planets was difficult enough. Trying to determine from aboard a ship in Underspace which were likely to support life was an impossibility.

There were many reasons why this was so, not the least of them being that the presence of an oxynitro atmosphere was not necessarily a prerequisite for the development of intelligence, the heliox-breathing Chirinaldo being the most prominent exception to the usual but far from absolute atmospheric rule. Then there were the amphibious Lepar, and another intelligent but not yet mature species who extracted all their oxygen directly from water.

Nor could the possibility of encountering even more exotic sentient types be ruled out. Among the allies of the Amplitur, for example, was a race of methane-breathers. So every system that boasted planets had to be closely inspected, lest a potentially useful . . . or dangerous . . . world be overlooked.

He rarely showed the uncertainty he felt. It was not easy being less experienced than many of those he was expected to command. But being Massood, he appeared naturally jumpy and nervous to others, and so it was impossible for any but members of his own kind to tell when he was feeling uneasy. The extremities of a Massood were in constant motion: twitching, curling, quivering. Movements were jerky and swift, not smooth like those of a Hivistahm or languorous in the manner of the Wais.

There was no hesitancy in the orders he issued, however, and the ship sped on through Underspace devoid of troubles mechanical or psychological.

Upon reaching a new system and emerging into real space, a well-defined procedure was followed. Whether the subject to be studied was a gas giant, a moon thereof, or a smaller independent world, the ship would assume an orbit a safe several planetary diameters out. Masking would be engaged so that they could not be observed from the surface. The process bent light around the ship. In the unlikely event its location was crossed by astronomers or other observers on the ground it would not occlude any stars, thereby preventing detection.

Usually it was only necessary to execute a single slow equatorial and a backup circumpolar to establish that a world was uninhabited. The presence of nonintelligent life could be duly noted and recorded from orbit, much to the dismay of Hivistahm biologists eager to examine and collect specimens from every new ecosystem.

Caldaq sympathized with his scientific staff, but time could not be allotted to pure research. There were too many systems to be searched. The sum total of all such studies would be rendered meaningless by a final Amplitur victory. Their assignment was to seek out potential help, however limited. To find out potential allies. Not to learn.

There were times when he questioned the work himself. Not because he was not doing what he'd been trained to do, which was fight, but because he was afraid he might not be doing his work well enough. In combat it was easy to determine if one was performing. His present assignment provided no such simple hallmarks from which to judge accomplishment.

It was the same with running. He moved his legs, fought gravity, and the clock charted the degree of his success. Much more difficult to decide if he was, for example, settling arguments properly.

There was constant trouble between the Hivistahm and the Lepar. It was in the nature of the Hivistahm to criticize, and they were particularly rough on the slow amphibians. Though patient, the Lepar would take such abuse only so long before reacting. Then there would be a fight, with the bulkier, stronger

Lepar unable to get a grip on the slighter but far more agile Hivistahm. This only raised the Lepar's level of frustration.

Caldaq found himself spending much of his time mediating such confrontations, which nearly always ended harmlessly if noisily. The skills he was forced to call upon differed greatly from those demanded of a fighter. He was much more comfortable in the role of combatant than referee, especially when members of another race were involved.

The usual result was that the Hivistahm would trot off muttering and whistling to itself while the Lepar would sulk back to join its fellows as if nothing had happened, leaving their commander to wonder if his intervention had done any good at all. At least when dealing with Massood you always knew where you stood following an argument.

Whenever his sense of inadequacy or insecurity grew too great to internalize, Jaruselka was always there to comfort and reassure him, and Soliwik to offer sound, practical advice. He could also turn to his other seconds, the S'van T'var and Z'mam.

That was one thing about the S'van: If you wanted them to be your true friends, all you had to do was plead ignorance or confusion and ask for their advice. They loved to give advice. Some postulated it was a physiological necessity for them, like inhaling. It was bearable only because the advice was usually sound.

The troubles the expedition experienced fell well within the range of the anticipated. Things were going as smoothly, Caldaq thought, as even an experienced captain could have wished.

They surveyed many dead worlds but also a surprising number that supported some form of life. One system of seven planets consisted of two outer gas giants, two inner seared rocks, and three worlds in between, all of which harbored life: an unprecedented occurrence.

The Hivistahm and S'van scientists all but mutinied in their desire to examine the remarkable trio, frantic to compare evolution on one world with its neighbor, to measure similarities and differences. Once again Caldaq was required to deny their requests.

Each of the three worlds was studied from orbit, and then it was time to move on. The grumbling of the scientists continued in Underspace, but the volume of complaints soon subsided. Everyone knew it was useless to argue with a Massood. Had a

S'van been in charge there at least might have been some intelligent debate on the issue.

Their reaction was not lost on Caldaq, whose admiration for Regional Commander Brun's abilities rose another notch.

The science staff's disappointment was forgotten when the next system they entered proved to be home not merely to life but to intelligent life.

The newfound species resembled the Hivistahm physically, but they were far too immature to be of any use in the battle against the Amplitur. They were living in tribal groups, primitive hunter-gatherers stuck at the spear-and-axe level of technology. Contact revealed a language primitive enough for the Wais to decipher in a couple of days.

The natives treated the visitors as gods, refusing to accept that they were as mortal as themselves. It was conceded by the Hivistahm that these people would require several millennia of maturation on their own before they would be able to help in any way, a pronouncement rendered with more Hivistahm solemnity than usual.

The ship continued on, burrowing through Underspace to check one world after another, following the complex course programmed into the ship's navigation system by the very best of the Weave's astronomers. Frustration levels among the crew waxed and waned with clocklike regularity, leading Caldaq to believe a psychologist should have been appointed captain rather than a fighter.

The only member of the crew who never gave him any trouble was Pasiiakilion.

On those occasions when he felt the need to get away from everyone else, including Jaruselka and Soliwik, he would go and visit the Turlog in its dimly lit artificial burrow. Squatting in a corner, it would regard him with one eye from the tip of its supportive stalk while the other concentrated on another task entirely. Though it appeared to be ignoring him, Caldaq knew the alien was devoting as much attention to him as it was to its studies.

An inflexible, crustaceanlike exoskeleton gave Pasiiakilion little range of motion. The large, clumsy claws were hard put to operate the simplest switches and controls. Special amplifiers magnified as well as translated the scratchy Turlog voice. Compared to Pasiiakilion, the clumsiest Lepar on the ship was the very picture of grace.

It had admitted him without greeting, neither rude nor accommodating. Caldaq responded to the subsequent silence with measured words delivered in an unchallenging tone. He was rewarded by a response, however unenthusiastically delivered. He could not tell how much of its attention the Turlog was devoting to his visit and how much to its reading, but at least Pasiiakilion responded. Its usual reaction was on the order of abyssal indifference.

Sometimes he wondered how the Turlog might have evolved had it developed a more flexible body. As it was, they were highly dependent on sophisticated instrumentation to help them carry out the most menial personal tasks. Nor did he care for the Turlog's quarters, feebly lit by faint reddish light.

But it was quiet there. He could relax, isolated from the numbing details of command, and talk via translator with the one member of his crew who never gave him trouble.

Sometimes he even received a reply.

Discouragement and ennui finally gave way to excitement and expectation among the crew when the ship reached a small world circling a star of medium age, which was home not merely to intelligence but to a real civilization.

Orbital observations revealed that while they had not yet acquired the ability to travel through Underspace, or indeed even between the worlds of their own system, the inhabitants had achieved a level of technology amenable to formal contact. There was ample evidence of the presence of aircraft and other sophisticated means of surface transportation. Furthermore, the natives responded to the eventual appearance of a shuttle above one of their principal urban centers with an appealing mix of curiosity and shyness.

Contact was made with the leaders of the new species and formalities exchanged, whereupon S'van and Wais specialists landed to pursue further contact in person. Caldaq did not go, nor did Soliwik. Newly contacted peoples often became uneasy in the presence of the physically imposing Massood. They were much more at ease dealing with graceful Wais and short S'van. So T'var acted in his stead, daily apprising his captain of developments below.

Caldaq's concerns were exacerbated by the ever anxious Hivistahm. The contact party was virtually helpless without any Massood to protect them, though the S'van *could* fight if absolutely necessary. Their versatility was another of their admirable traits. If the natives were intent on deception, T'var could probably manage a successful retreat.

His fears were groundless. The natives quickly demonstrated their maturity and friendship. Soon representatives were routinely shuttling back and forth between the surface and the ship, where they marveled at the achievements of the Weave and listened somberly to the history of its confrontation with the Amplitur.

Such information was not restricted to the local elite, but was disseminated by domestic means of communication to the populace at large. Caldaq's people spent a good deal of time educating and explaining. They were rewarded when the natives decided unanimously to join with the Weave and support the fight against the Purpose. Their enthusiasm was exhilarating and gratifying. The long voyage had not been in vain. Caldaq grew emotional.

The natives possessed good mechanical and learning skills. Upon the introduction of Weave technology and training they would be able to make a significant contribution to the war effort. Fighters they were not, but that would have been too much to hope for.

There was a considerable outpouring of honest affection when it came time for the ship to finally depart. T'var left their new allies with the promise that Weave ships would soon be calling in large numbers. The natives looked forward to receiving such visitations as soon as possible. Their eagerness to help was touching. It was also only sensible, of course, since if they failed to join the Weave they would eventually find themselves dominated by the Amplitur.

Acquisition of a new, intelligent ally was enough to render the expedition a complete success and justify its expense. They would return to applause and commendation. All those good things that Soliwik had told him could come from such a journey now seemed within his grasp.

But it was not yet time for Caldaq to enjoy them. Their mission was not completed. Eleven more systems remained to be scanned and examined before they could begin the long Underspace journey homeward.

With success already assured, the atmosphere on board improved noticeably. The Hivistahm grumbled less and ceased provoking the Lepar. The S'van relaxed, and even the bored Massood were cheered. The latter looked forward to returning to combat, promoted and acclaimed.

They had reached the limit delineated by navigation, a region of few stars and sterile worlds, when to everyone's surprise and delight instrumentation detected what might be communications signals.

There was nothing remarkable about them. They possessed no extraordinary range or power. Very typically stratified electromagnetic pulses. Nothing to suggest true civilization, of course. That would have been too much to hope for. But they did hint that another world had been located on which electronic means of communication had been developed.

As soon as they arrived masking procedures were initiated and the ship established itself in a safe orbit several planetary diameters out. Initial anticipation fell rapidly when no indications of space-traversing capability were noted.

Everyone was tired, Caldaq knew. Many besides the Hivistahm now spent much time thinking of home, and a predictable but nonetheless very real letdown had followed the discovery and cementing of an alliance with the inhabitants of the world previously visited. Surely any species they encountered subsequently could not be as helpful or friendly. He was tired himself. Despite his twice-daily workouts on the ship's track, he felt himself steadily losing the muscle tone so carefully established through years of training.

This world could be similar to the last one, but that was too much to hope for. More probably it was less advanced. In any event he knew he was unlikely to see the surface. Formal contact, should the locals prove advanced enough to handle it, would be managed by the S'van. The prevailing attitude on board as survey preparations were begun was one of hopeful boredom.

Preliminary observations produced at least one astonishing discovery: the principal landmass of the planet had disintegrated. For once, the geologists had something to be excited about.

Debate as to whether intelligence could even evolve in such a bizarre setting was resolved for a time by initial data which was, disappointingly, predictable and unsurprising. Urban centers and extensive agriculture were present, as were communications relay satellites. Only the distribution of population centers seemed slightly unnatural. More to study the remarkable geology of the planet than the works of its inhabitants, it was decided to add a diagonal circumnavigation to the standard equatorial and polar.

As observation proceeded, further deviations from the anticipated norm were noted. Caldaq was informed of the presence of unusually large population concentrations in regions where, at least from orbit, there appeared no reason for them to exist. Similarly, areas that should have attracted heavy settlement were practically deserted.

Such exceptions were to be expected. The developmental history of each species was different from that of every other. Land use was a subject for a follow-up expedition equipped to carry out advanced studies. Certainly this world, with its unique topography, would draw considerable attention from the specialists.

The level of technological sophistication achieved by the locals and whether it might exceed that of the Weave's recently acquired new allies quickly became a matter for debate. A certain amount of wagering on the question took place among the Massood, who were prone to that particular amusement. The Hivistahm considered gambling a waste of time, the Lepar did not understand it, and the Wais regarded it with tolerance. The S'van never participated because they might win.

Additional observations resulted in another finding no one could have imagined.

"It certainly is odd," said T'var. All three Seconds were present at the staff-study meeting.

The Hivistahm chief-of-study whistled into his translator while the others present adjusted their ear-mounted receivers.

"S'van understatement. So far we have documented at least fifteen distinct patterns."

Soliwik's nose twitched rapidly. "I see nothing remarkable in that. There are a number of worlds on which that many dialects are spoken."

"These are not dialects," Chief-of-Study insisted. Light flashed off her metallic green skin. She wore no personal adornment to the meeting save the ubiquitous eyeshades favored by her kind, tinted to spare her sensitive pupils. "Each a distinct language is, as distinct in some cases as S'van from Hivistahm or Massood is.''

Caldaq had come to the meeting prepared to listen to the usual statistical recitation. Now, on top of the planet's impossible geology, there was this. He found himself scratching nervously at his left flank as he straightened his tall frame in the high-backed chair.

"You're quite certain they are not dialects?"

"Absolutely," said the S'van second-of-study. "Not only have we examined the relevant recordings thoroughly and repeated computer analysis of our findings run, we believe even more individual languages may be encountered as our observations continue."

Caldaq swallowed. "Surely there could not be more than fifteen."

"There should not that many be." Chief-of-Study shifted in her seat. "The largest number of distinct languages developed by any known intelligent race is six, by the Wais. The idea of fifteen or more being spoken on one world is incomprehensible. Yet our observations to that conclusion inevitably lead."

"Well, we are not here to study languages." Caldaq regarded the crammed agenda screen in front of him. "The universe is a vast place where any number of sociological aberrations may be expected to be encountered eventually. Perhaps even a world where more than the usual number of languages are in use.

"The Massood have always done nicely with one and its accompanying dialects. Possibly not all these you have recorded are used for general communication. Perhaps some are devoted to specialties. A language for science, another for commerce. Although I am no linguistic historian, I believe there is some precedence for that." He looked up. "What say the Wais?"

"We are baffled." Translator-Chief gazed superciliously back at her commander. Bracelets clinked melodiously on her wrists, and her flowing cape was decorated with innumerable personal insignia and designs. All of exquisite taste, of course.

"Your notion, Captain, that certain languages may be used for specialized purposes may prove correct. But initial analysis by my colleagues and I seems to suggest otherwise." Familiar with the unintentional air of superiority the Wais sometimes affected when imparting information, Caldaq was able to ignore it.

"Admittedly, these are preliminary conclusions, but they are based on the many precedents present in our computer. At least five of the languages recorded thus far are utterly different in structure from the rest and from each other, yet sufficiently complex in content to constitute an efficient means of communication unto themselves. Among the remaining ten there are recognizable relational patterns and soundings, too many for each to constitute a separate language of specialization. In addition there are unexpected cross-references between otherwise utterly dissimilar tongues."

"Despite which you think there may be even more?" murmured Caldaq.

The Wais stared back at him. "Even as we sit here my colleagues are recording suggestions of such. The only way we will know for certain is to initiate a far more intense examination of the population."

"There are clamorings in other departments," said T'var, "for exactly that."

"Each new world prompts a similar ritual." Caldaq tried not to sound irritable. The whiskers on the right side of his snout flicked upward. "We will do only that which is necessary and we will follow procedure." He scanned the Hivistahm present.

"Enough of primitive babblings. Have we learned anything more about this world's unusual appearance?"

Chief-of-Geophysics adjusted her eyeshades. "It is tectonically far more active than it ought to be. The extraordinary physical environment may to a nonstandard ecology rise have given." She hesitated. "We have the presence of active volcanoes noted. There is also evidence of unpredictable violent movements within the crust and mantle."

"On an inhabited world," T'var murmured aloud. "Incredible! How do they cope emotionally?"

Caldaq motioned for his Second to be silent, gestured for Chief-of-Geophysics to continue.

"The single large landmass surrounded by water and small islands that is the norm elsewhere has been replaced on this world by something else, something very different. One can easily note this through a port, without special equipment. This world a treasure house of geologic abnormalities is, such as high mountains on the edges of landmasses instead of near the centers.

"Initially it was thought that perhaps the central landmass had by cometary impact been shattered, but further study a tectonic explanation suggests. The proximity of a moon much too large to be orbiting so small a world another likely influence is."

Chief-of-Study bobbed her head. "Of course, it is far too soon on a matter of such controversy final judgments to render. When contacted, it may be that the inhabitants themselves will some light on their unique environment be able to shed."

Caldaq assented with both ears.

"We'll know more when the remote returns. I know we should complete all three observational passes first, but I think we can bend procedure that much." He adopted a warning tone. "Staff will do the programming, as always, but according to prior preop. No department gets more space than normally allotted." He noted the objection gesture from Chief-of-Geophysics and responded. "On later flights we can assign time according to need, but not on this first one.

"I realize there is much knowledge to be gained here, but that cannot be allowed to obscure our objective. Our first task is to make contact with the inhabitants. It would be overwhelming to make contact with not one but two potential allies on a single expeditionary journey, even if neither has advanced far enough to have independently achieved Underspace capability.

"I will not tolerate any interstaff squabbling over time assignments. Everyone has their job to do, myself included." He eyed Chief-of-Study. "I am depending on the Hivistahm to follow procedure precisely, as always." She blinked acknowledgment.

Caldaq leaned back in his chair. "No matter what is suspected or theorized, I will not allow the linguists and geologists to assume preference over, say, the botanists or hydrologists or anyone else. We have just begun the study of this place and it is too soon to try and predict what discoveries may prove to be the ones of greatest importance. Am I understood?"

Everyone present touched a finger or claw to their translator receiver to indicate that he was. He gave the order primarily for the benefit of the Hivistahm, who tended to be argumentative. The Wais and the S'van would simply comply.

The meeting was at an end.

Fifteen languages, separate and distinct. His head twitched to the left as he tried to embrace the concept. What species needed fifteen languages in order to communicate effectively? It made no more sense than this world's shattered topography.

Hopefully the first remote would return with an explanation. The ship carried several of the small, self-contained atmospheric vehicles, each capable of extended flight through calm or turbulent weather, each able to carry out detailed observations of a planetary surface.

The presence of low-flying aircraft had been noted during the early orbits, but the remote would simply avoid them, going about its business without contact. It would scan one, perhaps two of the distinct landmasses and then return to the ship. After careful study of its recordings they could decide how, when, and where to send down a shuttle to initiate contact. With luck, the natives might even have more to contribute than an unnatural diversity of languages.

★ VI ★

They woke him in the middle of his rest period. He had no answers for Jaruselka as he slid off the high sleeping platform and dressed rapidly below her. Not that he was especially alarmed or nervous. A Massood did everything hurriedly. He washed his eyes and groomed himself as best he could.

T'var was waiting in the corridor. He apologized as soon as the captain emerged. Caldaq contained himself. The call had not interrupted anything since Jaruselka would not come into heat for another half time period, but he was still upset. Sleep was important to the Massood because they expended so much nervous energy simply by being awake. They could not go long without it.

As they took the lift to Command Central he used his remote to order a meal. Food could temporarily substitute for lack of rest. Sensing his mood, off-shift personnel hastened out of his path. Running to keep up with his captain, T'var began to pant hard. Caldaq finally took notice and shortened his stride, shamed by the oversight.

"This had better be important," he muttered irritably.

"Would I wake you if it wasn't?" The S'van sounded hurt, a specialty of theirs.

"You mean, if *you* did not think it was. That is not the same thing." Caldaq was in no mood for S'van subterfuges, verbal or otherwise. "Explain."

"It's the survey remote."

"Back already?" Caldaq's lips drew away from his teeth. "Too soon. Did someone decide there was not as much to see as they thought?"

"No. It's not that."

They stepped off the lift at Command. Caldaq noted immediately the unusual agitation of the Hivistahm staff, an uneasiness mirrored by their S'van and Massood counterparts. O'o'yan line techs fluttered among their larger colleagues like so many arthropod nectarsippers.

"What then?"

"It didn't come back at all."

Caldaq halted. So intent were the technicians and specialists on their conversation that they had yet to notice the approach of their captain and Second.

"What do you mean, it did not come back?" Designed to function under difficult, unpredictable conditions on unexplored worlds, survey remotes contained inbuilt multiple backup systems and redundancies. They were supposed to be fail-proof. That, however, was a specification, not an immutable fact.

"Is that what you woke me for?" Caldaq did not allow T'var time to reply. "This is a situation any Second should be able to deal with. Send another remote to see what happened to the first. Has anyone bothered to consider the possibility of mechanical failure?"

"Staff does not think this one failed, Captain. They aren't sure, but . . . some disquieting final transmissions were received."

"Disquieting? How?"

"Visuals." For the first time since he'd been awakened it struck Caldaq how much T'var was unlike his usual jovial self. "They are somewhat self-explanatory."

Caldaq bared his teeth as he strode forward. Crew and officers made room for him as he stormed into their midst and demanded explanations. Meanwhile T'var was murmuring in rapid S'van to Z'mam. Caldaq did not admonish his Second for speaking so. He wanted this settled quickly so he could return to his mate and his bed.

An officer beckoned him to a screen. "This is what the remote observed before contact was lost, Captain." Caldaq leaned forward.

He was traveling at high speed over mostly flat, forested terrain. The ground was only intermittently visible because of thick, scattered cloud cover. The view was peaceful, even normal.

As the journey progressed the remote passed above several small urban centers. Unexceptional lines radiating outward from the alien communities suggested the presence of limited surface transport facilities.

Without warning the image lurched wildly, then steadied again. Caldaq addressed the officer and the staff gathered close by without taking his eyes from the screen.

"What was that?"

An O'o'yan tech squeezed between two Hivistahm, his translator humming. "At first we thought heavy local winds might be responsible, then equipment failure. As you can see, the remote righted itself and resumed course as plotted, though it gained altitude while so doing."

"This is the awkward part," murmured the officer. "Here . . ." The Hivistahm reached out and adjusted the instrumentation.

The image slowed at the officer's command. As it did so one of the other Hivistahm pointed to the screen with a clawed finger. "There, see . . ."

A small object came into view in the upper right corner of the screen. Soon after, the image rolled violently again, the land and the cloudscapes whirling wildly. Very little additional real time passed before the screen went black.

Caldaq straightened. "I still see nothing to suggest other than mechanical failure."

An impatient officer, momentarily forgetting that the captain was not S'van, spoke sharply in the negative. "If the remote had crashed it would have continued sending audiovisual information until the moment of impact. Detailed study of the last available data clearly indicates it was airborne when final failure occurred."

"Some kind of lethal atmospheric phenomenon, then."

"We have reason to think otherwise." Z'mam stepped up to the console. Caldaq watched as the Second ran back the last images transmitted by the remote, finally seizing on one and enlarging it substantially. From the flat view thus selected he chose a small area and enhanced it to three dimensions. The alien object he'd isolated hovered motionless above the console: cylindrical, metallic, and winged.

"This was traveling at high speed proximate to the remote," he explained. "Immediately after it appeared, the probe commenced its gyrations. As you saw, total failure occurred shortly thereafter.''

A Massood off-shift officer spoke up. ''All remotes are programmed to take evasive action if and when an airborne alien device should approach to within a prescribed distance.''

Caldaq looked at the soldier. ''Surely you do not think the natives destroyed it?'' No one said anything. ''I have studied the preliminary reports. Even allowing for certain deviations, the perceived level of technology of this planet's inhabitants is much too low to include the ability to down an advanced survey probe.''

T'var cleared his throat, brushed at his impenetrable black beard. '' 'Perceived' appears to be the operative word here, Captain. 'Deviation' may also enter into it. The evidence would seem to suggest . . .''

''None of this is conclusive,'' Caldaq said impatiently. ''Send down another remote, but with a different program. There may be something special or unique about the particular area the probe was observing. This time run the survey over a different landmass.''

Strange to be talking about multiple landmasses on the same world, he mused. A mystery for the geologists to solve. A sudden thought worried him.

''Something not yet discussed. Could there be an Amplitur outpost here?''

One of the S'van spoke up. ''That was one of the first things we checked. There's no indication of it. Though somewhat sophisticated, the satellites in orbit around this world are of strictly alien design and execution, and insofar as we have been able to determine, utilized strictly for surface-to-surface communication. No information is being directed outward, and no interspatial transmissions have been detected save for occasional bursts being sent to and from tiny mechanical devices located elsewhere in the system, none of which resemble anything the Amplitur or their allies employ.''

''Does not make much sense, does it?'' Caldaq asked rhetorically. ''Be quick with that other remote.''

He did not return to the rest he so dearly desired. Instead he spent the following time periods in Command Central, watching and waiting as the second probe was ejected from the ship and sent on its long, curving course planetward.

From the time it entered atmosphere the probe functioned according to its programming. Therefore, unless a better explanation came to the fore, the loss of the first remote would be recorded as an isolated incident of probable mechanical failure.

The second survey probe went about its business without interruption, recording information day by day and sending it back out to the ship. It was about to be recalled when it vanished in a manner similar to its predecessor. Intensive analysis pointed inexorably to the same explanation: it had been destroyed by artificial means.

It was a more solemn than usual Chief-of-Study who addressed the assemblage in the gathering room. "In the event local sentients attempt to contact a remote, the device is designed to respond to the inquiry. Yet there is no evidence of such an attempt in these two instances. Is that correct?"

"That is so," said Third-of-Study, who supervised the remotes. His scales gleamed. "As near as we can determine, neither probe was contacted. Both were simply destroyed."

"I feel we are missing something." Caldaq studied the tense group of multiracial techs and officers. "I worry still about Amplitur influence."

It was infuriating not to know anything for certain. He was so nervous he was unable to control his snout and had to turn away often to conceal the violent twitching from the others. In that he worried needlessly, since everyone was quite familiar with the by-products of the overactive Massood metabolism.

The ship had gone to third-stage alert when contact with the second probe had been lost. They could not stay such forever.

"Our options are limited. We can continue with our survey until we run out of remotes, we can return directly home to report all we have learned and let Weave Authority decide how to deal with this world, or we can fulfill our responsibilities here by whatever means necessary." He regarded his advisors evenly.

"I did not accept this command with the intention of failing in any aspect of our mission. We have accomplished great work. I will not allow it to be marred by incompleteness.

"The remotes are good at observing and recording. They are not designed to react to circumstances for which they have not been programmed. That requires observational capability backed by greater flexibility. Since mechanicals have failed to provide us with understanding, we must seek it in person."

Murmurings in several languages filled the room, whistles and words and demonstrative clicks careening off one another anxiously. One of the Hivistahm verbalized the obvious.

"If both remotes were destroyed by artificial means, a crewed shuttle could face the same danger."

"I have given the matter some thought." The arguments ceased and he knew he had their attention. "Both probes kept to programmed courses and altitudes. We will go straight down, minimizing the opportunity for surface-based hostile observation or reaction. A shuttle can manage partial masking and once on the surface can be more completely concealed.

"Assuming the inhabitants were responsible for the destruction of the two remotes, it remains that it took them some time to track the first and considerably longer to destroy the second. It may therefore reasonably be assumed that their detection capability or their response time or both is limited.

"In addition, both remotes were programmed to fly over heavily populated regions. We will be more selective in choosing a place to touch down."

Soliwik had no objections. T'var and Z'mam voiced cautious agreement. Chief-of-Study and Third-of-Study thought it a bad idea, but being Hivistahm their response was predictable and Caldaq had allowed for it without in any way attempting to minimize the danger.

"I want a mixed landing party," he declared. "S'van and Hivistahm to observe and record, a Massood squad in case of trouble on the surface, and Wais to translate. Appropriate arms and equipment.

"Keep in mind we may be wrong in our conclusions. Meteorological interference or some other natural phenomenon unique to this world may still prove to be responsible for the failure of the remotes. The presence of a native aerial device in one of the recordings does not preclude those explanations. We may even be dealing with some kind of large, dangerous flying creature."

Even the S'van were impressed with his thoroughness, which they would have expected from one of their own kind but not from a Massood. Caldaq had no time to bask in their unspoken approval. He wanted answers.

"Soliwik, you and Z'mam will command in my absence." He looked to Chief-of-Study. "We will want to set down near one of the urbanized landmasses the remotes were studying without duplicating their paths. Close enough to observe, but isolated from immediate detection. It must be a place where the shuttle can be effectively hidden without restricting the range of our instrumentation. One where there is hopefully a diversity of habitats we can study."

Chief-of-Technicians objected. "It will be difficult to find a site meeting all your requirements from so far out. If we could approach the upper atmosphere . . ."

"Do the best you can," Caldaq told him. "We remain ignorant of the natives' capabilities. Until we know more I will not risk moving the ship closer. The techniques used in masking are imperfect and work best when well away from a surface." He turned to T'var.

"Assemble the landing group. Bear in mind we will be carrying a heavy load of instrumentation. I want techs who are not afraid to contemplate originalities." He glanced over at Soliwik. "And fighters who will pause to think before shooting."

Despite the necessary sense of assurance he was projecting, Caldaq was proceeding uncertainly at best in an unprecedented situation. He was simply giving orders fast enough to forestall serious dissension. Neither T'var nor Soliwik would have trouble finding crew eager to participate, regardless of potential dangers. After so long aboard ship, the chance to experience real gravity and breathe unrecycled atmosphere would be embraced enthusiastically.

Another captain might elect to leave well enough alone and return home without determining what had happened to the two lost survey probes, but he could not.

He explained as much to Jaruselka, who naturally requested to go along and who, just as naturally, he refused. There followed a barrage of traditional Massood verbal combat which resulted in her remaining on board to continue her own work and a strengthening of their mating bonds. He assured her he would take no unnecessary risks. He, too, wanted cubs.

The selection of a landing site provoked intense discussion among the scientific staff. Each department had its own priorities, its own agenda. To make progress Caldaq had to remind them that until they better understood the nature of the world below, scientific concerns would have to be relegated to the background.

Someone suggested that the planet might be home to several different intelligent species, which would go a long way toward accounting for the astonishing multiplicity of languages. This possibility was discarded as soon as native visual broadcasts could be analyzed. There was only a single dominant form, bipedal and apparently mammalian. Given the exceptions already noted, the very ordinariness of their appearance was remarkable.

Caldaq was relieved. The natives were not monsters. They resembled the S'van in certain ways, the Massood less so, while clearly distinct from either.

Selection of a landing site proceeded. The deep oceans would have been ideal for concealment, but too isolated for purposes of observation. Compromise among the members of the study and scientific staffs eventually produced a site.

It was located south of the landmass where the first probe had disappeared, proximate to the heaviest concentration of electronic transmissions and aerial transport but well clear of their paths. Both could be studied from a safe distance. Caldaq declared himself pleased.

It was unusual for the captain of a vessel to participate directly in such a sortie, but given the unprecedented nature of this world Caldaq felt strongly that his particular abilities might be of use. He was not leaving his command understaffed. Soliwik and Z'mam were more experienced and competent at shipboard administration than himself. If anything happened to the landing party, they would have no difficulty guiding the ship back home.

Having three Seconds gave him considerable flexibility. Furthermore, if it became necessary to employ the talents of the Massood, he wanted to be there to direct his own people. There would be twelve fighters in the squad. That should be sufficient to deal with any minor problems on the ground.

By avoiding urbanized regions where the two probes had vanished, they hopefully could avoid any such problems themselves.

They went down at the height of the nighttime phase, dropping uncomfortably fast toward the designated site and slowing only as they approached the surface. Preliminary observations confirmed the accuracy of the painstaking work which had been done in haste on board ship.

Below lay a multitude of shallow places surrounded by deeper water. All were uninhabited. Surface activity was nonexistent and communications transmissions feeble and infrequent. It was only a matter of choosing the site which best suited their requirements.

Personally Caldaq would rather have set down on land. The Massood were not water-lovers, and there was entirely too much water on this world to suit him. Only the Lepar would be comfortable in this place, he decided. But shallow seas offered the best opportunity for quick and easy concealment of the shuttle.

They entered the water as silently as possible, coming to rest on a firm bottom with sufficient clearance between the top of the ship and the surface. Since they had chosen an enclosed, protected area they would not have to worry about dangerous currents or wave action.

The tiny islets that encircled the landing site boasted modest vegetation in the form of dense bushes and tall branchless trees. The biologists went to work immediately, and it wasn't long before one discovered that the islets themselves were composed not of solid rock but rather of the decomposed skeletons of minute marine organisms.

Their chemical composition was quickly analyzed. It proved to be a simple, straightforward series which the shuttle's computer programmed into the onboard camouflage instrumentation. Working feverishly, Hivistahm and O'o'yan techs directed Lepar workers in the erection of an electrified grid around the shuttle. Thus stimulated, calcareous growth immediately began to form on the gridwork. In a few days the shuttle would be enclosed by a hard mantle indistinguishable from the reef surrounding it.

New information enabled the technicians to accelerate the process. Lepar sculpted the blossoming camouflage to better mimic the original, and the brightly colored local aquatic lifeforms which throve in the vicinity did their part by readily moving into the new rills and ridges materializing unexpectedly in their atoll home.

From the site it was possible to monitor major transmissions in several of the major languages without having to utilize high-gain reception equipment. The Wais worked overtime breaking down structure and grammar, their computers churning with correlations and analysis. Theirs was a talent Caldaq did not have, and he was grateful for their ability and persistence.

What a world this must be, he mused. Multiple languages, splintered lands, volcanic activity: the wonder was that any intelligence could triumph over such natural handicaps.

But it *was* a beautiful world, both above and below the surface. The ambient temperature was pleasing, the winds light, the amount of ultraviolet reaching the surface tolerable. If only the oxygen content were higher. Breathing would require more effort than usual. Still, he was impatient for a chance to leave the shuttle and feel solid ground beneath his feet again. It would be difficult not to take off running, for all that the little islands did not provide much room.

Given the opportunity he would have to restrain himself. The vegetation looked harmless enough, but no one could imagine what hungry or toxic creatures might lurk among the bushes. The same was true of the chromatically colored life-forms which swarmed in such profusion in the waters outside the ship.

Eventually a camouflaged access tube was constructed to the nearest islet and members of the crew were allowed outside at night, for exercise and by way of reward. The Lepar had preceded them, luxuriating in the warm water as they worked. You could envy them in their ability to breathe both in and out of the water, but that was about all you could envy them for, Caldaq reflected.

That first night he found himself gazing at the sky and its myriad unfamiliar stars. He did not worry about overflights by native aircraft. There had been none since they had landed.

There was a sandy beach. He started running along it, in the opposite direction from his fellow Massood, several of whom had been allowed to accompany him. He would meet them shortly, he knew. The island was small. But for a time he could be truly alone.

That was a luxury not to be imagined aboard ship. The objections of some squatty, hairy dwarfs were not about to keep him and his people from their first good run in months. Running was as vital to the Massood as sex. Besides, T'var would let him know if any native vehicles entered the area. That was unlikely, since research had confirmed the natives' preference for diurnal travel. In any case there would be ample time to return to the shuttle.

Vatoloi bobbed in the calm water nearby, his equipment belt secured around his waist, watching the Massood dash madly around the tiny island. Idly he plucked a strand of water growth from his external gills and flicked it aside. He did not understand what the Massood were doing. The activities of Massood ranked high on the list of things he did not understand.

Their pace was impressive, one he knew none of his kind could come close to matching. They might continue for much of the night, he knew, running round and round in circles until they exhausted themselves, until their long tongues were hanging from the sides of their mouths. It was of great importance to them, but for the Life he couldn't understand why. An immense amount of energy was being expended to no discernible purpose.

Perhaps it was a kind of joke, a humor. The Massood were fond of such, though they were not so incomprehensible as the S'van. Humor was something else Vatoloi did not understand. Of course it was not necessary that he understand. Enough to do his work, sleep, eat, reproduce.

As always there was the persistent feeling that he was missing something. It would help if he were as smart as the Massood, or the O'o'yan, or Life forbid, the S'van. While many races could make one feel inferior, only the S'van did it with empathy. That was a gift of the S'van. In a sense, Vatoloi thought, the structuring of an analogy giving him a headache as it always did, the S'van ran with words as the Massood did with their legs.

The Lepar possessed no such gifts. Nor did they have the technical skills of the Hivistahm or the delicate touch of the O'o'yan. They simply had the ability to work, steady and uncomplaining, so long as the task at hand was not too complicated and required no original thinking.

Ducking beneath the surface, Vatoloi's body effortlessly made the transition from breathing air to extracting oxygen from the surrounding seawater. As always he marveled at the intense colors of the local marine forms, many of which generated their own light at nighttime. He had collected specimens for many of the scientists, bewildered by their comments. But they praised his efforts, and he felt warmth.

No time to gawk now. He had to help Haoupi, who was checking the gridwork above the shuttle's antennae. Other Lepar swam by, and he acknowledged them with appropriate gestures and grins, his tail pushing him effortlessly through the clear water.

Haoupi was glad to see him. It was a great aid to one's labors when a supervisor like Vatoloi was available to tell you what to do when you weren't sure. The work was finished in good time. Because Vatoloi was so smart they did not even have to ask advice of the supervising Hivistahm. That pleased Haoupi because the Hivistahm were always impatient. They often said things that made you feel bad.

Making decisions was the hardest part of being a supervisor, but Vatoloi had accepted it because it had been asked of him. At least when you were a supervisor no one laughed at you or complained too loudly. But there were always the looks, the looks every Lepar had to live with. You dealt with them, as you dealt with the rest of existence.

This was a lovely place, he thought, the concept of beauty coming to him without struggle. And it was good to be able to go outside artificial walls. He preferred swimming to walking, no matter how many Hivistahm referred to it snidely as devolutionary.

He dove deeper, examining something crawling slowly across the sandy bottom. The first few days his tail had ached from lack of use, but now it was strong again.

They had heard the stories of the multiple languages and deformed geology of this world, but that did not mitigate its beauty for him. Of much more concern was the disappearance and possible destruction of the two survey remotes. Now crew had come to this place to try and find out what their machines had been unable to tell them.

Like everyone else, he was afraid of what might be out there. The Lepar were afraid much of the time. It was not an emotion so much as an endemic condition. They had come to this world, as they had gone to many other new worlds, in hopes of finding more help against the Amplitur. The Lepar feared the Amplitur far more than any of their allies, far more than the dark, lightless waters of their own world.

So they worked, kept working around the clock without complaint or objection or the quality of their work suffering, to help in their small way to defeat the Amplitur, who if not stopped would steal their selves. Smart the Lepar were not, but they were experts at enduring.

★ VII ★

By the fifth day they were still on the floor of the lagoon, their craft now comfortably concealed by calcareous concretions. No native had come anywhere near. Viewed from above, the shuttle was merely an extension of the extensive reef system. The local marine life found it much to their liking.

The Wais made progress in language analysis. They had identified and isolated three additional languages, bringing the total to eighteen. By this time Caldaq and his companions had passed beyond linguistic amazement.

They had also decided they could progress no further without making one of two choices. They could raise the ship and move nearer an urbanized area.

Or they could acquire a specimen.

It was easy enough to choose the latter course. They needed to increase their store of knowledge about the inhabitants as rapidly as was feasible. Working with a live specimen instead of confusing visual recordings would aid them in doing so.

Examination of those recordings confirmed initial impressions: the dominant race was mammalian and bipedal, surprisingly varied in size and coloring. As yet researchers were unable to tell if the latter reflected biological structuring into distinct categories such as workers and drones, for example.

At least they were not utterly alien. The S'van and the Massood were mammalian bipeds. The Hivistahm, O'o'yan, and others were at least endothermic.

But each spoke one language. Given the astonishing multiplicity of languages on this world it was remarkable that the natives could communicate effectively with one another at all.

A S'van had spent some time with Pasiiakilion, who had spoken of "geosociology." To the best of Caldaq's knowledge that was not a recognized discipline. The Turlog was struggling to find a way of describing the unique world they were studying.

They would try to isolate a healthy individual, a task which would require luck as much as care. If these people were as gregarious as the S'van, removal of an individual from its familiar social context could result in trauma or worse. Pity they weren't like the Turlog, he mused. One Turlog cared not a whit if another of its kind lived nearer than a light-year away.

It would not matter if the specimen chosen was male or female. The biologists would want to examine both, but any isolated couple might prove to be a mated pair. In that case the attempt to acquire could conceivably arouse mutually protective instincts, something which would be interesting to observe but contrary to the greater object of trying to secure a specimen's cooperation.

Four Massood would attempt the acquisition under cover of darkness, accompanied by a Wais to translate and a single Lepar to act as mechanic. The scientific staff protested at their exclusion, but not strongly. Memory of the disappearance of the remotes was still strong in everyone's mind.

The small submersible was silent and efficient. It was also virtually unsinkable. This was a great comfort to the Massood, who were not good swimmers. The thought of allowing Lepar to carry out the mission by themselves naturally occurred to no one.

It was decided to try to acquire a specimen from one of the native boats which occasionally passed close by the concealed shuttle. Infrequently, they actually entered the lagoon. The problem was that the smaller the craft, the more likely its crew was to notice the disappearance of someone in their midst.

It was decided first to try and find a vessel with three or fewer individuals aboard. To Caldaq the chances seemed slim. What fool would set him- or herself to sail a vast sea with so little companionship or assistance? But perhaps this close to land, in a small craft . . . It was worth a hopeful wait.

Days passed. A number of vessels entered and left the lagoon. All were crewed by a minimum of four beings. It was fascinating to observe their antics from the submersible instead of having to rely on recorded visual transmissions.

The natives wore little clothing, which made it easy to distinguish males from females. Their bodies were largely devoid of fur, an omission Caldaq and his fellow Massood found distasteful. In some ways the natives more nearly resembled the Lepar, though they had no tails and their skin was not slick. But they boasted similarly flat faces. Of course, so did the S'van.

There was no need to don heating packs since the temperature was quite warm even in the middle of the night. He lay prone atop the slightly curved surface of the submersible and studied the native vessel through a magnifier.

There were six of them, all gyrating beneath the oversized moon. Raucous modulations burst rhythmically from the vessel's central cabin. Caldaq gazed in fascination at the muscular but crude dances they were performing, wondering at the origin of the ritual which gave rise to such exertions. Males and females changed pairings frequently.

It was all very impressive from a biosocial viewpoint. However, it did nothing to advance their aims.

They had much better luck the following night.

The vast lagoon was empty when the double-hulled craft entered and anchored, but what drew them to it initially was not its isolation so much as the music that began to emanate from it that first night. It but fitfully resembled the dissonant native sounds that had been previously recorded. The music emerged from the craft in irregular bursts and snatches that changed and shifted unpredictably. Barbaric and uncivilized, though somewhat less so than what they had heard before. Also, the volume fell within the tolerable range. The boat could be approached in safety.

Since there were no other native craft present in the lagoon at the time, it was decided that a preliminary inspection might be efficacious.

Visual scan showed an empty deck. The sail typically employed to propel native craft was fully reefed, and it was secured to the lagoon bottom. Artificial illumination brightened the large central cabin.

Caldaq had Denlaca execute a tightening spiral around the craft. The deck remained empty, a hopeful sign suggesting a small crew at most. Nor were the internal lights regularly occluded by the movement of people within. Their pickups continued to record music. The sequence of harmonic variations was unlike anything previously noted in native transmissions. It was as if those on board knew what they wanted to hear, but not how. Caldaq was anxious to have a look at the inhabitants. Anxious enough to discuss the situation with his fellow Massood.

"This is the first time in several time periods the lagoon has been occupied by only a single native craft. It presents us with an excellent opportunity, but first we must ascertain how many natives are on board.

"If we wait until they show themselves, other craft may arrive and communicate with this one, thereby destroying its useful isolation. Given that the natives often appear only in daytime, that is a real risk. As we cannot observe during the day because our submersible would be easily visible in this water, I propose to board the alien craft now, in hopes of securing a count without exposing ourselves."

One of the soldiers proposed an alternative. "The Lepar can swim close to the craft."

Caldaq's nose twitched. "The ports are too high. He would not be able to see inside."

There were no other suggestions. Caldaq took upon himself the distasteful task of being the first to make the short swim from the submersible to the native vessel. Dropahc volunteered to accompany him.

The natives tended to be at their most inert in the dark hours just prior to sunrise. The Massood waited on board the submersible, discussing alternatives that ranged from the benign to the disastrous.

Then it was time to proceed.

Caldaq and Dropahc removed their clothing. Each donned an expendable service belt that contained emergency supplies, communicator, translator pack including the new program for the dominant local language, and small sidearm. The latter was not for confronting natives. Large carnivores had often been observed feeding in the waters around the shuttle.

Once outside the submersible, both Massood slipped into the warm water. Swimming was an unnatural activity. The Hivistahm and O'o'yan could not do it at all. Caldaq's lips drew back at the uncomfortable sensation. The native craft lay close by, motionless in the protected waters of the lagoon.

Muscles protested painfully but the distance involved was very short. Both soldiers soon found themselves clinging to the stern of one of the twin hulls, each of which had been fitted with horizontal slots to form a ladder. The vessel itself was of an interesting but not remarkable design, principles of primitive waterborne transportation being relatively universal.

Dropahc insisted on going up first. Water pouring off his fur, he turned to whisper back down to his captain.

"The back end is open and I can see into the central cabin. Nothing moves there. The music comes from the other hull."

Fancying large meat-eaters swimming through the darkness beneath them, Caldaq hastened to join his companion on the deck.

Between the two hulls lay a large, raised cabin. Behind it was an open compartment dominated by a wheel-like device and some simple instrumentation. Caldaq advanced until he was able to step down behind the wheel and peer into the cabin.

The interior was well lit. An unseen device hummed softly, doubtless the machine which provided the craft with power. The door to the cabin was open, allowing the music emanating from within to assail his ears unobstructed. It was not as painful as he'd feared, but it was far from pleasant.

Inside he saw another wheel and more instrumentation, along with furniture and decorations whose functions he could only guess at. Keeping low, he turned to his companion.

"Come close. There is no one here. Only the music."

Dropahc stepped down to join his captain. His ears lay flat against his head and his lips were drawn back, exposing his teeth. Whiskers quivered.

"The noise hurts my head."

"Mine as well, yet it is easier to bear than similar sounds we have recorded previously." He hesitated, then gestured at the open doorway. "We have to look inside."

"Exercise caution, Captain."

Caldaq turned in the opening. "We know what they look like. They are not physically imposing."

"Many toxic creatures have innocuous appearances," Dropahc pointed out.

"I will be careful." Caldaq bent and entered the cabin.

The low ceiling required him to bend slightly at the waist. His nose twitched at the end of his snout. The room was ripe with alien scent, strong and strangely sweetish. There were openings on both sides, leading down into the twin hulls. He turned toward the one from which the music came.

Bending double, he looked warily to his left, then his right. At the far end of the long narrow chamber he saw the native. It was seated, its naked arms and hands working with multiple devices. The music emanated from twin boxes fastened to opposite walls. Its back was to the doorway and it was oblivious to Caldaq's presence.

Personal observation confirmed what they had learned from their study of native visual transmissions. They had five bare digits on each hand, one more than the Massood, two less than the O'o'yan, the same as the Hivistahm. Otherwise they resembled the Hivistahm not at all. Their skin was almost entirely hairless, soft-looking and fleshy, not hard-scaled like that of his best technicians.

Up close the discordant sounds were almost more than Caldaq could bear. How the native stood them he could not imagine. It must possess hearing organs of remarkable tolerance, he decided.

He retreated to the central cabin for relief. Dropahc emerged from the opening that led to the other hull.

"Deserted," he murmured softly.

"I have found only one," Caldaq replied. The painful chords lingering in the air served to mitigate his enthusiasm. A particularly dissonant eruption made Dropahc wince.

"How can anything sentient stand such sounds? No wonder it is alone."

"It has kept its back to the opening, so I cannot tell the sex. Tell the others to come aboard, and bring the translator."

Dropahc eyed him questioningly. "Is that necessary, Captain? Surely the two of us . . ."

"I do not take chances with the unknown. I want everyone present."

Still Dropahc hesitated. "What if the Wais will not come? It cannot swim."

"The others can carry it through the water. We may need its services. Vatoloi can help."

Dropahc indicated acknowledgment and turned to go, hesitating in the doorway. "Who will watch the submersible?"

"Vatoloi." In response to Dropahc's questioning look he

added, "The Lepar does not have to operate anything; just stay with it."

Dropahc's nose twitched and he vanished silently into the night. Caldaq did not even hear him slip back into the water.

He returned to the opening and gingerly peered back inside. The native was still sitting before its devices, generating sounds no sane being in a civilized setting would have tolerated for more than a moment. Caldaq flattened his ears, hoping Dropahc and the others would be quick.

An F-sharp gave Will Dulac pause. He leaned back in the chair and stared moodily at the array of instrumentation assembled before him. The quiet hum of the synthesizer was the only sound in the port fore-cabin.

He ran the fingers of his left hand through his dark, wavy hair. It was shrinking yearly, retreating from his forehead and concealing itself somewhere down the back of his collar. That steady subsidence, like a glacier in retreat, was partly why he had chosen to grow the outrageously bushy sideburns. Also he wanted to do something distinctive and different with his appearance, just as he did with his music.

The first half of *Arcadia* was done and the remainder sketched in. But the scherzo that led into the concussive concluding allegro energico was giving him nothing but trouble. Not the music itself: the notes were there, dark and immutable, within the laptop's program. It was the orchestration that was driving him crazy.

He'd planned from the outset to begin the scherzo with flutes counterpointed by a single bassoon. The result would be driving yet comical, a bit of musical black comedy Berlioz or Bartók would have appreciated. Then have the second violins and the basses pick it up before segueing into the neat little toccata for brass he'd put together. The toccata worked fine, but for the life of him he couldn't figure out how to get from the end of the adagio to the scherzo. He was at an orchestral impasse.

Nothing sounded right. The flutes seemed lost and the bassoon, instead of protruding mournfully, came across like a dyspeptic tuba, a refugee from the Saturn movement of Holst's *Planets*.

He stared angrily at the MIDI board and the tangle of cables on the desk. What if he went with a sax instead of the bassoon?

The orchestration was complicated enough already, getting real expensive. Adding a sax player wouldn't encourage penurious small-town orchestras to play the finished work.

Dammit, Ravel had found the effect he wanted! So had Debussy, and Griffes. If a bunch of early-twentieth-century Frenchmen and a sickly American could create the sound he needed, why couldn't an experienced academic from New Orleans?

Maybe he'd subconsciously avoided use of the saxophone all along because the last thing he wanted was any jazz overtones. Coming from that part of the country, it was something he'd had to fight in his work all his life.

"Oh, yeah, you're that composer from New Orleans. Your work must be, has to be, cannot be anything *but* jazz-oriented. Right?"

He shook his head even though there was no one present to observe the gesture. Amazing and disgusting how people could generalize. Just because he was from Louisiana, critics and public alike *assumed*. He had no intention of being the second coming of Louis Gottschalk.

His work had nothing to do with jazz, everything to do with his Cajun heritage. It would have been much easier to do something simple for a first large-scale orchestral composition. A folk-song suite, perhaps, utilizing the tunes and fiddling he'd grown up listening to in the parish. Some simple orchestrating and he'd have a piece worthy of recording.

But that wasn't what had been swimming around inside his head for the past fifteen years. Oh, he'd make use of those tunes, you bet. But as bits and pieces, useful fragments and jumping-off points for the real composition.

No, his intent, his aim was greater than that. He was striving for nothing less than a synthesis of Cajun folk music with contemporary symphonic tradition. There were minimalist overtones, sure, but plenty of echoes of modern American music in the tradition of everybody from Hanson to Glass. John Vincent's wonderful symphony had been a particular inspiration to him, perhaps because Vincent had hailed from Alabama instead of Los Angeles or New York.

He'd thought taking off in the boat for a few weeks would help to break the instrumental logjam in his brain. There were too many distractions in the city, or even out on the Lake or the

Gulf. He knew that he needed to get farther away, much farther. Away from the casual camaraderie of the bookstores and the chatter of the University, away from the restaurants and lectures. Too simple to put computer aside and head to the Café du Monde for café au lait and beignets. Too easy to cut the power and spend the night hanging around the Quarter watching the tourists gawk at the locals and vice versa.

If he was going to make any real progress, if he was going to finish this monster which had taken over his life, he knew he had to go somewhere devoid of entertainment or intellectual intercourse. Since he didn't have much money, that meant taking the boat out.

What kept him going was Dorbachevski's interest in the project. The orchestra's director had half promised to premiere the piece with the symphony as soon as its composer had it whipped into publishable shape. A performance by the Philharmonic would not only give the composition instant legitimacy, it would be a qualitative leap over what the University orchestra could do.

Dearborn, the head of the department, had offered him a full professorship on more than one occasion. To the amazement of his colleagues he continued to turn it down, explaining that he preferred the independence conferred by part-time teaching and tutoring. Infrequent but well-paying guest conductorships and occasional TV work kept him afloat, if not in a position to begin collecting Fabergé eggs. It was not so much that he favored the life-style of a gypsy academic, he just wanted time to compose.

Of course, if he couldn't solve *Arcadia*, he would have to seriously consider giving Frank Dearborn a call.

Not to think of that now. Better to remember Dorbachevski's promise, to think of the completed tone poem filling Symphony Hall with sonorous prosody, its grand finale capped by a cacophonous coda of applause.

If only the fucking flutes would cooperate.

So far his tenuous claim to fame consisted of forty-five seconds of music he'd composed for the news department of the local NBC affiliate and the score to a documentary on Louisiana bird life for the Baton Rouge PBS station. If only the documentary had been on oil drilling or chemical refining, he might even have made some real money on it.

Arcadia was going to be his breakthrough: a symphonic poem utilizing Cajun themes, full of richness and power and hope. He'd put everything from memories of his childhood to all his technical knowledge into it, resisting the temptation to engage in trendy minimalism or shocking atonality. The finished work would be modern yet approachable.

It would not, however, be heard unless he could solve the bedeviling orchestration. It was as if someone had put a gris-gris on him, yes.

So he'd stocked his catamaran, cranked up the winches, loosened up the roller furling, and set sail south. No sampling the tawdry temptations of Cozumel or Cancún this trip. They were too redolent of his hometown. He wanted, needed, to get away from such distractions.

Only when he'd reached Lighthouse Reef did he select a mooring inside the lagoon and drop anchor. No one was likely to disturb him there for weeks. Only passing boats visited this place, sixty miles off the coast of sweltering, unglamorous Belize. Shoot, there were only a hundred and sixty thousand people in the whole country. More than half spoke English, which made it easy for him to replenish his supplies during his intermittent forays into Belize City or Monkey Town.

He was able to anchor in one place, taking the occasional break from the burden of composing by snorkeling in the warm waters of the enormous lagoon. The nearby islets were blessedly free of mosquitoes, though small biting flies did their best to fill the ecological niche their slimmer cousins had abdicated.

The weather remained good and as hoped, his work had taken a quantum leap forward. But now he was stuck, mired in the scherzo which should have been among the easiest parts to finish.

He resisted the urge to skip ahead to the allegro by covering his uncertainty with timpani. Better to junk the whole ten pages, and that he refused to do. Why couldn't he be like Strauss or Mozart, effortlessly cranking out masterwork after masterwork, the music already fully orchestrated in his head? Why couldn't counterpoint come naturally to him, instead of requiring such rigorous mental application?

If he was ever going to command more than a line in Baker's or Grove, he was going to have to complete something really worthwhile. That he was in the books at all, right between Dukelsky and Dulcken, was a triumph of sorts. But he wanted more from the compilers. He wanted admiration, he wanted commentary. He wanted *footnotes*.

DULAC, WILLIAM L.: born Slidell, Louisiana, 19 . . . well, not too many years ago. Marital status—single (but not forever, hopefully). Major works—two string quartets, assorted songs, music for television, the overture *Jambalaya*.

He smiled at that, memories of his first real success. Who but a Cajun would have had the audacity to compose a work of twelve minutes' duration for full symphony orchestra inspired entirely by food?

He read on in his thoughts: various minor works . . .

Arcadia would change that. In its present form the symphonic poem was fifty minutes long. Let them try to ignore him after *Arcadia* . . . if he could ever finish the damn thing.

Lips tight, he glared at the keyboard as his fingers manipulated the keys. The bassoon vanished, kicked aside by a newly installed saxophone.

Go with your instincts, his teachers had always told him. Don't let technical proficiency and expertise get in the way of what *feels* right.

He leaned back and contemplated. By damn, it even looked better up there on the screen than that stupid bassoon. He hit ENTER, listened to the CD-ROM track, then ordered playback. Instant synthesized orchestra replied through the speakers.

There it was, sensuous and mournful: daybreak fog the sun had yet to burn off the swamp. Spanish moss hung limp and damp from the arms of the cypress just as the sound of the sax clung to the trills of the flutes. Much better, he told himself. Much better. If he could just get through the scherzo, the allegro would be a breeze: all brass and bass and supple supportive strings.

Smiling with satisfaction he swiveled in his chair to find himself staring at something that had to bend double to peer through the passageway leading to the main cabin.

⋆ VIII ⋆

It was very tall and covered in short gray fur. Wide, dark eyes with vertical pupils stared back at him from either side of a triangular, protruding snout at the end of which whiskers and a black nose twitched ceaselessly. The one visible four-fingered hand was huge but small-boned. A small rectangular device hung from a necklace or strap, and a gold button was fitted inside one ear. Other equipment was attached to a thin belt above the hips.

A gaping Will thought he could make out a second face crowding close behind the first, and beyond it a hint of a giant bird with a crest of brilliantly hued feathers. It gazed back at him with the same intelligent interest as its hairy companion.

No one moved until the creature in the back squeezed through the opening and past the others. As it approached the composer its lips drew back, revealing grayish gums and rows of sharp, pointed teeth. It looked powerful and vicious and when it reached for him, Will instinctively knocked the menacing arm aside. He struck quickly and without thinking.

To his surprise the creature let out an incongruously high-pitched yelp and stumbled backward, straightening convulsively and banging its head against the cabin ceiling. It clutched at the wrist Will had swatted.

Though shocked, Caldaq reacted swiftly. He drew his sidearm and aimed it at the native. Behind him he heard the Wais gasp softly. He ignored it. Unexpected circumstances called for unprecedented reactions.

The native's response confirmed the correctness of the action.

It looked first at him, then at the sidearm, and stopped moving, correctly interpreting the device's function. Experience had demonstrated that even very primitive peoples understood that something pointed at their midsections should be regarded with caution.

Dropahc retreated to the large central cabin and sat down on the floor, grimacing in pain and holding onto his right wrist. Caldaq motioned with his sidearm for the native to follow. It did so, noting as it complied the presence of the Wais and the two other Massood. There was ample room in the cabin between the two hulls for everyone.

When standing, the native was slightly taller than the Wais, taller than any Weave sentients save the Massood and the Chirinaldo. Its face was even flatter than that of a S'van.

"I think it is broken, Captain." Dropahc looked up, mucus dripping from his snout. "Did you see how quickly it moved?"

"I saw." Caldaq did not take his eyes from the native. He couldn't conceive of killing it, but neither would he allow it to injure any more of his people. He could not understand the violence of its reaction to Dropahc's friendly approach.

"Perhaps this is an unnaturally belligerent individual," the Wais suggested shakily, "and that is why it has been isolated from others of its kind."

"The music itself is belligerent," said Dropahc.

Caldaq glanced briefly at the injured soldier. "Get outside. You cannot do any good in here and if there is further trouble you will only be in the way."

Lips quivering, Dropahc signed affirmation and exited.

The four remaining crewmembers confronted the native, which stared back. The Wais remained in the background. If it came to a fight, Caldaq knew she would be useless.

"If it makes a move toward any of you," he murmured, "shoot it." He ignored the shocked looks of his subordinates. "We will search elsewhere for a more tractable specimen. We do not know what these things are capable of and I will not have anyone else hurt."

The native had backed up against the large wheel device. It watched Caldaq as he spoke, understanding nothing of what was being said in its presence.

"I did not see." The Wais regarded the specimen out of soft, limpid eyes. "You say that Dropahc attempted to extend greetings and it simply struck and injured him without warning?"

"If it spoke first I did not hear," said Caldaq. "Nor did I see its mouth move."

"Surely it is not," muttered one of the other Massood soldiers, "like the Amplitur?"

"It reacted physically, so I would think not. We have an aberration here and we must find a way of dealing with it."

"To strike out like that without first attempting to ascertain what was wanted of it, to do actual physical damage . . ." Caldaq saw that the sensitive Wais was in danger of going into shock. To forestall that he spoke sharply to her.

"Find out what it wants."

The glaze vanished from the ornithorp's eyes. She signed a response, once more a fully functioning member of his crew. As she stepped hesitantly forward, Caldaq made certain his own translator was functioning.

The Wais found herself switching smoothly from fluent Massood to the chosen native language. It resembled Turlog and S'van as much as anything else.

"Please relax. We mean you no harm."

Will's head jerked around and he gaped at the tall bird-thing. It had spoken to him in perfect, unaccented American English. Nevertheless, it was hard to concentrate on what it was saying due to the presence of the three tall, toothy monsters who had surrounded him. Each was pointing something short and machined in his direction. They might be wands of peace, or devices for sampling the atmosphere or measuring his body temperature, but he didn't think so.

Nor was he anxious to find out. He realized that the alien which had left holding its wrist had been injured and that he was responsible. But he hadn't struck out that hard. It had only been his intention to brush the groping paw aside. Clearly he'd done more than that.

What more natural, then, than for these creatures to treat him as hostile? But he wasn't, he wasn't hostile at all. How else did they expect him to react, bursting in on him in the middle of the night?

Where had they come from? His imagination was working overtime. They smelled of the lagoon but none of them looked built for an aquatic life-style. They were not a bunch of his students come all the way to Belize to play some incredibly elaborate practical joke on him. Even if they could be human beings inside gray fur suits, there was no room for anyone inside that bird body, not even a child.

He wondered why it was the only one speaking. It was downright voluble, talking to calm and reassure him. All of which was dependent on him believing what was happening. Which he was starting to do. He just didn't *want* to. He found himself edging back toward the doorway which led to the portside hull.

"This is crazy," he mumbled aloud.

"Careful," said Caldaq. "It is moving." He raised his sidearm slightly, trying to decide which part of the native body would be most receptive to a nonlethal charge.

Abruptly, the creature changed direction and dove through the passageway that led into the other hull. It executed the maneuver with incredible speed, too rapidly for any of the soldiers to react.

"Watch out!" Wouldea shouted. "It is trying to get away!" Despite their concern, no one fired.

Instead they attempted to follow, greatly encumbered by their height. The Wais glided along behind, frantically issuing a stream of what should have been reassuring words in the local tongue. When these had no effect it switched desperately to a second native language, then a third.

"Why are you running? There is nothing wrong. *No problema aquí, señor. Was ist mit ihnen los?*"

Will went up fast through the hatch, shutting it behind him and looking around wildly. The foredeck was deserted. He stepped out on the trampoline suspended between the twin bows. If he could make it to Goff Cay and hide out there till morning, he might be able to signal his distress to the single elderly government employee stationed at Half Moon Cay. Half Moon was a bird sanctuary, and tourist boats sometimes put in there.

Not that anyone would believe his tale of being accosted in the middle of the night by four creatures with bodies like gibbons and faces like giant rats who let a glamorized emu do all their talking for them, but he didn't much care about that. All he wanted was to put distance between himself and his nightmare.

He was standing on the edge of the trampoline when they began to emerge from the hatch. Now he could see how tall they were, all except the bird-creature standing at least six-foot-six.

"Wait, please wait!" The bird-thing sounded almost plaintive. He wondered how it could form English words so well given that encumbering heavy beak.

The nearest alien was waving one of the pointy, lethal-looking devices in his direction. That settled it.

Caldaq slowed in surprise as the native leaped into the water. Gingerly he and the others approached the front of the craft. A quick inspection showed no sign of the specimen.

"Surely it is not amphibious. I saw no sign of gills."

"No." Wouldea pointed to the right of the boat as the native broke the surface. It was heading for an impossibly distant island.

"Great Stride," muttered the other soldier. "Look at it move!"

Caldaq raised his sidearm. They could try to stun it, but what if it wasn't a water-breather? It might sink and drown. The more unanticipated abilities it demonstrated, the more anxious Caldaq was to examine it.

He pulled his communicator and gave the necessary orders.

Will paused momentarily, breathing hard and treading water. Behind him his catamaran was an angular silhouette in the moonlight. He could see the three monsters lined up on the trampoline. They were staring at him but gave no sign of pursuing. The bird-creature stood nearby. Either they didn't want to follow him or else they couldn't. He relaxed a little.

The water was warm and comfortable and he was already a third of the way to his destination. From previous snorkeling expeditions he knew there were coral heads in the vicinity, but only a few that scraped the surface. If he didn't let his legs dangle he ought to be able to pass over the rest in safety.

As he turned to resume his crawl a face emerged directly in front of his. Less than a foot away, it was bulbous and glistening, with a mouth that nearly split the skull in half. Something like pink seaweed clung to both sides of the neck, and a pair of small black eyes stared into his own. It had a tail and webbed hind feet and wore some kind of body suit and belt. The fact that it was smaller than him did nothing to minimize the shock of its appearance.

Uttering an inarticulate cry, he tried to swim around it. Darting effortlessly in front of him, it blocked his path to the island.

Despite the creature's smaller stature, its mouth was wide enough to encompass Will's entire head. That intimidating orifice gaped as it made burbling sounds at him. When a second attempt at slipping past proved equally futile, he swam in place and studied his opponent.

Noting the webbed feet, gills, and tail, Will had no illusions about trying to outswim it. It didn't seem hostile: just curious. The vast mouth was devoid of teeth. There was also something about the tiny dark eyes, about the whole aspect of the alien, which was reassuring.

It burbled at him afresh. Not a pet or domesticated animal, he decided. The instrumentation it wore on the belt was proof enough of that. Its attitude was easygoing, but not indifferent.

Turning in the water, Will pointed back to his boat, then looked questioningly at the creature. He was not surprised when it lifted a dripping hand and mimicked the gesture.

"All right," he said tiredly. "I get the idea. You could probably swim circles around me till I sank." Reluctantly, he started swimming back toward the cat.

As he swam it struck him that the aliens already on board could have shot him at their leisure. They hadn't done so when he'd bolted from the cabin, when he'd jumped overboard, or while he'd been trying to swim to safety. Whatever their intentions were they apparently did not include immediate dismemberment and vivisection.

If he needed additional proof, he got it when he swam around to the back of his boat.

Long, slim fingers reached down for his. He found himself gazing up past whiskers and teeth into eerie catlike eyes.

The water alien was right behind him. Will reached up and took the proffered hand.

"I cannot do it." The soldier spoke to Caldaq. "It is much heavier than it appears."

Wouldea came over to aid his companion. It took their combined strength to help the native back aboard. Caldaq and Dropahc covered them as they retreated. At a sign from his captain, Vatoloi swam back to the unoccupied submersible.

Will climbed down into the cockpit, stood there dripping as he studied his captors. They were spread out, no doubt to cover him more effectively should he try to flee a second time.

"Take it easy." He raised both hands. "It's cold out here at night when you're wet. I just want to get a towel."

"Go right ahead."

Will regarded the Wais admiringly. "Damn but your English is good. I've got students you could tutor."

The Wais responded to the alien's words with a cocky flip of its feathery plume before turning to Caldaq.

"It does indeed speak the principal language. My earlier words were understood. I surmise it could think only of flight."

"Why?" Caldaq was genuinely puzzled. "We made no hostile gestures."

"I believe its reaction was based solely on our appearance."

"That makes no sense. Why should the way we look frighten it so?"

"I am a translator, not a xenopsych." The Wais spoke again in English. "Go and get your 'towel.' Believe me when I tell you that we mean you no harm. There was no reason for you to flee."

"Say you, yeah. I maybe think otherwise, you bet." Aware he'd momentarily slipped back to the patois of his childhood he added, "Just give me a minute to dry off. What is it you people want, anyway?" He entered the center cabin. His visitors (that was better than "captors," he thought) followed.

"Just to talk," said the Wais.

"Ah sure. Where are you from?"

In place of the nonexistent English equivalent, the translator substituted a descriptive term. "The Weave."

" 'The Weave.' As in someplace up there?" He gestured skyward with a thumb. The Wais flipped its plume again, curious to see if the native would interpret the gesture correctly.

"And you just want to talk?"

Caldaq could stand it no longer. He stepped forward. The native flinched, then allowed the taller Massood to place the translator around its neck and a corresponding lightweight receiver atop its head. It tightened automatically. At first the native bared its teeth. Then it relaxed.

"We have many things to tell you." The native's eyes widened, hopefully an indication it was receiving properly.

It responded hesitantly, mimicking the captain by directing its voice to the translator now dangling from its neck. The machine responded by converting the grunting speech into intelligible Massood.

"I don't know what you have to tell me. I'm more interested in the fact that you don't want to shoot me."

"Why would we want to shoot you?" asked the Wais. Catching Caldaq's expression, it hastened to add in Massood, "My apologies, Captain. I did not mean to . . ."

"Never mind. I am interested in results here, not protocol." He turned to the native. "We have to tell you about the Weave. About the Amplitur, and about . . ." he paused, not wanting to panic the specimen unduly and giving the translator time to catch up. "About many things."

"Fine." Apparently the native was not given to lengthy replies. "So long as you're not going to shoot me."

"You persist with that," said Dropahc. He held his sidearm in his undamaged hand. "Why would we want to shoot you? You are an intelligent being, we are intelligent beings. We have only just met. Why would we respond with weapons?"

"What do you call what you're doing right now?"

"You struck first, in anger."

"I wasn't angry: I was scared."

"But why?"

Will sighed. "This isn't getting us anywhere." He indicated Dropahc's weapon. "I'll stay frightened as long as those things are pointed at me."

Dropahc looked at his captain. With deliberate slowness, Caldaq resecured his weapon at his belt. His companions did likewise.

"That's better." Will went over to a locker and found a clean towel, dried himself off. He was very close to the inside helm. Also the radio and cellular phone, but if he decided to make use of those it would be better to do so when they weren't watching him so closely.

He spoke while mopping his back. "Look, I'm sorry if I hurt you," he said to Dropahc.

An apology for the violence committed, Caldaq thought. That was a hopeful sign, but far from conclusive.

"Will he be okay? By the way, my name is Will Dulac."

"Two names?" said the Wais.

"Yes."

"Dropahc will heal. Our medical staff has means for speeding his recovery."

The native was staring past him, astern. "Medical staff. You must have a pretty good-sized ship out there somewhere, right?"

"A shuttle. Our main vessel is presently situated between your world and your unusual moon." Caldaq was puzzled. Just when he began thinking of the native as perceptive it would betray its ignorance with a stupid comment or question. It was a nest of contradictions.

"Are you by any chance," Wouldea asked, unable to restrain himself any longer, "a fighter?"

"A fighter?"

Wouldea asked again. The translator program obediently essayed alternative semantics.

"A soldier." The native sat down on a long, padded seat. "Hell, no. What makes you think I might be a soldier?"

"You struck. You caused injury."

"I told you, I was scared. I wasn't fighting. When your friend came toward me I tried to push his hand out of the way. That's all. Maybe I was a little sharp, but I swear I wasn't trying to hurt anybody."

"Why should you want to push his hand out of the way if you are not a soldier?"

Will found the whole line of questioning exasperating. "Wouldn't you?" was all he could think of to say.

"Of course not." Wouldea responded instantly, startled by the very notion.

"I'm not a soldier," Will informed them brusquely. "I'm a composer, a musician."

"We heard your 'music,' " Caldaq declared. "It is not to our tastes."

"Sorry to hear it." There was no reason for Will to be upset by the admission. What did these creatures from elsewhere know of symphonic music?

Wouldea pushed his translator aside and spoke to Caldaq. "I saw Dropahc's hand, Captain. If this is a race of musicians and teachers, what might they be like if they chose to fight?"

"Think it through," Caldaq warned him. "Remember that

we are dealing with a single specimen in isolated circumstances.''

No, not quite, he reminded himself. There remained the matter of the two missing survey drones which had brought them to this place.

''Merely because some of their music is violent does not mean they are suited to combat.''

''They are physically able,'' Wouldea argued, unwilling to concede his optimism. ''Dropahc can attest to that.''

As the tropical night warmed his body Will watched the two aliens converse. No question but that they were as interested in him as he was in them. He was still not convinced their intentions were altogether peaceful, but he felt he was in no immediate danger.

Studying them, he was conscious of his naked flesh. The three tall ones with the ratlike skulls sported short gray fur, while the English-speaker's feathers covered nearly all of its body, some of it garishly. It looked like a cross between a secretary bird and Einstein as it fiddled with the instruments suspended from its belt. The large soft eyes were peridot green.

He didn't consider it dangerous at all, as opposed to the other three. Not only were its mannerisms unthreatening, so was its strange, mellifluous voice. This despite its appearance, which was far more alien than that of its taller companions.

He hung the towel around his neck. The two aliens, one of whom appeared to be in charge, continued to argue. Would they notice if he leaned casually against the helm and manipulated the radio sufficient to send out a general mayday? The unit would report his position automatically, bringing any yacht or power-boat that picked up the signal to his side. It might frighten off his visitors. They might not want the attention.

Or did they have the means to cope with that, too?

By now curiosity was starting to replace his initial terror. He peered through a port, wondering what had happened to the seallike creature which had intercepted him in the water. It had tried to talk to him without the benefit of a translating device.

Now all three of the tall aliens were arguing while the bird-creature continued to fiddle intently with the instruments attached to its belt. Will had no doubt that he was the subject of the animated debate. Were the clever little language devices designed to respond only to directed input, or were they deliberately excluding him?

He used the time to examine the equipment they carried. Besides the maybe-weapons and the translators there were a number of other instruments, fashioned of shiny, opaque materials. Plastic, perhaps, or some dull metal. Maybe something more exotic like metallic glass. He could only recall what he'd read in the general press and try to imagine, his education in the hard sciences being woefully deficient.

Simultaneously they ceased their high-pitched chatter and turned back to him. The hand which had been edging toward the radio froze. He smiled, wondering if it would mean anything to them. The one who was clearly in charge stepped forward. His whiskers quivered almost comically, but there was nothing funny about those teeth.

"Tell me something," he heard himself saying. The tall alien halted. Encouraged, Will continued. "Have you been here before this? Visited our world previously without our knowing it?"

There was concern in the alien's reply. It was not what Will had expected. "You have received previously extraplanetary visits?"

"No. At least, I don't think so. I mean, rumors about UFOs have been around for some time. Not that I believe in them myself, of course." Until now, he added silently.

"No one from the Weave," the alien told him, "has been to this world before us. We have not been studying you." It seemed to Will that the alien spoke slowly and with extreme earnestness. "You are saying you have had no confirmed encounters with any intelligence other than your own kind?"

"That's what I'm saying." Will wondered what all the concern was about. He did not need the services of a translating device to sense the tension in the cabin.

It evaporated with his reply.

"It is important to us to be sure that we are the first to visit your world," the bird-thing said in English. Will wondered why it was so important but didn't have the chance to ask because the one in charge was speaking again.

"My name is Caldaq, of the Massood." The name was not translated but instead came across as a short squirt of consonants interrupted by spit vowels. It was almost as much whistled as spoken, Will noted. The translator struggled with it. "I am in command of this visitation. I am a fighter by training, captain by avocation, runner by choice, male by gender. I am once-mated and have no cubs. My lineage is an important one. I am an ascetic omnivore.

"Now I have told you about myself. Tell us of you."

Why not? Will mused as he sat down on the couch. His life wasn't a state secret. "I'm thirty-eight, male, and single. I do some teaching, I'm trying to gain recognition as a serious composer, and this boat is my home, a choice of life-style which makes me suspect among my more conservative friends." He was staring at the alien leader. "Are you always this nervous?"

"Nervous?" said Caldaq.

"I've been watching you and your friends. Your faces are in constant motion: mouth, lips, ears, whiskers, nose. Don't you ever stop twitching?"

"It is a natural function of our physiology," Caldaq explained. "Does it trouble you?"

"No, it doesn't trouble me. But we don't do that and it's kind of hard to get used to."

"You are isolated." The bird-thing was speaking. "I am Wais. Our faces are not capable of such a range of motion." Will looked on with interest as one delicate hand wove an intricate pattern in the air.

"Every species," Caldaq went on, "has its own distinctive characteristics. Those which are natural and familiar to one may appear strange and even unpleasant to another."

"Ah. Like me brushing your companion's hand aside."

Caldaq was willing to concede the point. The more they conversed with the native, the more genuinely apologetic it seemed.

"What else can you tell us about yourself?"

Will spread his hands. "Not much. Once you get past my music, there's not much else to talk about. I'm half Cajun, though I don't guess that would mean anything to you. We call ourselves Humans." He gestured toward the nearest port, at the calm water of the lagoon and the uninhabited islets that ringed it.

"We call our world Earth. Right now we're offshore from a small Central American country called Belize." Pointing that out called a question to mind. "Why'd you land here, anyway? Why didn't you set down in Washington or Moscow or someplace important?"

Would this isolated native know anything about the missing

remotes? Caldaq doubted it, and decided not to bring up the matter just yet.

"We have a procedure for exploring new worlds. We feel it is best to approach quietly, to study and learn certain basics before announcing our presence. Particularly when that world is home to a sentient species."

"Of which there are more than a couple, right?" said Will. "I mean, there's us, and you, and the Wais there, and then there was that thing that cut me off in the water. That's four right there." He shook his head. "We've always wondered if we were the only ones. The only intelligence around, I mean."

What an extraordinary conceit, Caldaq thought. "There are dozens of intelligent races."

"I see." The native was very quiet for a long moment. Finally he asked, "With all those intelligences out there, how come it took until now for you or anybody else to make contact with us?"

"The majority of older, developed worlds lie nearer the galactic center, and not in a straight line from your system, either. Exploration has historically concentrated on systems that lie close to one another. Yours is situated in a different direction entirely."

Caldaq did not mind answering questions. The native was acting sensibly and they were learning much simply by observing him. Curiosity was a hallmark of the higher intelligences.

"May we have a look around your boat? Your home?" the Wais inquired politely.

"Sure, why not? I can't stop you anyway."

Again! Just when the native began behaving normally it would say or do something irrational.

"Why would you want to stop us?" Caldaq asked him.

"Well, I mean, it's my boat, isn't it?"

"Yes. But we would not harm it or take anything from it."

"I didn't mean to imply that you would. It was just a natural reaction, a figure of speech, okay? Don't get uptight about it." Will wondered how efficient the translator devices were.

"But it is not a natural reaction," Caldaq replied even as Dropahc and Wouldea disappeared into the starboard hull. He wished for the expertise of a xenopsych. The sooner the native was examined by a specialist the more real answers they would have. Until such time he would have to muddle along as best he could, utilizing the minimal training he had in such fields.

"You assume the possibility that had you chosen to deny us permission to examine your craft we would have done so by force if necessary."

"You mean you wouldn't have?"

This automatic inclusion of the negative in the native's reply struck Caldaq as most distressing. Were they really communicating? He asked the question of his translator.

The Wais checked her instrumentation. "All devices are functioning optimally, Captain."

"What about misinterpreted colloquialisms?"

"I have detected none."

"Then you confirm from your own knowledge what I am hearing?"

A hand fluttered in the humid air of the cabin. "My mastery of this language is not perfect and there are contradictions which my colleagues and I have yet to thoroughly resolve. For example, these people utilize an excessive number of verbs to convey very simple concepts. It is almost as if they luxuriate in an excess of action beyond what is necessary to communicate a concept. But while we may be missing certain subtle shadings of meaning I do not believe anything is being misconveyed by your unit."

Caldaq's upper lip rippled. "Very well. Unless you inform me otherwise we will proceed on that basis."

There was a single chair in the cabin. Caldaq eyed it speculatively, chose instead to sit cross-legged on the floor, resting his long arms on his knees. As he did so the corners of the Human's mouth twisted upward. It was very near a similar S'van expression, Caldaq thought.

"When your lips arc like that does it mean something pleases or displeases you?"

"I'm smiling, if that's what you mean," Will replied. "The expression is one of amusement."

Better to find something humorous than threatening, the captain mused. "What is it you find amusing?"

"The way you're sitting. You look like you're getting ready to start meditating or something."

"No. I am simply sitting." Actually there was more to it than that. It had been shown that certain peoples felt more comfortable when they were physically able to look down on someone they regarded as a potential threat. Lowering his height, Caldaq knew, might help to put the native more at ease.

He decided that the action which had resulted in Dropahc's broken hand had been an aberration sparked by their sudden appearance. Since then the native had been physically placid. In a way it was too bad. But then they hadn't really expected anything else.

Still, there was intelligence here, and technology of a level yet to be determined. A second potential ally for the Weave. Truly the expedition could be counted a great success.

"Have you any objection to additional questions?"

Will leaned back against the couch. "If you're after top-secret information I can't help you. I know synthesizers and boating and that's about it."

"Answer what you can. We will not be displeased if you cannot."

"Sure." Will looked outside. Indifferent to what was happening on the cat, phosphorescent marine organisms were turning the water astern a pale lavender blue. The natural phenomenon was soothing and reassuring to mind as well as eye.

Caldaq made certain the Wais and the one soldier who had not gone below were both alert before speaking anew.

"Before we landed here, before this encounter, we sent down two small drone craft to execute preliminary surveys of your world. This is part of the procedure I spoke of earlier. Both of them vanished. We would like to know what happened."

Will was thinking hard. "Where did they come down? I mean, where were they surveying? Over the U.S.?"

"I do not know what that signifies. They were programmed to study two of the most highly developed landmasses: one just north of our present location, the other nearly on the opposite side of the planet."

The native was bobbing its head, no doubt attempting to communicate something via the gesture. Fortunately he enhanced the unsuccessful attempt verbally.

"If they couldn't or didn't identify themselves, then they were probably shot down."

" 'Shot down.' " Will looked on as the alien conferred with the bird-creature, the Wais, in his own language. "You mean they were destroyed."

"Yeah, sure. Both of them probably entered sensitive airspace. What else would you expect?"

"They were doing no harm. They were simply observing."

"But there was no way for the people on the ground to know that. What else would you expect them to do?"

"Observe back. At least try to first ascertain if the drones had any hostile intention."

"Just being there unannounced could be interpreted as hostile."

"Why?" Caldaq leaned forward earnestly. "Why would their presence be so interpreted? They were unarmed, could cause no damage."

"I told you: There was no way the people on the ground could know that."

Despite the Wais's reassurance Caldaq still wondered if the translators were functioning properly. He was talking with the native, but not communicating.

"That is precisely why there was no reason to assume the drone presence was hostile, and—" He stopped. Clearly there was nothing to be gained from this line of questioning. It was something for the xenopsychs and the linguists to hammer out.

"Your best guess, as an inhabitant of this world, is that the drones were destroyed by artificial means?"

"Yes. Both of them probably went where they shouldn't." Will's gaze shifted from the alien leader, Caldaq, to the Wais. "What is it you want here? To study us?"

Caldaq shifted his legs slightly. The native had asked the question. He had only to explain.

"I have told you that the galaxy is home to many intelligences. I am of the Massood. The Wais you know, and the Lepar you encountered in the water. Aboard our vessel there are also the Turlog, the Hivistahm, the O'o'yan, and the Chirinaldo. There are many others who together comprise the Weave.

"Then there are those who are not of the Weave. Those who are independent, and those who align themselves with the Amplitur." He waited.

The native stared at him, finally asked. "From the way you've been talking I take it there's something unpleasant about these Amplitur?"

Caldaq was pleased. Curiosity, technology, intelligence. All seemed present in this native. They would not leave here without making allies of these people.

"To understand the Weave you must know about the Amplitur. And to understand the Amplitur you must know about the War."

Caldaq studied the native carefully, watching for expressions and gestures. It did not move, did nothing to reveal what it might be thinking.

At least it wasn't smiling, the captain thought.

★ IX ★

With the aid of the Wais, Caldaq proceeded to explain the history of the conflict between the Weave and the Amplitur, the war that had absorbed the attention of a hundred intelligences for more than a thousand years. He spoke of the all-consuming Purpose which drove and motivated the Amplitur, of the struggle to remain independent of their manipulations and demands despite their unique ability to project their thoughts and desires into the minds of other sentients.

He told of how they imposed their will on other species, if necessary through mental control, later by means of skilled genetic engineering. He explained that both sides in the conflict were searching constantly for additional peoples: the Amplitur to incorporate them into their Purpose, the Weave seeking help to combat the Amplitur's encroachment.

"It is rare to find a new species capable of contributing significantly to the resistance," he said. "Rarer still to encounter one able to participate in the actual fighting."

"Why is that?" Will asked ingenuously.

"The will to fight, to be able to take the life of another intelligent being however necessary it may be, to shed bodily fluids and cause physical harm is abhorrent to the majority of sentient races. It is regarded as anathema to the very idea of intelligence. I realize that you probably find the concept equally alien, but we search always in hope.

"The Weave is very strong, very powerful in many ways, but there are never enough to do the actual fighting. It is the same with the Amplitur, but they have been able to alter the genetic code of certain subject peoples to make them more aggressive.

It is not enough just to have better weapons. Computers and electronic predictors can accomplish much, but they cannot win a war. Individuals must do that.

"My people, the Massood, are in the forefront of most combat. It has always been so. We are not fond of what we do, but we are very good at it. More so than any other Weave race. We have accepted this role because there are none who can replace us. The Wais, for example," and he indicated the translator standing silently nearby, "are incapable of combat, as are the O'o'yan and the Yula and the Bir'rimor. The Hivistahm and the S'van can fight a little. The Turlog might but choose not to, and there are not enough of them to make a difference anyway.

"Besides the Massood only the Chirinaldo are considered true fighters, and because of their physical stature they are not truly effective in the close-quarter combat that is so important."

"Wait a minute." Will sat up straight. "I wouldn't think that in a conflict spanning millennia and whole areas of space there'd be much in the way of hand-to-hand fighting."

"War is an extreme form of debate." Caldaq hoped that his translator was conveying these concepts correctly. "If you kill someone they cannot join with you.

"In this regard the Amplitur are even more restrained than the Weave. If they were to stand off a world and render its surface sterile, they would have defeated an enemy but sacrificed potential converts to their Purpose. They avoid wholesale loss of life whenever they can, though they have made at least two exceptions that I know of. Both times they perceived a greater threat than gain.

"As to your comment, combat in space is an extraordinarily difficult proposition. Ships move in and out of Underspace at unpredictable intervals. You cannot linger long in real space because both sides possess weapons capable of quickly obliterating the largest vessels. It is simpler, safer, and more effective to fight on the surface."

"It is a question of persuasion." The Wais clacked its beak. "The Amplitur seek to integrate all intelligences into their Purpose, while we strive to convince their allies to rebel and join us in fighting against their former masters.

"The problem is that in many instances these subject peoples do not see the Amplitur accurately. Some regard them as teachers without really understanding what it is they are being taught.

Some of their oldest allies, like the Crigolit and the Molitar, have been so thoroughly biologically reengineered they are no longer capable of independent thought as we think of it."

Will sat motionless for a long while before replying. "And that's what you want here? You want us to join your Weave?"

"That is what we hope for whenever we contact a new species," Caldaq told him. "Your level of contribution would depend on your capabilities. These remain to be determined. For example, what we know of your technology thus far we find puzzling. Certain aspects seem unnaturally primitive while other obscure areas appear to have been highly developed. For example, you have many more orbital relay satellites than you must need, yet we detect no evidence of travel beyond your own world."

"We've been to the moon," Will said almost defensively. "Robot probes have visited all the planets."

"We detected no evidence of this."

"It's been pretty intermittent. There'll be a flurry of interest in the space program, ours or the Russians', and then interest will flag for a while."

"You do not advance steadily? There is no constant progression?"

"I'm afraid not."

Caldaq eyed his translator, confused. "What do you mean when you speak of 'you,' and then 'the Russians'?"

"Well, we have our own space program here in the States. The Russians have theirs. So do the Europeans and the Japanese."

"I still do not understand." Caldaq's lips drew back in confusion. "Who are these 'Russians' and 'Europeans'?"

Will wondered what the problem was. "Different peoples."

The Wais interjected gently in lucid Massood. "I believe that the native may be referring to local tribes."

"Ah." Caldaq's heart sank. If despite their level of perceived technology these people were still living a tribal existence, they would be of absolutely no use to the Weave. "You speak of your tribes?"

"We call them countries."

"Your various tribes . . . countries . . . each have their own programs of exploration and development and do not cooperate with one another?"

Will sighed. "As a general rule, no."

More confusion. Caldaq looked yet again at the Wais. She responded with words and gestures.

"This is a new species. Given their unique multiplicity of languages nothing in the way of communication can be guaranteed. However, I have observed nothing to suggest we are failing to make ourselves understood."

Caldaq hissed softly. Another subject to be put aside for the specialists to ponder, another matter he would have to leave unresolved.

"We seek you as allies. If you have indeed sent remote probes to the far reaches of your system, that would indicate you have capabilities we have as yet been unable to validate."

"Just because you didn't see them," Will said, "doesn't mean we didn't do it."

"Perhaps there may be other aspects of your technology we have yet to encounter," Caldaq added hopefully. "The means by which the two drones were destroyed, for example. That would constitute an astonishing achievement for sentients not in conflict with the Amplitur or a neighboring species."

The conversation was interrupted by the emergence of the two soldiers from below. Will could only sit and wonder what they were talking about as they chattered animatedly in their own language.

Before long he was moved to ask, "What did they find?"

"More of the very sophisticated alongside the bafflingly primitive," Caldaq informed him. "In that regard your craft appears typical of what we have observed elsewhere.

"Everything suggests that your species is at a critical stage of technological transition: one where great achievements have been made in isolated fields while in others the mundane is the accepted norm. For example, the devices you utilize to produce music seem reasonably advanced, whereas those employed to generate light are extremely primitive metal filaments surrounded by glass."

"I take it you use something more advanced than incandescent bulbs."

"There are infinitely simpler and cleaner means of producing illumination."

"I'm sure. There are also infinitely simpler and cleaner means of living. It's been fascinating to meet you, to know that there are other intelligent races out there, that we're not alone. But if you're still fighting wars then you're not so very advanced after all, and I can tell you right now we don't want anything to do with it.

"Like me, most of my friends abhor war. We're more like the Wais over there than you. War's an idea whose time has passed. Your allies are right: it's not compatible with real intelligence. I don't think we're going to be able to help you. Certainly not against something like these Amplitur you describe. I don't want anything messing with *my* head, and neither will anybody else with half a brain.

"I mean, look at me. You don't see fangs and claws. We're soft-bodied and not very big. Not real good soldier material, you bet. After five thousand years or so we're just starting to get our global shit together. The last thing we need is to take off on some kind of interstellar crusade. We've got plenty of problems to solve right here." He leaned forward intently.

"Look, you say no one's made contact with us before this because we're way out on the fringes of everything. Can't you just sort of forget, maybe, that you found us? Forget that you came here, and leave us alone? We don't need to be dragged into some crazy galactic conflict. We've got literature to write and art and music to perfect and we sure as hell don't know anything about how to fight an interstellar war. Can't you just back off and leave us alone?"

"There is no shame in being unable to fight," Caldaq assured him. "As I have said, only we and the Chirinaldo are able to do so. But logistical support is vitally important. Without that the Massood could do little.

"If you agreed to provide that kind of noncombat assistance the benefits that would accrue to you would be substantial: the sharing of Weave technology, the blessings of intercultural exchange . . ."

"And a piece of your war," Will said, interrupting. "I can't imagine what we could do for you. Seems to me our technology is pretty primitive compared to yours."

"In certain areas. Perhaps not in all. This remains to be determined."

"We can't build ships for you."

"The Hivistahm and Yula and O'o'yan build ships. Your own contribution to the war effort can lie elsewhere."

"Dammit," said Will, raising his voice, "we don't *want* to contribute to any war effort! Why can't you just leave us alone?"

"We could do that." Caldaq's reply was solemn. "The Weave could ignore you. The Amplitur will not. They leave no intelligence alone. You are a part of their Purpose or you are opposed to it. Either you integrate into their greater society or you face the extinction that was the fate of the two exceptions I mentioned earlier."

"What if we choose not to be integrated *or* eliminated?"

"You cannot resist the Amplitur alone. If they are allowed to land on your world they will put whatever they wish into your minds. Then their biorevisors will go to work on your genes."

"You're asking me to buy an argument that my own people have used on themselves for hundreds of years. All I know about these Amplitur is what you're telling me. I have no way of verifying any of it."

Caldaq saw he was not making adequate progress. "We must talk more. Tomorrow I would like to bring specialists aboard your craft, to examine it more thoroughly."

"And me," Will added.

"One can learn only so much from impersonal transmissions. Do you object?"

"I couldn't stop you if I wanted to, could I?"

Caldaq contained his exasperation. "You are an individual sentient. We would not do anything against your will. You do not make an ally of someone by forcing them to do something they do not wish to do."

Will sat there wondering how much truth there was to what this rat-faced alien had been telling him. It was simultaneously frightening, fascinating, and hard to accept. Worst of all perhaps was the knowledge that if he got out of this intact no one would believe what had happened to him. His would be one more UFO fairy tale. If he was lucky he might get a thousand bucks for it from one of the tabloids.

He wondered what their music was like. The thought perked him up. If he paid attention, this might provide the inspiration for an overture, or a symphonic suite. Maybe even another symphonic poem. Since he couldn't run, he might as well open his mind and observe.

The tall alien insisted all they wanted was to talk and examine.

If it was vivisection they had in mind, why speak of coming back tomorrow? Why not simply take him now?

"What the hell, the orchestration is driving me nuts anyway, you bet. Come back in the morning and bring whomever you want. I look forward to meeting some more interesting shapes."

"Thank you," said Caldaq simply.

Will watched his visitors slip over the stern. There was no sign of the aquatic creature which had confronted him in the lagoon, but he did see a dark, streamlined shape advance to meet the hesitant swimmers. They disappeared within.

Once again he was alone in the cat's cockpit.

A light Caribbean breeze cooled him and he tilted his head back to regard the universe, a tapestry of shattered magic.

The aliens had not warned him against contacting others. There was nothing to prevent him from using his radio to call other boats, the big cruise ship anchored off the Turneffe Islands, or the Belizean coast guard. Nothing to prevent him from raising sail and silently departing.

He wondered why the aliens had chosen him. Because he was alone? Would they try to stop him if he started the engines and headed for Belize City?

There was no inspiration to be had in Belize City.

A rare thing, inspiration. Impossible to buy, difficult to find. Why not go to bed and see what the morrow would bring? The world would look different in the light.

At first he feared that his boat had drifted onto the reef. Then his visitors began to emerge from an opening in its surface. He intended to ask Caldaq how they managed that trick but he didn't have time. Moments later they were back on board, all of them talking at once.

The Wais translator was present, and Caldaq, and another Massood, but this time they had company: supple reptilian beings called Hivistahm with bright green skins, large eyes, sharp teeth, and an insatiable curiosity, and a couple of short, swarthy individuals whose faces were almost hidden behind thick black hair. They scattered through the catamaran, prying and poking, paying particular attention to anything electronic.

Closer inspection revealed that not all the reptilian visitors were of the same race. Besides the Hivistahm there were members of a still smaller species Caldaq identified as the O'o'yan.

Will's translator struggled with the sounds. Rather than search on their own, the O'o'yan seemed to follow the Hivistahm everywhere, assisting instead of initiating examinations. They did not render such assistances to the two squat, hairy individuals.

Caldaq tried to divide his attention between the busy Hivistahm techs and the native who was watching them work. His communicator buzzed insistently.

It was Soliwik, communicating via shuttle relay. "Good to talk to you," he said. "How is Jaruselka?"

"Busy, like the rest of us," replied his Second. "She says to tell you that the affection you share does not require confirmation in the form of trite words or spatial communication." A warm sensation spread through Caldaq.

"My captain, progress continues in the interpretation of the wealth of electronic transmissions emanating from this world. Seven new languages have been isolated."

Another seven, Caldaq marveled. He was beyond astonishment.

"In light of continuing discoveries, those responsible for making translation programs are concentrating their efforts on what appear to be the most important ones.

"Progress in other areas has been slowed by the contradictions which are present in all transmissions. Some are quite disturbing. The xenopsychs regularly work through the night shift. They do not wish to leap to unfounded conclusions but . . ." She broke off, which was not like Soliwik at all.

"But what?" Caldaq watched Hivistahm techs fiddle with their eyeshades as they conversed. His gaze lifted to the nearest island. The view set his legs to tingling in anticipation of a good run.

"Does your specimen have a native visual receiver on board his craft?"

"I believe so." Caldaq eyed a corner of the central cabin. "Yes. I can see it from here. It is fairly primitive."

"Never mind the technology. You should have him activate it so you can view some of the transmissions."

"Which ones?"

"Any of them. I will not prejudice your reactions by telling you what the xenopsychs are saying. Every independent evaluation is valuable."

They talked about the situation on the ship, which was stable, and that on the surface, which was in hopeful flux. Then Caldaq closed his communicator and belted it before he walked over to stare at the visual receiver.

"Television," Will informed him. "Nice one, too."

"Could you activate it? I would like to see how it operates."

"Give me a minute to raise the dish."

Caldaq watched as the native adjusted a boxy instrument atop the receiver. Through a fore port he could see a small circular antenna raise and align itself. Lights on the box and the receiver glowed.

"There we are. That's Galaxy Six," Will told him. "One of our satellites." Caldaq gestured acknowledgment and then took a moment to explain the gesture. The native looked pleased.

One of the Hivistahm techs drifted over to join them. So did the Wais, who was always close at hand.

"What would you like to watch?" Will asked them. "Wait, I know. Let me find CNN." He operated a remote-control device.

The screen went black; then an image appeared of another native. Caldaq noted with interest that the male's skin was much darker than that of their host. The images alternated between the man, who was seated at a desk surrounded by other natives, and diverse scenes from around the planet.

Caldaq observed calmly until a sequence appeared that caused him to straighten involuntarily. "Wait, stop that, go back!"

The native was apologetic. "I can't. I have no control over the broadcast. If you want we can record it for playback later."

The shaken captain steadied himself, once again ducking to clear the ceiling. Avoiding the translator, he spoke haltingly to the Hivistahm in its own language.

"You saw it, too?"

"Truly I did," the tech replied. "Most strange it was."

"I, too, saw it clearly," said the Wais. Her voice was pure and steady as ever, but her beak was clicking. A pair of bluest feathers fell to the deck as she ran nervous fingers through her chest. "The reality must be other than as it appears."

Will's gaze flicked from one alien to the other. "I know how you feel. Sometimes the news makes me uncomfortable, too." He returned his attention to the remote device. "Let's find a movie or something."

He jumped through several films, from an old John Wayne on

TBS to more contemporary offerings on Showtime and Cinemax. The reactions of his guests were instructive. They varied from calm and composed to visibly agitated and anxious.

"Anything in particular that intrigues you?" he finally asked, knowing that there was. When no reply was forthcoming he started to switch the receiver off. Caldaq had learned enough from watching him to realize what he intended and hurried to forestall him.

"No, we would like to observe some more. Put it back on 'news.'"

Will obediently switched back to CNN, which was currently reporting on the troubles in Libya. After several minutes the Hivistahm turned and left.

Caldaq gestured at the screen. "This is not unusual?"

"What, the news? Or the movies? No, I'd say everything we've seen so far is fairly typical for a Tuesday morning. My reception isn't as good as I'd like it to be, but that's about as big a dish as you can put on a boat this size, you bet."

"The subject matter is confusing."

"I didn't have any idea what you might want to see, so I just tried to run through as many channels as possible."

"That was fine," Caldaq assured him. "Thank you." He understood now what Soliwik had meant.

He bellowed an order. Moments later they were joined by one of the two short creatures who had come aboard with the Hivistahm. It might have been more humanoid than any of the aliens, but Will couldn't tell for certain because you couldn't see much behind the body suit and the incredibly dense blanket of curly hair. It was the same height as the very different O'o'yan; barely three feet tall, but much stockier of build.

"What's this?" he asked undiplomatically.

"One of my Seconds. T'var is a S'van. They are mammalian, like myself and I believe like you." He turned back to his assistant. "Have a look at this, T'var, and see what you think of it. I am still forming my own opinions." He stepped aside so T'var could see the screen clearly.

The S'van studied the colorful flat images. Will noted that he did not twist and fidget in the manner of the Massood, nor were his eyes in constant motion like those of the Hivistahm and O'o'yan. He stood without moving and stared at the screen as intently as a professional critic.

Half an hour passed before he looked away. "It's all very strange."

"Mild, compared to some of what we saw earlier," the Wais informed him.

"My initial reaction," said Caldaq, "is that if these transmissions are representative of the general population, then this species is beyond our comprehension."

"Possibly he is attempting to deceive us with the abnormal," the Wais suggested.

"There is no reason for him to do so," the captain responded, "nor do I think he is that clever."

"I agree." Caldaq was gratified by T'var's concurrence.

Will watched as they conversed without the use of the translator devices. "What's going on? Something the matter?"

The Wais stared at him. "The violence. There is violence in almost everything we saw."

"I know, but except for the news it was all fiction. You know . . . make-believe?" He was somewhat taken aback. "Is that what's upset you? I don't get it. First you tell me you've been fighting a war for a thousand years and now a little movie byplay has you all flustered. That doesn't make any sense."

"The quantity of the violence is surprising, but that is not what we find confusing." The Wais preened uneasily. "We did not choose to have war; it was forced on us by the Amplitur. And the Massood and Chirinaldo do nearly all of the actual fighting. But even the fiercest among them would be appalled by what you have shown us.

"Unless, of course," it added hopefully in perfect English, "what we have witnessed just now is generated to serve some as yet unexplained philosophical purpose."

"The news is the news. It's reality, even if I don't like most of it myself. As for the movies, they're only intended as entertainment." Will stared at the bird-thing. "It's the violence that troubles you, but not the amount? What then?"

"The direction it often took," the Wais explained. "In both the documentary and entertainment sequences Humans were shown killing other Humans."

Will frowned. "So?"

"You fight among *yourselves*," Caldaq said, speaking slowly to insure that the translator conveyed his response accurately.

"Yeah, we do that. We're not proud of it." He rested a hand

on the humming TV. "I'm missing something here. You've been battling these Amplitur for hundreds of years. Why are you so upset to see that we do the same kind of thing?"

"You do not understand. It is conceivable that one species may come into conflict with another, but once it has achieved a certain minimal level of technology it is not possible for members of the same species to continue to war with each other. It is contraevolutionary."

T'var spoke up. "Catastrophe theory proves that a species which fights among itself cannot long survive. It will quickly reduce its numbers below the level necessary to maintain a civilization. This is axiomatic."

"All I can tell you," said Will, "is that we've been fighting ourselves since the start of recorded history, and that unfortunately we're still at it."

"Impossible." The Wais repeated the comment in a number of languages.

"I'm afraid it isn't. We're still here, though whether we've reached your 'minimal level of technology' I don't know." He stood there, the warm sun heating the interior of the cabin, regarding these representatives of a vast civilization unimaginably far away, and wondering why the hell they couldn't see the obvious.

"You're telling me that though you've been going at it with these Amplitur for hundreds of years, none of you has ever fought among yourselves?" In the subsequent silence he turned to Caldaq.

"You told me that the Massood are your organization's principal warriors. Are you saying that even early on in the history of your kind you never fought one another?"

"On an individual basis, yes. In small extended family groups, yes. But as soon as the first tribes grew large and settled they began to cooperate. That is a fact of nature obvious to the most primitive peoples. Cooperation is the only way for any race to advance out of barbarism. It is impossible to achieve a reasonable level of technology if energy is dissipated in internecine warfare." Caldaq wondered why he was having to spend so much time explaining the self-evident. It was going to take strong minds to interpret this unusual world and its even more peculiar people.

"The notion of a civilized race warring among itself is inherently contradictory. It is as bizarre as your geology."

"Oh. Now there's something wrong with our geology?" Will hardly knew what to say. The situation demanded the presence of experts. But they weren't and he was.

"A world is divided between land and water," said T'var. "This is the accepted, the anticipated norm. Imagine our surprise when we began to examine your world and found its principal landmass broken into many pieces."

"That's because of something called plate tectonics." Will strained to remember his college sciences. "I think the continents all used to be part of one big landmass, a long time ago, but internal forces drove it apart and set the pieces drifting."

"Land is not 'driven.' " T'var glanced at Caldaq, then back at the native. "Land remains where it's formed. It doesn't move around."

"It does here," declared Will confidently.

"I've never heard of such a thing." T'var muttered in uneven Massood.

"Do you think," Caldaq said abruptly, "that the unnatural hostility these people bear toward each other could in some way be related to their remarkable geology? The development of a multiplicity of languages suggests that their society has fractured. Might this not be the consequence of a fractured geology?"

"I know of no instance where the culture of a species has been heavily influenced by geologic forces. It's not my area of expertise." T'var found the notion unsettling. What might the effect be of a perpetually unstable world on the people maturing there? Would the society that eventually emerged somehow mirror that instability?

"It is no one's area of expertise," Caldaq pointed out. "There is no precedence for it. We must inform the staff on board ship. It will be interesting to see if the native's explanation solves any of the topographic puzzles that have been bedeviling them."

Will was speaking again. "So on your worlds you don't have separate continents?" The translators struggled with the concepts.

"Each planet has the land, where life evolves and develops, and there are usually some islands," T'var told him. "The land accretes into one large mass. It does not fragment. Your world is unprecedented.''

"Mayhap it has something to do with the moon."

"What?" Caldaq and T'var both turned to look at the translator. One did not expect scientific speculation from a Wais.

She gazed back at them. "Its mass has been remarked upon. It is much too large for a planet of this size. More appropriate to describe them as twin worlds. I was simply thinking that its size and proximity may have in the past had something to do with the fracturing of the land."

"A worthy hypothesis which we must leave to the geophysicists to explore." Once again Caldaq experienced a need to trade the incomprehensible for that which might be understood. He studied the native thoughtfully. Since its initial violent reaction to their arrival it had been calm, even cooperative. Still, he readied himself in the event his next question provoked another unpredictable reaction.

"Will you consent to a physical examination?"

"Of what? *Me?*" Will switched off the satellite receiver and the television. His mouth was dry.

The fridge held a six-pack of pineapple juice. He inserted the accompanying straw into one and sucked, conscious of the fact that he was alone on his boat with a dozen or more aliens. Maybe Caldaq had told the truth and the majority of them weren't fighters, but that still left him badly outnumbered. He was no fighter himself. And he'd already found out that he couldn't swim to freedom.

"What if I say no?"

The alien captain managed to convey the feeling that he'd just been insulted. "Then nothing will happen."

"You're not planning anything like exploratory surgery, are you?"

"No. You are an individual sentient. Why would we want to do anything to harm you?"

Will slugged down the last of the pineapple juice. "Then I guess it can't hurt. Where do you want to do this?"

"If you would not mind, we have facilities on our shuttle."

"The ship you landed in? I think I'd enjoy seeing that."

"Everything can be arranged."

⋆ X ⋆

Will was fascinated by the shuttle, which was much larger than what he'd expected. A fair amount of the interior was comprehensible. A chair, for example, was a chair regardless of how outrageous its size and shape. But other constructs left him puzzled.

"I see what you mean about our lighting." He extended a finger toward one of the illumination bands that ran across a wall like so much electrical tape. It was cool to the touch.

"Please feel free to ask questions about anything that interests you," said T'var, who together with the female Wais constituted his escort.

They ended up in a small chamber crammed with instrumentation and devices Will could not identify. A number of Hivistahm and O'o'yan techs were present, along with a couple of S'van. There was a small oval platform fastened to the center of the floor. Will knew that had his visitors been so inclined they could easily have brought him to this place by force, but he was still apprehensive.

"You're sure this isn't going to be painful?"

"No." T'var wondered at the question. "Why should it?"

"Clearly you've never visited my doctor." The joke did little to ease his nerves. "There aren't any straps or anything?"

"Restraints? Why would we need to restrain you?"

"Exactly my point." He inhaled deeply. "Where do you want me? Up there?" He gestured at the table.

"If you would be so kind," said the Wais.

Will gingerly lay down on the smooth, slightly warm platform. The overhead light was bright but not intolerably so. Several Hivistahm came over and looked down at him. It was impossible to tell from looking up at their toothy faces what they were thinking. The eyeshades of this group were not decorated. O'o'yan skittered about adjusting controls.

None of them wore translators, so they spoke through the Wais, who requested that he remove his swimsuit. He did so, wondering if any of his examiners were female and then realizing it didn't matter.

A thorough inspection followed. He was prodded with devices he didn't recognize, scanned by instruments whose function he could not imagine, poked with digits that were not human. None of it was painful or discomforting. They gazed into every part of him, asked him to manipulate his eyes and mouth, to flex and stretch. He obliged, asking more and more questions of his own as the examination proceeded.

Caldaq came in and stood silently next to T'var, watching. A senior tech broke away from the examiners to join them. As the only Wais present was otherwise engaged, they were forced to rely on their translators.

"Truly a strange structure. An unremarkable appearance conceals numerous surprises."

"For example?" Caldaq inquired curiously.

The Hivistahm tech regarded the platform somberly as his colleagues continued with the examination. He murmured to a nearby O'o'yan, who gestured deferentially and rushed to comply with the order. On the table Will whistled and twisted, breathed deeply and rolled his eyes in response to a steady stream of requests.

"Cranial peculiarities there are. Beyond that we cannot say. Results are limited by our instrumentation and the fact that we have no other specimens available for comparison. We could do better on board ship."

"Perhaps you will have such an opportunity soon. What else?"

"Again, assuming that the specimen representative of its kind is, it would appear that for their size extremely strong bones and a very dense musculature they have. Neural response time is exceptional. It is possible these developments may constitute an evolutionary response to their abnormal history. This is a preliminary hypothesis only. We can only begin to guess how fighting constantly with members of one's own kind has affected their physical development.

"Excellent day vision across the normal spectra and quite serviceable night vision they have, depending on the standard one judges it against. The daytime vision of the Hivistahm, for example, is slightly sharper, but little at night can we see. This is true of most other races. Human night vision may be another defensive response to an inimical evolution."

Massood night vision was considered excellent. "Would you say that their nocturnal visual acuity was greater than my own?" Caldaq asked the tech.

"Yes. It may also exceed that of the Massood in daytime." In response to Caldaq's reaction the tech added, "There is something more remarkable still. Examination suggests and the native confirms verbally that they are capable of limited distances underwater seeing, on the clarity of the liquid environment depending."

That gave T'var a start. "Without artificial lenses?" The tech indicated assent. "Surely they are not like the Lepar?"

"No. They are not amphibious in any way. While comfortable and agile in water they are, also strictly air-breathers are they. Furthermore, the native indicates that his people spending time in the water enjoy."

"We have recorded proof of that." Caldaq's snout quivered at the unnatural thought.

The tech wasn't finished. "Whether such activity is an evolutionary or social development we cannot as yet say."

"Then what we have here," said Caldaq as he gazed at the occupied medical platform, "is a sentient who can see better than a Massood, is stronger than a Hivistahm or Bir'rimor, and can swim better than any known sentient species save for the Lepar, who are slow and clumsy when out of water."

"Physically they would appear to be extremely versatile and adaptable, yes," agreed the tech.

"You spoke of exceptional neural response time."

"The specimen's reactions to certain stimuli are superb. When something is thrust toward it, for example."

"We have witnessed that, too," said the captain.

"Reasonable digital dexterity they possess, but in this area they are not remarkable. I would rate their manipulative abilities the same as the Massood or S'van, considerably below that of

Hivistahm or O'o'yan. While superb is hand-to-eye coordination, other movements are quite clumsy, a possible consequence of the development of exceptional strength in nontraditional areas of the body.

"Also the ability to adapt well to climatic extremes they have. I venture to say cold that would be fatal to a Hivistahm or heat that would fell a Massood they could survive. Their lungs process oxygen with great efficiency. Coupled with the structure of their bones and muscles and a redundant mass of ligaments and tendons, I see them as capable of great feats of endurance compared to, say, one of my own kind."

"Or to a Crigolit?" Caldaq asked quietly.

The tech's reply was deferential. "Possibly."

T'var spoke up. "This Will insists he is a musician, an artist who has no interest in fighting. He says that his friends feel similarly. This is contradicted by the evidence of their visual transmissions. Their daily activities, their forms of art and entertainment are all suffused with violence unimaginable in our respective societies."

"Only to our results so far with this single specimen can I speak," said the technician. "I cannot vouch for the truth of what it says, but I attest to its physical versatility. That is what is intriguing to me. The Chirinaldo are stronger, the Hivistahm see slightly better, the O'o'yan are far more dexterous, the Lepar better swimmers."

"And the Massood?" Caldaq asked slowly.

The tech hesitated, glanced back at the platform. Three Hivistahm and an O'o'yan were recording and observing as the naked specimen did sit-ups, performing the remarkable feat of touching its elbows to its knees. It was something only a Massood could have duplicated, or perhaps an Ashregan. The native executed the maneuver repeatedly.

The tech's teeth clicked. "The Massood run faster."

Caldaq felt relieved without knowing why. It was absurd to compare racial attributes. One could only make honest comparisons among members of the same species.

"Without better instrumentation and more elaborate tests involving multiple specimens impossible it is to verify these preliminary conclusions." The tech adjusted an eyeshade.

T'var asked the big question. "What of their battlefield potential?"

"Physically it is considerable, as just indicated have I. Mentally I cannot say. You report that the native decries combat. It therefore to the accepted norm among intelligent species conforms. Yet the visual transmissions viewed thus far would appear the native's claims to contradict.

"The fact that they have evolved fighting each other may have engendered in them an abhorrence or fear of doing battle with representatives of any species other than their own. May be self-confining their madness. I do not know. Not a xenopsych am I. And other problems there may be." He picked at his teeth.

"While judgment on a species based on observations of a single individual we cannot render, I must confess I and my group in this one a wealth of contradictions find, both physical and mental. Contradictions imply unpredictability, and the Hivistahm find unpredictability unnerving. To be a life-musician dedicated to peace and his art the specimen claims, but even his music full of violence is."

"I wonder," T'var murmured, "what he would think of some of our music?"

"Truly an interesting thought." The tech pushed his eyeshades back on his head and rubbed gently at his wide eyes. "I will propose the experiment, though I do not expect it to resolve anything."

"If analysis proves difficult we will proceed a little at a time," said T'var, "but proceed we must." The tired Hivistahm indicated agreement.

Will declared much of what they played for him lovely and charming. When the last strains from the alien device had dissipated in the cat's main cabin he sat up on the couch and smiled at his visitors.

"Delightful, but pretty simple rhythmically."

"Appreciation of music is wholly subjective." T'var did not waste time on tact likely to go undetected. "We find yours . . . rough."

"My stuff's pretty mild compared to what some of the so-called popular groups put out. You should hear an outfit called Cadmium. I have to admit I like strong rhythms and lots of percussion, but I'm by no means considered dissonant. Your music, though, it's like Bulgarian folk chant or Palestrina. None of which means anything to you, of course. Why are you playing it for me?''

''You are a musician,'' said the Wais. ''We thought you would find it of interest.''

''I do. Very much so.'' He leaned back on the couch, hands behind his head. ''Play that first part for me again, the piece that sounded like electric bells.''

Aboard the shuttle, as Will submitted to more testing, Caldaq greeted the chiefs of his scientific staff. T'var was also present, along with the omnipresent Wais.

''Time runs. We have a decision to make, one of vital importance. I must know if these people are potential allies and if so, to what degree. Might they be trained to participate in the actual fighting, even a little, or are there other functions they could perform? Or does this perceived instability of theirs render them useless to us? Naturally we welcome assistance of any kind.''

''We'll find out what we need to know only by acquiring and studying additional specimens,'' T'var said, ''or by probing this one more deeply.''

Second-of-Medicine protested. ''Too soon it is to subject a native to advanced procedures.''

''I disagree.'' T'var objected with un-S'vanlike pugnacity. ''Look how cooperative he's been so far.''

''Some of you have alluded to potentially useful aggressiveness. I see no evidence for that,'' Caldaq commented.

''Truly it broke Dropahc's wrist.''

''The creature claims it was an accident. The incident proves only that it is strong and clumsy, not necessarily feral.''

Second-of-Medicine was still troubled. ''A cooperative, helpful specimen we have. Dare we risk that cooperation by performing risky procedures whose results we cannot with any accuracy predict?''

''In case anyone's forgotten,'' T'var pointed out, ''there's a war to be fought, a war that has been going on for longer than any of us can imagine and which will doubtless continue following our deaths. Shortening that is worth the loss of a single native's cooperation. All precautions will be taken, but we must be willing to take certain risks.

"As you say, he has cooperated well. Until he demonstrates otherwise I believe we must rely on him to continue to do so."

With its clever words and ingratiating manner, Caldaq knew that a S'van could secure a commitment to cooperate from a rock. If anyone could persuade the Human to participate in a difficult procedure, it would be T'var.

"Examinations of further complexity would require the consent of the native."

"Naturally." T'var looked up at his captain. "We have done all that can be done with our limited facilities here. We must be allowed to continue them aboard ship."

Will Dulac sat up and swung his legs over the side of the platform as the floor shuddered slightly. His busy entourage did not pause in its work.

"What's going on? It feels like we're moving."

Second-of-Medicine addressed the native via her translator. "Truly it is deemed necessary that to our ship we return."

"Hey, wait a minute." An alarmed Will slid off the platform, scattering a pair of O'o'yan as he grabbed for his swimsuit. "I said I'd try to help you out here. Nothing was said about going to another ship."

The Wais smoothly interposed itself between the native and the agitated Hivistahm physician. "A semantic discrepancy. To us 'the ship' means all of its individual components, of which this shuttle is but one."

"Then I agreed to visit this component." Will struggled with his suit. "That's all."

T'var joined the conversation, all energy and shared enthusiasm. "Wouldn't you like to see our ship? To be able to look back and view the whole of your own world?"

Will looked down at the squat speaker. Beneath the profusion of hair it was more humanoid than any of the other aliens, including the tall, shrewish Massood.

"Sure, all this is fascinating, and I'd like to help you out, you bet. It's just that nobody said anything about any long-distance commuting. You're not kidnapping me or anything, are you?"

"Kidnapping?" The translator struggled with the term. T'var glanced up at the Wais but it clacked its beak to indicate it, too, was confused.

"Taking me somewhere against my will."

"This obsession with compulsion by force." T'var stroked his beard in exasperation. "It is as characteristic of you as your hairlessness. Why would we do that?"

"To get what you want from me."

"We want your cooperation, which we already have. Therefore the use of force would be redundant as well as repugnant. Have you learned nothing of our society?" He spoke in Hivistahm to the group of attendant technicians. "I begin to despair of these creatures. It may be they are not civilized."

"Truly truly of such possible contradictions I warned." Second-of-Medicine hissed softly. "Their behavior remains utterly unpredictable."

T'var indicated acknowledgment, turned back to the native. "I assure you we will do nothing against your will. If you wish to leave now, you are welcome to do so."

Will looked at him. The unblinking stare made the S'van far more uncomfortable than he would have thought possible. You could stare back at a Lepar, an O'o'yan, even a Massood without experiencing the same sense of unease. Yet this native had repeatedly emphasized its commitment to nonviolence. *Why, therefore*, T'var wondered, *do I feel so uneasy in its presence?*

"I can leave? Right now, and go back to my boat?"

"Certainly," said T'var. "By doing so you will deny yourself an experience beyond your imagining, but that's your choice. I'm sure we can find another of your kind willing, even eager, to accompany us." He hoped the translator would make it sound intriguing and not patronizing.

The native appeared to hesitate. Then its lips curled upward slightly. It really did possess a remarkably flexible face for a vertebrate, T'var mused.

"Hell, I've come this far. One of my old composition teachers used to say inspiration is where you find it. Okay, I'll go with you. If you promise to bring me back to my boat when I'm ready to return."

"We promise," said T'var. As if anyone in the room except the native could conceive of doing anything else, he thought. Was it individuality they were dealing with here, or species insanity? More than ever he felt the need to subject the specimen to a proper examination.

* * *

The native was visibly awed by the interior of the ship, though less so than might have been expected from a member of a non-space-traversing species. It was as if it was impressed by the ship itself but not its existence. Caldaq included the observation under the burgeoning file labeled "Human."

Members of the crew invariably paused to gawk at the strange creature as it was escorted through their midst. When they finally reached the heart of the ship's research facilities, Will found himself directed to a low but comfortable lounge. He'd been anticipating another platform. The plush informality of the lounge was greatly reassuring.

"More examinations?" He reached for the waistband of his trunks. "Want me to get undressed again?"

"Not necessary will that be." For a Hivistahm, Chief-of-Medicine had a commanding tone.

Will smiled. There was a dreamlike quality to the chamber in which he found himself, soft and reassuring compared to the improvised examination room on board the shuttle. He climbed onto the lounge, which was large enough to hold two people, put his hands behind his head, and let himself relax.

Caldaq, Soliwik, and T'var were among those looking on as the examination proceeded, while Z'mam tended to routine ship operations. They stood in the observation room which overlooked the chamber. Soliwik was outspoken in her comments.

"What ridiculous-looking creatures they are. Though no more so than a S'van."

"Thank you," said T'var dryly.

"Look at it! That absurd little clump of fur atop the skull and practically none anywhere else. The tiny eyes, hardly bigger than a Lepar's. The flat face and useless teeth. I grant the defined musculature, but otherwise it strikes me as very poor design." She turned to Caldaq. "How do you think it will react to the scan?"

"I do not know." Caldaq stood very close to the glass. "It does not know about that. Chief-of-Medicine thought more uncontaminated results could be obtained if the subject was kept ignorant as to its purpose. I am not certain I agree, but I am not prepared to overrule him. I try to avoid making decisions outside my field. However, Second-of-Medicine expressed similar reservations, which she felt she was not yet ready to explain. I find her hesitancy more interesting than the reservations themselves."

The cerebral scan was a technique that allowed Weave technicians to simulate the projective abilities of the Amplitur. Its development was a triumph of Weave technology, complicated by the fact that in the entire history of contact only a few Amplitur had been captured alive. Study of such captives was an extremely dangerous and difficult proposition which had to be carried out sufficiently outside the Amplitur's projective range to insure the safety of the examiners.

Much of what the Weave knew of the Amplitur and their peculiar abilities came from those who had been captured by the enemy and subjected to their control. Or to communication, as the Amplitur preferred to call it. Hundreds of years of intense study of the matter had failed to produce the hoped-for artificial means of shielding a mind against an Amplitur probe. But work went on, driven more by hope than expectation. If such a device could be constructed, it could significantly affect the course of the conflict.

Soliwik gestured toward the room. "They are starting. The native appears uneasy."

Indeed, they could hear and see the specimen protesting as two of the technicians attempted to slip the mesh over its head.

"I'd better get down there." T'var excused himself. Moments later they saw him enter the room and hurry to loungeside. Edging aside the Wais, he began talking to the Human. The native promptly lowered his arms, his head nodding slowly, and eventually allowed the technicians to proceed with their work.

"I also wonder at Second-of-Medicine's inability to elaborate." Soliwik stood watching. "The Hivistahm are rarely reluctant to express themselves."

"I believe she is worried about proceeding too rapidly. We have no choice, of course. The Amplitur will not slow their advance to accommodate our studies."

"I see no danger. From what I have seen and heard, this species is barely civilized."

"They are difficult to categorize. Just like their planet. It is premature to say if that will render them unsuitable as allies. Second-of-Medicine may think so, but I am convinced that among the staff her opinion is in the minority."

"Do you believe that, or is it wishful thinking?"

Caldaq eyed his Second sharply. "You know me better than that."

Soliwik stared through the transparency. "It looks like they are ready to proceed."

The operators were at their stations. One sat in a chair to the left of the lounge, close to a monitoring console. Her head was covered with a mesh pickup very similar to the one the native now wore. An O'o'yan bustled about her legs, busying itself with redundant checks of readouts and instrumentation.

Both the interfacer and the native closed their eyes as the scanner eased them into respective sleep states. A pale nimbus appeared around each mesh as the scan commenced. Off to one side, T'var chatted idly with the Wais. Technicians sat at their stations, seeking the memorable while recording the mundane, striving to learn through intense application and imperfect machinery what a single Amplitur could accomplish effortlessly in a few moments.

As time passed uneventfully Caldaq let his mind drift to other matters. He was startled when Soliwik nudged his leg with hers, a traditional Massood means of gaining another's attention. She was pointing into the room.

"Did you see that?"

"See what?" He blinked.

"Watch the scanner interfacer. There."

Caldaq saw the mesh-capped technician twitch slightly. Had she been Massood Soliwik would have ignored the reaction. But she was Hivistahm. The Hivistahm might shake, but they did not twitch.

Concern on its reptilian face, the attending O'o'yan reached out with his free hand to adjust one corner of the mesh.

Caldaq jumped as the interfacer lashed out with her left arm, sending teeth and blood spraying from the technician's face. You could hear the sickening contact through the transparency. The technician landed on his back, his hand console flying across the room as the interfacer went berserk, legs kicking convulsively, arms flailing. Beneath darkened shades, eyelids twitched and fluttered.

Nearby the sleeping Human turned onto its side, then rolled the opposite way on the lounge. One leg kicked out repeatedly, striking air.

The terror and fury it was experiencing was wholly and unashamedly delineated in its twisted expression.

★ XI ★

Emerging from the momentary paralysis brought on by what they'd seen, several physician-seconds rushed to the aid of the bleeding, sputtering O'o'yan. Others attempted to restrain the interfacer, who was hissing violently as she continued to strike out in all directions.

The bravest rushed the lounge. One O'o'yan threw himself on the native's left arm. The specimen reacted with a loud moan and threw the technician aside. A Hivistahm caught a foot that sent her tumbling.

Swearing, Caldaq and Soliwik abandoned the observation chamber and rushed to help.

By the time they arrived the technicians had the mesh off the interfacer and were gently lowering her motionless form onto a medical pallet. Chief-of-Medicine himself was squatting over her, carefully running a diagnost around her head. Blood trickled from one nostril, running the length of her snout.

"What happened here?" Caldaq's tone was short, clipped.

"Truly truly most truly we do not know." Second-of-Medicine looked stricken.

A technician arrived with a small readout. Caldaq grabbed the device, called up a preliminary interpretation in Massood as someone placed a funnel-shaped respirator over the interfacer's snout. Gas hissed.

"I cannot make sense of this."

Second-of-Medicine took the readout and peered through his eyeshades at scrolling information. Delicate fingers made demands of fine switches.

"Look here," she said, speaking through her translator. "Everything normal at the beginning. Nothing out of the ordinary. Alien but not abnormal sleep pattern.'' Nervously she looked over her shoulder at the examination lounge. The Human was still asleep, no longer kicking but still wearing a strange expression. The technicians had managed to remove the mesh from its head.

''Through the usual prescribed stimuli we ran, starting slow and imprecise at first, analyzing and recording as we proceeded. Different species react to different stimuli and in differing fashion.

''As study proceeded and stimuli grew more actively intrusive more atypical reactions we began to note.''

''A difficult observation to argue with,'' Soliwik muttered.

''Besides the physical, I mean. Buildups far out of the ordinary. For example, an astonishing increase in cortical electrical activity there was. Right off the chart.''

''What type of stimuli?'' Caldaq asked.

How abrupt, how terse. How like the Massood, Second-of-Medicine thought. With a long, slim finger she traced patterns on the readout's screen.

''A mildly threatening episode, here. See the parallel lines used for comparison purposes? This one would be expected of a Hivistahm, this nearly straight line for a Lepar. This is what we got from the native.''

Caldaq leaned over to examine the jagged scribblings. It was the kind of recording one might expect to take from the mind of an insane sentient. The native Will Dulac was many things, but he was not insane. Yet the readout was real, not an invention. It had monitored *something*.

''What happened to her?'' Soliwik gestured toward the interfacer, now resting quietly on the medical pallet.

''Truly we do not know yet.'' Second-of-Medicine regarded her unconscious colleague with concern. ''Preliminary diagnosis is cataleptic shock.''

Caldaq's nose and ears were twitching sharply. ''From what?''

The Hivistahm craned her neck to look up at the towering Massood. ''In the absence of alternative explanations, one must assume it involves the feedback she received from the native. Still checking we are, but thus far nothing to indicate mechanical failure was involved is there.

''Whatever the actual cause, the result was an incredibly violent episode. Chief-of-Medicine says she has never witnessed the like.''

"Neither have I, but then I do not spend much time in labs." Caldaq tapped the readout's screen. "The native insists it and its kind are peaceful creatures. Can it have been lying to us outright?''

"Possibly, but if it had something it wished to hide from us I do not see why to these tests it agreed to submit.''

"I see no explanation for the contradiction," Caldaq muttered.

The Hivistahm looked thoughtful. "At the time of the episode in deep sleep was the native. It remains so. Therefore we must conclude that what occurred was not the result of conscious effort but was instead an instinctive reaction by its mind and body to the intrusive stimuli." She dug at an ear opening with a finely manicured claw, scales glistening in the bright examination lights.

"I am by this more troubled than if the native of its own conscious volition had reacted. It suggests there is a portion of its nervous system over which it has no control.''

"I am glad to hear that," declared Caldaq. "It indicates to me that the native did not intend to harm the interfacer.''

"Yet she has truly been harmed.''

"But you cannot yet say exactly what happened?''

"A lot of data there is to be analyzed. Most importantly, the corroboration of her own testimony we need. I look forward to her recovery.''

"Surely," Soliwik commented, "the shock cannot be so severe?''

"Treating her now they are." The Hivistahm looked on worriedly as her colleagues worked on the unconscious interfacer. "I hope you are right, Second-of-Command.''

The interfacer came out of it a little while later. Came out screaming and whistling shrilly as if being pursued by one of the great carnivores of the homeworld. Attending physicians and techs quieted her with medication and reassuring words, manually darkening her eyeshades. At her insistence they also removed her from the examination chamber to another part of the ship.

Two hours later Will Dulac rolled over, yawned, and opened his eyes. The nap had left him refreshed, relaxed, and wondering why he'd made such a fuss over the harmless probe. In response to questions from the Hivistahm and S'van he replied that he had felt nothing, remembered nothing. No nightmares, no unease. His neck was a little stiff, but otherwise he had slept comfortably. The intensity of their queries puzzled him.

In response to his request they provided him with food. Some of it was Massood, the rest S'van. Studies indicated with a good degree of certainty that his body would find all of it nourishing. Taste, however, was much more difficult to quantify. Some of what they were certain he would enjoy he set aside in disgust while dishes Caldaq would not have touched the native appeared to find quite palatable.

It was a good deal later when Chief-of-Medicine reluctantly allowed the injured interfacer to be interviewed.

She lay on her side on a clean medical pallet, a thermoletic sheet covering her body. Both Chief- and Second-of-Medicine were present along with several specialists, Caldaq, and all three Seconds-of-Command. Caldaq would have liked to have had Jaruselka present as well, but it would not have been proper. Anyway, he could discuss the findings with her later.

"What can you tell us about what happened?" he inquired as gently as possible. The interfacer's shades had been blacked out and he could not see her eyes.

Her voice was wispier than normal, her breathing terse. "Truly truly I do not know. The probe commenced without incident or abnormality. I encountered no resistance. There was the expected strangeness at first but otherwise nothing remarkable. The mind of the native open and clear remained. Particularly unsophisticated I thought it." She hesitated and sipped liquid from a tube before continuing.

"With the prescribed sequence of stimuli I proceeded. Then chaos without warning. It was as if into the nether pit of the universe I had been plunged. I . . . I do not think at this time an adequate description of the experience I can render." She looked up at Chief-of-Medicine. "Please do not ask me too much to remember. Not now, not yet."

"It will not be required." The older Hivistahm bent over the interfacer and murmured something too low for the translators to pick up. As he spoke he repeatedly ran an index finger from between the patient's eyes up over her head and down the back of her neck. She relaxed visibly. Her voice grew softer still.

"As if my brain was on fire it was," she mumbled finally. "The horror, the sheer hatefulness." Unexpectedly she sat up and pushed back the darkened eyeshades. "Instinctively homicidal are these creatures. They hide their natural selves beneath a veneer of civilization. Inside as bloodthirsty and primitive as a Stachc they are."

"We still do not know for certain during the scan what happened," said one of the specialists. "On personal experience only is based your interpretation. This species is manifestly not primitive."

"Technologically no," argued one of his colleagues, "but sociologically it is a different matter. They fight among themselves, which for a species that has achieved their level of technological sophistication is unprecedented."

"There's also the testimony of the specimen itself." All eyes turned to T'var. "It cooperates with the scan and any other examination we wish to perform. It speaks only of peace and friendship and insists that's the ultimate goal of its people. It alludes to the astonishing infighting of its kind by insisting the activity is in rapid decline."

"Species infighting has been recorded elsewhere," a tech pointed out, "but only in societies that in a pretechnologic stage of development are."

"Yet the implications of our studies thus far in light of what has happened today are profound," argued a colleague.

Another captain might have injected his own opinions by now. Not Caldaq. Very early in life he had realized that it is difficult to learn anything with one's mouth open. On the other hand he knew that if left to run unchecked the debate could continue well into the night shift.

"Something important has taken place here. I am not as interested in why or how as much as I am in whether or not it can be used against the Amplitur."

"*No!*" Startled, he turned along with everyone else to the medical pallet. As if stunned by her own outburst, the interfacer put her head down against the backrest and repeated more softly, "No. This species as an ally we do not want. Anything to do with them we do not want!" Her eyes flicked wildly from one astonished onlooker to the next.

"Dispose of this one and depart before we are detected. My recommendation that is. I am not in command, but that is what I would do."

"Calm yourself you must," Chief-of-Medicine urged her. "Still subject to the aftereffects of the shock you suffered are you. Do not try to analyze. Dream instead of home."

"Truly do not patronize me." The interfacer added something in rapid-fire Hivistahm. What little of it the translator could cope with shocked Caldaq. The response was extreme and unnatural for a Hivistahm, much less for a trained technician.

As if conscious of his reaction and knowing that the final decision was his to make, she looked straight at her captain.

"Kill it," she said bluntly, "and this system leave alone."

"Dream and recover." Chief-of-Medicine muttered orders to a specialist, then led the group out of the room. Like everyone else, Caldaq carried his own confusing thoughts away with him.

In the examination chamber Will Dulac was doing his best to participate in a kind of signaling game with a pair of intent technicians. They chatted back and forth, the techs having to wait for their translators to deal with the guttural alien tongue. Though Caldaq could not interpret the native's expressions, it seemed to him that it was relaxed and at ease, perhaps even enjoying itself.

"On one hand we have the testimony of the interfacer," he said to his Seconds, "and on the other this reality." He gestured at the scene on the other side of the transparent wall where Will was doing whatever the pair of techs asked of him. Elsewhere a S'van was taking readings and two O'o'yan were checking instrumentation. At the rear of the chamber a Lepar was doing some routine cleaning. The scene verged on the bucolic.

"It is impossible for me to shake off the feeling that we stand on the brink of some great revelation. I cannot, I will not abandon that to the frenzied recommendation of a single injured specialist."

Soliwik observed the examination in progress. "The native insists its people are inherently pacifistic and will have no part in resisting the inroads of the Amplitur. Yet despite repeated declarations of its own peaceful nature it has shown the ability to react to specific stimuli with both physical and mental violence.

"Perhaps that is a key. It does not act; it reacts. If we could somehow convey the extent and depth of the Amplitur threat, perhaps it would react usefully to that.''

''Usefully to what degree?'' Caldaq wondered.

''I do not know,'' Soliwik hesitated, turned to look at him. ''My captain, I have been in service all my life. I have witnessed much and heard more. But I have never in all my experience seen anything akin to what occurred earlier today in this chamber.

''I am no scientist, no technician. I am a fighter and a leader of fighters. But I know the interfacer suffered something. Whatever it was shocked her values as well as her mind. Did you hear how readily and insistently she said to kill the specimen? That is unlike a Hivistahm. Truly,'' she added in a slight attempt at levity.

Caldaq indicated acknowledgment, looked down to his left. ''T'var? You have been unnaturally subdued through all this.''

The S'van spoke carefully. ''At present I find myself ambivalent on the matter, but I'd tend to side with you, Captain. Aside from the morality of 'disposing' of an intelligent specimen, I still feel we have much to learn from it. There's value in all knowledge, and where this species is concerned we still have a dearth of it. We can't simply depart and leave our work here unfinished, even if these people prove ultimately to be useless to the Weave. I could not be party to ambiguous flight.

''Clearly Soliwik is right when she says there's a capacity for violence here. The Hivistahm do not have it. The Lepar do not have it. My people do not have it. That is a resource as much to be desired in a new species as rare metals or great ships. What we have to ascertain is how much of what the native says is contradicted by its reactions and whether or not there's anything in that apparent contradiction which we can usefully exploit.

''We need to find out if there's a way to induce these creatures to fight on behalf of the Weave instead of among themselves. The *potential* for combat is certainly present; if not in this specimen, then possibly in others.'' He eyed Caldaq speculatively.

''I should even venture to say that this potential matches or exceeds anything the Massood are capable of.''

Caldaq did not bristle at his Second's observation. Some of his troops might have reacted more strongly, but he did not. Perhaps it was a consequence of his unique temperament.

"Second-of-Medicine's comments pose a problem. She suggests that if this capability is indeed present, it may not be consciously controllable by the native individual. If it cannot be controlled, I do not see how effective use cannot be made of it."

"Her observations may be clouded by personal experience," T'var responded. "Indeed, it would be unnatural if they were not."

"If this potential can only be unleashed when the native is surprised or asleep, then it is useless." Soliwik rested a hand on the transparent wall. "Most of you were focused on the interfacer's reactions when the episode occurred. I kept my attention on the native. I saw no overt signs of violence, nothing to suggest it was defending itself in its sleep. A few slight twitches and a jerking of one leg. There was nothing to suggest, from a physical standpoint at least, that it was aware of what it was doing. As you know, the native confirmed all this upon awakening."

Caldaq considered. "We must find out what it is capable of when awake. Defensive mechanisms and reactions that engage only when it is unconscious are clearly of no use to us." He sniffed, sucking air and uttering a whistling exclamation.

"We are not leaving this place until we know if there is anything of use here or not. Studies will continue. We must summarize and analyze what we have learned about his species and proceed accordingly. It is self-evident they are capable of violence against themselves. That does not concern me. It is an aberration for others to dissect.

"In contrast our mission is entirely practical, and it is to practical ends we must be devoted." He reached down to put a hand on T'var's shoulder. The S'van was surprised by the physical contact.

"I leave it to you, Second, to see to it that the scientific staff concentrates on practical matters and does not drift into the Underspace of pure research. We need results I can act upon, not more theory." He straightened and stared into the chamber, regarding the native thoughtfully.

"We have debated this matter among ourselves. Let us discuss it with the specimen."

T'var was uncertain. "It may find the subject provocative."

"That is what I am hoping."

Caldaq's hopes were not fulfilled. Not only was the native not provoked, it demonstrated a distinct reluctance to discuss the matter at all. It showed more interest in the plants which brightened the relaxation lounge to which they had all moved.

Passing crew glanced only occasionally in the direction of the little group. A pair of Lepar ignored them as they cleaned the bubble that protruded into another part of the ship. The benches on which they sat were made of curving plastic. Different heights accommodated the backsides and legs of different species so that a S'van might sit comfortably in the company of a Massood.

T'var was remonstrating with the indifferent native. "We've explained that few Weave races are suited to combat, the Massood and Chirinaldo foremost among these. Our efforts against the Amplitur are severely restricted by this limitation. Neither the Massood nor the Chirinaldo have high rates of reproduction. Efforts have been made to increase these but . . ."

"If you're looking for someone to breed soldiers for you then you'd better look elsewhere," Will told him.

T'var's expression was submerged in the depths of that great black beard. "I offer apologies if I've offended."

Will sighed. "It's not that. It's just that in spite of what you think we're not suited for what you want. I realize that our history might suggest otherwise, but we're getting better at peace. We've been working toward it for thousands of years and we're almost there. People have started to realize it's simply not practical, in an age of weapons of mass destruction, to go on fighting one another. There can't be any victors." He smiled, without considering the effect it might have on his audience.

"The last thing we need, the last thing we'd want to do, is export our failures. I don't know why we've fought throughout our history. You've said it's not normal, and if it was up to me I'd agree with you. I can't give you any explanations. It's just the way we developed."

"As a species matures toward civilization the normal sequence of events requires that individuals band together to cooperate against natural forces." T'var ran thick, stubby fingers down the weft of a nearby broadleaf plant. "Your people seem to have done exactly the opposite. We would like to know why."

"So would we," said Will feelingly.

"Some of our specialists have suggested that your abnormal development may be related to your extraordinarily active geology. On all other sentient-inhabited worlds the species has evolved on a single large landmass. This is conducive to cooperation and joint development. We find your planet as fractured as your society.''

''You may be right about that,'' said Will. ''You may be right about everything . . . except us being ready to participate in your war. Besides, didn't you tell me that the hallmark of a truly advanced, mature civilization is one that has given up large-scale conflict?''

''And so we all had, until the advent of the Amplitur.'' Soliwik leaned forward earnestly. ''Don't you think we tried talk and intelligent debate before taking up arms against them? You *must* realize that neutrality is a concept alien to the Amplitur. You are a part of their Purpose, living and developing under their suzerainty, or you are opposed to them.

''You must believe this.'' Cat eyes burned into his. ''You will not be given the luxury of avoiding a choice. If you decline to join with us, the Amplitur will eventually find your world. They will not permit you to decline.''

Will was quiet for a long moment. ''Why us? Why are we suddenly so damn important to you? We have so many problems of our own, we're so different, as you've repeatedly pointed out. We don't know anything about starships or interstellar drives. Of what use could we possibly be to you in a galaxy-wide conflict?''

''Allow me an apparent misconception to correct,'' said Second-of-Medicine. ''You apparently believe that interstellar conflict consists of great armadas of heavily armed vessels dueling in deep space. A physical impossibility this is. Ships traveling in Underspace cannot be tracked. Ships moving in normal space are separated by vast distances and unless locked in near atmospheric orbits are too far apart from one another to engage with on-board weaponry.

''Nor is there by destroying a ship much to be gained, even if a target could from fleeing into Underspace be prevented.''

''The war is to convince and persuade, not destroy,'' said Soliwik. ''Most fighting takes place on the surfaces of contested worlds. Care is taken to spare the local ecology and civilization insofar as is possible. The objective is to destroy the Amplitur, not the worlds on which they hold dominion.''

Will leaned back against the sculpted foam of the bench.

"You're still trying to tell me that after a thousand years of combat and the development of advanced weapons and ships capable of traveling between star systems, both sides do most of their fighting hand to hand?"

"It's not practical to fight in space," said T'var. "There's nothing in space to fight *for*. Do you begin to see why species with a proclivity or at least tolerance for combat are so sought after by both sides? Of course, the Amplitur have an advantage we can't match, both for reasons of morality and science. They can modify certain species the better to fulfill their requirements."

Will frowned. "Modify?"

"Biologically alter." T'var gazed hard at the native. "Naturally each species is convinced everything they do is of their own free will and volition. Despite continuing efforts we have been unable to convince any of them otherwise. How do you convince a sentient that it has been genetically reengineered if it has been reengineered to believe otherwise?

"The Amplitur themselves do not participate in combat. If not for their allied races, some of whom, it must be admitted, joined them voluntarily, we could end this war in a few years."

Will was shaken by the images thus called up, but not sufficiently to alter his convictions. "I sympathize with your situation. I really do. I just don't know how else to put this except to say it.

"Humans don't like to fight. We've been forced into it, whether because of stupidity or history or geology or whatever, but we don't like it. We now realize how wrong it is and we've been trying hard not to do it anymore. You've said that it's aberrant, uncivilized behavior. We're coming to realize that, starting to mature, as you put it. I don't think anything you can say is going to change people's minds."

"There must be a way to test this." Soliwik turned away from her translator so that her thoughts would not be conveyed to the native.

Caldaq indicated agreement, looked at Will. "You may be right. Please be patient with us if we strike you as overly insistent. Remember that we have come a long way and it will be difficult for us if we have to return disappointed." He did not mention the other intelligence they had previously encountered, which had enthusiastically agreed to ally itself with the Weave.

"If the truth of what you claim can be proven, then we will depart unobtrusively. However, you must understand that, given our position, we cannot leave until what you say has been verified beyond a doubt."

"That seems fair enough." Will eyed the alien commander. "What kind of proof would be sufficient for you?"

"I am sure that as an intelligent individual it is clear to you that it is impossible to pass judgment on an entire species based on the actions of a single specimen. We must acquire a larger, representative sampling of the population and put the same questions and tests to them that we have put to you. We need to see how they will react, speak, perform in specified situations."

Will considered. This was becoming as complicated as one of his Uncle Dan's bourrées. "I take it you'd like me to help you find some people?"

T'var nodded. "I think it's self-evident that we can get this over with a lot faster if you'd agree to serve as intermediary for us."

"Why should I help you?"

"Because," said T'var, "the sooner we've obtained and tested our sample, the sooner we'll depart forever if your analysis of your kind's reactions proves correct."

"All right. I'll do what I can. It's going to sound crazy to most people but I'll try. One thing, though: no professional soldiers, no military personnel. No people who have been trained to fight other people. You want a representative sample of the general population; that's what I'll try and get for you."

"Agreed." Caldaq's ears bent forward and his upper lip curled back.

"There's just one problem," Will told them. "I have no idea how I'm going to get anybody to cooperate."

"You have," Soliwik pointed out.

Will looked at her. "Not enthusiastically, if you'll remember. And you found me alone and isolated."

"You mean," said a puzzled Second-of-Medicine, "you will have difficulty finding people who will agree to help? On a mature world individuals would naturally wish to cooperate."

"I told you: this isn't a mature world. But you won't take my word for it, you want to test other people. Fine. I just have to figure out how to convince some of them to go along."

"Based on what we have learned of your civilization," said

Caldaq, "it clearly would not be effective for us to appear in a town and make the request ourselves."

"No. That's why you need me." Will looked thoughtful. "I might be able to find a few people willing to meet aliens, talk with aliens. The possibility of contact has been in the news for so long that some people are probably ready for it. But locating people willing to come to your ship and submit themselves to a battery of tests, that's another matter entirely. I don't know how to start finding people like that."

"If it is a true test of your people's potential to be," said Second-of-Medicine, "you should adequate specimens everywhere be able to find."

"Easy for you to say. You have your own definition of civilization. I don't think it fits ours. If you're right, though, I suppose I should be able to sail my boat inshore right here and find the people you need. What if I can't?"

"Then we will have to find another way of running the necessary tests," said Soliwik.

Will chose not to ask what the alternatives might be. Instead he muttered aloud, "If I had some way of convincing people instead of just asking them to trust me . . ." He looked at his audience. "You don't just ask Humans to do something extraordinary for you. It's customary to offer something in return for services rendered."

"That is an operative part of most civilizations. The idea of 'paying' a sentient to serve as a test subject is not." Caldaq turned to his colleagues. "That is not to say that under the present circumstances it is unworkable. The transfer of Weave technology is not an option. What else might be acceptable?"

"I'd like to keep away from counterfeiting. If the work wasn't perfect it could lead to trouble. Precious stones would be acceptable but most people would think they were fakes." Will looked at the captain. "How about gold? It doesn't matter what shape it takes. Just so long as it's the real thing."

After brief discussion the request was put to the scientific staff. Initial dismay gave way to relief when it was found that the necessary element was present in extractable quantities in the planet's seawater. The same method which had been used to camouflage the shuttle could be modified to extract gold instead of calcium.

This will all find its way into a grand symphony some day,

Will kept telling himself. He would title it "Contact." Now if they would only continue to provide him with samples of their own music . . .

He was surprised and disappointed to learn that what music the Massood possessed was simple and straightforward. In contrast, the Hivistahm and particularly the S'van utilized highly developed musical languages and were delighted to supply him with examples.

Listening to a S'van contrapuntal song cycle through an expandable playback device as the shuttle dropped away from the ship helped him to forget that he was traveling through empty space. The music was soothing, relaxing, like listening to a brace of waterfalls engaged in friendly debate. Easy to see why his own music had shocked them.

It wasn't the dissonance. There was plenty of that in the recordings they gave him. It was the rhythmic progressions that made them uneasy.

What am I doing here? he thought abruptly as the shuttle bumped through cloying atmosphere on its plunge toward a looming Caribbean. I should be composing, not recruiting the unsuspecting for a visit to an alien lab.

If not him, he knew, they would find someone else. Someone who might have a less sophisticated view of the world than himself, who might unconsciously perpetuate a false impression. It was incumbent on him to see this through.

It shouldn't take much to convince Caldaq and his people that they were wasting their time here. He would simply pass over anyone in uniform, anyone who even looked like a soldier. Ordinary people, that was the ticket. Not that Belize was a hotbed of military tradition anyway.

People would disbelieve him, might even laugh at him outright. More than one would assume he was some kind of smuggler. But he had been supplied with enough gold to overcome the reluctance of a few. These would follow him out of greed if not curiosity. If they bolted at the sight of Caldaq's people, so much the better. It would only serve to reinforce his thesis that a parochial humanity would be useless in any interstellar conflict.

Whereupon the representatives of the mysterious Weave would depart, leaving him to get on with his composing and his world to practice its increasingly peaceful ways. As for the driven Amplitur and their unfathomable Purpose, it was not unreasonable to assume they might be defeated by the resolute forces of the Weave long before they ever encountered mankind. Hadn't Caldaq admitted that Earth lay far off the beaten interstellar track?

No, they would be shown conclusively what Will had been trying to tell them all along and then they would go, leaving him with a little gold of his own and, if he was lucky, recordings of their music to inspire and infuse his work with the exotic for the next twenty years. He felt no compunctions at keeping both. Teaching paid next to nothing, while the history of musical patronage was old and respected. Wagner had his Ludwig of Bavaria. Will Dulac had the Massood.

★ XII ★

It took the shuttle crew several weeks to reestablish themselves in the protective lagoon and extract from its warm waters a toolbox full of yellow persuasion. The gold was produced in the form of thick-walled straws. Will assumed it had been condensed around some kind of tube or wire. The toolbox was sturdy enough to hold it all, but he worried about the handle breaking. It was heavy enough that he had to shift the load repeatedly from one hand to the other.

"You're sure you trust me with this?" he asked T'var. "I've got a small fortune here. I could go ashore and disappear and you'd have to start all over again."

"Why would you do that?" wondered the short Second-of-Command.

"You're right: I wouldn't. You have your cause and I have mine. I'm going to use what's in here to prove to you that you're wasting your time on my world."

The Human was very confident, T'var mused. His words repeatedly contradicted the claims of the xenopsychs. Claims were not proof, however, of either thesis. That would come only with additional study.

This world, he realized, represented a great gamble. Too great, if an injured interfacer was to be believed. Second-of-Medicine was of similar mind, but the concerns of two members of the medical staff counted for very little in conference. For now T'var found himself agreeing with the majority. This world offered confusion, but not danger. If its mysteries could be unraveled then its promise might be fulfilled.

The shuttle carried a tender, an air-repulsion craft designed to give a survey crew the ability to explore the surface of new worlds. It was not large, but it would serve to transport Will to the mainland under cover of darkness.

He'd never been farther inland than the port of Belize City, but he knew that the country was mostly undeveloped rain forest and swamp, a steamy refugee from a Somerset Maugham novel brought forward from the 1920s and set down whole and intact in the present day. Air traffic was sparse and the main roads little traveled. They should have no difficulty crossing the coastline unobserved.

They set him down near the main highway, promising to meet him at the same spot in a week's time. Will was not sanguine about his chances.

"You may find me waiting for you by myself," he told T'var, "the gold notwithstanding. But I'll do my best."

"You will choose a *representative* sample of your people." The Wais was speaking to insure that at this critical moment there were no misunderstandings. The bird-thing looked more comfortable than the S'van.

"Of course," Will lied. He had no intention of being so imprecise. There might be a number of soldiers on leave in the city. The British maintained a substantial garrison in their ex-colony, to keep chauvinistic Guatemalans at bay, and the Americans used the country as a base for training their own soldiers in tropical warfare. The last thing Will wanted was to recruit a mob of poorly paid would-be soldiers of fortune.

No, the people he picked up would be much more selectively "representative" than that. Soldiers and even ex-soldiers he would avoid like the archaic attitudes they represented.

The ship's techs wanted several dozen specimens. Will patiently explained that a group that large would invariably attract unwanted attention, even in laid-back Belize. He did not add that the greater the number of people he brought back, the more likely it was to include one or two individuals of the aberrant type the scientists were looking for. So he had several reasons for wanting to keep the group small.

If he could convince enough people, the Weave would have its representative sampling of Humanity . . . only it would be a sample acquired and filtered through William Dulac's convictions and beliefs.

He could not recruit outright pacifists. If he was that obvious then his alien patrons might abandon him and begin again else-where. He had to satisfy them that the people he brought back were truly representative of their species.

The absence of nocturnal traffic which had allowed the shut-tle's tender to set him down unobserved meant that he would have to lug the toolbox and its heavy contents all the way into the city. His legs were threatening to give out when a white-bearded farmer driving a pickup truck nearly as old as himself offered a ride the rest of the way in. So grateful was Will for the lift that he readily climbed in back with the load of bananas, heedless of the large tarantulas that often traveled with them.

The ride into town was hard on his spine but mercifully devoid of arthropod companionship. He hopped off, gave the old man a U.S. dollar, shouldered his backpack, and hefted the toolbox as he headed up a narrow dirt street flanked by multistory build-ings of stucco and clapboard.

Belize was a backwater country full of poor but charming people whose hopes throughout history had been repeatedly devastated by hurricanes and indifference. The city was crowded with citizens unable to find work on the plantations, fishing boats, or in the nascent tourist industry. A few Victorian struc-tures and stolid churches which had somehow survived the city's repeated inundations were bright spots among the otherwise ramshackle architecture.

A small but clean hotel offered temporary refuge from the tropical night. Hiding the toolbox as well as possible he col-lapsed on the bed and slept till late morning.

After a meal of broiled fish and bottled water he was ready to go to work.

Streets which had been deserted the previous evening were full of people going nowhere in a great hurry. Clumps of vacant-eyed men accreted on street corners, waiting for destiny to tap them on the shoulder. Women chattered and popped in and out of tiny storefront markets, juggling groceries and babies with equal agility. Children skipped like water bugs around and through the surging mass of adults, laughing because they could not comprehend the poverty in which they dwelt, finding joy in a muddy puddle or an empty liter bottle of 7-Up.

Lebanese immigrants with S'van-black mustaches hammered and sawed on a new store in the shape of a mosque. A dread-locked Rastafarian stumbled up the street, unable to surmount the half-foot-high curb. No one spared him a glance. A little man who looked like a Mayan bas-relief sprung to life sat on a corner of cracked concrete, arms crossed atop his knees as he uncomprehendingly observed the bustle of a mobile civilization.

The faces of Belize City were a microcosm of Humanity, stained with an abnormal amount of sweat. The country was a dumping ground, the depression at the bottom of the Caribbean funnel where the adventurous and disaffected ended up when there was nowhere else to go, no more islands to hop. Representative of Humanity, yes. The lower end.

It owed this legacy as well as the prevalence of the English language to the British colonial government from which the present independent administration was not far removed. The country was full of British and other expatriates who had found in this corner of Central America their place in the sun. American and German tourists lingered in the few souvenir shops, in a hurry to purchase something, anything of local manufacture so they could get back to the contemporary beach resorts and air-conditioning of Ambergris Cay. Sunburned, healthy young Scandinavians in lederhosen and too-heavy hiking boots smiled painfully at everything as they marched energetically up and down the streets.

There were Hindus; descendants of small brown men who had been imported to the Caribbean to work the sugar plantations; Meskito Indians fleeing insurrection in Nicaragua; even blue-eyed natives who were the descendants of Confederate settlers arrived here on the heels of the Civil War. They had come hoping to reestablish the grandeur that had been the Old South.

But there was no grandeur to be found in Belize, unless it was in its mountains and jungles, rivers and reefs. Certainly there was no grandeur in Belize City, a community built on land so low that high tides periodically washed the raw sewage which flowed down the river right back up the main streets.

He avoided the two stores where he occasionally purchased supplies for his boat, concentrating instead on what passed for the touristy end of town. Broken gold straws crammed into the deep pockets of his pants rested heavily against his legs as he ate lunch in a bad Chinese restaurant and studied the crowd. How to approach someone, and who to pick? People shambled and shuffled past his table, alternately staring at the ground or conversing with companions.

It was too crowded here, in the center of town. Paying for lunch and praying for his digestion, he decided to try the insipid waterfront, soon found himself strolling along the unimpressive breakfront which held back the sloshing, garbage-laden ocean.

He sat down on a smooth-topped stone and stared out to sea, wishing he was back on his boat working with his MIDI and keyboard, wondering how to proceed, wishing he'd never heard of Massood and S'van, O'o'yan and Lepar, the Weave and the Amplitur and their eon-old conflict.

But heard he had, and it was up to him to keep not only himself but the entire Human race out of it. That's not for us, he knew. We still have plenty of our own problems to sort out. We haven't time to deal with someone else's troubles.

"Mister, you got a dime?"

Turning atop the rock, Will found himself face-to-face with a boy who looked to be about twelve but was probably closer to fifteen. Skinny and malnourished, he wore a torn short-sleeve shirt and frayed shorts. No shoes. A second boy, aged too soon, stood nearby. He might have been sixteen, or twenty-five. Both looked hungry, and not just for food.

"Sure." Will smiled and dug into a pocket. His fingers encountered a four-inch length of gold pipe. "That your friend over there?"

The boy gestured with his head. "That my bro, mon. Got a dime for him, too?"

"Your parents know you two are out begging?"

The boy smiled ingenuously. "Of course, mon. You think we orphans or som'ting?"

"You kids going to school?"

"Hey look, mon." The youth retreated a step. "You got some money, we thank you. Don't give us no lectures."

"Take it easy." Will smiled back. "I'm no preacher." He lowered his voice conspiratorially. "You kids ever get to the movies? You know, cinema?"

"Movies?" The boy regarded him warily. "Sure, mon."

"Who do you like?"

"Who you think, mon?" Skinny arms and legs wildly assaulted the air. "Chuck Norris, mon. Bruce Lee. All those guys."

"You like to fight, huh?"

The boy hesitated. "Sometime, maybe. What you want, mon? My bro and me don' do no weird stuff."

"How'd you two like to make some real money? How'd you like to meet some . . . aliens. Like in the movies. You know . . . people from another world?"

"Hey, we seen stuff like that. Our friend, he's got a VCR. You crazy, mon."

"Am I?" Will drew one of the gold straws from his pocket, showed it to the boy. In the dim tropical light it shone like the sun. His eyes grew wide.

"Hey mon, that ain't real, is it?"

"Call your brother over. I have a business proposition for the two of you."

By the end of the third day he had recruited not only the two orphaned brothers but a friend of theirs, a powerfully built fisherman who sometimes gave them shelter. He was also the blackest black man Will had ever seen, as black as the water beneath a Mississippi pier on a moonless night. There was no color in him whatsoever, not a smidgen of beige or chocolate brown.

There was also the middle-aged expatriate he had encountered in his own hotel, originally from the southeast of England but lately of many local bars. He'd been elegantly drunk, though not so drunk that he failed to identify the gold Will showed him as the real article. Whimsically he agreed to participate. "It will be a real lark," he laughingly insisted. Will wondered what his reaction would be when he found himself confronted by Caldaq.

The man had come to Central America on sabbatical and had chosen to stay, held by cheap liquor and the certain knowledge that he was accomplishing absolutely nothing with his life back home in Surrey. So there was plenty of time to indulge in whatever diversion a crazy American could concoct, right? When sober enough he could identify every country together with its major cities, principal exports, important topographic features, and fifty-four different local brands of beer. A useful addition to Will's group, yes? He was ready for whatever adventure happened to come his way so long as adequately noncorrosive booze was made available in modest quantity.

There was the young man with the dreadlocks, a Rastafarian—like the one Will had seen stumbling down the city's main thoroughfare, a cannabis smoker for sure, yes mon, but not stoned when Will talked to him—who readily embraced the opportunity to meet some real as opposed to smoke-induced aliens. Will smiled to himself as he contemplated what Caldaq's reaction might be to this particular specimen of Humanity. It would be interesting to watch the Wais attempt to translate when the man's every alternate word was well nigh incomprehensible. Will only hoped he would remember to show up at the hotel at the appointed time.

Another pair of candidates materialized in the form of a pair of students from Sydney, would-be intellectuals out to experience the world before returning home to make as much money as possible while vegetating on the beaches of the Gold Coast pretending they were doing something for the future of mankind. Will ignored their pretensions as readily as he welcomed their presence.

Seven was a good number, but Will wished for a few more and he was running out of time. Tomorrow night the shuttle's tender would return to the place where he had been dropped off, eighty miles up the central highway. He and his flock would be expected to be there to meet it.

His recruits seemed to arrive in pairs, like Ken Woods and Tamy Markowitz. They were a painfully earnest young couple who were, in Markowitz's words, "scouting out potential honeymoon sites."

"So we won't waste our time and money on a place where we don't think we'll have a good time," Woods added.

Their particular jejune brand of insensible preyuppie reasoning was precisely what Will was looking for, but he had a hard time convincing them to come along. Eventually they agreed. Not to meet aliens, which they didn't believe for a second, nor for the gold. They agreed because they found fascinating the people Will had already recruited and Markowitz turned out to be a would-be professional photographer. It would be a wonderful opportunity for her to observe and photograph a diverse collection of people in a restricted setting. Will wasn't even sure what she looked like because he rarely saw her face. It seemed as if a single-lens reflex was all that existed above her neck.

They would probably bolt when the tender arrived, he thought, and certainly when Caldaq or T'var put in an appearance. He kept them anyway because that reaction in itself would be instructive.

Nine, then, as motley and unlikely a group as one could imagine even in Belize, assembled outside the hotel the following night. He'd rented a full-size van from a local car-hire, though for the amount of gold he'd slipped the attendant on duty at the time he could probably just as easily have bought the vehicle outright.

After seeing to the stowing of luggage on the van's roof rack he put the mumbling Rastafarian in the front seat next to his own, the two local youths immediately behind with their fisherman friend next to the door, where he would have a little extra legroom. The two Australians struggled into the back, where they could chat with the expatriate teacher. Woods and Markowitz obligingly split up.

He was climbing into the driver's seat when an old woman confronted him.

"Excuse me, sir." Her voice was soft, her English good, and she was overdressed in broad-beamed hat and clean white dress, as if for church. Beneath one arm she carried a large wicker basket.

"Can I help you, granny?"

She smiled, a gentle upcurving of the corners of her mouth. "There are stories in the city of a white stranger who carries gold."

Will looked around, suddenly wary. It was dark out and even here, in front of the hotel, sufficiently desperate men would not hesitate if they thought the prize commensurate with the risk.

"Belize City is full of stories." Even in the poor light he could see that she was missing all four front teeth.

"It's not drug money, is it? That would be an offense against God."

"I've nothing to do with drugs."

"Good," she said firmly, hefting her basket. "I hear also that this stranger wants people to go with him for some mysterious purpose, and that for this he pays handsomely." She indicated the van and its noisy inhabitants.

He did not wonder where or how she had heard. The Human telephone in Belize City was far more reliable and accurate than its electronic counterpart.

"I already have enough people."

"I don't take up much space," she said, a plaintive note in her voice. "I want to go, too, if there is any chance to make some money."

What would the Hivistahm scientists make of this one? Will mused. Still he hesitated, studying her carefully. He didn't want anyone to die on him.

"Excuse me for saying so, but you don't look very—" He hunted for a polite word. "—strong." He checked his watch. Still ample time to make the rendezvous.

"I'm stronger than I look, sir. I've worked all my life. Just because I'm small and old don't think I'm not strong. I do not know what it is you have in mind for your people, but I can tell you that I am a widow. My husband passed away two years ago. I have a son who works in San Pedro and he has a wife. By them I have, God be praised, two grandchildren, a boy and a girl. A third died last year.

"They cannot visit me because they have no money. I have no one in this city. I want to go with you, sir."

Will softened. "Do you understand what we're going to do? We're going to meet people from another world and travel on their ship to a much bigger ship that waits in space halfway between here and the moon, where they will look at you and ask you questions."

"Sir, I do not care what it is you want of me, if there is some money involved. I have never been out of Belize City in all my life, save for two trips to the capital. I want to make enough money to live close to my son and my grandchildren. I will do whatever you ask."

Some good was going to come of this after all, he thought. "See if you can find room in back." He looked into the night. "What about your luggage?"

She held up the basket. "I have everything I own in here. What else would I need?"

What else indeed, Will thought.

She started around to the other side, paused to look back at him. "Bless you, sir."

Feeling better, he climbed in and shut the door behind him. "Don't say that until you see what you're getting yourself into." In her own way, he knew, she was as blind to the reality of what was happening as the Rastafarian and the teenagers.

Gunning the engine, he turned around and abandoned the waterfront for a main road, trying to find his way to the central highway in the dark. Behind him his charges nattered away meaninglessly, ten Human beings chosen at random who would unwittingly do their part to convince Caldaq and his Hivistahm xenopsychs of mankind's unsuitability as potential allies.

The half-drunk teacher expounded on irrelevancies to the Australian students while Markowitz snapped meaningless pictures like mad. The Rastafarian mumbled to himself, oblivious to the jokes the two teenagers made at his expense, while the dark fisherman stared silently out a side window.

It was late and they encountered very few oncoming lights. There had been none at all for more than half an hour by the time Will spotted the big tamarind tree he'd chosen for a landmark and pulled off the highway onto a dirt road. A bumpy mile beyond, the track ended in a shallow swamp. Of the tender's previous touchdown there was no sign, the resurgent muck and resilient water plants having obliterated all evidence of its earlier visitation.

Will killed the engine and stepped out. "This is it."

The eldest of the two teenage boys confronted him. "This isn't it, mon. Where's the gold you promised us?"

"Don't you want to see the aliens first?"

The younger boy walked to the water's edge, his tone more credulous than his brother's. "Where are they?"

Will tilted his head back, scanning the dark cloud-filled sky. "They'll be here. So will the gold." He looked over at the older boy, whose expression eloquently declaimed that the whole world had conspired against him since the day of his birth. "Why don't you give me a hand with the luggage?"

"Hey, mon, do it yourself, you heah? My bro and I, we already got ours." He held up a package secured with twine.

Ken Woods gave Will a hand. So did the silent fisherman, whose body seemed fashioned of black rebars welded together.

When the pile of luggage had been unloaded Will checked his watch again. Things could get interesting if the tender failed to materialize. He didn't look forward to spending the night at the edge of the swamp, fielding accusations and indignant inquiries while watching nervously for patrolling fer-de-lance.

As time passed complaints filled the air with increasing frequency. He knew he couldn't hold them much longer. Eventually he would have to pass out the gold in the toolbox, turn the van over to his disgruntled recruits, and remain behind to greet his alien acquaintances with confessions of failure instead of the promised specimens.

Then suddenly, without any warning, there it was: a massive dark outline suspended in sky, slowly lowering toward them. It sang like a troll humming its babe to sleep, a deep-throated mechanical counterpoint to the oohs and aahs that now began to rise from his companions.

⋆ XIII ⋆

The expatriate stumbled and lost his Panama hat, while the old woman from Belize City crossed herself. Elevating his mumbling to a higher level, the Rastafarian gaped at the silently descending tender. The fisherman stood nearby, staring, silent as when Will had first set eyes on him.

The suddenly sobered British schoolmaster staggered over to stand next to Will. He held his recovered chapeau tightly in one hand, running the other through what remained of his graying hair.

"I . . . I thought it was a joke, what you said. You know, an evening's entertainment. Something to tell the friends back in Tunbridge Wells someday."

"I think you'll find it entertaining enough," Will told him, "but it will involve more than an evening. As I said." He eyed the older man thoughtfully. "You can run if you want to. No one will try to stop you."

The expatriate did not take his eyes from the descending vessel. "No. No, I think I will stick around for a while yet."

A slight puddling of water marked the tender's touchdown. A ramp extended from its flank to dry land, and the door above retracted. Figures appeared in the opening.

Will overheard the Australian girl questioning her male companion. The tall, freckled redhead had a voice like a Dickensian waif.

"How come they're different sizes?"

"They're not just different sizes, luv. They've got to be different species. Say, have a look at that tall one in the back. That's

153

a sheila for sure, even if she is hairy as a possum.'' He pointed to the advancing Wais. "I don't know *what* that is.''

Caldaq and the S'van assistant captain Will knew as T'var were accompanied by three Massood soldiers and a Wais translator. As greetings were exchanged Will saw that Caldaq's attention was not on him but on his recruits.

The latter stared and mumbled among themselves as the realization that this was not a joke, not a set piece being staged for unseen television cameras, began to take hold. None of them broke and ran. Somehow Will wasn't surprised when the old lady, the one he'd allowed to come along as an afterthought, was the first to walk up to the towering Massood and extend a wrinkled black hand.

"I am pleased to meet you, sir. My name is Annalinda Mason.'' She whispered to Will, "He is a 'sir,' is he not?''

"He is,'' said Will, simultaneously realizing that despite all he'd been through he had yet to explain the meaning of a handshake to the aliens. He proceeded to rectify that omission, watching as the captain's long, slim fingers enveloped those of the elderly woman.

At the same time, Caldaq's gaze roved over the edgy onlookers. "This is the best you could do?''

Will had determined to stick to his guns. "You wanted a representative sample, remember? No professional soldiers, not even any soldier-types. Just plain folks, so you could determine what kind of people Humans are. Well, I've brought you ten representative Human beings.''

The irrepressible T'var did not sound half as discouraged as his captain. Come to think of it, Will had yet to encounter a depressed S'van.

"That is what we wanted and that's what you have brought us. We must learn from what is made available to us.''

The group watched his approach with interest. As he was nearly two feet shorter than the shortest of them, in addition to being the most nearly humanoid of all the aliens, no one was intimidated by his inspection.

"The variance in coloration is interesting. It is more substantial than your visual transmissions suggest.''

"Our visual transmissions,'' Will told him, "very rarely reflect the true nature of our society. That's what I've been trying to get across to you all along.''

"This is for real, isn't it?" Ken Woods was muttering.

"As real as the gold." Will kept expecting someone to break and run, but their fascination with the aliens continued to exceed their concern. Perhaps, he thought, society had been so conditioned by now by the deluge of speculative fiction and films to the possibility of intelligent visitors from other worlds that the reality no longer had the power to shock. Certainly the tall, polite Massood and the feathery, supremely elegant Wais were far less intimidating figures than some of the ravening creatures which had appeared in popular movies.

T'var was peering up at the Australian couple. They in turn gazed down at him, intrigued by his bright eyes and bear fur. The young man looked over at Will.

"What's with the goofy-looking midget, mate?"

Will winced. "That's T'var, one of the assistant captains."

He needn't have worried. If anything, T'var was equally amused by the confrontation. "I am not offended," he said through his translator. "S'van are not easily insulted. We have made not being offended a survival trait. Others are envious enough of us as it is."

"Yeah?" said the youth challengingly. "Why would anyone be envious of you?"

"See," murmured one of the escorting soldiers behind Caldaq, "the staff rumors are true. Even in manners and speech they are belligerent."

Will's earplug conveyed the soldier's words and he hastened to correct her. "No, no. They're just curious, is all."

"I am called Caldaq." The captain stepped forward. "I command a vessel that is presently located halfway between here and your moon. If you agree, all of you will soon have the opportunity to see it for yourselves." He went on to deliver a capsule explanation of everything Will had been told about the Weave, the Amplitur, and the great war, concluding with an explanation of why they were on Earth and what they hoped to gain from their visit.

"For us to properly determine if you can be of real assistance to us will involve a journey outside your own solar system. You will be well treated, properly cared for, and amply supplied upon your safe return home with the gold you value so highly. No harm will come to you, and you will have experienced things your kind has not yet imagined." Showing how much he had learned, he added with visible effort, ''We would not force any of you to do this against your will. If you choose not to accompany us, you may depart whenever you wish.''

The fisherman picked up his simple pack and strode wordlessly forward, followed by the Australian students and the old woman. The others followed en masse.

Will inhaled deeply, took a last look at the familiar night sky, put the keys to the van on the driver's seat, and strode up the ramp into the hovering transport.

The tender returned to the reef and was secured aboard the shuttle. As preparations were being made to depart, Caldaq confronted Will.

''You are not going with them, Will Dulac.''

Will nodded knowingly. ''I hadn't planned on it.''

''And neither am I,'' the Massood continued, surprising him.

''What do you mean, you're not going?''

''I sense your confusion. The speci . . . the people you have brought to us will be taken to the nearest Weave world equipped with appropriate study facilities. That work must be complemented by continued research here.

''Because of your world's extreme contradictions and unusual potential it has been decided to expand our present base here. It will be small but well equipped and will consist of a shuttle and whatever facilities we can build around it. It is my option to go with the ship or continue work here. I have chosen to remain. It is my personal request that you continue to help us with our observations.''

Will was shaking his head slowly. ''You can't just throw up some big complex and expect the locals not to notice it.''

''Everything will be concealed as effectively as our shuttle was when first you encountered us.''

''You're going to stay here in the lagoon? This strikes me as a pretty isolated place from which to begin a study of all mankind.''

''Our instrumentation is sophisticated. We will manage. The isolation will allow us to make occasional onshore forays when required. We will have the use of the tender, which as you have seen can travel partially masked.'' Cat eyes stared hard at Will.

''Your continued assistance and cooperation, of course, would be of inestimable value to our labors.''

Will considered. He'd had it all worked out. As soon as the

aliens had departed with the recruits he was going to put on sail and start back to New Orleans, washing his hands of the whole business and resuming work on *Arcadia*. The remaining gold in his toolbox would allow him to take a nice, long sabbatical from teaching, something he'd dreamed of for years. He'd be able to finish the tone poem, do some short stuff, maybe try a couple of chamber pieces, and get a start on the cantata.

If he stayed to help Caldaq, there might not be much time for composing. Contrariwise, he would be able to study and absorb a wealth of alien musical influences.

"The composition of the study team has yet to be finalized," Caldaq told him in reply to his next question. "There will be Massood additional to myself, Hivistahm and S'van technicians, probably a few Lepar. No Chirinaldo."

"I've noticed that your people aren't as technically oriented as, say, the Hivistahm."

"It is not that so much as the fact that the Weave includes many skilled sentients but few fighters. The Massood fight because they can, not because they want to. We do this for the good of the Weave. Until the Amplitur forced combat upon us, Massood society was as sedate as that of the S'van."

Will felt a tug at his waist. "I've requested to stay also," T'var told him.

"Captain and assistant captain? Who'll run your ship?"

"Two other assistant captains," Caldaq explained. "Soliwik, who is actually more experienced than I, and Z'mam. Except in matters of actual combat, the Weave possesses great flexibility in matters of organization."

"How long do you expect them to be gone?"

"As long as it takes to learn what must be learned. I am not concerned. My mate will return with them. Meanwhile there is much to be done on your world." Something on his instrument belt beeped softly.

"We have to go now. As soon as you have returned to your boat we will ascend. In several days time we will be back to begin our work here." He hesitated.

"You may not be a fighter, Will Dulac, but you are strong of opinion. The Massood respect that. I hope you will be here when I return. We could continue our research without you, but you know something of us and our aims. It would be far easier to work with you than to begin anew with another of your kind, who might not be as intelligent or understanding.''

But I'm against everything you're after here, Will thought. Aloud he said, ''I'll think about it.''

Just before departure the teacher handed him a hastily scribbled letter to friends back in England. The couple from Connecticut passed along a similar message. Will promised to mail both at the first opportunity.

From the cockpit of his cat he watched the darkened shuttle rise above the mirrored sea, turn slightly, and begin its silent climb heavenward.

Caldaq stared out one of the shuttle's ports until the view of the Human's watercraft was obscured by dark clouds. In another part of the shuttle, he knew, ten Humans were doing likewise, chattering excitedly as they clustered together to get a glimpse of their world receding beneath them.

''Who do you think is right?'' he asked T'var. ''The Human Will Dulac or the xenopsychs?''

''If I could answer that there would be no need for extended study. Personally, I don't think these people understand themselves.''

''How can a race not understand itself?'' Caldaq straightened. ''That is a contradiction in terms.''

''Which is just what we have on this world: a biological contradiction in terms. Are these people civilized or not? We may have to invent new terms to describe them. Our studies here must proceed on the assumption that the abnormal is the norm and that we'll encounter only the unexpected.''

Not for the first time Caldaq wished he could borrow the mind of a S'van. A Massood proceeded directly from point A to point B. It was usually left to the S'van to explain what was happening at point C.

T'var's words troubled him all the way back to the ship. They worried him as he watched the Human guests being made comfortable, worried him as preparations were made for Underspace entry while the shuttle, which was going to remain behind, was loaded with equipment for the incipient base.

It even troubled him on the return journey to the surface of the bright blue-and-white planet, until he made himself put it out of mind. There was too much to do now to waste time on worry.

He was more relieved than he cared to admit when they found Will Dulac's boat anchored where they'd left it. The Human was waiting to greet the shuttle as it descended. Perhaps he'd been working on his strange music, Caldaq mused.

Will was standing in the cockpit when Caldaq stepped out of the shuttle's submersible onto the cat's deck. The moon was bright, allowing him to see the bubbles that emerged from where the vast dark shape was settling into the lagoon. Caldaq remembered the Human hand-shaking gesture of greeting in time to extend his fingers.

"I saw the shuttle," Will said, "but where's all the material for constructing your base?"

"It is begun even as we speak."

Will looked over the side, wondering if his big spotlight was strong enough to illuminate anything beneath the clear surface. Not that he intended to try. The intense beam might draw the attention of a passing fishing boat or yacht.

"You saw how we camouflaged our craft previously," Caldaq reminded him, fingering the translator unit hanging from his neck and hoping it could command the necessary terminology. "It is called electrophosphoresus. Lepar are already erecting the framing. Chemicals will be extracted from the water to create structures which will be attached to our vessel. The gold you value so highly was obtained through the same process. With Lepar setting the frames the work will go quickly."

"Yeah, the Lepar. That's the thing that intercepted me when I was trying to swim away."

"Yes. Your agility in the water was quite a surprise to us. Few Weave species do well in water. Our biologists were startled to see an air-breathing bipedal mammal swim so efficiently."

Will nodded, even though he was at best an average swimmer. "But the Lepar?"

"The Lepar are amphibious. In fact, they are unique in being the only known amphibious species to have developed true intelligence, though they are still—" He hesitated. "—slow in many ways. But they are very dedicated and work very hard. Being so different from the rest of us, they tend to keep to themselves. Even the Chirinaldo, who breathe supplemented heliox and are too massive to move around much on the ship, are more sociable.

"In a situation such as we face here, the ability of the Lepar to work underwater is of obvious value."

"What a coincidence that there happened to be some in your crew."

"Our ship was commissioned for exploring. To cope with unforeseeable contingencies, as diverse a crew as possible was assembled. The Lepar do certain things better than any Massood, the Massood have their advantages over the S'van, and so on."

"And you think we might do something better than anyone else?"

"Or hopefully at least as well. That is what our studies are intended to reveal."

Will spent plenty of time in the water watching the base take shape. He didn't relax until the shuttle once more resembled part of the reef. His only concern was that the work might be noticed by a low-flying plane, though the likelihood of that was small. What air traffic there was in this part of the world ran north–south along the coast of the Yucatán down to Honduras. Lighthouse Reef was sufficiently far out not to be overflown by commercial traffic.

Once the basic structure was complete the base began to sprout imitation coral heads and shelves, branches and caves. Even the colors matched those of the surrounding living reef. Lobsters and urchins began to move in, making new homes in the artificial coral's inviting nooks and crannies.

Will came and went as he pleased, utilizing the same airlock employed by the Lepar. Some nights he used the cat's dinghy to ferry anxious, quivering Massood to the nearby islands, where they spent hours running off accumulated nervous energy. They seemed to flow across the sand, their long legs scissoring effortlessly as they completed endless circuits of the palms and ironwood bushes.

It was Caldaq who explained to Will the sheer joy the Massood took in running and jumping, in competing against gravity. It was their heritage, their tradition.

Will was therefore somewhat surprised to note that while they could run forever, none of them seemed particularly fast or able to jump especially high. Though he was in his thirties and only in fair shape, he thought of matching his speed against theirs, then decided it would be tactless if he happened to win. Nor did he mention that any competent Human sprinter could run circles around the fastest of them.

The Hivistahm and O'o'yan, the S'van and the Wais did not seem at all athletic. It made him wonder.

He worked hard at convincing the techs who had been assigned to the base that mankind was hopelessly far down the road to peace and contentment. His words were contradicted by much of what they recorded from standard television broadcasts, so that he often found himself explaining the differences between reality and fiction. Even if Humans bizarrely fought among themselves that did not mean they were ready to go to war against an alliance of aliens they did not even know existed and who had never done anything to them.

No, all mankind wished was to develop the kind of advanced civilization the S'van and Hivistahm took for granted.

They listened with interest to everything he said, noting with approval and occasionally admiration Human accomplishments in art and music, literature and theater. Examples of Human efforts at working together to achieve harmony and understanding were everywhere.

Yet contradictions also abounded. Much of mankind's music was as acrimonious as it was affecting. The same could be said for his art and theater. Certain aspects of Human sport were as violent as the war between the Weave and the Amplitur, makebelieve or not. Even Human humor seemed as mordant as it was amusing.

Patiently Will explained, interpreted, elaborated upon. The idea was not to laugh at someone but with them. Not to injure on the playing field but to compete, just as the Massood competed at running and jumping.

There was much in what they heard and observed that severely troubled Third-of-Study, who had been placed in charge of the xenopsych section.

"Are you saying," said Caldaq in the privacy of his tiny cabin, "that you agree with the Human Will's assessment of his kind, or disagree with him?"

"Both."

It was difficult for Caldaq to envision the technician's true thoughts. The Hivistahm relied far more on gestures than on their limited range of facial expression. He stood there, eyeshades down, delicate fingers locked together. A Hivistahm could stand motionless like that long enough to drive a Massood crazy.

"Everything the native says is true, and everything he says is a lie."

"Well, that will make a fine definitive report," said Caldaq sarcastically.

The technician unlocked his fingers. "Truly I do not know how else to put it. Sometimes my people and I feel that the dumping ground for every contradiction in the universe this world is. Even their weather a study in extremes is."

"So I have heard." Will had tried to explain what they might face come hurricane season, though Caldaq had difficulty fully grasping the enormity of his description. Hurricanes, as Will called them, were a feature of uninhabitable gas giants, not civilized worlds.

Abruptly Third-of-Study began to pace. Caldaq sat a little straighter. The Hivistahm did not pace. That was a Massood characteristic.

"Do you the reaction of the technician who was damaged by the cerebral scan remember?"

"I do," said Caldaq.

"Less certain am I with every passing day that her reaction, while extreme, was unjustified."

Caldaq indicated displeasure. "That is not a scientific attitude."

"Truly this world renders mental detachment difficult. It is the unpredictability of these people that troubles me, and I am not alone in this opinion. To utilize the unpredictable in warfare, whether being or machine, to court disaster is."

"You may see them as unpredictable because we do not yet understand them."

"That may be so." Third-of-Study halted. "But even those species capable of fighting, such as the Massood, can in predictable fashion to a known set of circumstances be expected to react. That cannot be said of these Humans. They cannot say it of themselves, as our prime specimen repeatedly pointed out has. That is a dangerous quality to have to deal with in a time of battle. If these people do not know how they might react, what they might do, how can they within the existing command structure be accommodated?

"This is true even of our first contact and erstwhile native friend, Will Dulac, who never tires of violently reminding us how peaceful his people are. His voice grows loud and his gestures swift.'' Behind the lime-tinted shades the eyelids of the Hivistahm blinked nervously. ''Truly I find it impossible to believe that these contradictions have entirely your notice escaped, Captain.''

Caldaq put aside the lightscribe he'd been working with. While capable of irony, the Hivistahm were not spendthrift in its use.

''They have not.''

''Even assuming that the native Will is wrong and that his people serviceable fighters prove to be, do we really want such creatures as allies? Might not their mental instability as much a liability as benefit render them?''

''The fact they do not know themselves is one of the characteristics that makes them unique. Let us first find out if and how they can be useful to the Weave. Then we will deal with any related problems. It may be possible to structure their integration in such a way as to minimize their awkward unpredictability.'' When the Hivistahm showed signs of pursuing his objections, Caldaq irritably waved him off.

''It is for you and the S'van to decide if these Humans can be helpful and for the Chirinaldo and Massood to determine whether and how. Confine your determinations to your specific discipline and leave tactics to me.''

The technician seemed about to say something more, abruptly decided not to. He pivoted on wide sandals and headed for the doorway.

Weeks passed before Third-of-Study felt confident enough to confront his captain again.

''Truly something else concerns me.''

Caldaq was not in the mood. He hated administrative work and there was much to deal with. ''What is that?''

''It may be as Will Dulac says, that if presented with the choice his people would choose not in the great conflict to participate. But what if they are not given that choice?''

Caldaq's whiskers twitched as he regarded the technician. ''What do you say?''

''We could what the native says accept, that his people inherently peaceful and unwarlike are but have acted otherwise because of historical circumstances they are to learn how to control just beginning. We could depart, all evidence of our visit obliterating, preserving the ignorance of this world. Left to develop by themselves these people progress toward true civilization might well make.''

"They might also destroy themselves utterly," said Caldaq. "There are indications they may yet do that."

The Hivistahm gestured elaborately. "Truly. And if we intercede, if they come to know the Weave and share all that it stands for, that will not be permitted to come to pass. They to destroy themselves will not be allowed."

"Make your point, supervisor."

"If we leave they will either achieve civilization or destroy themselves. If we stay they will not destroy themselves but truly civilized may never become. The native Will speaks of the inexorable progress of his people toward peaceful coexistence. Our presence here disrupts that. Do our needs, the needs of the Weave, give us the right that to interfere with, with perhaps permanent effects? Do we the right have to deny these people the peace they have sought for so long simply because we feel are more important our needs? *Do we the right have to interfere on such a scale with the development of a potentially civilized race?*" The technician paused.

"It is such matters that glad make me."

"Glad of what?" Caldaq asked softly.

"That I am not the one who such decisions must make." Whereupon Third-of-Study departed, leaving Caldaq to silent contemplation of his glowing, waiting lightscribe.

★ XIV ★

Will sat in the cockpit listening to T'var as the S'van assistant captain toweled himself dry. Of all the Weave peoples he felt most comfortable around the S'van. Because of their intelligent rodentlike visages and continual twitching he often found the Massood intimidating in spite of themselves, while the Hivistahm and O'o'yan who comprised the bulk of the staff at the burgeoning base were too reptilian in appearance to warm up to.

In addition to being mammalian, the S'van were gregarious and talkative. They also possessed a highly developed sense of humor which transcended species, adroitly juggling inference and innuendo with a skill Will could only admire.

There were also several Lepar at the base, but they were so quiet and reserved he doubted he'd know how to initiate a conversation even if he encountered one of them in a hall or in the water.

Also, it was difficult to fear someone barely three feet tall. Sometimes he wondered what S'van faces looked like behind the thick black beards common to both sexes. The same dense curls covered head and arms, hugging the barely visible coffee-colored skin. Leaning against the back of the cockpit, T'var looked like a dark-eyed kitchen scouring pad.

Will turned down the volume on George Lloyd's Twelfth Symphony, grateful for the company. Unlike Caldaq and the Hivistahm, who came solely to ask questions and make recordings, the S'van actually seemed to enjoy his company.

"You're excited by something," the S'van commented.

Will nodded. "I've come to an important realization, T'var.

See, I've been trying everything I can think of to convince your commander and his staff that my people simply aren't suited to participation in this war of yours. But it's not because I'm right and their observations are wrong. We're both right.

"One of your Hivistahm technicians spent hours yesterday discussing Human unpredictability with me. He thinks it makes us more unsuitable for participation than if we were a planet of congenital pacifists. I hadn't looked at it like that before, but I think he has a point. I'm going to raise it with Caldaq."

"The topic is already under discussion," T'var informed him. "It may make no difference. You are still likely to be deemed useful."

"Damn! What's it going to take to convince them to leave us alone? We're trying to put thousands of years of insensate primate violence behind us. How can I make Caldaq realize that?" He looked so sharply at T'var that the second-of-command jumped slightly.

"How about you, T'var? What do the S'van believe?"

T'var studiously examined the short stubby fingers of his right hand. "The S'van find it judicious not to offer up too many judgments."

"Yeah, I've noticed that." Will squatted next to the wheel, lowering himself so that he was eye to eye with his visitor. "What is it with you people anyway? You seem willing to let the Massood and the Hivistahm and the O'o'yan make all the decisions while you hover in the background with your mouths shut."

Had there been a smile behind the black forest Will would not have been able to see it. "You are perceptive. But then, you've made use of your own opportunities for study these past months.

"I'll tell you something, Will Dulac. It is something I can say more freely in your company than in that of my crewmates. The simple fact of the universe is that the S'van are smarter than the Massood and the Hivistahm, the Wais or the O'o'yan."

"Then how come you don't make the decisions? Why do you leave them to others?"

"We do not simply stand back and let events progress. We suggest. We influence. We make our opinions known. You should understand that even in a great civilization it is not always beneficial to be perceived as the smartest, particularly when one is small in stature and numbers.

"Because of our abilities we occupy a disproportionate number of important positions in the hierarchy of the Weave, though we constitute a very small percentage of the total population. This gives us great influence while also exposing us to remnant primitive emotions. So we're careful to minimize our exposure. For example, we keep to our homeworld and do not choose to colonize in the manner of the Hivistahm or the Bir'rimor."

Will frowned. "You feel threatened by your own allies?"

"The Weave is not the monolithic front you perceive. Within its structure there is more conflict and dissension than you would believe. It's grown so large that without the universal threat posed by the Amplitur I for one am convinced it would disintegrate of its own unwieldiness. This is our greatest danger.

"There's no internal fighting as you think of it, but there are other means of expressing dissatisfaction with one's neighbors. Civilized means. Because of our vulnerability we're very careful to let the Hivistahm, the O'o'yan, and the Wais make the decisions. To let the Chirinaldo and the Massood do the fighting while we offer advice. It's not important to us who receives credit for making the right decisions; only that they get made." Heretofore he had been speaking rough English. Now he resorted to his translator.

"There are emotions which are common to many peoples. Jealousy is not unknown among the peoples of the Weave."

Will was nodding to himself. "I appreciate the confidence you're showing me. But that doesn't tell me what the S'van believe."

"Persistent as well as perceptive." Will didn't know whether to take it as a compliment or criticism. "I will not speak for other S'van, but as for myself I tend to agree with Third-of-Study. Your unpredictability renders you unreliable in a combat situation. Whether that makes you useless is another matter."

"Why not come," Will said abruptly, "and see for yourself what we're like, instead of asking me the same questions over and over and relying solely on television broadcasts? Come to the mainland with me."

Unpredictable, yes, T'var thought. "I?"

"Why not? Let me show some of you what our everyday life is really like. Television dotes on and magnifies the violence in our society. It doesn't show the joy we take in just living, the love we have for the world that surrounds us. You can't feel that, can't experience it from broadcasts.'' He straightened and stretched.

''This is something I've been thinking about for a long time. I can't take Caldaq. Even if I could rig some kind of disguise for him, the Massood are just too big and conspicuous. The O'o'yan and Hivistahm are too lizardlike in appearance. A Wais would be able to converse with anyone we encountered, but their body shape is impossible. Whereas a S'van just might be able to bring off an impersonation. You wouldn't draw much attention, being . . .''

''Short,'' T'var finished for him. ''I do not consider myself short. The description applies only when compared to a Massood or a Human. We do not think of it in the pejorative, as you seem to.''

''I could shave you some,'' Will said thoughtfully, ''although it's probably not necessary. Not here. And the hair is something of a disguise in itself. With the right clothes you'd look a lot like a short Human. You might be noticed, even remarked upon, but not followed.''

''You realize that the local climate is not to our liking,'' T'var reminded him.

''Who else could I take? A Lepar?''

''Your idea has merit, despite the risk.''

''We can go ashore in the dinghy,'' Will told him, planning. ''At night. Nobody'll spare us a second glance. You'll have a chance to experience Humanity in person instead of relying on broadcasts and me.''

''I am an administrator, not an observer. Such an expedition should include trained observers.''

''I don't think that would work. You, maybe one other, but no more. Two midgets walking with a man will attract some comment. Half a dozen would draw a crowd.''

''Very well. Despite the potential discomfort I will come, together with a companion. *If* I can convince the captain.''

Will toyed idly with the wheel. The cat's twin rudders creaked slightly. ''From what I've seen the S'van can convince anyone of anything.''

''Ah, if that were only true.'' T'var ran thick fingers through his beard, stroking the black ringlets. ''Then we would convince the Amplitur to leave us alone, there would be no war, and we could depart and leave you to the peace that you insist you are working toward.''

When presented with the notion Caldaq was understandably reluctant, but as Will surmised T'var eventually succeeded in persuading him of its value.

The two S'van would trail Will and try not to draw attention to themselves. Special shoes were fabricated which added inches to their height without impairing their mobility. Loose, floppy hats covered the dense hair while adding to the illusion of greater stature.

When all was ready Will inspected his charges and pronounced himself satisfied. Imitation reefwalkers covered alien feet, while gloves masked their hands.

"This is Belize," he told them. "People wash up here from all over. One of the first things they learn is to mind their own business. I don't think we'll have any trouble."

The rechargeable electric motor powered the dinghy inshore beneath a sliver of silver moon like a pared fingernail. Will tied up at a commercial wharf, there being no marina facilities in Belize City. This was not a favored anchorage of the yachting set.

They did indeed attract some stares on the busy wharf front, but no questions. The drunks did not panhandle them, and the dopers shied clear. Further inland they encountered people interested only in each other: couples strolling arm in arm, young people laughing and dancing, tourists watching Miami at Pittsburgh via pirated satellite signal.

Children sought diversion in muddy streets while dogs yapped at indifferent alley cats of adamantine expression. Music blared from crowded bars. There were no guns in evidence, a fact of Belize which Will was counting on to impress his companions and contradict much of what they had seen on the evening news broadcasts.

It would have been harder to make his point in Mexico, or Guatemala, but here there was a pervasive feeling that life however poverty-stricken was at least decent and might improve. He could see that T'var and E'wit were impressed by what they were seeing, E'wit's fingers busied with his concealed instruments as he recorded and noted everything they saw for in-depth study back at the base.

Their path eventually brought them back to the waterfront. Will pointed out two couples seated on separate benches. They ignored everything as they cuddled, staring out to sea.

"What are they doing?" E'wit kept his recorder humming.

"Just being together." Will's chest hurt. There were women in his own life, and he'd been spending a lot of time alone on the catamaran or in the company of aliens. "They might be married, or just friends. Humans need each other's company."

"Not so much unlike us," murmured T'var. He turned to his left. "What is that?"

Will stared in the same direction, along the narrow roadway that separated buildings from the seawall. "Music. Let's go see."

A crowd had gathered to listen to a local band serenade the tourists staying in a waterfront hotel. The three men calypsoed harmoniously, one singing while his companions hammered on steel drums slung from their necks. Tourists and locals alike clapped appreciatively after each song. The security guard stationed at the hotel door grinned and tapped his left foot in time to the music.

Despite his circumstances, a part of Will listened and absorbed, filing away the rhythms for possible future use. Music had been his personal salvation. Perhaps it would contribute to that of the Human race as well.

They stayed till the band left and the crowd dispersed. Only when the sun threatened to put in an appearance did they return to the dinghy for the long ride back out to the reef.

Will was trying hard to expand upon a melody derived from an O'o'yan seduction theme when the tiny communicator the visitors had installed in the cat buzzed for attention. Irritated by the interruption, he put instrumentation and the creative process on hold while he answered. He recognized T'var's uncertain English.

"Interesting news, Will Dulac. Our ship has returned."

"I'm happy for you." The ship was overdue, Will knew, and there were those among the aliens who had begun to worry. Interception by a hostile vessel in Underspace was a practical impossibility, but accidents were not.

As for himself, he had settled into a daily regimen he was in no hurry to see disturbed. As the visitors felt increasingly secure in their base they had less need of him. This allowed more time for composition. He'd long since finished *Arcadia* and faxed it home. Response from fellow faculty members had been enthusiastic. More importantly, the conductor of the symphony had read the score and scheduled it for performance in the fall season. His success was assured.

When informed that he was hard at work on a new project, the tone poem *Othervisions*, the head of the department insisted he extend his sabbatical for as long as was necessary. After all, the creative process was a fragile thing, and having a published composer on the faculty was a coup for any southern university. Did he require a stipend? No, Will had assured him. His own resources were sufficient.

More than sufficient, thanks to the visitors and their ability to accrete twenty-four-karat gold straws out of seawater. Not only was he living better than ever, he'd been able to equip the cat with the kind of equipment he'd only dreamed of when he'd bought her. Satnav and twin sonic drives, full scuba gear, everything he'd ever wanted. All in return for answering a few questions each day.

Now that comfortable routine was about to come to an end. The ship had returned, bringing to those who had been left behind fresh supplies, news, familiar faces, and just possibly, some answers.

He stepped outside, into the familiar damp heat, and stretched. Daylight enough remaining for a swim, he slipped on his fins, mask, and snorkel, made certain the translator was secure in his ear, and climbed down the portable steps into the water. A school of yellowjacks darted over, looking for a handout. He waved at them and they scattered lazily, unafraid.

Several minutes later he became aware he was not alone, and swam over to watch the Lepar at work.

It noted his presence immediately but did not acknowledge it. He had been told that while the Lepar were willing to talk they preferred to keep to themselves. Their vocabulary was limited. This was generally not a problem since they rarely had anything to say.

This one kept eying him as he floated above the base, outlined by the evening sun, breathing through his snorkel and watching. Finally it stopped and with a flick of its hind legs and tail shot upward to join him, the wide-mouthed face breaking the water next to his. Will pushed his mask back on his forehead, wiped saltwater from his eyes.

"You're not Vataloi, are you? I know a Lepar named Vataloi."

"No. Vataloi is a supervisor. I am Otheleea." The translator made English of the impenetrable gurgle.

"What do you do, Otheleea?" Will kicked his fins, treading water.

"Fix things. Mostly underwater. No other people can work in water and air."

"We can. Maybe I can give you a hand."

"I have heard that you swim well. But you are an air-breather only." The Lepar's tiny black eyes flickered.

"That doesn't mean I can't work underwater."

Otheleea reached out to finger Will's snorkel. "You are carrying no air supply, and this is not a rebreathing device."

"No, just a tube. But I can hold my breath. Please. I'd like to try and help."

"If you injure yourself blame will come to me."

"Nonsense. It'll be my own responsibility. And I'm not going to injure myself."

"A Massood could not do this."

Will smiled. "I'm not Massood."

The Lepar regarded him, its expression unreadable. "No, you are not," it finally declared before sinking beneath the surface.

Will pulled down his mask, cleared it, then arched his back and straightened his legs, doing a porpoise dive straight down. He couldn't use his translator while holding his breath, but the Lepar's gestures were easy enough to understand. He was able to assist a little in between trips to the surface for air, holding tools and in one instance helping to support a large piece of plastic glass that Otheleea was welding in place.

When the work was done they surfaced simultaneously. The Lepar stared.

"You were right. You did help. No other sentient could have done even that much."

"We just like to swim, that's all."

"It did not trouble you to work with me?"

"No. I enjoyed it. Needed the exercise. Composing is a pretty sedentary activity."

"You helped not because you had to but because you wanted to."

"That's right, I—hey!" All Will saw was a flash of flattened tail and webbed feet as the Lepar vanished beneath the surface. He ducked in time to catch a glimpse of the torpedolike shape disappearing around a corallike corner of the base.

He shrugged mentally and headed back to the cat. T'var was right: the Lepar were hard to figure.

He brought out a set of clean clothes, wanting to look his best for whoever stepped off the shuttle that was due down later that night. In many ways he would be sorry to see the base shut down and its inhabitants gone, now that their tests had doubtless shown them what unsuitable allies Humans would make. He'd made friends among the visitors: Caldaq and T'var and others. He'd even managed to establish a casual relationship with several of the perpetually grumbling Hivistahm.

Life would go on. He had his music, the Massood and the S'van and the rest had their war. He would immortalize their visit to the best of his abilities, and perhaps someday in the far future when the war had ended their descendants would return to this world, startled to find themselves hailed by music imbued with themes taken from their own past and reworked for Human instruments. That would be the finest memorial of their brief stay on Earth anyone could ask for.

⋆ XV ⋆

Caldaq could not stop pacing. His nose was twitching so rapidly, Will thought as he watched the Commander, it must surely snap off the end of his snout. Pointed ears flicked rapidly, like tiny hirsute semaphores.

T'var stood nearby, scanning the night sky along with Chief-of-Study, another Hivistahm Will did not recognize, an O'o'yan attendant, and the ever-present Wais. A Lepar technician waited patiently in the base submersible just offshore.

After a while T'var strode over to stand next to Will, and the two of them studied the stars together. "There's something you must know," the S'van said through his translator. "It involves what occurred on the world Vasarih a number of months ago."

Nearly a year had passed, Will reflected, since Caldaq's ship had departed the solar system. It did not seem so very long. They had learned a great deal in that time, with Will assisting them in their work as best he could. Yes, he would be sad to see them go. His had been an experience unlike any other save perhaps that of the ten Humans now returning. He had been informed that all ten were coming back. Whatever tests and examinations the Weave had subjected them to could not have been very harsh.

"Vasarih is a contested world," T'var was saying. "Your fellow Humans participated in that conflict."

"What?" Will's contemplation of the Caribbean sky was shattered.

"They accepted training and used it."

Will stared down at the S'van. "How could your people do something like that? How could you put a bunch of unprofessional strangers, kids and old people, into a combat situation? I know the whole purpose of this was to test Human fighting potential, but . . ."

"Apparently," T'var said calmly, "when the situation was explained to them they all volunteered to help. No one was 'forced.' Do you still understand us so little?"

"Volunteered?" Will was taken aback. "All of them?"

"Yes."

It was instructive to observe the Human's reaction. T'var knew well where Will Dulac stood on the matter of his people's cooperation with the Weave. He was sympathetic. The S'van would have liked nothing better than to have been left out of the war effort, to continue their own lives in peace. But if the Amplitur were going to be pushed back, everyone was going to have to assist in the pushing, including the less than enthusiastic. That included the S'van. Did it also include Humankind? That had yet to be determined.

The masked shuttle was revealed when it had drawn near enough to occlude a number of stars. It settled gently into the shallow water of the lagoon alongside the submerged base and Will's dimly lit catamaran. Light appeared in its flank above an extruded ramp. Figures began to emerge, walking toward the little island on which the greeting party waited anxiously.

Caldaq stopped pacing and waited at the base of the ramp. It was difficult to discern individuals in the dim moonlight, but at least two were Massood. One was Jaruselka.

Their intense reunion was marked by intriguing digital and verbal byplay, but Will hardly noticed. Likewise he paid no attention to the greetings exchanged by Chief-of-Study's companion and one of the Hivistahm from the ship. Any other time he would have watched raptly, making mental notes and seeking sources of inspiration. Not now.

His attention was on the column of Humans who stepped off the ramp onto the dry white sand of the beach. All were similarly clad. It took him a moment to realize that their clothing was a modification of what the Massood normally wore: a dark brown jumpsuit sort of arrangement crossed with bright slashes of yellow.

Leading them was the young trio from New England. Trio because Tamy Markowitz carried a child in her arms. Will stared as she carefully placed the swathed infant on the sand. As her husband knelt next to her he noticed the staring musician.

"Dulac, wasn't it? William Dulac?"

"Dulac, yeah, that's right."

Ken Woods looked down at his son. "This is Robert. Beautiful, isn't he? First Human being born off the planet." He grinned. "If we'd known Tamy was pregnant we might not have gone. Turns out it didn't matter. The Hivistahm technicians studying us were ecstatic. We got better care than we would've had at Mt. Sinai General."

Tamy Markowitz had found a periwinkle in the sand and was pressing it into the child's palm. Tiny fingers curled around the shell.

"Yes, darling, you're home. This is your home, this is Earth."

Will watched them coo over the infant a while longer before turning his attention to the others, who had gathered in a group nearby.

The change in the teenage brothers he'd recruited from the slums of Belize City was astonishing. Not only were they a year older, they had definitely matured in other ways. Young physiques had filled out with muscle. Gone was the hesitancy and fear he remembered. Their movements were assured, confident. As he stared they broke away from the rest and headed up the beach, accompanied by a slightly older man. Recognizing one of the Australian students, Will began searching for his companion.

He found her standing, not by herself, but close to the dark fisherman. When they saw Will approaching the man extended a hand and smiled electrically. There was none of the sullen anger Will recalled so well.

"Hello, mon. I remember you. I can' thank you enough what you did for me." Slightly dazed, Will shook the gnarled, powerful fingers. "I didn' talk much that time back ago, but that was before. Before the big sky trip; before Lea." The woman smiled and put her arm through his.

"We married, mon. This whole business"—and his arm described an arc against the night sky—"change my life."

"Too right. Changed everybody's life," the young woman added.

Will looked up the beach. She noted the direction of his gaze. "Steven? I've never seen him happier. You know we weren't in love or engaged or anything like that. We were just traveling around together, seeing some of the world. It was convenient. But after I got to know Matthias here, well, Steven didn't mind. He got involved in the training and the studies to the exclusion of just about everything else.''

"It's none of my business anyway," Will muttered.

"Hey, mon." Matthias clapped him on the back. "How been the old world while we gone? It miss us?" He laughed heartily. "What about you? You have a good year?"

Will was more than a little taken aback by the formerly silent fisherman's effusiveness. "Okay, I suppose. You . . . all of you seem so *happy*."

"Mon, you just don' know." He beckoned. "Hey, Eleroy, you come talk to this mon, you heah?"

The Rastafarian stepped out of the darkness. Gone was the glazed stare, the slight jerkiness of movement, the raging dreadlocks. His hair was cut short and close and he stood straight as any of the palms on the little islet. He studied Will's face carefully, as if trying to decide whether it was real or counterfeit.

"I know you, mon. I owe you my life."

Questions overwhelmed Will's ability to ask them. So many, he had so many. This was not what he'd been expecting, not what he'd been expecting at all.

"You've changed."

"Everybody changed, mon." Eleroy nudged the fisherman in the ribs. Lea laughed and clutched his arm tightly. "All my life I was nothing, mon. Nothing. I go with you because I don' know what happening to me any of the time. These people, they fix me right, you see? They make me feel important, give me something to do. They say I helping them a lot and that make me feel real good, real good.

"First thing, I ask them for ganja. They don' understand but we talk. Then they ask questions, especially those big lizards. They take my blood and break it apart and they give me something else in return. Made me feel good, mon. Then we talk some more, and I learn things, and what they give me make me proud to be a man. Now I don' have to get high all the time to feel good. I got something lot better."

"Like what?" Will asked him.

The Rastafarian gave him a tight-lipped grin and clapped a hand to the device secured at his waist. "A purpose, mon. To fight for the Weave. To protect this place, my home. Your home, too.'' He indicated the island, the ramrod palms, the calm waters of the lagoon.

"I never had anything to fight for before. I don' even like to fight. But it all explained to us, mon. These Amplitur things out there, they want to take away everything that makes a man, everything that makes you real.''

The woman spoke up. "We have no choice, really. We have to fight, or we'll end up sacrificing our Humanity. The Amplitur will come and take it away from us. Fair dinkum.''

"But we do have a choice,'' Will insisted. "We can stay out of it. We can . . .''

The Rastafarian exchanged a sad look with his friend the fisherman. "He don' know. He don' understand because he ain't been Out There.''

"No,'' Matthias agreed, "but he will.'' He looked past the nearly submerged shuttle which had brought them down and inhaled deeply. "I missed this. I missed the smell. Not just of the sea.'' He gazed back down at Will. "It this whole place, mon. This planet, this Earth, this our home. I been other places this year gone and no other of them smell like this.'' He smiled at his companion. "Come on, sweet woman. Let's take a walk.'' Hand in hand they headed inland.

Will was shaking his head. "What did they do, brainwash the lot of you?''

"No, mon,'' said the Rastafarian. "They just show us the truth. Somebody they smack you in the face with it time after time, pretty soon it impossible to ignore, you know? They show us the truth about everything, including ourselves. Matthias, he find his truth. I find my truth. Sooner or later you gonna find your truth.'' He gazed out across the water, toward the mainland.

"I got some sisters somewhere. Not here, down in Monkey Town on the coast. I got to find them and share the truth with them. The Massood boss say I can' do that just yet, but maybe soon. Maybe.''

He started to walk away. Will reached out for him, was stopped by a new voice and a hand on his arm.

"Let him go.''

It was the expatriate teacher, and he was not alone. Next to him stood the old woman who'd been the last to join the group.

Their brown-and-yellow uniforms fit surprisingly well. Will had to smile at the sight of the battered Panama hat perched incongruously on the man's head. Like its owner, it looked none the worse for wear.

"Come on, old chap. Let's find a place to have a sit and we'll explain the lot of it to you."

"The young ones." The old lady was nodding to herself as they walked. "They all impatient, and they have reason to be."

"You see, William . . . that is your name, isn't it? I've seen so much this past year that this old head is quite crammed with detail. It's the way we're made, how we're fashioned. At first it was all a big joke to us. Then when we saw how serious things were we found ourselves turning serious as well. After that we found things out without having to go searching for them."

Will listened to him but his eyes were on the old lady. She looked ten years younger. No longer the shriveled, worn-out woman who'd begged to go along, she stood straight and proud. Age lines in her face had been replaced with others suggestive of hidden strength brought unexpectedly to the surface.

"We each of us had our own reasons for agreeing to your peculiar request," the teacher was saying. "We all thought we knew what life was about, oh, yes. Then we were forced to confront new things, both within ourselves and without."

"Such new things." The woman rested a hand on the expatriate's shoulder.

"You see, old chap, when you spend a lot of time talking to things that don't breathe as you do, or even what you do, and you start learning the true universal constants, why then your own little personal problems start to acquire this rank air of the petty about them. You find out what really matters instead of what you thought mattered and see some significant differences. All my life I'd been told that travel was broadening. What they don't tell you, can't tell you, is that the farther you travel the more broadening it becomes."

"I heard that you were involved in some fighting. How did they get you into that?"

"Why, they didn't get us into anything, young man." The old lady eyed him reprovingly.

"Once we learned about reality, saw how things were, naturally we wanted to help," the teacher told him.

"Your clothes." Will gestured weakly.

"Ah, yes." The man looked pleased. "We sort of put them together ourselves, based on what those Massood chaps wear and what I remembered from my days in the service. That young lass from down under is something of a designer. Working with her, our hosts had no trouble running these off for us. They were most accommodating when they saw that we wanted to help."

Will said nothing and the man continued.

"You know, I never had much of anything. I was a poor teacher at best, bleating away back in Surrey at indifferent young sods who were much more interested in the latest football scores or music vids than in anything I might have to tell them. That's why I left England. There was also a small matter involving some funds in a school account.

"I thought I might salvage what little remained of my self-respect. Instead I left all that behind, along with my wife, a bland but decent woman far better off without me. No children, thank God. Haven't communicated with her in twelve years.

"I drifted, and like many of my countrymen I ended up here, in Belize. They need teachers badly, so obscure portions of my résumé were not brought into question. Not that I was a better teacher here than I'd been Surrey. Liquor has this way of complicating one's classroom manner.

"I was drinking rather more than I was teaching when you materialized with your offer of an evening's entertainment. What I did not expect to receive was higher education, which I was firmly convinced I had put far behind me. I acquired fresh knowledge, and something rather more than that. I acquired a cause. Because, you see, these Amplitur really are the cold soul of evil.

"I also regained my self-respect because I found something that I was good at."

Will eyed him guardedly. "Like what?"

"Why combat, of course. Oh, yes. That girl Lea, for example, is quite the Amazon, as tough as her paramour and those boys you found in Belize City. The couple from Connecticut are not bad and the young Australian fellow, Steven, is something of a born strategist. I don't know if you've had occasion to notice, but most of these alien chaps aren't any good for fighting at all. Only the Massood, and some other fellows called Chirinaldo. They're big, but middling slow afoot. The Massood have

a lot of endurance, but they've little natural quickness and despite their size they are not very strong.

"The S'van and Hivistahm who studied us kept talking about
our neuromuscular structure and how it was tied into our peculiar endocrine system." He waved a hand. "Don't ask me to
explain. It was quite technical." He reached into a breast pocket
and withdrew the familiar shape of a translator. "These gadgets
don't function as effectively when scientific terminology is involved."

"I don't understand any of it at all," said the old woman. "I
only know that these are good *people*, despite what they look
like. They need our help. It made me feel good to be able to
help them, even a little."

"You see, old chap, I spent some time in the military. I'm
good at planning things. Annalinda and I have a lot of experience that the young people need. Their initial successes tended
to make them impulsive. Steven understands that. It's why they
put him in command."

"I've seen fighting all my life," the old woman said. "I'm
no good at it myself. I have a lot of control but no ability. But I
can tell others of what I've seen. Those two poor boys you
brought along are like my own grandchildren. They need good
advice."

"Do you know what it's like," the teacher was saying, "to
have a great lot of important individuals tell you how wonderful
you are, how important you can be, how much they need your
help? It does something to you, makes you feel good inside.
Just like these uniforms."

"That's enough for now, Edward." The old woman took his
arm and started up the beach. "We'd better go find the boys
before they get into some kind of trouble."

"Quite right there, Anna. After all, this isn't Vasarih." He
winked at Will, cocked the tired Panama tight on his head.
"Think about what I've said, will you, old chap?"

Numb and confused, Will watched them hike up the beach in
search of the three young men.

"I'm pleased, of course." Caldaq sat on the sand, legs crossed,
arms resting on knees, inhaling the now familiar aromas of this
world as he watched the prodigal Humans chatter and cavort.
They were so childlike in their enthusiasm, so easily pleased,

and these few, at least, a little less ignorant of the state of reality. In their jumpsuits they looked very much alike despite the usual variations in individual coloration. Jaruselka sat close, ignoring the sand in her fur.

Chief-of-Project stood nearby. She was an elderly Hivistahm entitled to much respect. At night she was able to dispense with the dark shades which during the day were necessary to protect eyes grown sensitive with age.

"Truly we all are. These people the potential to be of use beyond our wildest dreams have. Weave Command is ecstatic over what little they have been told."

Caldaq's gaze roved the palms, the odiferous sea beyond. "Then the isolation of this world is to be ended?"

"No. Is that not a strange decision?"

"I do not understand."

"You were not there. You did not see." Jaruselka shifted on the sand. "Because of what has been learned the evaluators are torn between caution and hope.

"Individually and as a group, these creatures graded out more suitable for combat than any people of the Weave, including the Massood."

This revelation inspired no jealousy or envy in Caldaq. A considerable part of being civilized involved the ability simply to see truth.

"This is difficult for me to accept, my mate. While I have not seen what you have seen, I have spent a lot of time on this world, observing, studying, learning. It leads me to believe that much of what our friend Will Dulac says about his people is true. They do love music and peace and very much aspire to the Weave definition of civilization."

"Truly they may aspire, but it is not what they are best suited to doing." Chief-of-Project was remorseless.

"It has been postulated," Caldaq argued, "that if left to develop by themselves they might be able to overcome that fact."

"Quite likely." Chief-of-Project took several steps toward the water, her sandals leaving broad triangular impressions in the sand. Sharp nails flicked against one another as she spoke.

"Undisturbed they might achieve the same level of civilization as the O'o'yan, or the S'van, or the Wais." She did not mention the Massood. Caldaq chose to regard it as an oversight.

"Truly it is conceivable that they could overcome the instinctive combative tendencies which they now so ingenuously display to become as peaceful as, say, the Hivistahm.'' She turned back to the two Massood, slitted eyes bright in the moonlight.

''However, a certainty that is not. There is equal evidence to suggest that such inclinations will continue to manifest themselves even as their technology advances. It is intriguing to postulate what direction their society might take if such tendencies are encouraged instead of decried.''

An angry Caldaq rose. Jaruselka stood beside him. ''I will not be a party to such a thing. It reeks of the immoral. These people must be allowed to find their way to civilization.''

''Even if that way to mutual self-destruction leads them?''

''Do not try to hide what you want beneath a layer of fatuous altruism.''

To her credit, the elderly Hivistahm was obviously uncomfortable. ''Truly I am not unaware of the contradictions posed by this dilemma.

''If we allow these creatures to achieve the kind of civilization which would permit them entry into the Weave, then sacrificing a great weapon we may be. Of what use would such a civilization be to them if subsumed into the Amplitur Purpose it is eventually?

''If we instead allow, even encourage them to vent their natural combative tendencies not against each other but against the Amplitur, then great things accomplished may be. Do not forget, Captain, that the future of many races and not just that of Humans is in the great contest at stake. The Weave survives because the good of all it considers.

''Adjustments to Human inclinations in the future can be made, after the Amplitur we have defeated. Time enough then to embrace these creatures and to the heart of Weave civilization clasp them. Truly first everything possible we must do to insure a civilization there is for them to join.''

Caldaq's anger at an immutable injustice was already fading. ''It has already been decided, hasn't it?''

Jaruselka eyed him sympathetically. ''It was not our decision to make. I am told that the Council agonized long over it.''

''The full Science Council,'' Chief-of-Project elaborated. ''The General Council of this world's existence is not yet aware.''

Caldaq gestured tiredly, resumed his seat on the sand. "And they have already participated in actual combat?"

Chief-of-Project's claws dug at an itch. "On Vasarih. A cautious test in hope executed of confirming results otherwise difficult to believe. Only those who volunteered were involved, the youngest and strongest, though they received advice from their seniors as well as from our own people in the field.

"The Amplitur force on Vasarih consists mainly of Crigolit with a smattering of T'returi largely providing logistical support. Truly also there are the divided Vasarih themselves."

"And what happened?" Caldaq pressed her.

Chief-of-Project hesitated briefly. "Conflict these creatures transforms in ways they themselves are unaware of. They take to combat as to a narcotic. Their endocrine and nervous systems function differently. The fact that for the first time in their racial history they were fighting creatures other than their own kind seemed only further to energize them.

"Vasarih a minor theater of conflict is, but in the sector where they were introduced their impact immediate and devastating was. Not only did they wreak havoc themselves, their attitude and presence inspired the Massood who were present safely through any trouble to shepherd them."

"They fought alongside Massood?" Caldaq said.

"Yes." Jaruselka put a hand on his shoulder. "I witnessed this myself."

He eyed her sharply. "You participated? You did not say . . ."

"It would only have worried you. Should I have not? I am trained as any Massood, and I was one who had dealt with the first specimen, Will Dulac. I understood more than those Massood who had never encountered a Human before.

"Chief-of-Project speaks endless uncomfortable truths." The Hivistahm was gratified by the support of the Commander's mate. "When these creatures are thrust into combat they seem to enter a different state of consciousness. They are transformed."

"They fight like machines." The elderly Hivistahm searched for the best way to convey her feelings. "Not out of control but not as we would fight, either. This is not a conscious choice they make but something with them instinctive, something in their racial psyche deeply ingrained. Out of the other mature species civilization has bred it. Even the Massood must make themselves fight.

"These people do not have to force themselves. They enter into combat with positive delight." Her reptilian visage seemed almost to contort into a true expression of amazement. "Do you know that we actually had to employ force to extricate them from the field? They *wanted* to remain and fight on."

"That is absurd," Caldaq insisted. "No one wishes to fight when one can withdraw without sacrifice."

"Truly you have not observed these creatures in combat. More astonishing it was than you can imagine. The unobtrusive administration of medication was required several of the younger specimens to calm."

"And this is what the Weave wants to encourage?" Caldaq threw a shell into the water. "Does everything we have learned here carry no weight? What of our studies that show Humans as serene and peaceable, on the verge of true civilization?"

"Our own civilization we must preserve before we can theirs assist. Remember that none of the specimens were compelled to fight. All volunteered willingly: indeed, enthusiastically."

"Because they were not made aware of alternatives, of the duality of their nature which they do not yet fully understand themselves," Caldaq argued.

Chief-of-Project's voice turned cool, as though she was tired of debating the matter. "A duty we have here, Captain. Curious I am to know how this Dulac has influenced you."

"He has not influenced me." Not for the first time Caldaq felt the urge to strike a Hivistahm. A S'van could argue with humor and disarming wit whereas a somber, remorseless Hivistahm speaking to the same point usually came off as insufferable. He forced himself to relax clenched fingers.

"I am a captain of the Massood, commander of a Weave vessel. We fight a common enemy, but they have yet to make enemies of these people. That is an issue not easily to be dismissed."

"Truly ten of them they now have as enemies," Chief-of-Project pointed out.

"Ten individuals do not constitute a representative sample."

The elder gestured agreeably. "This is why we have with the supplies and equipment necessary to expand your base here returned."

"Expand? But if the Council has already made its decision . . ."

"The Science Council only," Chief-of-Project reminded him. "You are not the only one of the moral ambiguities of the situation aware, Captain. Or of the dangers. The Council desires more information, additional studies.

"For reasons of which I was not completely informed they do not feel the time is right to make a wholesale appeal for assistance to the people of this world. Partly it is felt that their uniquely suspicious nature against their cooperation might mitigate."

"Then what is to be done?" Commander or not, Caldaq was confused. He had landed on this world thinking one way, only to find himself convinced otherwise by Will Dulac and by what he had seen and learned this past year. Now other studies contradicted what he had come to believe, yet this caution on the part of the Council seemed to contradict its own findings. What did they want of this world? And of him?

Jaruselka was comfortingly close. "I know it is difficult, lifemate. We must trust in the wisdom of those more highly trained than ourselves."

"They have not seen these creatures, as I have, in their natural environment."

"Who is to say what constitutes their 'natural environment'?" Chief-of-Study was remorselessly self-assured. "There is nothing natural about this bizarre world of theirs. Perhaps their proper environment lies elsewhere."

"Do we have the right," Caldaq reiterated intently, "to influence these people in such a fashion?"

"That is a question to philosophers best left." The elder Hivistahm was relaxed now. "It need not those most involved in military matters concern."

The Military High Council was composed largely of Massood and S'van. Caldaq gazed at his mate. "What do our immediate superiors think of all this?"

She responded without hesitation, her whiskers all but motionless. "They are aware of the possible moral contradictions but believe it to be in the best interests of the Weave as well as these people that they be engaged as allies in order to alleviate some of the burden of actual fighting that at present rests almost exclusively on the shoulders of the Massood and the Chirinaldo.''

''The Chirinaldo do not have shoulders.'' Caldaq's ears were in rapid motion. ''Whatever personal reservations I hold, as the commander on site I must carry out the orders of the Council.''

Chief-of-Project tried to ease his anxiety. ''Truly you will have much to say as to the manner of their actual execution.''

''I will not,'' the captain added, more for his own benefit than that of his mate or the Hivistahm, ''employ any orders as cover for the abrogation of my own moral principles.''

''Truly no one is expecting that you would.''

''Then what does the Council wish here? How can we make allies of these people without requesting their help?''

''Impossible that is not.'' Chief-of-Project deferred to the captain's mate.

''The ten specimens,'' she explained, ''often exhibited those inexplicable contradictions that were noted here during our initial studies. Their enthusiasm for combat may yet prove transitory. If they were committed in large numbers to an important battle and suddenly lost their taste for conflict it could prove disastrous.

''Therefore studies are to continue while we expand recruitment.'' She nibbled the side of his snout in an effort to relax him. He snapped at her, but affectionately. ''Not by the usual means of announcing ourselves to the world at large. That cannot be done here anyway because these people have no one capital, no center of power.

''Since Humans exist in a fragmented society, we are to deal with those fragments on an individual basis without alarming or involving the populace as a whole. This has never been done before, but if one disregards the inherent inefficiencies there is no reason why it cannot be pursued adequately.''

Caldaq regarded her narrowly. ''So we are to continue to study and analyze and observe while simultaneously attempting to integrate them into the war effort on an individual basis? What is there to motivate individuals to fight?''

Chief-of-Study spoke up. ''Some seem to find worthwhile the cause itself, belying their apparent immaturity. Others on the excitement of combat appear to thrive.''

''That is sick,'' Caldaq murmured.

''Then truly it is a useful sickness. If you think that alien, consider that there are also those willing to fight in return for mere medium of exchange.''

It was almost too much to accept. Yet his mate was beside him, confirming everything the Hivistahm said. ''You mean they are willing to degrade themselves as sentients, to risk their actual existence for something as insignificant as—''

''I know incredible it is, but do not forget that they are uncivilized in the Weave sense, that not only their personalities and biology but their environment and geology is skewed. If you promise them enough metallic gold it seems they will almost anything do.

''How widespread this unbelievable phenomenon may be is for additional study another matter. From our observation of the selected specimens it appears widespread to be but not all-inclusive. As you have so deftly pointed out, the sample too small to be representative is.''

Suddenly the moist night air struck Caldaq as foul. ''If they fight for something other than the cause how can we be sure of them?''

''We cannot.'' Chief-of-Study was full Hivistahm somber as she scratched behind an ear opening. ''All we can do is make the best use of them that we can while we their activities and reactions closely monitor. To gain the aid of instinctive fighters to take certain risks we must be prepared. Truly.''

''I am still not convinced they are that.''

''Believe it, lifemate,'' said Jaruselka. ''Because the high command does. We are to recruit even as we seek answers, something that has never been done before. But then, there has never been a world like this, sentients like this.'' When her mate did not comment she continued.

''There was a report.'' She nipped lightly at his cheek. ''Three of the specimens—two of the dark ones and one of the light—took sidearms and without waiting for orders or directive entered an area that the Crigolit had been monitoring. Against all common sense they rushed from behind totally inadequate armor to obliterate an entire enemy squad. Believing themselves safe, the Crigolit hardly had a chance to respond. By civilized standards they *were* safe. But not against Humans.

''That is not the most amazing thing. What is most astonishing is that the report claims the Humans involved enjoyed the experience.''

"These creatures," said Chief-of-Project, "have less regard for personal safety than any sentients known."

"Surely," Caldaq mumbled, overwhelmed by repeated revelations, "their lives are important to them?"

"Truly. But when they in the grip of this fever are, this endocrine imbalance which makes them such superb fighters, they lose control completely. It is as if in their brains is suddenly thrown a switch which turns off logic, reason, and common sense except insofar as those values relate to combat. It is regrettable they were not fitted with instrumentation able to fully monitor the neurochemical changes that within their systems took place while under fire they were. That oversight will with future specimens be corrected."

"Bravery," Caldaq said weakly, "is a useful trait."

"It is more than bravery, lifemate," Jaruselka told him. "More akin to controlled insanity. The Amplitur can override the instinct for self-preservation in their clients by means of mental projection. These creatures do it instinctively, as part of their physiochemical makeup."

"Is needed more study." Chief-of-Project turned to face the sea. "I need to know if you feel that your personal reservations your ability to carry out council directives here will compromise." It was a typical Hivistahm inquiry: straightforward and tactless.

"No. Our friend Will Dulac will disagree with the study group's conclusions. He will continue trying to convince us otherwise."

"Let him. His objections as well as his cooperation instructive are, and it is very useful the assistance of a native to have who is familiar with us. Keep him comfortable, Captain."

"I am a ship Commander."

"The Council requires that you operations here continue to supervise."

Caldaq's lips curled back. "Which I will do, under protest." He shook off Jaruselka's attempt to mollify him. He was angry as well as confused and wanted to be certain Chief-of-Project understood.

The elder Hivistahm regarded him thoughtfully out of bright, bulbous eyes. "I presume you have noted that in one area Human technological achievement has far surpassed itself?"

"In the development of arms. Do not worry. Our presence here remains secure. I am more concerned about *my* ship."

"We have brought advanced masking instrumentation back with us. It will your security here enhance and that of the ship insure."

"Then my professional concerns are satisfactorily addressed," Caldaq conceded stiffly.

Decisions had been made without him. Even though he knew it would have taken too long to consult with him, the oversight still rankled. He could not let it trouble him, however, and the council could hardly be blamed. Not if half of what his lifemate and Chief-of-Project had told him was true.

Will Dulac reacted to the same information much as Caldaq expected. As he listened to the Human protest, the captain found himself noting the violence of the man's words and gestures.

They were in one of the new assembly chambers which had been added to the base. Construction was proceeding energetically in four directions, spreading out beneath the floor of the lagoon as well as into surrounding islands. Multiple levels were being added with large areas earmarked for research, for communications, for training. Above it all fish swam and crustaceans crawled, blissfully unaware.

Work halted only when the occasional yacht or fishing boat entered the lagoon. None possessed even the simplest detection equipment. When they moved on, work resumed. At night shuttles ferried equipment and personnel from the great ship floating in space down to the languid reef.

Caldaq let T'var do most of the talking, a talent the captain envied no less than any Massood.

"These things are true," T'var was saying. "You must accept them."

"I can't. I won't." Will popped one of the decorative rose-hued bubbles rising from a floor spigot. It burst, leaving a tremulous E-flat lingering in the air. "I don't know what happened to those ten people out there. Maybe it had to do with the fact that they were far away from Earth, isolated among aliens. Maybe they felt they had no choice but to try and please their hosts by showing that they could fight if they had to."

Z'mam had returned with the ship. He'd been on Vasarih. "There was no coercion, Will Dulac. When reality was explained to them, they saw the universe in its true light and were eager to help.''

''Then I chose the wrong bunch.'' At his touch burst bubbles burbled a rising cadenza.

''I tried to choose people who had little to lose by going, people who seemed to be drifting through life. I guess you gave them something, though I don't understand the completeness of the transformation. In any case, they weren't as average as I thought. Those were the kind of people I tried to recruit for you, but I guess the very fact that they went along stamps them as atypical.

''If you study happier people, prosperous citizens, people with an appreciation for the finer things of civilization like art and music, people in love with their work and their lives, you're going to find that they're much more interested in peace and contentment than in taking off to fight a bunch of aliens they don't know exist and could care less about.''

''All that you say may be true,'' T'var responded soothingly, ''which is a major reason for the expansion of our facilities here.''

''I thought you were expanding to make room for more Human recruits,'' Will said bitterly. He slashed a whole column of bubbles with the edge of his hand, releasing perfumed discord.

''We hope for some response,'' T'var admitted, ''but study will also intensify. It may be that your thesis will be proven and that Humans as a species are unsuited to wider participation in the conflict. This is after all the main reason why we are here. Should it be determined that you are correct, then our facilities here both new and old will be obliterated or returned to the ship and we will depart in silence, leaving you to the isolation you desire.'' The two S'van exchanged a glance, eyes flashing beneath dense black brows.

''Your personal presence can only accelerate our learning curve.''

Will turned away from the decorative bubble generators. ''I won't have anything to do with the recruitment of mercenaries.''

''No one is asking you to,'' said Z'mam cheerfully.

Will's gaze narrowed. ''Don't tell me the S'van are going to go ashore and set up an enlistment booth?''

''Not at all. Several members of the group we have already trained are more than anxious to assist us in this.''

Will shook his head. "Won't work. They're not sophisticated enough."

"I think you underestimate your own people. The older Human of the peculiar headgear, the couple of contrasting color, and our three Vasarih heroes strike me as sufficiently intelligent for the task."

"Maybe." Will saw clearly now that if he was going to stop this he was going to have to convince the Weave scientists and not its administrators. He couldn't do that by running away.

"All right. I'll continue to help you with your research. But only because I still have to convince you how futile it all is.

"I've no doubt you'll find some people you can use, but there are always exceptions. Individuals and couples. You can buy people who have nothing, but there's a world of difference between that and recruiting all of mankind to your cause."

They expressed their gratitude, then left him to the bubbles. He toyed with them absently, the sounds they generated as they burst washing over him as he sat by himself and pondered.

He would continue to work on his music. Anything to relieve the increased pressure brought about by their revelations. He had no choice but to stay on. The more he cooperated, the more frequent the opportunity to persuade.

Had he refused to help they would simply have gone on without him. Somehow notifying the authorities did not seem the best way to convince them of mankind's peaceful nature. He would have to rely on example.

The task ahead was not impossible. After all, he was a professor, an educated, sophisticated man. The so-called recruiters the aliens intended to use consisted of an old drunk, an ignorant fisherman, and some poor boys taken literally off the streets. The rest were little better. Whose influence was most likely to persuade: theirs or his?

And this was Belize, Central America. Hardly the most efficacious recruiting ground for imaginative individuals.

Yes, the aliens would find a few Humans willing to fight for them, to do anything for a little gold. But their commitment would be shallow, temporal. They would soon tire of the exoticism of travel to another world, of the need to actually participate in combat. The ingrained Human wish for peace and tranquillity would soon lead them to demand they be returned home, thus conclusively demonstrating mankind's unreliability to the dedicated peoples of the Weave.

He felt much better after he'd convinced himself.

★ XVI ★

A distressingly steady stream of recruits poured into the base: poor cane cutters from Guatemala, surplus oil-field roughnecks from the Yucatán, subsistence farmers out of Honduras and El Salvador spiced with the occasional tourist couple or trekking European.

It did not matter. Before long they would start quitting, demanding to return with their gold to the world of their birth, to live out their lives in peace and harmony far from inexplicable alien altercations. Wait until they began refusing combat, he told himself. Until they started acting like the obstreperous polyglot bunch they were. The aliens would rapidly grow tired of Human eccentricities, as they would of Earth.

That they could recruit the poor no longer surprised him, but he was startled by the number of middle-class and wealthy individuals who agreed to participate. These were the people who came to this part of the world to fish or dive or sit on the white sands of Ambergris Cay. People who had no need of gold. Yet in fancy hotel bars and on the beaches they listened. Despite their money, their lives must be empty indeed, Will reflected.

Not everyone was ready to go. Even when confronted with alien technology and the aliens themselves there were some who still thought it all a trick, a complex promotion for a film or television show. When they realized it was quite real, some panicked and wanted out.

While the people of the Weave did not have the Amplitur ability to influence minds, they did possess a command of chemistry which enabled them to synthesize a drug that induced a selective amnesia. Reluctant recruits could be returned to their hotels or jobs dazed and confused but otherwise unharmed, and unable to reveal what they had seen. Their memories would be hazy and jumbled, full of colorful images of strange shapes and sand and clear water lush with bright tropicals. They would remember spending time in an attractive place of indefinite location. Lingering unease would vanish in the press to return to jobs, or farming, or vacation.

Uncertainties of a different kind continued to plague Third-of-Study as recruiting proceeded hand in hand with research. For the most part he kept quiet and did his job. He knew his was an overly cautious nature, a fact which his colleagues had remarked on more than once. Undoubtedly it had restrained his advancement.

Besides, the Hivistahm were not questioners. Argument and debate were usually left to the irrepressible S'van or temperamental Massood. Even the diminutive O'o'yan tended to participate in debate more often than the Hivistahm, who had not successfully settled thirty-five worlds by favoring dissension.

To avoid derision Third-of-Study preferred to voice his concerns during communal prayer sessions, sitting in the holy circle with his back to his fellows, all of them facing outward while looking inward. He kept his eyes closed as he spoke.

"Truly you worry needlessly," said a colleague. "Does not the performance of the second group of Human trainees only confirm that of the first?"

Third-of-Study had no reply. He had seen the same reports as everyone else.

Another technician continued. "Already these creatures have helped several significant victories to achieve, not only on Vasarih but on Sh'haroon as well. They have done everything asked of them and more. Indeed, restraining them is perhaps the most difficult task their Massood commanders have had to face so far."

"Truly astonishing," another admitted. "The more casualties they sustain, the more they wish to fight, which contradicts logic."

"In the face of which," murmured a senior researcher from the opposite side of the circle as she contemplated the shifting images on the encircling wall and compared them to those within her mind, "you persist in envisioning problems which Massood Technical has already branded inapplicable at best, frivolous at worst. How often do you have to be reminded that the need to defeat the Amplitur overrides even substantiated concerns?''

Third-of-Study persisted. ''I worry that on a species we do not sufficiently understand we are relying.''

''More important to be able to make use of them than understand them.''

''Truly,'' whispered a technician, ''will follow understanding as research and contact deepen.''

''What matters to me,'' said the senior researcher present, in her ethereal elder voice, ''is that the enlistment of individuals of this species in our cause means that fewer Hivistahm into combat need be pressed, or O'o'yan, or Lepar or Yula. Someday our discovery here may even ease the heavy burden borne so long by our beloved friends the Massood.

''I do not argue that represent these Humans a paradox, but it is a paradox of unending usefulness to the Weave.''

Silence in the chamber as each Hivistahm considered itself in relation to the universe beyond.

''A race that wears civilization like fair-weather clothing could to the Weave itself eventually present a threat.'' There, Third-of-Study thought. I have finally stated it without qualifications.

A technician riposted tiredly. ''Again to remind you: hundreds of years of effort have been spent confronting the Amplitur. Once that threat removed has been there will be ample time and resources available for dealing with lesser problems. Unless of course you mean to suggest that this uncivilized species a greater threat to the Weave presents than the Amplitur?''

The deliberate silence that ensued allowed the sarcasm to linger in the air.

''We know these creatures hardly at all.'' Third-of-Study was angry now but, being Hivistahm, did not show it. ''They with Weave forces integrate quickly. Some Massood commanders are already important battlefield decisions allowing them to make. They even empathize with the Chirinaldo.''

''Glad of that I am,'' said a technician. ''If they can with the Chirinaldo interact, it means we do not have to.''

Third-of-Study continued. ''Some fight only for material recompense. Uncivilized that is.''

''Also immaterial it is.'' The senior researcher shifted slightly in her crouch. ''Truly it matters not what motivates the Humans to fight, only that they do.''

"They are not for Weave membership ready."

"In that you are not disputed." She allowed her drifting thoughts to caress an image of pure effulgence. It warmed and relaxed her. "I would no more wish to see a Human visitation group on my homeworld placed than you on yours would. Though unconventional, our present arrangement ideal is because it allows us to make use of these creatures while the awkward question of actual membership and concurrent social interaction avoiding."

Third-of-Study nearly committed the unpardonable sin of looking at the speaker but caught himself just in time. "Then you *do* with my thesis agree, at least in part."

"Not at all. Our course of action here by abnormal local conditions is dictated. We improvise out of necessity, not choice."

"But as you say, you are not displeased by it." When no reply was forthcoming, Third-of-Study continued.

"Assuming continues to expand their commitment, what will happen when the Humans discover that being denied the membership in the Weave they are that is automatically extended to all other civilizations?"

"You assume they will want membership. Given the depth of contradiction we have observed thus far in their racial psyche that is not inevitable. They may content be in the conflict to assist while remaining outside the pale of Weave civilization. In such an instance I believe the Council would remonstrate with them but not, I think, too strenuously."

"That," said Third-of-Study tersely, "suggests a deliberate attempt a primitive people to delude."

"Do you as close friends and companions want them or are you fearful of them? Which is it to be? With yourself you argue, Third-of-Study. I prescribe less work and additional meditation." She rose, stretching.

The prayer session was at an end.

There was one individual at the base who wholly shared Third-of-Study's concerns, though for different reasons. The two walked together down a corridor the next day, each occasionally checking to make certain his translator unit was functioning properly.

"They have decided," said Third-of-Study, "not to offer your people membership in the Weave."

"Correct me if I'm wrong," Will Dulac replied, "but does that mean they're not going to expand their efforts here beyond this one base?"

"Truly that is so."

"Then if we're excluded from your civilization, the Amplitur shouldn't be able to find us."

Third-of-Study rubbed at the bony ridge above his left eye. "We will of course try to keep the location of your world secret from our enemies, but we do that with every world. It is difficult from the Amplitur to hide things. Since field troops have no inkling of your world's location give it away they cannot. It is inevitable, however, that some of your own people will eventually be captured and interrogated by the Amplitur. At that time learn about you they will."

"I thought you said they couldn't read minds?"

"They cannot. However, they might, for example, make the mental suggestion that it would be useful for you your extremities to immerse in a caustic solution. You would find your own body disobeying you. This they would do regretfully, with genuine sorrow, but would do nonetheless. Few such episodes required are to convince a prisoner to cooperate." They turned a bend in the corridor. A couple of O'o'yan scurried past, glancing briefly at the towering Human.

"You do have general ignorance in your favor. Few of the individuals recruited thus far display even the most rudimentary knowledge of astronomy and none whatsoever of the mechanics in celestial navigation involved. Of your world's spatial relationship to the Weave they know nothing. Even if any of them wanted to they could not for the Amplitur your world locate."

"How are your studies coming?"

"General research proceeds normally."

"Not that. Your own studies. You, personally. I know you've been saying to any of your kind who would listen that we're too potentially destabilizing to be trusted."

The Hivistahm's teeth clicked together several times in rapid succession, a sure sign he was startled. "You are not supposed to know of such things."

Will grinned. "I have more freedom here than most of your colleagues and everyone's eager to talk to me. It aids their research. I also have this." He tapped the translator hanging from his neck and indicated the matching plug in his ear. "I listen, I hear things."

Third-of-Study craned his neck to regard the Human. "My theories do not you trouble?"

"Shoo, we're on the same side, you bet. You think we're dangerous, I think we're on our way to becoming harmless. You want us left alone, I badly want you to leave. Maybe we can help each other out."

"I see." Third-of-Study relaxed. "How do you feel events will progress?"

"According to what I've been saying all along, natch. Your people don't know our history, our psychology. Your military techs see only the short-term help a few Human soldiers can give them. The people they're recruiting are either dirt-poor, bored, or iconoclasts. They might be useful for a little while but soon the novelty of what they're doing is going to wear thin. Then they'll want to come home. When that happens they'll say to hell with your silly antediluvian conflict. They'll have had it with war and bloodshed.

"Your military personnel, people like Caldaq and Soliwik, won't know how to handle that lack of commitment. That's when they and their superiors will decide that unreliable Earth isn't worth the effort. You'll abandon us and we'll be able to get on with our efforts at making peace among ourselves."

"What about the returnees?"

"Any who talk or try to sell the story of their experience will be treated as nuts. They can't prove anything anyway. In a few years they'll be forgotten. Life will go on as before, without outside interference." He stopped. "Tell me something, Third-of-Study. I'm Human. I'm a composer, an artist. I've spent a lot of time among your people. All I want is for you to go away and leave me and my kind in peace. You want exactly the same thing. But there's something I want to know.

"You're not afraid of *me*, are you?"

Third-of-Study reached out to gently clasp the incredibly soft, flexible Human hand. "Truly I am not," he lied.

★ XVII ★

Eventually Will sailed back to New Orleans. After so long in backwater Belize, life in the bustling, steamy, cosmopolitan city hit him like an ice-cold rag. He visited friends and colleagues, attended the triumphal symphony premiere of *Arcadia*, promised the anxious director that yes, another major work was forthcoming, made the acquaintance of a discreet and eager dealer in precious metals, and paid the anticipated pile of overdue bills. There were CDs to buy, films to catch up on, books to acquire. He dated but made no promises. It was flattering to be desired, but for a little while longer yet, he told more than one disappointed paramour, he had other priorities to attend to.

Many months later he tied up his affairs, restocked the cat, and fled the delta with his autopilot locked on a southerly heading.

It was impossible to imagine, he thought as he steered carefully back into the lagoon of Lighthouse Reef, that anyone was living there—much less hundreds of aliens and Human beings working together below the tranquil surface.

He made contact with a Lepar sent to check out the intruder and soon found himself strolling the familiar corridors of the base. Caldaq was genuinely pleased to see him again. The Hivistahm, O'o'yan, Wais, and the rest were more formal, more restrained in their greetings. Third-of-Study was the exception. He was as demonstrative as it was possible for a Hivistahm to be with one not of its own kind.

Attitudes, he explained, had not changed. Will was disappointed but not really surprised. It was too soon for boredom and dissension to have set in among the first recruits, he explained. Give them another year. Then things would begin to happen.

He was curious to see how their integration, though doomed to inevitable failure, was proceeding, much as one might approach a heavyweight boxing match with a mixture of fascination and abhorrence. The idea of paying to see two grown men, usually poor, usually black, beating themselves to bloody pulps for the delectation of the masses filled him with disgust, yet there was something about such contests that gripped people and made them reluctant to look away. In the same way, he needed to see how his fellow misguided Humans were doing in the service of the Weave.

Though Humans were being sent to several worlds it was on Vasarih where they were actively committed, Vasarih where they were seeing real combat. Will had been told it was not an important place. Despite the rhetoric of those doing the recruiting it was clear that the officers of the Weave were far from confident of their new soldiers.

Caldaq perfectly exemplified his superiors' uncertainty. While preliminary results and hopeful tests seemed to point toward Human effectiveness in battle, Will Dulac was ever present to energetically contradict every new finding by pointing out the flaws in S'van reasoning, by demonstrating what peace-loving Humans could accomplish in the arts, in music, in literature and drama.

Humanity was a mirror for the captain's ambivalence. There was no questioning the epic qualities of Human literature, for example, yet much of it turned on violent acts. Yet did not Massood storytelling utilize conflict as motivation and plot device? Will argued after studying numerous examples. Indeed it did, Caldaq had to admit.

What he could not get across to the Human Will was that the Massood did not enjoy fighting. It fell to them as members of the Weave because alone among Weave races they were capable of it. As for the Chirinaldo, one could never be certain what the massive heliox-breathers were thinking, except that their easygoing society was anything but combative in nature.

In contrast to the cultures of both Massood and Chirinaldo was the still unconfirmed possibility that many Humans derived positive enjoyment from combat. At his most persuasive, Will Dulac could not dislodge this option from the Commander's mind. So radical, so alien was the notion that the xenopsychs assigned to study the phenomenon went so far as to postulate the existence of two separate Human species differentiated only by a genetic proclivity for violence yet to be isolated.

Humankind was the embodiment of contrasting attitudes. At once peace-loving and warlike, civilized and barbaric, it confronted the Weave with an entirely new kind of intelligence the parameters of which the Hivistahm and S'van were struggling to define. It did not help that Humanity had spent much of its own existence trying and failing to accomplish the same goal.

"I keep trying to tell you," Will said, "that only a few aberrant individuals enjoy fighting. Most people despise war."

"Perhaps that is because heretofore they have only had their own kind to fight," Caldaq responded. "For the first time in your history that is no longer the case."

"It doesn't matter."

"Are you so sure of your own kind? It is claimed that any being which enjoys combat is by definition not only uncivilized but unintelligent. Yet your people are demonstrably intelligent."

"I know you find us confusing. We find ourselves confusing. Not long ago it was an admirable thing to be a soldier, to wear a uniform and die in battle."

Caldaq's nose twitched. "How can one be admired for volunteering for personal extinction?"

"Hey, I said it was history. My life is music."

"Which I would enjoy listening to." Caldaq was eager to change the subject. "I know you have been working hard on your latest composition."

"It's not ready yet. I'm still searching for a few basic themes for the last movement. When it's finished you'll be the first to hear the complete work, I promise."

"I look forward to it."

Caldaq watched the Human depart, wondering anew at the variation in size among individuals. Some stood taller than the Massood while others were as short as the average Hivistahm. Among the Weave only the Lepar exhibited as extreme a variation in adult stature. Another bizarre byproduct of Human evolution, he mused.

Absurd to think there might be any kind of biologic relationship between the soft-voiced amphibians and the loquacious land-dwelling Humans. But then, to whom were the inhabitants of this peculiar world most nearly related? The Massood? The S'van? Or perhaps some species not represented at the base?

Second-of-Medicine and Third-of-Study had their own reasons for siding with Will Dulac. They thought Earth a dead end, a place for the Weave to leave and leave alone. Their arguments and occasional impassioned pleas were offset by the reports that filtered halfway back across the galaxy. So far three groups of Humans had received Weave combat training. By now the third and largest was starting to make a real impact on the Vasarihan conflict.

Massood troops clamored to fight alongside their new allies, believing that with their help breakthroughs might be made in sectors which had been stalemated for years. Human soldiers insisted on leading assaults on enemy positions. If the reports were to be believed, they truly liked their Massood comrades. The Massood responded with admiration if not genuine camaraderie.

As for the other races, they had little reason to interact with these new fighters. Nor did Humans evince any particular affection for the Hivistahm, or the O'o'yan, or any of the other Weave species they came in contact with. They joked and chatted with the S'van, but the S'van got along with everyone. They had to. For their part the S'van were careful to keep their distance. It would not do for other members of the Weave to perceive an intimate relationship between the S'van and these rabid Humans, especially when none such existed.

Such suspicions and fears only emphasized what a miracle it was that the Weave had survived for as long as it had, Caldaq mused as he turned down a corridor.

Will was trying to teach Third-of-Study how to swim, a task more difficult than he'd imagined. For one thing, the Hivistahm's lungs were small in proportion to its physique, resulting in poor buoyancy and a concurrent tendency to sink rapidly as he exhaled. This made the Hivistahm's dislike of the water immediately understandable.

Third-of-Study was game to try, however, confident that the more he knew about Humankind the better the arguments he could make for leaving the species alone. Will Dulac he did not fear, having already decided that Humans acted like utterly different creatures when alone than when assembled in groups. The actual equation was simple enough: $5h(u) = v?$, wherein five or more Humans acting in concert in the presence of uncertainty resulted in violence of unpredictable dimensions, the degree of violence being a function of the number of Humans.

Third-of-Study had to work much harder than a Human in order to stay afloat. Since the delicate front arms and fingers provided little in the way of motive power he had to kick constantly to keep his narrow skull above water. He was doing his best close inshore when a slick, bulbous face appeared nearby.

The Lepar expressed its concern via the omnipresent translator. Third-of-Study explained that he was in the water by choice and that everything was well under control. Bulging eyes regarded Human and Hivistahm solemnly for a moment before the Lepar disappeared with a quick twist of its torso and a flick of its tail. Will watched it go, then lay down in the shallows, resting his back against the warm wet sand.

"Tell me about the Lepar," he said.

"Truly I suspect there is little you do not know." Third-of-Study joined him, delighting in the sunshine and glad of the chance to relax. His legs ached badly. "You have among us a great deal of time spent."

"That's so, but you hardly ever see a Lepar," he said into his translator. He had acquired a knowledge of Massood, and some select phrases in S'van, but Hivistahm with its whistles and clicks utterly defeated him. It did not make him feel incompetent. The only other aliens he saw speaking Hivistahm were the Wais, who seemed able to master any tongue. Someone had said something about dual sets of vocal cords.

"They prefer to themselves to keep, to out of the way of others stay." Third-of-Study's eyeshades darkened to maximum to shield the sensitive organs from the tropical sun. "Not only are they the only truly amphibious sentients, they are also among the least intelligent. That is not a criticism, merely part of my answer to your query. Certain things extremely well they do."

"That one was Vatoloi, wasn't it?"

The Hivistahm looked at him. "You can recognize individuals?"

"He was the first Lepar I ever saw, years ago. The one who intercepted me in the water when I was trying to swim away from Caldaq and his escort."

"Vatoloi a ranking Lepar is, if truly it were he," said Third-of-Study. "We do not much contemplate the Lepar. There is little to learn from them. They do not try to beyond their abilities extend themselves and attempt nothing unless they are confident of accomplishing what they set out to do."

"I never learned how many are working here at the base."

"I cannot a number give you." Third-of-Study was irritated at what he perceived to be a waste of valuable time. It wasn't often he was able to isolate the Human for moments of personal study.

"Truly I apologize for my feeble attempts at swimming. We Hivistahm are for the activity ill constructed. There is also the problem of buoyancy. Your bones are very light for their strength, more like those of the Wais than myself or a Massood."

"Shoo, I think you're doing pretty good."

"Thanks be to you."

"Why'd you want to learn to swim, anyway?"

Third-of-Study shifted onto his haunches. "To better understand your kind."

"The enemy?"

The Hivistahm clicked teeth. "I regard you as dangerous, not as an enemy. 'Enemy' implies directed hostility. I prefer to think of your kind as clumsy rather than inimical."

"Think of us any way you want. Just help me convince Caldaq and his superiors that it will be best for everyone if we're left alone."

"Such our common goal is, Will Dulac."

They contemplated the lagoon, the palms and bushes. Will's cat rode at anchor nearby, motionless atop the silver sea. Sergeant majors fluttered in the shallows, and Will thought he glimpsed the flash of a trio of squid, hunting chromatic prey. Beneath the sand on which they lay, the steadily expanding Weave base pulsed with activity.

"Are we really so full of contradictions?" Will asked quietly.

"Consider the manner in which you react to the combat you insist your people truly abhor. Massood advance or retreat but do not long the consequences of individual battles bemoan. Humans seem incapable of putting a past over which they no longer have any control behind them. They will about those they have slain become emotional, generating water from eyeducts and clashing sounds making. Then they will rise the next day to kill again. Only one other species reacts thus to the death of enemy: the Amplitur.''

''What's that?'' A surprised Will turned away from the lagoon.

''They do not become emotional in the fashion of Humans, or for that matter, Massood. At least, not insofar as we can detect. But the passing of their enemies they likewise lament because it signifies a reduction in the number of individuals available for incorporation into their Purpose.'' Sunlight glinted off emerald green scales.

''Perhaps you may somewhat the source of my personal concern understand, which I thus far have failed to my colleagues convey. We speak of Human contradictions. They are vaster than I think you yourself can imagine. The Weave a conservative organization is. It is uncomfortable with that which it does not understand. You say that your unpredictability ultimately renders you useless to the resistance. I say that dangerous it makes you. Truly it is much the same thing. On that I found my hopes.

''There are many in the study group who think you mad. That still in dispute is. What the honored Commander's superiors continue to debate is whether your madness is more useful than dangerous.''

''So you think we're crazy?'' Will picked up a small piece of bleached coral and chucked it into the water, heard the soft *bloop* as it sank to merge with thousands of dead cousins that littered the floor of the lagoon.

''Perhaps not in a conventional sense. Evaluating new definitions tailored specifically to the Human condition an ongoing team activity is. Too simple to call you mad, your society mad, your world itself mad.

''Take the matter of your multiplicity of languages. You must know that the development of a common language is considered a prerequisite for the maturation of any advanced civilization. Yet you advanced technology have achieved in spite of your linguistic fragmentation. To us this is astonishing and unprecedented. The evolution of your civilization has in every particular from the norm differed. It is what makes you so valuable to the military. It is also what makes some among them nervous.''

''Nervous? Why should they be nervous if Human soldiers are winning battles for them?''

"Because a soldier always uncomfortable is when dealing with a weapon whose workings he does not fully understand."

"I see." Will rolled onto his side. "What about me?" He tried to peer through the dark eyeshades. "You've said that you're not afraid of me. Do *I* make you nervous?" He was hurt but not really surprised when the Hivistahm hesitated.

"You personally? No. You made us of your own position aware from the very beginning, and I have seen nothing to suggest deviation."

Will knew he'd been the subject of study from day one, but to hear it stated so bluntly was still disconcerting. A S'van, he thought, would have put it more tactfully.

"Truly you are what you claim to be," Third-of-Study continued. "Nor are you an isolated example. Others of your kind have for a variety of reasons recruitment refused. Among them are some who have stated that they find war repugnant. More contradictions. The Massood abhor conflict yet all are willing to fight because they see the necessity. It is with the Chirinaldo the same. An individual Human can be as civilized as a Wais or primitive as a Vasarih. This unsettling dichotomy is present in you individually as well as racially.

"Psychologically you drift free. You have no mental anchors. An individual who refuses recruitment will later another of our people encounter and ask to join. Another who eagerly volunteered will its mind change and demand to be demobilized." Sharp teeth scraped against one another. "The latter will noisily proclaim its pacificism, utterly ignorant of its contradictory behavior." Third-of-Study leaned forward so suddenly that Will was startled. He'd discovered that the Hivistahm preferred to keep as far away from Humans as possible.

"Truly, Will Dulac, your kind does not know itself. You do not know what you want, what you are about, who you are. Your destiny an enigma shrouded in pain and confusion is."

Will stared at the tinted eyeshields. "That's my worry."

"No longer. It is ours as well. There is so much about you we do not understand. This obsession with gold as a medium of exchange, for example. Clearly it is to the inequitable distribution of resources among your kind related and is by your regressive tribal society exacerbated. People in one sector go hungry while food rots elsewhere. A few large, powerful tribes the consumption of energy dominate while others cannot light their cities.

"One of the basic hallmarks of true civilization is the reasoned distribution of elementary planetary resources. Individual wealth is among Weave species existing, but only after everyone has been minimally provided for. Like everything else we feel this aberration is to your proclivity for combat somehow related. It is not flattering to you.

"You must realize that many of my colleagues do not consider your kind civilized."

"I know that. I'm not blind."

"It is this constant preoccupation with conflict which concerns me and which simultaneously makes your kind in the fight against the Amplitur so valuable. Truly it every aspect of your society permeates, irrespective of tribe. It is present even in ordinary, daily conversation, in your mating rituals, in the way you apportion food and your offspring raise. It should have out of your species long ago evolved.

"Despite this you have a high level of technology achieved. Terms are to describe you being invented."

"I think you're overreacting, you and all your associates," Will replied. "If you took the weapons away from us we'd stop fighting."

"Are you so certain? I think not. I have some of your weapons seen. The small ones have what you call 'safeties' into them built, to from discharging accidentally prevent them. My colleagues anxiously for the safety inside the Human system search. They feel one exists. Less sure am I."

"You talk a lot about your fellow researchers. How does Caldaq feel about us?"

One eye swiveled to regard the lagoon while the other remained fixed on the Human. "Caldaq an honored commander is, captain of ship and expedition, and unusually thoughtful for a Massood. Very much a remarkable example of his kind. I believe he on the question ambivalent remains. As a Massood relieved he is when it is only required that he follow orders.

"That is not to say averse he is to venturing suggestions, which are highly valued. But he is not a philosopher. You must understand that unusual it is for a Massood a nonmilitary command to be given. Normally an expedition such as ours by a Hivistahm, Yula, S'van, or Wais is directed."

Will nodded at the lagoon. "How long do they think things can go on like this? Admittedly we're isolated here, but operations have to shut down when the occasional fishing boat or diving groups shows up. One of these days someone's going to give you away."

"Our ships effectively masked are and our transmissions here still unnoticed. Those who are recruited and their minds change respond appropriately to treatment and to their lives return forgetful of what they have seen and heard here."

"Sooner or later," Will argued, "some of those people are going to get together and compare notes."

"By that time I am certain will have been made a decision on whether to abandon Weave efforts here or to reveal ourselves formally to your people. Myself, I truly for the former pray."

"I'm glad we're working for the same end, even if it's for different reasons," Will told him. "When you leave, I'm going to miss some of you."

"I will miss some of you also," the Hivistahm replied, lying like a skilled S'van.

★ XVIII ★

Will had made friends with an O'o'yan willing to whistle traditional melodies for him. He was memorializing them on his pocket recorder when Caldaq and Jaruselka interrupted the session. Though mated, it was unusual to encounter them together outside their quarters, since their specialities required their presence in different parts of the base.

He shut off the recorder while the O'o'yan saluted in the manner of its kind and scampered nimbly out into the corridor.

"Something wrong?" he inquired curiously.

Caldaq took the seat next to the Human, his knees reaching toward his chin. Both ears twitched in unison.

"Three weapons are astray."

Will put his recorder aside. "What do you mean 'astray'?"

"Periodic inventory is made of all military equipment," Jaruselka told him. Not for the first time Will mused on the peculiar physiology of the Massood larynx. It was impossible to tell male from female by listening to them.

"Each unit is electronically coded so that it may be counted remotely. When a unit's power source weakens, it notifies inventory so that immediate replacement may be made. When the Lepar assigned to the task went to do so, she found the weapons missing.

"Follow-up revealed that the units read weak not because they are powered down but because of distance. They are on the mainland."

Will considered. "What of the S'van and Hivistahm who are conducting nocturnal field studies ashore?"

"None carry weapons. The power packs in communications

devices are differently coded. No Massood would take a weapon off the ship and anyway, all Weave personnel have been accounted for.''

Caldaq's tone was solemn. ''That leaves your people.''

''I suppose it does.'' Will put his recorder aside. ''Am I supposed to be surprised?''

''I do not understand what you are inferring,'' Caldaq replied. ''I know only that these weapons must be recovered. Humans have been trained in the use of Weave technology so that they may fight the Amplitur. This knowledge was not imparted for other purposes.'' Gray eyes came close.

''You will come with us to help resolve the anomaly.''

''Go with you?'' Will glanced at the silent Jaruselka, back to Caldaq. ''You're not going ashore? Remember, we already decided that the only ones who can remotely pass for Human, even at night, are the S'van.''

''When there are weapons involved, the Massood must be involved. None of my people are as experienced in dealing with Humans as I, so it falls to me to go. If it were possible I would take a Chirinaldo with me.''

''Easier to camouflage an elephant,'' Will muttered.

''I would be grateful for any suggestions.''

The musician considered. Viewed from behind on a dark night a single Massood might temporarily pass for a tall Human, but a cluster of them would be as conspicuous as a professional basketball team in Bangkok. Unlike the S'van, their furry, shrewlike faces could not be disguised. They would have to keep under cover as much as possible. Certainly they needed his help.

Besides which Caldaq had not offered him the option of refusing.

He was surprised when the fully masked shuttle came onshore south of Belize City and instead of setting down, continued inland. The missing weaponry had been traced to a point near the country's capital of Belmopan. It did not take long to get there, the entire country being small enough to cross by car in a single day.

Homing in on the weapons' power units, they tried to set down as close as possible to their location without revealing themselves to the citizenry. A vast auto-wrecking yard on the city's industrial outskirts offered a good landing site. The shuttle was able to touch down unobserved among the saurian skeletons of demolished buses and exterminated taxis.

As soon as it neared the ground, half a dozen towering Massood soldiers leaped from the interior to take up defensive positions behind a burned-out truck. Will followed more cautiously. Had they landed in the States there would have been dogs or watchmen to deal with. In Belize barbed wire was sufficient to deter would-be thieves.

He found a place where the branch of a tree had pushed down the single strand of barbs atop the chicken-wire enclosure. After checking as best he knew how to ensure it wasn't electrified he scrambled to the top and straddled the limb.

The Massood had followed. Now they milled about beneath him, murmuring among themselves. Anxiously Will scanned the yard.

"C'mon. What's the holdup?"

"We cannot do that," Jaruselka hissed up at him.

"Can't do what?"

"Climb as you have."

Will gaped down at her. The fence was maybe ten feet high, stout and easy to get a grip on.

She held up her right hand. "Our fingers are not strong enough to support our upper-body weight in such a position."

"The devil you say." The yard was still empty and silent. If there was a watchman, he might be asleep or drunk. "Burn the fence." He knew that the weapons they carried could easily make a hole in the chicken wire. They would just have to hope it wasn't noticed before morning.

Once through they advanced fast and quiet, the Massood hurrying along hunched over to minimize their great height. While Jaruselka operated the tracking device that was leading them to their quarry, Will mentally composed and hummed music appropriate to the moment.

They avoided detection by keeping to dark alleys and dirt paths, save for a terse encounter with a single tottering local who, upon encountering a group of giants in the middle of the night, thoughtfully turned and hurried away without uttering a sound.

Jaruselka paused alongside a wild hedge and gestured with the tracker. "They are in there."

The narrow alley served as backyard to a rambling two-story

wooden structure. Water trickled from a PVC pipe that protruded from the underside of the building, which was raised off the ground on two-foot-high concrete stilts. Mud and garbage glinted beneath. Mist coagulated on the corrugated roof and trickled earthward, collecting in rivulets that pooled up in the nearby drainage ditch.

Eight or nine wooden stairs led to a tiny covered porch and screen door through which a dingy hall was visible.

"Let me have the tracker," Will told Jaruselka. She hesitated, then handed it over. "There's a light in the hall. If anyone's moving around, you'll be seen. I'll go in and try to find out what the story is."

"They have the weapons," she reminded him.

"That doesn't mean they know how to use them. My bet is that they're thinking about selling the technology."

"I am coming with you," Caldaq whispered decisively.

"You can't. What if somebody sees you?"

"This is my responsibility. Remember who is in charge here."

"All right, it's your party."

Caldaq murmured to his people. One soldier stepped forward to join him. The rest concealed themselves behind and within the hedge.

The screen door was not locked. This was Belize, Will reminded himself. Not Chicago. Following the tracker, they entered and turned up a flight of stairs.

"What are you going to say?" Caldaq whispered from behind. "How do you intend to approach them?"

"Depends on their reaction. I'm not a Wais."

A naked low-watt bulb feebly illuminated the second-floor landing. The walls were shedding huge strips of cheap brown wallpaper that reminded Will of chocolate shavings on the side of a yellow cake.

The tracker led them to the rearmost room. After motioning for Caldaq and the other soldier to wait in the shadows, Will rapped on the door loud enough to wake but not alarm. When no response was forthcoming he tried again, louder.

The voice that replied from within was tentative and none too friendly. "You know what time it is? Already we pay for the goddamn room."

"My name's William Dulac. I'm not with the hotel, I'm from the base."

A pause, then, "What base?"

"It's too late for games."

The door clicked as it was opened. Will took a wary step backward. The heavyset, unshaven man who looked him up and down did not glance up the hallway.

"How did you find us?" Will sensed movement in the room behind the speaker. He didn't recognize the man. Not one of the original ten recruits then. For some unknown reason this discovery pleased him.

"You've got weapons from the base. Don't you know that no Weave technology is allowed to be brought ashore?"

"I hear something like that." He opened the door wider. "Look, *mes amis*, why don' you come in and we discuss it?" A smile parted the stubble. "You alone?"

"No." Will glanced up the hall. Caldaq and the soldier stepped out of the shadows.

The man slumped when he saw them. "Should've guessed. Hans think you might have way of finding us. All right, *entrez*, the lot of you."

The two Massood had to duck to clear the doorway. It was not much of a room. Sink, cracked mirror, a pair of rumpled beds.

"That's Hans," said the man who'd opened the door, indicating the lanky individual lying on the far bed. "Miyoshi's in the john. I'm Jean-Pierre. Have a seat and I explain." Will took a chair. The Massood remained standing.

"I ask again. How you find us?"

"All weapons from the base can be traced. You don't need to know how."

"You don' trust me, eh? Well, I suppose I can' blame you."

A toilet gargled behind a door, which opened to reveal a short, unattractive Oriental woman. She held a pistol in each hand. Caldaq's fingers eased toward his own sidearm, froze when she aimed one of the weapons at him.

The taller man slid to the floor and removed a pair of rifles from beneath his bed, tossing one to his companion while focusing the other on the Massood.

"We can't kill them here," the woman was saying. "If the bodies were found it would attract too much attention."

"They'll cooperate." Jean-Pierre eyed the aliens. "You don' want to give away your presence any more than do we."

"I do not understand," said Caldaq. "Why would you want to kill us? We do not wish you harm. Only to bring back the weapons."

"But you can' have them back." The man did not smile. "We took them because we need them, *ne c'est pas*?" He looked over at the woman. "As long as we have these they can track us."

"Let them try it in New York, or Nagoya." She gestured toward the door.

Will instinctively raised his hands and started for the exit. "I don't get it. What's the idea?"

The one called Jean-Pierre checked the hall before leading the way. Hans and the woman followed behind, their weapons trained on the three prisoners.

"We hear about you. You that musician fellow who been helping the rats and the lizards from the beginning. For a supposed smart guy you pretty slow. It never occur to you what somebody could do with a couple energy rifles and a field masking suit? Take out an armor car without breathing hard, my friend."

So there were no complex plans afoot here, Will thought. It was all very primitive, very basic. Very Human.

"These people are common thieves," he said in Massood. "They've taken the weapons so that they can steal money."

"Your obsession with artificial means of exchange again." Caldaq started down the stairway. "Do they want more gold? We can give them more gold."

"You don't understand. Some people can never get enough. Besides, I don't think they'd trust you."

"Why not? It would be a fair exchange from our point of view."

"They simply wouldn't believe anything you'd say, Caldaq. Or me, or anyone else. They'd be afraid of being tricked, having their memories adjusted like those recruits who change their minds and are returned to normal life. They're in control right now and people like this don't exchange control for promises."

"But I would keep the promise. It would be worth it to us."

"They can't understand that. People like this don't think like that."

Jean-Pierre paused at the bottom of the stairs, muttering. "Let's take them out the back. We can get a car, a truck, take them out and dump them in a swamp somewhere." He glanced at Will. "Good of you to come in to talk to us. We don' want any shooting in here. People might see things."

"Why not just give it up?" Will was trying to control his emotions as they approached the screen door. "Turn the weapons back in and rejoin your recruitment group. The Massood will forgive you. No harm done."

"*Non*. I think we stick with our original plan."

"Then let us go. We're not going to come after you. This isn't as important as what we're doing at the base. Surely you realize that much."

"We were told about the war," said the woman behind him. "We have our own scores to settle."

The only thing that surprised Will was that something like this hadn't happened sooner. Not all those recruited for training were altruistic or even merely greedy. There were malcontents and iconoclasts with shady histories. Unhappy folk, individuals trying to avoid the light of society, couples on the run from their pasts.

Thus far all had found a new direction, a new life in the service of the Weave. These three seemed suited to that task. Instead they had chosen, at the risk of their lives, to make war on their own kind. For money. He sympathized with Caldaq's confusion.

Jean-Pierre opened the screen door and stepped out onto the porch, checking the alley in both directions. Will held his breath. He beckoned for them to follow. It was excruciatingly difficult to avoid looking toward the hedge.

"Shoot them here," the woman said. "I'll roll them into the ditch and cover them up while you and Hans go look for a truck."

Jean-Pierre nodded, led them toward the bushes. "Nothing personal, *mes amis*, but we don' really have a choice."

"We'll be missed," said Will. "This is Caldaq, the base commander."

Jean-Pierre eyed the tall Massood sharply. "Commandant, eh? Too bad."

"They'll come looking for us," Will went on. "They'll find you no matter what you do."

"Better find us quick. We got a morning TACA plane to Mexico City. I got a feeling they can't trace these toys across the whole world. That wouldn' make no sense."

"You think you can smuggle guns like these through customs?"

"Why not? They don' look like real guns. We tell everybody they're movie props. Bet you it work swell." They were almost to the hedge. "I say we got nothing to declare, they don' even open our . . ."

He never finished the sentence. Massood materialized on all sides. Something made a noise like a giant electric spark. The humid night air was filled with the odor of burned flesh.

Never having had any military training, Will did the most helpful thing he could by dropping to the ground. Rifles and pistols had been knocked or pried loose, leaving Humans and Massood rolling together in the mud. One soldier went flying through the air. Someone yelped as bones broke.

To his horror Will saw that the three renegades were winning. The Massood had never faced their own allies before. They might be faster over a distance, but running counted for naught in hand-to-hand combat. The compact, heavily built Humans were not only stronger but quicker.

Caldaq and two colleagues managed to wrestle Jean-Pierre into restraints. The rest were having a difficult time with the woman. One Massood lay holding her broken leg while another lay unconscious in the drainage ditch. This left the one called Hans free to make a dash for his rifle.

Looking around wildly, Will spotted the pistols, which had been knocked out of the woman's hands. Instinctively he picked one up and pointed it at the tall German. It felt like a toy in his hand, light and featureless.

"Don't do it!" he shouted. "It's over!"

The younger man either didn't hear the warning or chose to ignore it. He picked up the rifle and started to turn.

Looking back on it later Will found he could not recall the exact sequence of events. He remembered the man aiming the heavy weapon at the three Massood clustered around the cursing JeanPierre. His finger rested in the notch on the side which served as a trigger. Both his posture and expression revealed his intent.

So Will fired first. A Cajun boy learns how to use a gun early. There was no recoil.

A thin purple line struck Hans as he was sighting the rifle. A sound like a fat man's suspenders snapping accompanied the burst.

Hans twitched violently, once, and crumpled to his knees. The muzzle of the peculiar rifle dug into the ground, supporting him briefly, before he tumbled onto his side, knees drawing into his chest as his muscles contracted.

Will rose, staring dumbly at the recumbent shape. It seemed that Caldaq was yelling at him. Then the tall, slim alien was alongside, his musk pungent in the moist air.

"Thank you, Will." Gray cat eyes and toothy snout were in constant motion, black nose twitching. "Are you all right, my friend?"

A stunned Will struggled to make sense of Massood words. "Yes. Here, you take this." He handed over the pistol.

A steady stream of curses in at least three languages issued from the two uninjured thieves as their restraints were secured. Caldaq barked an order and two soldiers hefted the body of the man Will had shot. Even though the coroner's department of the city of Belmopan might not be blessed with an extensive imagination, it was better not to leave anything that might inspire awkward questions.

On their way back to the wrecking yard the woman made an attempt to break free, kicking the soldier immediately in front of her behind the knee and hurdling his crumpling form before anyone could grab her. But she could not outrun a Massood, and with her arms bound behind her, her options were limited. She was hauled back, swearing in disgruntled Japanese, while a temporary crutch was rigged for the unfortunate soldier she'd injured. After that, the Massood watched their two captives more carefully.

It was a tired, hurting group that finally reboarded the tender with its prisoners. The pilot eyed the returnees nervously, anxious to be away. Masking was not half as effective in broad daylight.

The Massood were as exhausted emotionally as physically. They knew that if Will hadn't brought down the third Human they might have been overwhelmed despite their numerical superiority. Until now they had been the best, the Weave's front-line troops, the people the Wais and Hivistahm and S'van had relied upon to drive back the Amplitur hordes. Less than half their number of Humans had nearly wiped them out: Humans with preliminary training and no combat experience. What if the renegades had been experienced veterans of the fight for Vasarih? It had been a numbing, humbling experience.

But there had been only one death: a Human. Slain by another Human. This realization was not lost on anyone.

Will brooded all the way back to the base. As a child he had hunted in the back bayous, had killed for food, had watched his grandfather gut and flay critters for their skin and meat. He had intervened to save his friends as much as himself. Quickly. Instinctively.

It bothered him a great deal.

Several armed Humans were among those waiting to greet the tender upon its return to the base at Lighthouse Reef. They angrily took charge of their wayward brethren. Those few Massood who did not require medical attention followed behind. They strode slowly up the corridor, the familiar jauntiness absent from their step. The experience had cost them more than just energy and sleep.

It would be important to keep the incident as quiet as possible, Will reflected. Not to prevent a recurrence—a tighter watch had already been put on all sidearms—but to prevent a collapse of confidence among the Massood.

The bench he slumped onto hummed as it adjusted itself to his height. He'd stopped hyperventilating but was still sick at his stomach. The image of the man falling, curling into a fetal position on the ground, becoming motionless, replayed itself endlessly in his mind.

"You had no choice." Caldaq stood over him. "Had they succeeded in escaping to a large urban area it might well have proven impossible for us to go in after them. Everything we are doing here would have been jeopardized."

"I know that." Will's voice was barely a whisper.

The Commander sat down next to him and the bench obediently knotted in the middle to accommodate the second, larger frame.

"Where did you learn to shoot? Since first we met you have done little save tell me how much you abhor violence of any kind." Absently he felt of the large welt on his right thigh, where he'd been struck.

Will sighed heavily. "Where I grew up every kid learns how to hunt as soon as they can walk."

"I see." Caldaq looked up the corridor. The prisoners and their escort had vanished around a distant corner. "If you had not killed the man all might have been lost. Three against eight, and we would have lost. You did what was necessary." He paused.

"None of my people here have been on Vasarih. They have never seen a Human in combat. They were not prepared for—" He hunted for the right words, switched to the translator. "—for the ferocity of the resistance.

"Someday I hope to see what a fully trained Human soldier can do. Humans who have made a profession of soldiering against their own kind, who enjoy what they do and strive to be the best at it. It is a thought I find simultaneously exhilarating and frightening." The lips on the right side of his snout drew back to indicate humor.

"The Crigolit do the majority of fighting for the Amplitur cause. I think they are due a great surprise. I am not even sure I would take odds against an exceptional Human fighter in single combat against a Molitar." He looked evenly at Will.

"Perhaps this was a possibility from the beginning. You might have warned us."

"I didn't want to consider it. I thought all your recruits would be content with the gold. We're not all like those three," he said earnestly.

"Yes, so you have insisted all along."

"A small percentage. There's always an antisocial minority to deal with."

"Not among the other races."

All the long months of striving to convince Caldaq and the rest that man was an inherently peaceable creature were in danger of being wasted as the result of a single night of stupid, insensate tragedy. Will was heartsick.

"They were borderline insane to think they could get away with this," he muttered.

"Their behavior did not suggest insanity." Caldaq looked thoughtful. "I thought their actions quite rational."

He was going to have to work harder, Will told himself. Tonight was a setback, not a defeat. The images of violence and death could be overcome. Not for the first time he found himself wishing that he'd studied psychology instead of music.

He wondered what Caldaq was really thinking. So he asked.

"I am trained to captain a ship. That is what I would wish to be doing."

"And I'd much rather be spending my days composing. Circumstances have forced both of us out of our chosen professions."

Caldaq was quiet for a while. Then, "It is interesting to observe the change in the attitudes of primitive peoples when they are finally exposed to the immensity of the galaxy and the issues that rend civilizations. Perhaps it would be helpful for you to see what is happening firsthand."

Will was taken aback. "What do you mean?"

The Commander eyed him intently, his nose nearly motionless. "How would you like to go to Vasarih?"

Leave Earth? Watch the homeworld fall behind, lost in the immensity of space? Hundreds of recruits had done it. Could he not do as well? It would mean leaving his music behind, too, if only temporarily. And what inspiration, what cosmic themes might he encounter on such a journey?

"Your point is well taken."

"You can go out with the next group of recruits." Caldaq looked pleased.

✶ XIX ✶

He closed up the catamaran as best he could; disconnecting the solar chargers and batteries, reefing the sails tight, making certain both anchors were secure and leaving a note for the persistently inquisitive: "Gone ashore for a few days. Back soon." Hopefully that would convince any passersby that the boat had not been abandoned and that its owner was nearby and in good health. In any event, the cat would not be subject to the attention here it would have received up at Cancún or over in the BVIs.

Vatoloi came to assure him that he would monitor the craft personally.

The shuttle trip out was unexceptional, akin to riding a large plane in mildly turbulent weather. A sense of steady acceleration was accompanied by occasional slips and bumps. In contrast, the journey through what the S'van captain referred to as Underspace was actually boring. There was no sense of movement or motion, no feeling of speed.

There were several hundred recruits on board, all babbling and chatting excitedly. They had already seen enough at the base to make the journey itself seem anticlimactic. Though they hailed from dozens of different countries they had no difficulty making themselves understood, since the translators each had been issued had much less trouble with Spanish and English than they did with high Hivistahm or S'van.

Wais circulated smoothly among them, answering questions and reassuring the suddenly uncertain. Poor farmers from Guatemala, teachers and students, European tourists conversed eagerly, excitedly, discussing a future none could have conceived of months earlier.

Training sessions and orientation meetings were conducted at regular intervals. Will attended a few, came away discouraged by the military emphasis even though he knew full well that was the sole reason for the presence of Humans on board the vessel.

They paused first at a world called Motar. It was a measure of the respect his friends had for him that they had assigned to him a S'van aide, instead of the usual Hivistahm or O'o'yan. J'hai cheerfully explained the reason for the stop.

"This is where your people are receiving their primary battlefield training. The Motarians are extremely intelligent but their rate of reproduction is quite low. It's a wonder, actually, that they've been able to sustain their species at all. They're mammalian but resemble the S'van more than your kind, except that they're quite hairless and extremely corpulent." He barked amusedly.

"Though small in numbers they are supportive members of the Weave. They offer us their world, which boasts a great variety of terrain. It makes an excellent training ground. Nor are Humans the only peoples who receive instruction here." He glanced out a port. "It won't take long to offload your people."

Once again the huge vessel fell into Underspace. It took considerably less time to make the journey to Vasarih. For Will it hammered home how far Earth was from the body of galactic civilization.

Approaching Vasarih, however, was a far more serious matter than entering orbit around Motar.

"I'm told you have some familiarity with combat tactics?" J'hai murmured to him. Will indicated that he did. "Then you'll understand our caution. We must plan according to what we know of Amplitur assault patterns. The captain must select a section of space not frequented by enemy vessels lest one lock on as we emerge and fire upon us. By the same token the Amplitur can't gamble on challenging a superior force. It's all very much a matter of supposition and chance. Guesswork must be precise. Jumping in and out of Underspace is more than a matter of pushing a button. It takes time for drives and engineering to accommodate the requisite mathematics."

"It's been explained to me," Will told him. "Though I'm still not clear on why ships don't spend time in normal space destroying targets on the ground."

"All important bases on the surface are hardened. Nuclear

devices destroy that which both sides seek to preserve, and surface-based weaponry can find and destroy a ship before the ship can locate the mobile base. Starships are too valuable to expend attacking ground targets. They're needed to move troops and supplies between worlds. Even for an advanced civilization a ship such as this one is a complex and expensive undertaking, not to be risked lightly.

"Remember also that the Amplitur seek to convert people, not exterminate them. A world won through the use of nuclear devices is usually not a world worth absorbing. Better to beat your enemy off with as few casualties as possible."

"Has the Weave ever done that?" Will asked him. "Pushed the Amplitur and their allies off a world they controlled?"

"We've had our victories. Why, we inflicted a major defeat on them only two hundred years ago."

The confession failed to startle Will. He'd heard enough about the ancient conflict to grasp its vast dimensions.

"Subsequently the Amplitur regrouped and reorganized. Neither side has made a real gain since then. Each of us periodically acquires new allies, develops new weapons systems, but the balance of power is not significantly altered." J'hai glanced up at him. "We're hoping that your kind might make an impact."

Sorry to disappoint you, Will thought as he settled himself into the shuttle seat. J'hai ensconced himself in the one opposite.

"Which side are the native Vasarih on?"

"Ours." J'hai swiveled his seat to face the Human. "A few have gone over to the Amplitur side, though most want nothing to do with them. It's not always a matter of free choice on their part. You know that the Amplitur are capable of influencing thoughts?"

"I've been told." A cold chill tickled Will's spine. He wondered what it would be like to experience an Amplitur mind probe, to feel his own thoughts twisted like putty, bending to Amplitur suggestion. "Then there are Amplitur on Vasarih?"

"Wherever there's conflict with the Weave there are Amplitur observing, directing, controlling. Never in great numbers. But there are always a few around to offer 'advice' to their minions."

"As the Turlog advise the Weave?"

"It's nothing like that. The Turlog are allies. They provide suggestions and analysis. They wouldn't have anything to do with mind control even if they were capable of it, which they're not.''

Control takes many forms, Will mused. Aloud he asked, ''Who's doing the fighting here for the Amplitur?''

''Mostly Crigolit. There's also a Molitar contingent. You may see one or two among the prisoners. Big, impressive fighters though not the most intelligent. Ideal for Amplitur purposes. Both species have been allied with the Amplitur for so long no one knows if they were manipulated into the alliance or if they joined voluntarily. Not that it matters. Once allied, a race cannot break free.

''There may also be some Ashregan serving as point fighters.'' He looked sideways at Will as the shuttle disengaged from the mother ship. ''Have you ever seen an Ashregan?''

''No. Why?''

''Just wondering.'' Warning sirens sounded. ''We're preparing to drop. We may go straight in, or there may be an enemy warship in the vicinity and we'll have to duck back into Underspace. If you feel a surge in the engines, you'll know.''

It seemed to Will that they hung there forever, suspended in the big ship's gravity field like shrimp in a gumbo.

Then the darkness outside the ports gave way to dazzling light as the shuttle plunged like a stone toward the surface. Reflections from clouds, sea, and land created a pinwheel of color outside.

Just above a moderate storm the shuttle slowed and leveled off. A straining Will could see little but cloud; dense, impenetrable cumulus formed fairy towers that framed their descent.

As the shuttle continued to drop, land began to show through breaks in the cloud cover. Land and sea. Nothing to suggest that this world was a center of violent conflict between two great civilizations. J'hai was talking to him.

''The level of Vasarih technology is several orders below that of your own people. Contacts between urban areas are still infrequent. Since the major cities are all situated on the coastline most of the fighting has been conducted in a region known locally as the southern plains. The Amplitur wish the destruction of population centers no more than do we.

''The Weave discovered this world slightly before the Amplitur, therefore the majority of Vasarih are allied with us. They assist in the conflict to the best of their limited abilities, mostly with simple ground support such as food and the like.

"We'll be setting down close to the northwestern section of the contested area, in mountainous terrain. Local Vasarih fortunate enough not to have been caught in the cross fire have long since moved away. We have a major base there, dug into the foothills. That's where you'll have the chance to talk with your own kind."

"Fine," Will replied in S'van, startled to realize that circumstances were making him into something of a linguist.

J'hai glanced forward. "We monitor constantly during descent. You'd be surprised how much simpler it is to shoot down a vessel from the ground than from out in space. The vessel which brought us here has long since returned to the safety of Underspace.

"War is much more of a mental than a physical contest. In that we can be a help to the Massood. It's participation in actual combat that we and the Hivistahm and the rest cannot stomach." Behind the dense black beard the S'van's expression was unreadable.

"I'm personally glad I don't have to get any closer to the fighting than this."

"What are you?" Will realized he'd simply accepted J'hai's presence without ever inquiring about his companion's profession.

"Military intelligence, if that's not a contradiction in terms. I thought you knew."

"No. They just told me I'd have a guide."

They came in low over mountains so rugged that Will's breath twice caught in his throat. The strip of land on which they touched down terminated in a sheer granite cliff which unexpectedly parted to admit the compact craft.

Once inside the immense excavated cavern the warning lights dimmed, and Will was able to release himself from his seat. A dull thump echoed through the vessel.

"Attack." J'hai eyed the ceiling. "I expect we had a seeker on our tail. Must've blown up outside. Someone will be spending the afternoon cleaning up gravel."

A perspiring Will followed the S'van outside and into a bustling underground world. Aliens and vehicles were moving in all directions, intent upon unknown tasks. Their individualized attire was spotted and slashed with colorful insignia, some of which Will recognized, much of which he did not. Massood and Hivistahm, O'o'yan and Lepar were familiar to him, but there were also several physical types he had never encountered before. J'hai provided names and translator settings. Will fingered the unit that dangled from his neck.

As they made their way through the complex he searched anxiously for a recognizable Human face, saw none.

"Not many are assigned here," J'hai explained. "Most are out in the field, where their unique talents can best be utilized."

"But there are plenty of Massood here." Will pointed out a trio of the tall fighters.

"Their presence is a function of numbers. The Massood populate a dozen worlds. Only a very few of your kind have been trained."

"I was told I'd see Humans here."

"So you will, and soon," J'hai assured him. "I said they're out in the field. That's where we're going."

"Into combat?"

J'hai looked up at him. "Isn't that what you wanted? To see how your people were reacting to actual fighting? If that's what you wish then you'll have to take the risk of being shot at. I have no sympathy for your reluctance. Only my specialized psychological training allows me to accompany you beyond this point. Consider my situation for a moment. I am neither Human nor Massood.

"We won't be going to the front lines. Training or no, I couldn't handle that. If you want to change your mind we can depart on the next shuttle." J'hai sounded hopeful.

"No," said Will, dashing the S'van's hopes. "I hate war also, but I came here to see how the people who were recruited are doing. I'm not leaving until I've done that."

"Very well." J'hai made a disconsolate joke in his own language which had Will grinning. You could always depend on the S'van to leaven a tense situation with humor. "Your people operate from a forward base which is not far from here. It's located astride the route the Crigolit are using to advance westward toward an important Vasarih town. Humans were pressed into the fighting there to see how their presence might affect the outcome."

"How are they doing?"

"I don't know, having been away from here for some time myself. We'll find out when we get there." He was subdued. "Hopefully we'll arrive during a quiet period."

Will found himself envying the S'van and Hivistahm and all the other peace-loving races of the Weave. All he had to do was convince them to see Humans in the same civilized light.

They left the base via a smaller exit, traveling in an armored ground-repulsion vehicle that skimmed along several meters above the rocky ground. The mountains shrank behind them. Soon they were traveling down a winding gully through semi-desert terrain. A Chirinaldo weapons master bulked large in the weapons emplacement atop the machine, which in addition to its two passengers was ferrying medical supplies to the combat zone.

"The gully offers cover against long-range Crigolit detectors," J'hai explained. "This vehicle is too small to carry masking equipment. Aerial surveillance is limited to what both sides can keep in the air. Both sides put up orbiting observation satellites which are destroyed with great regularity."

The gully was beginning to narrow uncomfortably when they entered a smaller version of the main base. Weaponry was much in evidence and the proportion of Massood among the inhabitants considerably higher. But there was still no sign of fellow Humans.

One made her presence known soon after they disembarked, pausing only long enough to exchange a few words with the massive Chirinaldo as it was recharging its heliox-breather. Two silver stripes crossed her uniform, running from the top of her left shoulder across her chest to disappear beneath her right arm. Her skin was dark brown, her eyes and hair jet black. Will had expected someone tough, not beautiful. On reflection he conceded that the two were not necessarily mutually exclusive.

"I was told you were bringing an important visitor." She stared at Will while addressing the S'van.

"This is William Dulac."

Her eyebrows rose. "So you the legendary Dulac." Legendary, Will thought bemusedly. I write music. I'm a composer, not a legend.

She compounded his initial surprise by simultaneously shaking his hand and leaning forward to kiss him hard and strong full on the lips. Though he'd been anticipating a more formal greeting he professed no objections.

"I'm Captain Echevarria, Maria Echevarria." Her English was as heavily accented as her enthusiasm and energy were contagious. "*Muy* good to meet you, Señor Dulac. Everyone in this place know your name."

He felt a sudden overpowering urge to climb back into the vehicle and demand to be returned to the main base, thence to the ship and to Earth. This was what he had come for, and now that he'd found it, it wasn't at all what he'd expected or hoped for. His confidence level underwent a sudden drop, and he wasn't sure he wanted to probe further.

"You're a captain?" he found himself mumbling, unable to take his eyes from her.

"*Sí*. Isn't that amazing?"

"Where do you come from?"

"Mexico City. I originally went to the Coast to try and make some *dinero*, you know? My English pretty good, *verdad*?" Before he could reply she snapped something in S'van to his guide, who replied in kind and gratefully excused himself. Will looked after him as she slid an arm into his and dragged him away.

"It good to be able to do this once in a while. Can' do it in the ranks and still maintain order."

"So you're a captain." He couldn't think of anything else to say. Not with her pressed tightly against him. She was warm, but not soft.

"Sort of. We hav' to make up our own ranks. They not much on rank here. Suppervis . . . supervisorial positions, they call 'em. So I'm a supervisor-captain. Doné pretty good for myself."

The corridor was busy with Hivistahm and O'o'yan and Massood. He even saw a solitary Bir'rimor, but no Humans.

"Where's everybody else? And please don't call me a legend."

"You keedding?" She slid her arm free and lengthened her stride. "You start all of this, you give those of us who are here this chance. If not for you, none of us would be here. We'd be back on Earth, doin' whatever we'd been doin' when the recruiters found us." She startled him by spitting derisively into a corner.

"You were in the Mexican army?" he ventured, utterly overwhelmed by her ebullience.

She laughed, a rich, knowing sound that echoed down the corridor. "Who, me? You keedding? A woman in the Mexican army? Don' tell me you never hear of machismo, man. Where you from, anyway?"

"New Orleans."

"I hear that's a great town. Someday maybe I geet there. But I got a job to do here first. It not so bad, you know? They keep track of the gold you earn. At first everybody kind of suspicious about that, but here nobody seem to try and cheat anybody else. They not innocent, just different morals. I think, maybe better than ours."

"They're willing to let you do their fighting for them. I'm not sure yet how moral that is."

"Yeah, well, everybody got to believe the way they want, right? Hey, don' get me wrong. We not just fighting for the money. From everything I hear, these Amplitur are a bunch of *pendejos grandes*, you know? Me, I never seen one yet. None of us have. Mostly just damn Crigolit. They not so tough. They think they are, but that before they run into us. These Massood, they do pretty good, but they wouldn't last a week where I grew up. They too careful.

"I mean, when you out there, and you got two bugs with guns comin' at you, there no time to do strategic analysis. You just got to react. That not how the Massood like to fight. The Chirinaldo, those big guys are a little better, but they so big they make easy targets. So they operate a lot of the heavy stuff, like the e'ways and flaggers.

"The Crigolit guns are good stuff, though. If Pancho Villa had got some maybe we could've taken back California." She laughed again.

Will struggled to get a word in edgewise.

"Are you alone here?"

"Mostly everybody is out killing bugs, but there a few of the gang around. I was ask to meet you. You goin' to come out there? We take good care of you, man. No worries. Like I say, you responsible for us bein' here."

"No!" Seeing her reaction he softened his tone. "I'm *not* responsible. I got involved to try and *keep* people from being sent here. This isn't our business, isn't our fight. We shouldn't be involved. We need to get out before . . ."

"Before what, man? What you talkin'? The pay she's fine. Maybe these folk all look funny but they damn good to us. Hey, they *love* us. Nobody here give a damn what you be on Earth, what kind of person you were. Everybody here gettin' a fresh start, a new life. To the Massood, to the Hivisties and the S'van, we all just Humans. We fight for them and we do good. That all they care about." She gestured up the corridor.

"Most of these people here, at least the ones I command, they never had much. Not in their whole lives. Either they did shit work or got trapped doin' something they grew to hate. They came here lookin' to find themselves as much as for the *dinero*.

"I got three lieutenants under me." She giggled. "Not all at the same time, *comprende*? One sell insurance in Germany, another work for the IRS out of New York. His woman, she didn't do nothing there. She was bored pissless. She do something now, though. You ought to see her cut those bugs down with what we call here a cassion rifle. The last guy, he was turning into an old man chopping cane on Dominica.

"All of 'em are happy doin' the work here. The Hivistahm figure how to fake some of our food pretty good. I don' know what more anybody could want." Black eyes bored unforgivingly into his. "So why you say we should get out of this place?"

Her response had come hard and fast and it took him a moment to collect his thoughts and respond.

"Maybe a few people are suited for this, but we can't let the whole Human race get involved or . . ."

"Or what?" She wouldn't let him finish a sentence. They turned a corner. "Didn't anybody tell you *nada*? These Amplitur don' back out. You give 'em a meter, they suck you into this crazy damn Purpose of theirs." She illustrated by interlocking her fingers. He noted that the nails were painted bright red.

"That might be nothing more than Weave propaganda. We don't know that the Amplitur wouldn't leave us alone."

"Well, I know, mister. Because I seen the people they got fighting for them, the Crigolit and the Molitar. The Molitar are tough but they not real bright.

"I don' know how to say it in science words but it like they all got their brains scrubbed clean from the inside out. Right down to their genes. Me, I don' want my genes washed, *comprende*?

"I'd like to see an Amplitur, though. I understand they got pretty eyes and four feet and two big tentacle things comin' out of their faces. I'd like to see if I could squeeze one into another shape. You can' break their necks 'cause they ain't got no necks to break. They're invit . . . invertebrates. Hey, I can' even say that in Spanish." She laughed.

"I still don't understand why there aren't more of our people here. Are all Humans kept out on the front lines?"

"No, but I tell you something. Except for the Massood I think maybe we frighten these people a little bit. Or maybe they don' like us a whole lot personally." She shrugged. "It don' matter. Nobody give a damn if the Hivisties or the O'o'yan or those stuck-up Wais don' want to socialize with us. The S'van are better, but you can' really tell what a S'van is thinking, you know?

"I ask about it one time an' a S'van he tell me the other Weave peoples got 'delicate sensibilities.' I sort of understand. I mean, sometimes we're kind of loud, but hell, what do they expect? This ain't no fancy hotel lobby ball out here, it war. You can' blame somebody if it not in their blood."

"It's not in our blood, either," Will said angrily. "The danger of all this is that it's reinforcing a regressive tendency that mankind is just learning how to suppress."

"Hey, speak for yourself, man. Me, I been fighting all my life."

"Then you *have* done some soldiering." Now maybe her misplaced passion for fighting would be explained.

"Not what you'd call it, though I've spent some time with soldiers. I'm a professional *puta*, man. A whore, a prostitute. I leave Mexico City because my pimp was gonna kill me. All the time I hear about the rich tourists in Cancún, so I go there. One day this funny English guy come up to me and ask me some weird questions. Then he show me more gold than I ever see even in a jewelry store and he tell me I can get some for myself.

"For that much gold I do the stirrups from the ceiling, you know? But he say it nothing like that, and he talk a lot of crazy talk, and says why don' I give it a try? Well it not like I got much to lose, you know? So I say, why the hell not? I want to get as far away from Mexico City and the guy who's after me as possible, and Belize is farther than Cancún.'' She chuckled. ''Hombre, I had no idea how far away I was gonna get.'' She slapped him on the back.

''Hokay, that's Maria. Now you tell me about you.''

''I'm a musician, a composer,'' he replied without enthusiasm.

Her expression brightened. ''Hey, no keedding, really? I used to sing a little. I was gonna be a singer, you know? Got any idea how many poor girls there are in Mexico City? Sixteen million, man. And I think maybe half of them want to be singers. So hey, I was a lousy singer but a good whore. Now I find something better. And they make me a captain, maybe because I shoot straight, talk straight, and ain't afraid of nothing. What you think?

''Ranks-wise we got ourselves one colonel and a few majors, but that all so far. Maybe when more people get here we get some higher-ups. 'Major Echevarria.' I like that. What you think? Hey, you want to kill some Crigolit? We get you a weapon.''

''I don't want to kill anything,'' Will mumbled glumly. ''I just wanted to see how things were going.''

''Well they goin' pretty good, man, pretty good.'' She frowned. ''Hey, you want to meet some other soldiers now? I think maybe you don' like me.''

''It's not that.'' He looked over at her. ''It's just that . . .''

''Hokay, no problem, I understand. You just get here and this all a bit much. Tell you what. There's a squad due in pretty quick for some R&R. Maybe they here already. I introduce you to them.''

''How have they done?'' It was a question he didn't really want to ask anymore but couldn't avoid. Perverse curiosity, like the prizefight spectator. ''In the field, I mean?''

''Well, I tell you. The Amplitur forces were right on the outskirts of this big local city near here when the local command dump us in alongside the Massood. Since then we've push them back, oh, maybe a thousand kilometers. Soon we gonna push them right off this planet. That pretty easy to do here, you know? They got no Europe, no Africa. Just all the land in one place and water everywhere else.

''We gonna flank their whole forces and hit their main base of supply from behind, and if they try to come back on us we'll just slice them up into leetle pieces. Nobody thought like that before we got here. I mean, the Massood are good fighters but they too direct. They don' see things the way we do, and they stop to talk things over too much. By the time they finished talking, our people are wavin' back at them to hurry up and come on.

"I think maybe we too fast for them, you know? But they like us. Us being here and helping means not so many dead Massood. We could use a couple thousand more troops. How are things back on Earth?"

"The same," Will told her, not knowing what else to say.

"Be better if we could get more real soldiers here. We got a few. Recruited from vacations. One of our majors is a Russian. When they found out about us, he and his woman and kids all jump ship in Jamaica. He's a good guy. Speaks better Massood than I do."

"You speak Massood?" Will gaped at her.

"Sure." She rattled off a guttural stream for him. "Not so hard, though they don' swear enough. We teaching them some."

Will nodded to himself. The dissemination of Human culture had begun.

"Here's the lounge."

They entered a room in the shape of a half-moon. He remarked on the incongruity of the expansive window only to have her explain that it could withstand a tactical nuclear explosion and was polarized to dissipate any type of energy weapon. The furniture was clean and flexible while the room itself took the form of a series of descending concentric levels, like an intimate theater. Massood and Hivistahm sat and chatted and sipped liquids from exotic containers.

The lowermost level was full of chairs and couches. The Humans gathered there scrutinized flat screens the size of hand mirrors and laughed at what they saw. Echevarria led him down.

"What kind of casualties have you suffered?" Will inquired as they descended.

"We've had some people killed, some hurt. This is a war, man. You see your friend killed, it just make you want to fight harder. That something else I don' think the Massood understand. When they lose people they want to pull back. The more of us go down, the harder the rest want to fight. So maybe we do things a little backward, you know?'' She raised her voice as they approached the bottom.

"Hey, Joh, Chang! I got somebody I want you to meet. Come all the way out from Earth.''

For the second time Will was stunned at the reaction mention of his name produced. It seemed everyone wanted to shake his hand or kiss him. It was the last thing he could have anticipated, having come all this way expecting to encounter rampant homesickness and disillusionment. He wanted no part of their adulation.

Nor was any of it faked for his benefit in the manner of some of the music-ignorant matrons who supported the symphony because it was the sophisticated thing to do. This jumbled assortment of Humanity gathered on a far distant world meant every word they said.

A stockbroker named Davis had already made one recruiting trip of his own to enlist several of his friends. All had given up six-figure incomes to fight for the Weave.

"Making money is exciting at first," the man explained as he inhaled gas from a sealed flask, "but you reach a point in time where you realize it doesn't have much to do with real life. It just doesn't feel right. It becomes nothing more than dull routine to be followed mindlessly and unquestioningly." He gestured at the window. "There's nothing dull about what we're doing here.

"So you make a lot of money, so what? You buy a fancier car, a bigger co-op, you fly first class instead of coach, you stare dumbly at a bigger TV with a few extra buttons and knobs. What does that have to do with the meaning of existence? Not a damn thing.

"So you run for Congress or hope for an appointment to the Federal Reserve Board so you can lose yourself among thousands of other bureaucrats who can't accomplish anything worthwhile either. Is that a life's work?

"This—I mean, this conflict is about the structure of civilization. That's something worth devoting your life to.''

"That's what the aliens say," Will responded. Some of the smiles disappeared.

"You really don't know what's going on out here, do you?" the ex-broker said pityingly. "You're the one responsible for us being here and you don't know what's going on." He turned to Echevarria.

"Maria, has Will seen any of the prisoners?"

"No. He just get here."

Davis nodded understandingly. "Why don't you see if you can get him into Interrogation?" He turned back to the visitor. "Everyone here believes in what they're doing, regardless of where they come from or what they did back on Earth. We're all respected and appreciated in a way no Human beings have been respected and appreciated before, not in the whole history of our world. Have you heard about how the Amplitur treat those who do their fighting for them?"

"I've been told that they can exercise some kind of thought control."

"Thought control, yeah. Only it's more subtle than that, much more subtle. You won't meet any Crigolit zombies on the battlefield. The Amplitur aren't that blatant. This is much scarier. You know that they alter the DNA of subject peoples, insert traits that are passed on to all their offspring?" He glanced back at Echevarria. "You need to show him some of the prisoners."

"Yeah, show him," said an Oriental woman reclined on a maroon couch.

"Show him," suggested a dark man in the back, "those two Ashregan cavalry techs they brought in last week."

"Cavalry?" Will said.

"They use something like an airborne scooter," Davis elaborated. "Don't ask me to explain how they work. All I know is that they shoot along about two feet off the ground and can go over anything; water, mud, rock. Each one carries a driver and weapons specialist. They're real fast and they give us a lot of trouble, but when they take a hit everything pretty much disintegrates. On rare occasions we'll take one out and it'll come down soft.

"Usually they carry Crigolit, but sometimes something else will be aboard." He looked at Echevarria. "Introduce him to the enemy, Maria." The broker clasped Will's shoulder. "Come back afterward and we'll talk some more." His smile returned. "You're something of a legend here, you know? Not just among us. The Massood, the S'van, everybody knows your story."

"I don't want any part of anything like that," Will insisted. "It's all wrong."

"Doesn't matter. You can protest all you want to, but once a myth's emplaced it's tough to dislodge. I think you're stuck with what others perceive you to be." He sucked on his flask.

"Try and relax. Nobody's uptight here. The food's great and they keep inventing new kinds of entertainment for us. Got to keep the crazy Humans content." The glass flask he'd been sucking on slipped out of his mouth. Will could see where the tip had been chewed down, therefore it couldn't be glass . . . could it?

Davis noted his stare. "Some kind of perfumed inhalant. Gives a real nice buzz and it's nonaddictive. Imagine breathing strawberry sundae."

"Nostril nosh," one of the others quipped. Everyone laughed.

Maria took Will's arm, leading him upward. "See you later, people," she said over her shoulder.

"Yeah, take it easy, Maria." Similar salutations in half a dozen languages saw them off.

As they left the relaxation chamber behind, Will struggled to make sense of what he'd heard and seen.

★ XX ★

At a place where the corridor widened a line of oval, open-topped carts sat waiting. Inside was a control panel and two opposing flat benches. Echevarria touched several switches and the cart started down a side tunnel. Despite their speed no wind ruffled Will's hair. They were encased in some kind of invisible protective bubble.

"You look troubled," she said, searching his face.

"What gets me is that everyone looks so damn happy."

"They are happy, *compadre*. The people here, they come from all walks of life; different countries, different cultures, but here everyone is the same. We all foreigners in this place. They doing something worthwhile and meanwhile piling up gold like crazy. Who wouldn't be happy?"

"I wouldn't. How many do you think would keep fighting if not for the gold?"

"I don' know. Some yes, some no. Don' matter, because there *is* gold."

"Hasn't it occurred to anyone that the S'van and Hivistahm and the rest might not want to associate with you because you're all fighting for money?"

"Don' matter. They think we pretty strange anyway."

"When people start retiring back to Earth others are going to ask where all this gold is coming from. The secret will get out."

She shrugged. "Fine with me. You know, some of these people brought their kids."

"You mentioned the Russian."

"An' some have had kids since they been here. We got our own nurseries."

238

"Don't the parents care about schooling?"

"We got a couple of teachers taking care of that. Kids learn other stuff here, too. Take the Saki sisters. They speak Massood better than the Massood themselves."

"It's not fair to bring kids into something like this. They haven't the foggiest notion of the issues at stake. How old are they?"

"Nine and twelve, I think."

"They'll forget about Earth."

"Don' matter. They happy, too. Make good soldiers some-day."

Will shuddered. There had to be a way to put an end to the nightmare.

The cart deposited them onto a moving sidewalk deep inside the mountain. Massood here wore sidearms and glanced questioningly at the Humans. There was considerably less of the casual conversation he had noted on his arrival. This was a place of business.

As they walked Echevarria would occasionally address one of the soldiers, sometimes utilizing her translator, other times speaking directly in crude Massood. They passed Hivistahm and O'o'yan as well. A Wais flowed past, impeccable of attire, graceful of stride.

"How do you communicate out in the field?" he asked her.

"We start using English by default. It's easier than the translators."

"Nobody tries to push their own language?"

"Hell, everybody too busy trying to learn some Massood or S'van. Easier back here. Always a few Wais around to help out. They pretty nice folk. Me, I like 'em even better than the S'van. With the S'van you never know for sure if they laughing 'cause they like you or not. You get a reaction out of a Wais, you know it for real." She paused outside a doorway. Will was startled to see two Hivistahm guards bearing weapons.

"Those guns don' kill, only paralyze," she told him. "Can't spare Massood from real fighting for this kind of work." She grinned. "Course, they'd never waste a Human on guard duty. These lizards never have to shoot at anybody anyway. Nobody ever escape from this place."

She murmured into a wall pickup, waited until they were passed through to another gate. Behind the second checkpoint lay a high-ceilinged room full of unadorned furnishings. Echevarria put up an arm to restrain Will, ran her other hand along an invisible barrier.

The two prisoners had ample room in which to move about. "This place will hold four," Echevarria explained. "They don' like to put more than four in any one cell."

Will blinked. The plainly attired captives gazed back at him with equal interest.

Small eyes peered out from beneath protruding brows. An odd ridge of bone framed each recessed ear. The nose was flat, with twin openings. Though not large, the mouth appeared capable of opening wide. Perhaps the deep jaw was loosely hinged. The arms were long, the legs too short.

Those differences aside, both prisoners looked very, very Human.

"Ashregan," said Echevarria grimly. "Funny faces and squatty builds, but otherwise they don' look so different from us, eh? You never mistake one for a Massood or S'van, but they could pass for you. Not me. I was never that ugly."

One of the aliens approached the barrier and spoke softly. "He want to know who you are," Echevarria said.

"How . . . how do you know?" Will remembered the translators. Echevarria helped him adjust the setting on his own.

"You not wearing a uniform, so he's confused."

"These are allies of the Amplitur?"

"For about six hundred years. Long enough for the Amplitur to mess their genetic material around real good. Now all they can think of is serving their damn Purpose."

Will fingered his translator as he stepped up to the barrier. "You look very much like us."

"We have also remarked upon the similarities." The male had a thick, sweet voice. "I am only a simple soldier of the cause, and not very familiar with such concepts as parallel evolution. I would not presume to comment further." Shockingly, he smiled.

Will forced himself to reply. "Why do you and the Amplitur seek to conquer all other peoples? Why do you allow them to be your masters?"

The Ashregan exchanged an astonished look with its female companion. "There are no masters within the Purpose. We are all its servants. Each species serves to the best of its particular abilities. The Ashregan fight. The Amplitur advise.''

Echevarria leaned close. Her perfume was strong. ''Señor Davis, he told you they were subtle, eh? The Amplitur don' give orders. Only 'suggestions.' ''

The Ashregan overheard. ''We could argue semantics for days, months. Are Humans not receptive to the advice of the S'van? That does not make them your masters.''

''In the field we do what we think best,'' Echevarria shot back.

''In the heat of battle everyone improvises,'' the Ashregan responded.

''If you want to live for this Purpose of yours,'' Will put in hastily, ''that's fine, but why this compulsion to drag everyone else along with you?''

''Don't you think we know that it would be easier to ignore you? Would it not spare us much suffering and pain? But we who have experienced the Purpose could not think of ourselves as civilized if we failed to extend its beauty and benefits to the uninitiated.''

''Even so,'' Will insisted, ''what if the uninitiated don't want any part of it, don't have any need of its 'benefits'?''

The Ashregan smiled afresh. ''Look around you. What do you see? Humans and Massood, Hivistahm and S'van unnaturally allied in an effort to resist unity and peace. The Weave is a wholly artificial organism, held together only by a misplaced desire to forestall the inevitable advance of the Purpose. Without it the many species would quickly fall to fighting and bickering among themselves. Where such conflict and dissension exists there can never be real harmony, true contentment. I ask you, Human: On which side lies logic and truth?

''As for the Ashregan, we are content.''

''That because the Ashregan are brain-dead,'' Echevarria said with a derisive snort.

The male looked over at her. ''You confuse unhappiness with lack of choice.'' Small dark eyes turned back to Will. The voice was earnest, pleading.

''Your people are great fighters, of unique and astonishing ability. Certainly you are the most unusual opponents the Ashregan have ever encountered. Why perish on behalf of Weave folly when you could be enjoying all the peaceful delights of the

Purpose? You deny yourself true peace because you have been seduced by the lies of the S'van and others. The S'van are the most accomplished liars in existence. The manipulation of words is their art, the seduction of meaning their music. They are as accomplished at prevarication as you Humans are at warfare.

"Try to convince your brethren. The Amplitur cannot be defeated, the Purpose never dissolved. Thousands of years of history cannot be reversed. The destiny of your kind is the same as that of every other intelligence: to join in the Purpose and not in fractious, primitive alliances such as that of the Weave.

"The Amplitur will welcome you joyfully, all the more so because it will avoid the needless death of many. The death of a single sentient diminishes the Purpose."

Will was silent for a long moment—dissecting, considering, mulling over a simple soldier's eloquence . . . or programming.

"As I understand it," he said finally, "the end of this Purpose is to be the integration of every intelligent species into a single all-encompassing organization?"

"That's so." The Ashregan was pleased.

"To what final end?" Will asked sharply.

"The Amplitur surmise that when this integration has been completed, all unified intelligent life will make the jump to the next stage of evolution. Whether that is to be joint participation in some kind of universal overmind or something else no one, not even the Amplitur, know for certain."

"How many intelligences have to participate to produce this critical mass? How big does it have to be?"

"That the Amplitur do not know. They have been trying to quantify the necessary volume for thousands of years."

"But what if there's nothing at the end of all this? No next stage of evolution, no melting pot of a supermind? What if the Amplitur just go on absorbing one species after another to no eventual end?"

"But the end exists."

The female spoke up from her place on a bed. "What is your notion of the be-all and end-all of intelligence, Human? Does your kind have a better theory?"

Will was taken aback. He'd come here to rail against war, not discuss philosophy and metaphysics. "No. We just feel that it's better to be left alone to find our own destiny than to sacrifice our individuality to some kind of compulsive herd mentality."

The female sat up, imploring with both hands. Five fingers on each, Will noted, but no nails. Just smooth and rounded at the tips.

"There is a sweetness, a joy of completeness within the Purpose that one who is not part of it cannot imagine."

"All that notwithstanding, some people might prefer independence of thought and action."

"It is illogical and uncivilized," the male insisted, "to favor dissension above cooperation."

"Then it's our decision to remain uncivilized. It's the way we are."

"Only because you've known nothing better," said the male calmly. "I fear my arguments are failing to reach you. If there were an Amplitur present . . ."

"If there were an Amplitur here you'd see the Purpose soon enough." Echevarria had been leaning against the wall, listening. Now she straightened, gazing narrowly at Will. "It'd reach out and lovingly embrace you with its tentacles and look deep into your eyes with those beautiful ones of theirs. Then you'd feel a little tickling, you know? Right here." She tapped the side of her head.

"Pretty soon you see the light. You understand. That what they say the Amplitur can do to you. They done it to some poor S'van and Massood. Some got cured by treatment and others just died twisting in their beds." She gestured derisively at the prisoners.

"These things are the product of eight or nine hundred years of genetic manipulation. They wouldn't know an independent thought if it bit them on the ass."

"We do not expect to convince you." The Ashregan was not in the least upset. "We are only simple soldiers. All we can offer are our honest sentiments and the example of personal contentment.

"We have heard some things about your kind, Human. The Ashregan, too, used to fight among themselves, long ago. Now such unsupportable conflicts are a matter of history. We work together to serve the Purpose, and we are happy."

"Sure you are," Echevarria responded. "You better be happy, or the Amplitur will come and work on you some more."

"You wouldn't know happiness if confronted with it," the

female commented. "You refuse to acknowledge the possibility. You have not yet matured sufficiently to deal with the concept."

"Oh, I can deal with the idea of happiness," the captain told her. "What I have trouble dealing with is the notion of racial lobotomy. Come on." She took Will's arm and he allowed himself to be led away.

"Remember!" the Ashregan shouted after him. "There is independence within service and there is the independence that allows you to kill on behalf of meaningless abstraction." The alien voice faded from translator range as they reached the first checkpoint. "It is uncivilized!"

Out in the corridor Echevarria eyed Will questioningly. "What do you think?"

"I'm not sure," he replied slowly. "They were more thoughtful than I expected, and they look so much like us."

"Yeah, they do, don' they? Parallel evolution. Except they all brain-dead."

Will was shaking his head uncertainly. "They didn't act like zombies, or robots."

"Oh, they as independent as you and I," she agreed, "except when it comes to this Purpose business. Then it like their brains, their ability to think, goes flat like the line on a dead man's heart monitor. It only start up again when you change the subject.

"Speaking to which, you want to go out on a foray? I can get you a weapon issued. You can watch us push the Ashregan and the Crigolit back over the cordillera toward the sea. Soon as the next load of troops arrive we gonna make our big push." She whispered conspiratorially. "The Massood are still hesitating, but we're tired of sitting around. The major say it time to kick some butt. You know how to say that in Russian? And if there are any Amplitur around we gonna kick them, too. Course, they ain't got no butts." A wolfish grin creased her beautiful if slightly worn face.

"After we finish with this world we gonna go on to the next one. I don' know which, the S'van haven't told us. But we sure not gonna sit around here for a hundred years like the Massood been doing." Her open hand palmed his backside and he jumped slightly.

"You know, for a composer you got a cute behind. I never know a composer. Maybe if you get bored later, you want some company . . . *comprende*? It's nice when you don' have to do it for money."

"I'll think about it" was all he could find to say, caught off guard by the abrupt change of subject. "I've got a lot to think about, and J'hai wants me to see more of the base, and . . ."

"Yeah, sure." She gave him a friendly whack. "You want to know where I am, you just ask around, hokay?"

"Okay."

"Want to see something interesting?"

"Sure," he said warily.

She showed him her hand. It was slim, feminine. "Take a close look." She straightened her fingers.

"I don't see anything," he told her, feeling stupid.

"Don' you see? There's no lines." It was true: her palm was perfectly smooth. "These S'van are pretty smart, but for practicals you gimme a Hivistahm every time. If they weren't such pansies they'd make good fighters.

"Had that taken off by a zeit shell. Right here." With a finger she traced a line on her wrist two inches below the hand. "The lizards do real good regeneration. But you lose the lines. Fingerprints, too. The Amplitur now, they say the Amplitur can even grow your fingerprints back. They say the Amplitur can grow anything." She gestured toward the east.

"You get shot up out there, if they can find enough pieces, the Hivisties can put you back together pretty much the way you look before, even if you do end up with plastic guts. They take real good care of us here, you know? Maybe they don' like us a whole lot, but they take care of us."

They climbed into the little transport vehicle. "What about the S'van? I thought the S'van liked everybody."

"That what they say. Me, I never seen one be anything other than friendly. But it hard to tell about them. Sometimes I think maybe they joke around 'cause they got no choice. It hard to get mad at somebody who joking all the time. I hear there's not a lot of them. Hell, even the Lepar could chop them up pretty easy." She grinned. "Hey, you know how many Lepar it takes to load a photic charge?"

"No," Will mumbled as the vehicle sped along.

"One to hold the tube, one to load the charge, and a third to keep the first two from trying to eat the parts." She cackled uproariously.

"I kind of like the Lepar." The tension in his voice surprised him.

Her laughter faded. "Hey, don' get me wrong, man. I do, too. Everybody like them. They work their tails off to help everybody else. They so slow and dopey-looking, how could anybody get mad at one?" The vehicle began to decelerate.

"I'll take you back to J'hai. Sure you don' want me to have a sidearm issued to you?"

"No," Will said firmly. "There are too many guns around here as it is."

⋆ **XXI** ⋆

Thoughtful-quick-Probing had work to do and was irritated by the timing. It glanced up and around, the right eye swiveling independently on its short stalk to peer two-thirds of the way down the mottled orange back, where an irregular protrusion erupted from the smooth skin.

"Awaken, Thoughtful-new-Prober," the Amplitur insisted.

Miniature eyestalks uncoiled from within the fleshy eruption, tiny eyes shining wetly at the tips. The bud leaned slightly forward, attentive and expectant.

Another two time periods and it would be fully formed, at which point it would separate from its parent to embark upon existence as an independent entity, already well educated and mature. A successful budding was much to be praised, the complex process always to be coddled.

But such was the skill of Thoughtful-quick-Probing that despite its delicate condition its presence at the upcoming interrogation session had been requested by Command.

It was awkward. A maturing bud ought not to be disturbed while its body was embarked on the sensitive process of taking over its respiratory and circulatory functions from the parent.

The blood vessels and nerves of parent and offspring would be linked a while longer. Thoughtful-quick-Probing tried to be optimistic. The encounter would be educational for the new individual.

The bud responded to the thought by waving its miniature tentacles, exercising evolving limbs already capable of grasping small objects. The four legs moved only slightly within their

247

encasing skin. They would be the last part of the new individual to separate from the parenting body.

The room was crowded. Thoughtful-quick-Probing noted the presence of most of the Command staff together with a number of Ashregan, Molitar, and Crigolit officers. Assuming position to one side, it exchanged silent greetings with the others of its own kind while Bent-high-Commanding shifted forward. Immediately all Amplitur thoughts were stilled in deference to the presence of their mentally mute allies.

Bent-high-Commanding spoke aloud, struggling to convey its thoughts by means of the crude, wispy vocalizations that were utilized by all other sentient races.

"You all know that we have lost Vasarih. We are in danger of losing Aurun. Vasarih was always in question. Aurun we thought we had won. The Aurunians had forgone the deviancy of the Weave in favor of furthering the Purpose. Recent developments have adversely affected their outlook." The Crigolit set to muttering among themselves. Evidently this last information was new to them.

"The Weave has engaged a new ally, an extraordinarily effective fighting species which appears to embody a heretofore unencountered combination of high technology and primitive ferocity. They were first detected in small numbers on Vasarih and it was thought initially they might be native to that world. The presence of two intelligent species on the same world is not without precedent.

"Further encounters and new information have revealed that these beings are in fact native to a world of their own. The number participating in Weave actions is still small but increasing. Their modest presence on Vasarih has rapidly made our presence there untenable. There have also been deleterious side effects."

"Examples?" mused Thoughtful-quick-Probing, admonishing its bud to pay close attention.

"The Massood seem to fight better when placed alongside these creatures, who have the ability to make those in their company function more efficiently. It may be that their influence will extend to and include such as the S'van and Hivistahm, though there is as yet no evidence to support such a hypothesis.

"The threat they pose is therefore manyfold and complex. Those cadavers which have been dissected have not been especially informative, though I am told preliminary examinations suggest that their neuromuscular systemology is unusually dense for a mammalian life-form.

"As would be anticipated, the Weave has been extremely protective of them, doing its utmost to shield them from our observation. However, that has not prevented us from securing several live specimens. It is to these few that we owe what real information we have." Bent-high-Commanding deferred to Solution-pale-Overseer, who assumed the former's speaking position.

"The specimens have revealed exceptional physical abilities, but no daunting devices. Their weaponry is standard Weave issue. They bring with them no new superweapons, nothing we have not dealt with previously."

A Crigolit officer spoke up, not in the least deferential. "Well on our way to winning Vasarih we were, until these creatures arrived. Unorthodox methods of fighting they employ. The Massood we can predict and strategy devise to counteract, but not these. Unreasoning and illogic are their allies. One would think them not sane. Sacrifice themselves they will, and unpredictably."

Solution-pale-Overseer waited until the Crigolit's mind had cleared. "We have yet to formulate standards by which to judge these creatures. Each unit appears capable of functioning independently of higher supervision. This makes them extremely difficult to clear from a contested region.

"Physically they are remarkably powerful, yet agile. They have mastered Weave weaponry with impressive speed."

Another Crigolit stepped forward. "Aurun lost now as well. All but secure was that world. Guidance in this matter we must have, Learned Ones. Tactical decisions we must make."

"They will be forthcoming," murmured several of the Amplitur simultaneously.

"Time now for enlightenment," said Bent-high-Commanding. A door opened at the back of the room and many eyes of differing focus turned. Two enormous Molitar entered, escorting between them something only slightly shorter but far less massive. The Massood officer halted when his guards did, blinking at the lights and the encircling aliens. She was surprised to see the Amplitur.

One of them was about to bud. She wished fervently for the

simplest of weapons even though she could not immediately have made use of it. Her arms were bound to her sides by restraining foam.

They had provided her with a translator. "Why have you brought me here? What do you want?" She glared at the half-dozen Amplitur who were silently inspecting her. "I did not think you exposed your precious skins to the possibility of physical harm."

"You understand our abhorrence of violence," said Solution-pale-Overseer.

"You mean your desire to have others do your fighting for you."

"We serve as it is most efficacious for us to serve." Solution-pale-Overseer approached the captive. "Should I desire to do so I would not require the assistance of another life-form to aid in dismembering you." The Massood tried to shrink away from the dark, brilliant eyes.

"You have not been brought here to die," Bent-high-Commanding assured her in its strange sucking whisper of a voice, "but rather to provide information." The Massood steadied herself.

"We have had some difficulty on Vasarih."

"You have *lost* Vasarih," countered the prisoner, nose twitching violently as her fur bristled. Gray eyes met those of slitted gold.

"A not unreasonable assessment of the situation," the Amplitur admitted. "We have lost much not because of you but because of these peculiar Human creatures. You have found others to do your fighting for *you*, therefore pause before judging us."

The officer struggled against her restraints. "Massood fight alongside Humans. We do our own fighting."

Bent-high-Commanding gestured fluidly with a tentacle. "This cannot be permitted to continue. These Humans are disruptive. We can be patient and contain them, as we have contained others. But we do not like to step backward when we can advance. We would like for you to tell us what you know of them."

"I am sure you would," she responded, but with less bravado than previously. Her eyes kept darting from the one addressing her to the other silent, unblinking Amplitur standing silently behind it.

Bent-high-Commanding retreated, relinquishing its place to Thoughtful-quick-Probing. At its approach the Massood tried to retreat only to find her path blocked by the Molitar. Thoughtful-quick-Probing sighed inwardly and concentrated, eyes retracting on their stalks. A moment passed.

The Massood seemed to slump slightly. Her eyes gazed straight ahead, motionless in their sockets. Nose, ears, lips had ceased their normal twitching.

A mind was a void to be filled, Thoughtful-quick-Probing mused. Information inserted, suggestions made. No locks, no barriers. The officer responded to the gentle but irresistible probing of the six as directed by the one.

In a sense this was simpler than verbal questioning. No time was wasted dealing with objections or the identifying of subterfuges. No foolish curses or loud objections interrupted the steady flow of information. They inserted the queries and recorded the verbal responses. The Massood's mind responded as straightforwardly and efficiently as any instrument.

When it was done, Thoughtful-quick-Probing eased out. The Massood shivered and started to collapse, to be caught by the Molitar on her right. Thoughtful-quick-Probing discussed the completed procedure with its bud as it backed away.

"Take her back, treat her gently," said Bent-high-Commanding. "She has a good mind which someday may serve the Purpose."

"There are fewer than we thought," ventured another of the six.

"Which renders their accomplishments that much more impressive," said Thoughtful-quick-Probing.

"This danger cannot be underestimated." Bent-high-Commanding projected impatience combined with anxiety. "The Weave will take all steps to keep secret the homeworld of such a valuable new ally. This Massood does not know but suspects that they come from a remote region."

The eldest of the six spoke up. "Acquiring the necessary information will be costly."

"That is so, but the infection is virulent," said Bent-high-Commanding. "It must at all costs be contained before it can spread. I await advisement."

The Crigolit, the Ashregan, and the Molitar stood quietly as the Amplitur communicated among themselves. Tentacles wove abstract patterns in the air, eyestalks coiled protectively inward. In its silence the sight was impressive, even awe-inspiring. Not for what was visible, but for what was not. Not for that which was revealed but for that which was implied.

Eyes uncurled to regard the room. Bent-high-Commanding spoke.

"This species is new to Weave technology. On a world called Motar the enemy maintains a major training facility. We have minimal surveillance there. This will be increased. Energy must be expended to learn all that can be learned about these beings: whence they arise and how they come to fight alongside the deviant Massood."

"All setbacks are temporary. No defeats are final." Thoughtful-quick-Probing offered its opinion. "We will deal with this as we have throughout all history: by redoubling our efforts to eliminate the problem."

The Amplitur mutually concurred, signaling politely to their allies in the room that the conference had come to an end. The Crigolit and Molitar and Ashregan acknowledged, began to file out discussing what they had seen. Enthusiasm and energy had replaced their initial uncertainties. Some of it was genuine, some thoughtfully implanted by the tentacled quadrupeds they were leaving behind.

The Amplitur could not bear to see their allies unhappy.

★ XXII ★

Will was putting the finishing touches on the cantata. It was better than *Arcadia*, better than anything he'd ever done. Someday soon when the Weave had taken its misplaced leave of Earth he hoped to hear it performed.

Arcadia had brought him recognition. The cantata would secure his reputation. No more teaching, no more tutoring of tone-deaf young women from wealthy Southern families. The commissions would arrive en masse, hopeful and pleading. An opera next, or another symphonic poem.

Life was good.

Footsteps on the aft deck drew him out into the bright Caribbean sun where Caldaq stood, awaiting permission to enter. T'var followed, hidden by the Massood's bulk. After admitting them Will went to the secure locker, popped the combination, and withdrew the translator they had given him.

"Kind of unusual for you to be out in broad daylight." He directed his words to the base commander.

"I will not waste time," Caldaq replied somberly as he sat down on the floor, crossing his legs and leaning back against the navigation table. "We think that the Amplitur may have found Earth."

"Oh." All thoughts of opera and music fled as Will sat down heavily on the couch opposite the Massood. T'var had struggled up into a chair. "How?"

"We are not sure, but that does not matter. For some time they have been unusually active in the region around Motar. You will recall that that is the world where Human recruits receive their initial training. Now the Amplitur are assembling a considerable force near P'hoh. That is an uncontested outpost world, not worth a Weave attack, not worth defending heavily. The rationale for a gathering of such force there has been the subject of much recent speculation and study.

"P'hoh is the nearest Amplitur-visited world to your system."

"I see," said Will slowly. "What happens now?"

"The Military Council has been discussing the matter with the General Council. It has been decided to inform your multiple governments. The responsibility for deciding how to proceed must in this instance rest with them. It is a decision the Weave cannot take unto itself."

Will blinked. "I thought the idea was to keep everything a secret until I had a chance to convince you that my people are better off not knowing about your war, much less participating in it."

T'var gave a slight sideways twist of his head and beard. "That's no longer possible, Will Dulac. If the Amplitur come here, the Weave can help defend your world, but not if it is kept ignorant of what is happening. Being familiar with principles of contemporary warfare you know that we probably cannot prevent the Amplitur from landing at least some troops. As elsewhere, any decisive battles here will be fought on the ground."

Will had no reply.

"Several thousand of your people have had Weave instruction, are familiar with Weave weaponry and tactics. We are prepared to bring them back from Vasarih, even Aurun, to help train more of your kind. We are confident that your professional military will make the necessary adjustments far more quickly than the novices we have already successfully trained.

"The degree of readiness your world can achieve depends on how rapidly it can prepare and how long the Amplitur delay."

"But they may not even be coming here," Will argued. "They may not know about Earth."

"They've encountered your kind on Vasarih and Aurun," said T'var. "The Amplitur wouldn't commence this kind of buildup near a useless world like P'hoh without"—and the humor was successfully filtered through the translator—"a purpose."

Caldaq was watching Will closely. "There is an attendant possibility. Everyone up to and including the Council places great value on your personal opinion. If you choose to make a decision on this matter and let it be known . . .''

"No," Will stammered as the import of the Massood's statement struck home. "I can't make this kind of decision."

"Then we have no choice but to inform those of your people who do, which is to say, your governments. I know your feelings on this, Will Dulac. You can still make your presence felt. Your governments may feel as you do and choose not to prepare, to elect instead to try and reason with the Amplitur. Perhaps you will be successful where every other species has failed."

Will's mind reeled with the possibilities. At last the thief was abroad in the interstellar night. Should mankind talk, or take up arms? His own instinct was still to talk, though if Caldaq was to be believed, the precedents were less than sanguine.

T'var felt similarly. "The Amplitur know of your kind from Aurun and Vasarih. They see you as a serious threat. I don't think they are coming to talk."

Will bent forward, supporting his head in his hands. Memory of the soothing, uplifting music he'd been working with earlier had been shunted aside by dread and uncertainty.

"All right. I guess something has to be done. God knows I didn't want this."

"You were warned." Unblinking cat eyes regarded him coolly. "Years ago I told you that contact between your kind and the Amplitur was inevitable. We have delayed formal contact here largely because of you and your convictions. I must tell you now that you have yet to convince me that your kind is inherently peaceful. Not that it would matter to the Amplitur, though I cannot seem to make you see that.

"At the same time I am not as convinced as are some others of your people's usefulness as fighters. You have spoken of their unpredictability, and in this you have yet to be proven wrong. I remember clearly the incident involving the stolen weapons. Such a thing would never happen with Massood, or any other Weave peoples.

"It may be that your opinion will eventually win out. It is not for me to say. I am only an administrator. But any people facing the likelihood of Amplitur attack deserve to be informed of the possibility so that they may take such steps as they see fit."

"When?" a disconsolate Will mumbled.

"As soon as possible. It was hoped that you could advise us

on procedure. We have no precedent for dealing with such an aberrant sociopolitical structure.''

A pained expression crossed Will's face. ''You're an administrator. I'm just a musician. I don't know how to deal with politicians. Give me some time to think.''

Caldaq rose fluidly from the floor, automatically bending so as not to bump the ceiling. ''Remember that every day, every minute may be bringing Amplitur assault forces nearer your system.''

''And it may not. I'll keep that in mind.''

Caldaq and T'var left the Human to his thoughts.

Back at the base S'van regarded much taller Massood. ''It would be useful to convince the Human. You know what will happen. The Amplitur will arrive with sufficient force to impress the natives, but they won't attack. First they'll offer the philosophy of the Purpose. If Will Dulac is right about his kind, there'll be some who will listen.

''This cannot be permitted. If the Amplitur are allowed access to Human leaders, those individuals will soon find themselves uncritically espousing the Purpose. It's happened too often before, on other worlds. Our studies here have shown that Humans rely extensively on their chosen leaders to make decisions for them, often to the exclusion of individual thought.''

''I know, Second.'' The Massood commander was uncharacteristically contemplative. ''It is only that what is proposed will be a difficult thing to sleep with.''

''I don't see it that way. We're doing what is necessary to save lives: S'van, Massood, Hivistahm, and in the long term, Human.''

''I see that. It is only that I would prefer to do so honestly.''

''We're being truthful in all things,'' T'var insisted. ''This world would have been drawn into the conflict eventually.''

''I suppose so.''

''And consider this, tall Captain: Suppose the Amplitur had discovered this world before us? Imagine Humans as allies of the Amplitur, fighting alongside the Molitar.''

''No one fights alongside the Amplitur. They only fight for them. But you are right, my hirsute advisor. The notion is unpleasant.'' They parted, each to his station, each to his thoughts.

* * *

"I'm afraid I don't have any brilliant suggestions on how to proceed with this. What have you come up with?" Will sat in the chamber with Caldaq and Soliwik, T'var and Z'mam. He'd slept very little the previous night. "Do you want to make a show of force, or set shuttles down in the major capitals, or what?"

"Our studies suggest that your people are easily traumatized," said Soliwik. "We would prefer that you make the initial contact by way of a personal presentation." Both ears bent forward intently. "You must understand that the concept of multiple governments on a single planet, among a single species, is still new and alien to us."

"To alleviate local concerns insofar as that is possible," Caldaq added, "we will conduct simultaneous presentations for the two most powerful tribes."

"I heard about the Russian officer on Vasarih," Will informed them. "He'll probably do a better job of it than I will. I wish my Uncle Emile was here. He was an alderman, knew how to talk to politicians."

"You've known us longer than any of your kind." T'var's tone was soothing, reassuring. "You'll do just as well."

Thus committed, Will leaned forward, folding his hands on his lap. The back of his seat obediently flexed to accommodate him.

"How am I supposed to persuade people? They're not going to believe this no matter what kind of pictures or tapes I take with me."

"I will travel with you," Caldaq replied, surprising him. "T'var will come also, together with a Hivistahm recorder and a Wais in the event of translator failure. I think the four of us in person should be sufficiently convincing, don't you?"

"Not at first," Will said dryly. "At first they'll think you're refugees from a movie. But you're right: in the end they're going to have to accept the evidence.

"Accepting you won't mean acceptance of your agenda, however. You'll see. Once people realize there's fighting involved, a major conflict, they'll back off and demand that you leave." He was feeling more confident. Revelation, he'd decided, did not necessarily mean involvement. Considering how far things had gone, it might even be for the best.

"Oh, you might get some countries to mobilize defenses, but

no one will rush to send troops offplanet to help fight your war. You'll see.''

Caldaq was about to reply when he was interrupted by Z'mam. Only the extraordinary circumstances allowed the commander to ignore the breach of protocol.

"That will be sufficient for now," the S'van murmured. Caldaq eyed the squat being but kept silent.

"If we could get on television somehow . . ." Will was murmuring.

"No." Soliwik was insistent. "In order to be convincing this must be done in person. Your primitive visual transmissions allow for considerable electronic trickery."

"Be prepared for whomever we meet to be terrified of you," Will warned them. "Humans can be very paranoid."

"Your point is noted," she replied.

Will sighed deeply. "Can one of your atmospheric shuttles make it as far as Washington? I'll show you where that is on a globe."

"We know where Washington is," said T'var confidently. "While you've been busy with your music we've done our own work." He gestured with short, stubby fingers. "I personally could find my way to the Lincoln Memorial, the Smithsonian, and the White House."

"You know the city better than I, then," Will told him. "If I'm wrong about this and you people are right, then it means the end of everything. Art, music, culture, a unified, peaceful world. Everything."

"You sell yourself short," T'var retorted. "If anyone should sell themselves short it ought to be the S'van, and we do not."

Will had to grin at the diminutive alien. "Your kind would joke at the Apocalypse."

"It is our way." T'var was apologetic. "As you are well aware."

Will turned thoughtful. "I don't think we should set down on the White House lawn. We don't want to cause a panic. It has to be some place where the government can't lock us all up and study us at its leisure, either, or manage the news for their own purposes."

"Where then?" T'var inquired.

"I think I know."

★ XXIII ★

"Mr. Benjamin, sir?"

C. R. Benjamin looked up from his desk at the junior editorial assistant. Her face was flushed and her eyes wide. He leaned back in the recliner and put his hands behind his head.

"Let me guess. It's Cambodia again, isn't it? What is it this time?"

"It's not Cambodia, sir."

"Well, it better be something at least as important. I'm doing the final corrections for the Sunday. I can't be bothered every time somebody stumbles across a minor crisis they're convinced is worth an editorial. How the hell do they expect me to put out a paper? I don't spend all my time at parties and fund-raisers like *some* people. Unlike them I actually involve myself in publishing."

"I know that, sir." She hesitated. "There's a flying saucer on the roof."

He leaned forward, glanced absently at his computer screen. "That's not bad. Tell whoever's responsible that they've brightened my day. See, I'm smiling." His lips twitched infinitesimally at the corners. "Tell them also that what's funny once isn't funny twice, and if anybody bothers me again this morning they'll find themselves spending the rest of their career composing obits. I take it you're not responsible?"

"No, Mr. Benjamin, sir."

He returned to his work, but only for a moment. "You still here?"

"S-sir? There really is a flying saucer on the roof. There's a

259

man in it. He says his name is William Dulac, and that he's from Louisiana.''

C. R. Benjamin made a face. "Well. That explains everything, doesn't it?''

"That's not all, sir. There are four aliens with him. He says there are lots more of them waiting down in the Caribbean.''

"Really? What would they be doing there now when the season doesn't start till November?''

A large bald man in his fifties appeared in the doorway, and the assistant gratefully made way for him. Benjamin squinted at the new arrival.

"Marcus? Don't tell me they suckered you into this, too?''

The city editor had a deep, bemused voice. "It's for real, C.R. I mean, it's not huge, but you couldn't helicopter it onto the roof.''

"What is all this?'' Benjamin rose sourly from his recliner. "Can't I get any work done around here? If you people want to play jokes, fine, but have the decency and common sense to wait until lunchtime!''

The city editor edged into the room while the editorial assistant uttered a strangled sound and ducked into a corner.

Something tall entered, ducking to clear the doorjamb. Its angular form was covered with fine gray fur and a tight-fighting jumpsuit cut off at knees and elbows. Additionally it wore a belt studded with strange devices. Long arms hung toward the floor. A toothy elongated muzzle sniffed constantly at the air.

It was followed by something resembling a small tailless dinosaur, differently clad and equipped, which advanced with the stride of a nervous ballet dancer. In succession appeared an extremely hairy, muscular dwarf, an ostrich clad in haute couture, and a man.

"Should I call Security?'' The city editor hovered near a wall panel.

Silently C. R. Benjamin regarded his visitors, ignoring the rising clamor in the hallway beyond. Eventually his gaze settled on the sole Human among them.

"Tell me one thing, young man. Do you really have a flying saucer on the roof of my building?''

"It's only an atmospheric shuttle,'' Will told him. "It's not even saucer-shaped.''

"I see. You know how people are. Always reaching for the

easy description. That's why it's so hard to find good writers anymore. They all seem to use the same words.'' He glanced at his city editor. "No Security, Marcus. But do close the door.''

The city editor nodded, did as he was told despite the crowd that was now pressing tight around the portal.

C. R. Benjamin slowly took his seat. "We're not going to have any trouble here, are we, Mister . . . what was your name, son?''

"Dulac. William Dulac.''

"If you were in Nawlins right now, what would you likely be having for lunch?''

Will frowned but replied. "Oyster po'boy.''

The editor nodded approvingly. "Then you are from Louisiana. If you're a fraud, you're a Southern fraud, and at least they're more interesting than most.'' The noise in the hall was growing louder.

"Marcus, tell those people to get back to their desks and that everything in here is under control.'' The city editor complied. Gratefully, Will thought. The pretty editorial assistant accompanied him without having to be told.

C. R. Benjamin rubbed his hands together theatrically. "I like stories that walk into my office. It's cheaper than paying correspondents. Now then, if this is some kind of elaborate gag or stunt now's the time to enlighten me, son. You're not from the Fox network, are you? I know our reviewers been giving their new shows hell.''

"We're not from Fox, sir, and this is no gag. I sincerely wish it was. These people,'' and he indicated his silent companions, "really are from other worlds. Each represents a different species. They're united in an organization they call the Weave.''

Benjamin waved a hand. "I suppose you'll allow me time and means to confirm what you're saying? Right now I'm only operating on what I can see and hear, which is no way for a journalist to act.''

"My friends are amenable to physical examinations,'' Will assured him. "They understand your caution because they've encountered it before, on other worlds that they've visited.''

Benjamin grunted slightly. "Let's just for the moment proceed on the assumption that you all are what you claim to be. This Weave of yours, it's kind of like the EEC?''

"Sovereign and independent worlds united for reasons of

trade, commerce, and mutual defense,'' replied the Wais in ac-
centless English, startling the editor.

Will thought that under the circumstances the old man was
exercising remarkable self-control. Of course it was unlikely
that anyone would become editor in chief of one of the most
important newspapers in the United States without it.

''So this is the long-anticipated First Contact.'' Benjamin
thought to turn off his computer screen and activate the recorder
on his desk. ''With not just one alien race but four. I wouldn't
have thought there'd be four.''

''Sir, there are hundreds,'' Will informed him quietly.

''Hundreds.'' Benjamin considered. ''And they decide to
make contact here in my office. Excepting you, of course, young
man. They obviously contacted you a day or two earlier.''

''I'm afraid not, sir. Actually they've been here for a number
of years now, observing us, learning, working with some of us
in secret.''

''I see. I presume you will in due course enlighten me as to
the reason for this secrecy.''

''Yes, sir.''

Benjamin indicated the Wais. ''The one with the feathers
speaks better English than my sportswriters.''

''Linguistics is a Wais specialty, sir. However, all of these
here speak some Earth languages to some extent. I speak some
of theirs. And we have these translators.'' He held up the device
hanging from his neck, touched his earpiece.

''Well, if it's not the first contact it's still quite a scoop. Biggest of the past thousand years or so. And you're presenting it
to me. I'm very grateful to you, Mr. Dulac. How does a young
man from Louisiana come to . . . ?''

''Everything will be explained, sir,'' Will said, interrupting.
''Right now we have to deal with more important matters. And
you're not quite getting an exclusive here.''

''Oh. *New York Times*?''

''No, sir. The other major tribe.''

''Tribe?'' Benjamin frowned.

''*Izvestia*, sir.''

''I see. Well, I don't think that's going to cut into my circu-
lation much. I'm sure you have reasons for proceeding as you
are, which you no doubt will disclose in due course.''

''Yes, sir. We're here because there's information that needs to be disseminated, and fast. If it was up to me it would stay a secret, but that's no longer possible.''

"Very well. My organization will be more than happy to assist. But if I may inquire, why here, and why in this manner? It's not what I would have envisioned.''

"We need to get the word out uncensored as well as quickly, sir, devoid of possible government spin.''

"Then you chose well, son. If this is all for real you won't have to twist my arm to clear tomorrow morning's front page for you. Will tomorrow morning be all right for your purposes? That'll give us some time to work up articles, get some expert opinions, and take some pictures. You don't mind pictures?''

"Not at all,'' said the Wais.

"We will be accommodating. It serves our needs,'' added Caldaq in rougher but still comprehensible English.

"Excellent. Of course, if this turns out to be some kind of elaborate prank, I'm going to make everyone involved wish they'd never been born.''

"I wish it was just a prank, sir,'' said Will somberly.

"The reason for our presence . . .'' Caldaq said to Will.

"Not yet. He needs reassurance first.''

"Excuse me?'' Benjamin's gaze shifted from alien to man.

"Sorry,'' said Will, aware he'd been speaking in Massood.

"You spoke of hundreds of intelligent species. That's a pretty daunting revelation, son.''

"What's even more daunting is the fact that not all of them may be friendly.''

At that Benjamin's gaze grew narrow. Believing it would have more impact, Will allowed the Wais to explain the history of the Weave-Amplitur conflict, concluding with a summation of the current situation. When the ornithorp had finished, the editor sat silently in his recliner, trying to absorb the import of what he'd heard. Every light on his desk console was flashing for attention. Irritably he turned them off.

"We don't have to get involved,'' Will said carefully into the silence. "It's not our fight. We're not members of this Weave.''

"That's true.'' Benjamin noted the expectant stares of the four aliens. He could not read any of their faces, knew nothing of their expressions, but there was no mistaking the intensity of their gazes.

"The bird-thing said these Amplitur, the creatures who lead

the opposition, want every other kind of creature to believe exactly as they do. The people in this Weave feel otherwise. They've quietly recruited some Humans to help in the fight and that's why the Amplitur are coming here. To keep any more of our people from joining up."

"Something like that," Will admitted. "The question is, are they coming to fight or are they coming to talk? Or are they even coming this way at all?"

"No, son, those aren't the questions. The question is can we afford to sit around on our duffs and wait to find out without making any preparations? Now don't get me wrong: I'm as peace-loving a man as you'd ever want to meet. If you've ever read my paper you know I don't even approve of these little so-called 'surgical strikes' where we go in and clean out a drug lord or two.

"On the other hand, I don't much like the sound of these Amplitur, and I'm not sure I want them having anything to say about the way my grandkids believe when they grow up."

"You must join with us." Not trusting his command of the language, Caldaq relied on his translator. "If only to protect yourselves."

C. R. Benjamin's gaze shifted shrewdly back and forth between Will Dulac and the alien commander. "Do I detect a slight divergence of opinion here? No matter. Whatever final decisions are made I think it behooves us to at least look to our own protection. You see anything wrong with that, Mr. Dulac?"

Suddenly Will felt that all the years of work with the Massood and their allies meant little. That in a couple of moments his importance to them had been superseded by the old man behind the big desk. It had taken place so quickly that realization of the fact was only now beginning to set in.

"It is not required."

A startled Will turned on Caldaq. "Wait a minute. You said that . . ."

"What we said," replied Caldaq, speaking slowly to insure that his translator would have ample time to choose the best words, "was that the Amplitur may be coming this way and that given that possibility your world should be prepared to defend itself. We did not say that you would have to participate in that defense. It was recommended, not demanded. If necessary, the Weave alone will see to the defense of your world."

"We're not members of your organization," said Benjamin. "Why should you stick your necks out for us? Those of you who have necks."

"For years now several thousand of your people have been fighting on our behalf. Not a great number, but not an insignificant one, either. Some have died in Weave service, if not for Weave ends. It would not be civilized to abandon their homeworld to the Amplitur."

"That's very altruistic of you."

"It is not in any way altruistic." Caldaq had to wait on the translation. "We would do this because some of your kind have rendered us service and more may do so in the future. And because we see danger in allowing the Amplitur to have their way here."

"What if this Cajun's right?" The editor pointed at Will. "Suppose when the people hear about your conflict they *don't* want any part of it? Suppose they just want you and your friends to take off and leave them alone?"

"What is your opinion?" The Hivistahm recorder spoke for the first time. "What do you think the majority of your population will do?"

"I don't know. That's why we hire pollsters. And I can only speak for this country, not any others. What do you think these Amplitur will do if they come here?"

"First they will try and talk," Caldaq told him. "Then they will attempt to have close contact with your leaders, in order to adjust their minds. If they are prevented from doing these things, they will try to control you by force. Finally, if they consider you more dangerous than potentially useful, they do their best to exterminate you."

"The bird-thing said that in these cases most fighting takes place on the ground, and that it's virtually impossible to prevent forces from being landed."

"That is correct," said the Wais. "Captain Commander Caldaq can provide a more thorough explication. I am a translator. I have little knowledge of military matters." The Wais shuddered visibly.

"How would you defend us?" Benjamin asked.

"We would bring back the several thousand of your kind who have learned how to make use of Weave technology," Caldaq explained. "The remainder of the defense force would be composed of Massood, with appropriate support from the rest of the Weave. The Amplitur forces will not land in your urbanized areas, whose populations they will wish to preserve intact. They will fight to take control of your defense installations, power facilities, and food supplies to compel capitulation."

"It's your individuality they wish to destroy, not your lives or prosperity," T'var added. "Whenever possible they will contest resistance in open country or small towns, until they have defeated all forces sent against them."

"Seems very civilized," said Benjamin.

"There, you see!" exclaimed Will excitedly. "So who's to say we can't talk them into leaving us alone?"

C. R. Benjamin scratched his forehead. "If any of what I've been hearing is true, they don't seem much on leaving anyone alone."

"Precisely." Caldaq took a step forward, unable to remain in one place any longer. A Massood with less self-control would long since have been pacing the room. "You are for their Purpose or against it."

"The Amplitur have their own art, their own aesthetics," Will found himself arguing. "Why can't we try sharing with them instead of fighting them?"

"But it's all directed toward honoring this Purpose of theirs, right?" Benjamin asked. "Seems pretty restrictive to me. I like editors and writers who disagree with me. Keeps things lively. I don't know that I'd care for a homogenized world, however peaceful."

"We don't know that they'd restrict diversity," Will insisted. "For years these people have been telling me that our society's unique among the inhabited worlds. If we can convince the Amplitur of that, I think there's a good chance they'll leave us alone."

"Maybe. Maybe. But I don't see how we can ask a bunch of folks from somewhere far away who don't even know us to do our fighting for us . . . assuming there's any fighting to be done," he added to forestall Will's protest. "In any event, that's not a decision to be made by me, or you, or anyone in this room."

"You've heard our history. How do you intend to proceed?" asked T'var.

"I'll see that you're given a forum. That's *my* job." Leaning forward, he activated an intercom on his desk.

An agitated voice quickly responded. Will could overhear other voices talking in the background. "Mr. Benjamin, are you all right?"

"Calm down, Mattie. Everything's under control."

"What are those . . . ?"

"Questions later. We've got a paper to get out. Tell Elena I want the front page wiped."

"Mr. Benjamin, the whole front . . . ?"

"All of it, right up to the damn masthead. And I want plenty of space inside. No, forget that, leave it as set. We're going to do a special insert. Gives us more flexibility. When you're through ring Prestwick at CBS: I owe him one. After that get me the president's press secretary. Then see if you can put me through to General Maxwell over at the Pentagon." He grinned up at his visitors.

"Joint Chiefs of Staff. We'll see if we can't pull a quick session together, either here or there. They don't usually let visitors sit in on their meetings, but I think in your case they'll make an exception." He redirected his voice to the intercom.

"Tell Maxwell it's C.R. at the *Post*, and call my wife and tell her I'll be working late tonight."

"Yes sir, but . . ."

"That's all for now, Mattie. More later." He clicked off, leaned back in his chair, and folded his hands across his belly. "We have a few minutes. Maybe we'd better go over what you're going to say to the power brokers.

"You know how to talk to these visitors, Mr. Dulac, but I know how to talk politics. Different languages. We don't want anybody thinking yes when somebody means no."

"Do you think they will listen to us?" Will asked him, suddenly tired. "Do you think they'll believe any of it?"

"They will when the biologists I'm going to call in a minute from now reveal the results of their examinations. You've seen too many old movies from the forties and fifties. Watch how closely they pay attention after you tell them that an identical encounter is taking place in the Kremlin."

Despite the old man's confidence Will wasn't sure what to expect. Discord certainly, then debate, resistance.

* * *

There was all that and much more. Humanity had to accept not only first contact with an intelligent alien race, but with hundreds. Immediately thereafter man was confronted with the intimidating revelation that he was about to be plunged headlong into a millennia-long conflict the existence of which he had evolved in ignorance of.

As argument raged across the face of the planet as to how mankind should react, hundreds of Weave-trained Humans began returning from Vasarih and Aurun. They were not politicians, or professional soldiers, but ordinary souls recruited off the streets of Central America.

They scattered to their countries of origin, where each had his or her moment in front of the camera. Expressions of dissatisfaction were few. Among the exuberant majority the rationale for their contentment varied considerably.

Or as a cane cutter from Trinidad put it, "It not like shooting other people, mon. Dee Crigolit dey ugly things. So are dee Molitar and dee Acaria. Dee Ashregan got funny faces and dee all been brainwashed. That what dee Amplitur do to you if deh get you. Wash out your brain till dere nothing left except dere crazy Purpose. And dee pay, she's damn sight better dan for cutting cane."

Will and others of like mind looked on helplessly as public opinion shifted with astonishing speed from paranoia to combat fever and the world began to mobilize to meet the perceived threat. Weave specialists patiently explained why they could not predict when and where the enemy would arrive, and why they could not prevent it from landing troops. They might set down outside Manhattan or in the heart of Africa. There was no way of telling.

At least Earth would not suffer the fate of those primitive worlds which had been forced to face bombardment from orbit. Within months several dozen Weave warships had taken up stations around the blue planet. The Amplitur would be forced to attack Earth in the same fashion as they might assault any developed Weave world: by winking into normal space, offloading troops as fast as possible, and fleeing back to the safety of Underspace before their ships could be targeted and destroyed. They would also have to deal unprepared with Earth's unique and confusing geology.

It developed that because of intense fighting elsewhere, Massood troops could be spared only to assist in training the natives and not for actual combat. But the Hivistahm and Yula made certain that Weave weaponry in abundance was made available to the multiple Human armies. Huge transports materialized in orbit to offload vast quantities of material and supplies.

For the first time in mankind's acrimonious history, all the armies of the Earth were united against a common foe. Together with their intent, fast-learning Human counterparts, Massood professionals devised multiple strategies designed to contest any enemy landing. Coordination of worldwide defenses proceeded at a most satisfactory pace.

Will was in the expanded communications and study center at the base, watching as Weave technicians simultaneously monitored dozens of domestic television broadcasts. They recorded everything for in-depth offworld dissection, from the sublime to the absurd.

"The Amplitur will be at a considerable disadvantage when they arrive." Caldaq was leaning against a rail, observing the busy technicians below. "The distance they have to travel is extreme, and they can know but little of your world's peculiarities."

"We can't count on that," Will pointed out.

"That is true. But it is one thing to hear that a world's landmass has disintegrated into many sections, another to cope with the tactical problems it poses. The Amplitur will be forced to learn as they fight." He turned from the rail. "Friend Will, I read disappointment in your expression."

"I thought there'd be more debate. I thought more people would be reluctant to make preparations for war." He laughed bitterly. "I thought that the Soviets and Americans would at least hesitate before trusting each other. The two armed forces practically fell into one another's arms. After so many years of spying on each other they knew exactly how best to integrate their units." He looked up at Caldaq.

"I heard that the president was miffed over how you deployed your ships."

"He was not alone," Caldaq admitted. "Many of your tribal chiefs were upset that we did not first discuss the matter with them. At the time we did not realize it was a question of social propriety, thinking it purely a military matter. Command did not wish to waste time." He hesitated. "Often I find myself believing that your people need to be protected against themselves.

"The Amplitur will find their work here difficult. Consider the business of trying to secure planetary power sources. Normally a landing force will seek out and attempt to take control of the few important fusion facilities. But you have no such centralized power sources. Your energy grid is as fragmented as your society. Power is derived from a few nuclear plants and a multitude of small, inefficient facilities that burn fossil fuels." His lips curled behind the twitching black nose.

"Your society is founded upon confusion. If an artist were to propose it, it would not be believed. Imagine a species achieving your level of technology and still burning irreplaceable hydrocarbon deposits simply to generate energy! The illogic of it numbs the mind. Fortunately it will confuse the Amplitur as well. I am told there is not a single fusion plant on the entire planet."

"We've had trouble cracking the problem." Will was apologetic without knowing why.

"Astonishing. Had you matured normally you would of course have acquired the technique long ago. Instead you have dissipated your energies in endless petty tribal quarrels.

"That may now turn to your advantage. The Amplitur will find you as puzzling as did we when first we began to study your society. I would very much like to be in their command center when they burst out of Underspace preparatory to landing troops only to find that your population is scattered across six landmasses instead of the familiar one. There is also the matter of your extreme, unpredictable weather.

"No, they are going to have a very difficult time. Which is not to say," he added darkly, "that their failure is guaranteed. Fighting may continue for some time. But have no fear. The Weave stands beside you, even as some of your people have stood by the Weave."

For gold, Will thought. Most of the recruits who'd returned from Vasarih and Aurun could care less about the Weave, their rarefied pronouncements on television notwithstanding. He knew it would be useless to point that out. People girding for possible battle would always prefer an encouraging fiction to an uncomfortable truth.

"So you have no way of knowing when they're likely to arrive here?"

"Not at your world, no. A ship traveling through Underspace generates an immensely diffuse distortion wave around itself. In interstellar space this is not detectable. But when it encounters something as dense as a solar magnetosphere the disruption can be detected. It is akin to an object traveling underwater. In deep water it is not noticeable, but as the water becomes shallower waves may be produced on the surface.

"Many vessels entering your sun's magnetosphere will produce considerable distortion. With luck we may have one or two weeks' notice of the enemy's arrival."

"A couple of weeks," Will murmured. "That's not much time to get used to an idea."

"The majority of your species appears to be coping with the possibility quite well."

Will shrugged. "I suppose. A lot of the world's been waiting quite a while for the bug-eyed blood-sucking monsters from space to show up."

Caldaq's puzzlement was evident. "The Amplitur are not bug-eyed. Nor do they suck blood. If one discounts the fact that they are invertebrates they are physically quite attractive. It is their philosophy that is repugnant." He turned thoughtful.

"But I believe I understand the reference. It is as if your entire species has been waiting thousands of years for a conflict of this nature. I have heard individuals speak of preparing to fight the armies of the 'Devil.' "

Will shrugged. "People employ whatever metaphors reassure them. When they think they're going to war, they need something to hate."

"But we of the Weave do not hate the Amplitur. Hate is an unnecessarily excessive emotion. Disagree yes, envy yes, dislike surely, but not hate. Hate wastes protein. Even primitive predators kill without hating their prey. Hate is . . . immature."

"What did you expect from us? We're not a mature species. Your own specialists have pointed that out repeatedly. Speaking of which, I've a question for you.

"It looks like that in spite of everything I and those who think like me can do, we may end up fighting for the Weave's cause. We're receiving Weave protection and assistance. But no one's discussed our actually joining the Weave yet.'' He eyed the tall Massood sharply. ''Why is that, Caldaq?''

''The General Council believes,'' the commander replied smoothly, ''that the task at hand is to prevent your world from falling under the sway of the enemy. Matters of social integration must wait until that is assured.''

''I suppose so,'' Will agreed. But the evasiveness of his friend's reply troubled him.

He peered over the railing. Hivistahm and O'o'yan bustled between stations, impacting on clusters of S'van. Lepar delivered messages or scoured one corner of the expansive chamber. A single Wais swept grandly through an exit, trailing feathers and perfume.

''Do you think they'll attack here? After all, this is still the center of Weave operations on Earth.''

''I think we are reasonably safe here. They must first secure a landhold before they can think of fighting on the water, and your world generates sufficient electronic background noise to make things difficult for their detectors. But I cannot promise that they will overlook this place. Their instrumentation is very good. I wish I could convince you to accept a sidearm.''

''I'll tell you the same thing I told a woman on Vasarih: I'm not into guns. I don't like guns. Plenty of other Humans feel the same way, despite what you've been seeing on the national broadcasts these past months. Driving off an invasion is one thing, but once that's over and done with you'll see how fast they choose to put their weapons aside. People are like that after every war. They throw themselves mindlessly and wholeheartedly into battle, only to experience mass revulsion near the end. It wasn't always like that, but we've matured a lot during the last half century.

''If you think you're going to get a united planetary government to permanently mobilize against the Amplitur on the Weave's behalf then I think you're in for an unpleasant shock.''

''You are so certain of your species, Will Dulac. Have you forgotten that not long ago you yourself used a gun, and against your own kind? You killed.''

Will shivered slightly at the memory. ''I did it to save the lives of my friends. I'd do it to protect my family, if I had any family. That's a helluva lot different from taking up arms against someone whose philosophy you happen to disagree with.''

"The Amplitur Purpose is more dangerous to you than any weapon."

Will turned toward the doorway. "Let's not get started on that again. I'm not carrying a sidearm, and that's final!"

Caldaq did not smile. Instead, his upper lip rippled rhythmically. "No need to get violent about it."

"I'm not getting violent." He spoke sardonically to his friend. "Sometimes I think you people are just as tricky as the S'van. You just hide it better."

"No one is as tricky as a S'van," Caldaq corrected him. "I was merely pointing out the obvious."

"Yelling because you're upset about something and picking up a gun with the deliberate intention of shooting another intelligent being can't be equated. They're not the same thing."

"Aren't they?"

"I don't want to argue about it."

"Naturally not. Since we first met you have made noble claims for your species, but I fear they reflect more of your personal philosophy than Human reality."

"We'll see." The doors parted to allow Will egress. "When this is all over, maybe even before it's over, we'll see."

∗ **XXIV** ∗

Weave ships monitoring the solar magnetosphere recorded the approach of the Amplitur fleet a little more than two weeks in advance of its projected arrival in Earth orbit. Despite the extensive preparations mankind had made, the announcement was still greeted with shock around the world. The Weave warships in orbit went on heightened alert. As for the natives, there was little they could do except continue their preparations, wait, and watch the sky.

When the enemy armada finally materialized above the central Atlantic it was to disgorge a fusillade of troop shuttles surfaceward, not to talk. There followed a frantic, amazingly brief exchange of projectiles and high-energy-beam weapons at the outer fringe of the ionosphere which reminded farmers in the Azores, who were directly below, of the occasional rare wintertime visit of the aurora borealis.

The massive mutual discharge of energy produced very little destruction. One of the defending warships was damaged. One of the attacking vessels was totally destroyed.

Ground-based forces obliterated several of the rapidly descending shuttles, overwhelming their defensive capabilities. The rest achieved touchdown, landing on four of the six populated continents. From then on victory or defeat was a matter of hourly reports.

Despite his newly bestowed official appointment as a high-ranking liaison-at-large, Will felt eerily divorced from the conflict. There was little for him to do except answer the questions of the occasional reporter visiting the base looking for an angle. Will knew little of combat, communications, or international relations, and right then the services of a composer were not much in demand.

He took to wandering aimlessly through the greatly enlarged base, whose functions had in many ways been superseded by outposts in Washington, Moscow, Brussels, Tokyo, Rio, Nairobi, and Sydney as Humanity sought to coordinate the defense of its world. International communications were regularly disrupted by the invading forces. The battle quickly became fragmented as central control was lost.

This did not quite result in the demoralizing disruption the Amplitur had anticipated.

The Crigolit unifer slowed her floater and waited for the rest of her unit to catch up. One by one they cut their drives to study the terrain ahead. Individual scanners showed nothing but sandy yellowish hills devoid of all but rudimentary vegetation. It was an unpleasant place for a fight but an important one, for not far ahead lay an important hydroelectric installation.

This entire miserable planet was an impossible place to fight, she reflected. No landmass as she knew it, no unified power grid, and dozens of tribes to contend with instead of a central government that the Amplitur could bloodlessly take control of. Why, you couldn't even speak properly to the enemy, who spoke hundreds of languages. It was civilization as asylum.

Other units were supposed to be swinging down from the north to prevent native reinforcements from arriving. Of course, the installation could have been destroyed by long-range fire, but then it would someday have to be replaced. Much more practical to capture it intact.

They had encountered no opposition since leaving the base. Hopefully any local defenders had been shipped north to contend with the descending force. Local farmers hid when the unit shot past, except for the grubs who threw rocks and sticks which invariably missed their intended targets. The Amplitur would change that, the unifer knew.

The assault would have been easier from the air, she reflected, but native technology included a bewildering and surprisingly effective plethora of surface-to-air projectiles. In fact, the immense store of native as opposed to imported Weave military weaponry had been a disconcerting surprise.

As yet no one had been able to supply a rationale for the

existence of so many native weapons. The planet showed no signs of conflict. It was almost as if the natives found something aesthetically appealing in the design and construction of mass weapons of destruction, which were far more sophisticated and deadly than their overall level of technology seemed capable of producing. Their architecture was primitive, as were their agriculture and art. Only in the manufacture of weapons did they excel. While this aberration was intriguing, it posed unexpected problems for those charged with local pacification.

She pushed the scanner up on her head, to the base of her antennae. Hardly surprising that their tactics should be as unconventional as their civilization. One never knew what they might try next. A unit in the field had to be prepared for anything.

She was just issuing the order to advance when the Tuaregs erupted from their self-contained foxholes to obliterate ninety percent of the invaders. The rest were caught as they attempted to retreat.

Distribution of the recently developed air-conditioned foxholes by a Japanese-American consortium had begun only a few weeks earlier. They were impervious to enemy scanners and completely portable. The Tuaregs collapsed them and radioed for pickup while floaters exploded on the surrounding sands and immolated Crigolit popped and crackled. A couple of the robed fighters scavenged among the alien corpses, much as their ancestors had done a thousand years earlier in the wake of ambushed caravans.

It was time to return to base, the subjoiner decided, no matter what the damned command group said. Her troops could not advance through soggy ground that threatened to swallow them in their field armor. They needed aerial transport. The trees around her were so close together and the vegetation so dense that floaters could not maneuver through it.

Perhaps the natives could walk on mud, but her fighters could not. They had been told that this would be an excellent location for a forward base from which to infiltrate nearby urban concentrations, one that could easily be concealed from the air and expanded at leisure. Resistance in the region was spotty and poorly organized. With good reason, the subjoiner thought. No one voluntarily makes their home in hell.

Their landing had gone unopposed. They had encountered none of the screaming, madly gyrating native aircraft that had so devastated other landing parties, nor any of the heavily armored ground vehicles with their projectile weapons and big guns. Who could have imagined that a world not part of the Weave or the Purpose would wait groaning beneath the weight of unused war material? It defied reason as well as experience.

Behind the scout team, engineers were already digging in, or trying to. Solid ground was a scarce commodity hereabouts. But with time they would overcome the initial difficulties, providing a base from which attacks could be launched on the major urban centers to the east. Then control of at least one portion of this world's shattered landmass would be assured.

A call sounded from up ahead. The subjoiner strode forward, made her way slowly and cautiously between the huge trees and their buttressing roots.

A procession of fallen forest giants blocked the way. It would be simpler to go around than take the time and energy to cut a path, she decided. Flipping her visor back down she examined the surrounding jungle, eyescanners searching for any large infrared splotches that might signify the presence of a sniper or enemy scout.

Something made a wet splatting noise against the side of the subjoiner's armor. She looked down to see liquid spreading where a pellet of some kind had burst. As she drew her sidearm her squad hunkered down in the muck.

A simple gesture of defiance in the absence of effective opposition, she decided. Common enough among disorganized primitives.

Suddenly she dropped her weapon and began dancing on all four legs, screeching madly and slapping at her side. The pale liquid was dissolving her body armor, hissing its way through the flexible shielding. She fought to free herself before it ate completely through.

Instead of rendering assistance, her subordinate joined the rest of the squad in racing for the nearest armored transport. Once inside and safe from anything up to and including a tactical nuclear strike, she made her way grimly to the operations center of the huge vehicle.

"How many of them are there?" she asked the technician in charge.

"We cannot say. This region is alive with life, much of it Human-sized. The readout is confusing. Certainly there are some out there. I . . ." She stopped, began to wheeze loudly. The subordinate turned nervously.

"What is it, what's going on?"

"Air's failing!" yelled another tech. "Right on top of us they are, plugging the ventilation system."

This is ridiculous, the subordinate thought wildly. This one transport boasted enough weaponry to level a small city. But there was no small city to level outside, no concentrations of enemy troops or vehicles, no low-flying aircraft. Only a few natives. Hisses of frustration filled Operations as Ordnance let loose with a variety of weapons.

None of which were of much use when those responsible for aiming them couldn't breathe. The recycling system kept the air inside the transport clean and pure in the presence of radiation, biologic agents, or toxic gas, but the external vents had to be clear. Coughing and choking, she tried to give orders.

"Use the armatures!" Those mechanical limbs were designed to clear just such blockages, but something had jammed them as well. The subordinate realized they had no choice but to go outside to clear the obstructions.

As hatches popped and the Crigolit began to emerge, the Bantu fighters were waiting for them.

The Ashregan officer in charge of the expedition hated fighting in the mountains as fervently as did his troops. It was cold, and while one's body armor maintained a respectable internal temperature the terrain and climate combined to make the going difficult. Some of the canyons where they were operating were narrow and winding enough to intimidate the most experienced floater pilot.

The leader buzzed for attention as he activated his rapid-fire cannon. "Only a few of them," he reported as he checked his visor scan. "Off to the right twenty degrees."

"We'd better have a look." The officer angled his floater and his squad followed.

There were four of the natives, living in what had to be a temporary abode: a small domed structure fashioned of some thin, light material. Stakes secured it to the ground in the middle of the meadow. Though only one native was visible, the scanners had no trouble sensing the others through the thin fabric walls.

As soon as the floaters swung into view, the juvenile made a noise and ducked inside.

The officer was the only one equipped with a translator programmed to interpret the local language. As his squad set down near the shelter, he activated the unit and waited for the natives to emerge.

There were two adults and two juveniles. They huddled together as the officer and two flankers cautiously approached. The rest of his squad waited on their floaters, nervously scanning the surrounding terrain.

The adults were taller than Ashregan or Crigolit. With the exception of the Molitar they were taller than any of the civilized races. Their size did not intimidate the officer. They were not armed. The adult male had his arm protectively around the female.

"What is it?" the native asked uneasily. "What do you want with us?"

"We know that an important military installation is located in this vicinity," the officer declared through his translator, "deep within one of these mountains. Scattering devices have prevented us from pinpointing it." The juvenile male favored the Ashregan with a succession of contorted expressions. The officer ignored him.

"Do you know where this facility is?"

"I'm just a fireman," the native replied. "We're just up here camping out. I had three days' vacation coming. You gotta have some time off, time to get away from things. Especially with the invasion." He looked past the officer, at the hovering floaters.

"Where'd you guys come from? There aren't supposed to be any of you around here."

"Why don't you go back where you came from?" the female said before her mate could silence her. "Why don't you leave us *alone*?"

The officer decided that this was neither the time nor the place to explain the beauty and nature of the Purpose to her. When the Amplitur arrived they would do it more efficiently. Dissemination of the Purpose was not his assignment.

He told them as much, hoping they might understand. They

were intelligent, even if their society was hopelessly primitive. But not their military organizations, he reminded himself. This world was a study in bewildering contrasts.

"We don't know what you're talking about," the man muttered. "I'm just a fireman. We're just camping out."

The officer raised his sidearm and aimed it at the juvenile female, who clung to her mother's leg. "If you do not tell me what you know of this installation's location I will kill your youngest offspring." The Amplitur would have disapproved, he knew, but there were no Amplitur in this forlorn place; only him and his troops.

The adult female gasped and clasped both arms around the juvenile, who began to make loud wailing sounds while generating moisture from her eyes. Native fear reaction, the officer surmised. The adult male took a step forward, halted when the two flankers pointed their weapons at him.

"Listen to me. This won't gain you anything. Do you know what a fireman does? When things burn I put them out. I'm not a military man, I'm not even in the Reserves. I don't know anything."

"You are lying. All of you people are familiar with your local military facilities. Your entire society has organized for this conflict."

"Not us," the native insisted. "Is there any fighting in this area? Do you see any guns? You can check our tent if you want."

"We are interested in information, not weapons." The officer gestured and one of his flankers went to check the shelter. He was back in a minute.

"No weapons or communications devices, sir."

The officer indicated acknowledgment, again directed his attention to the natives. "I see that you are afoot. That tells me that you live in the immediate area. Difficult to believe therefore that you would be unaware of a major military installation."

"Why? The army doesn't publicize the location of its bases. Why the hell should I know anything about it?"

The officer fired once, scorching a black line on the ground close to the feet of the juvenile female. The older one screamed, looked frantically at her mate.

"Tell them! Go on, Jeff, tell them. They'll find out anyway, sooner or later. It's not our job to shield the installation. They're the ones with the weapons. Let them do the fighting."

"I can't do that, Trace." The man was obviously wrestling with conflicting emotions.

The officer aimed the muzzle of his gun at the juvenile female's forehead, whereupon the adult female began remonstrating with her mate even more violently.

The man hesitated, dropping his head along with his voice. "It's in the south flank of Mt. Harrison." His eyes came up, burning. "It won't do you any good. It's heavily defended. There are Massood in there, too. And they put in some new stuff a few weeks ago that you bastards don't know anything about."

"Mt. Harrison," the officer murmured, consulting the topographic schematic on his visor. "Which one is that?" He gestured with the sidearm. "Quickly."

The man gestured defiantly. "About a mile west of here this canyon forks. Take the north branch and follow it to its end. From there you can see several peaks. Harrison is the highest."

The officer considered shooting them all, but his training in the Purpose decided him against it. These four presented no threat. Without communications devices they could not warn their fellows, and from what the officer knew of the region it would take them days to walk to the nearest facilities. By that time heavy weapons would have targeted the enemy installation and extirpated it.

They reached the side canyon rapidly and turned north. The cliffs were steep but not vertical, so the floaters were able to make good progress. Scanners reported only bare rock ahead.

They had been fortunate to encounter the isolated family group. The officer could empathize with their desire to escape the pressures of combat. Under identical circumstances and without the Purpose at stake he might have acted similarly. The two juveniles would make fine converts someday, peaceable and understanding. Unlike their barbaric, unenlightened parents.

Wheeling smoothly around the canyon's curves, they never saw the fine net that blocked their way. It was fashioned of new ultraweb mesh, invisible to their visor scanners. At the speed they were traveling, the last of them could barely slow in time to avoid smashing into his fellows.

Not that it mattered, once the massive weights at the corners of the net were sent tumbling into the canyon. Entangled floater pilots fought helplessly within the mesh, struggling to find a way out. Floater engines stalled and flared. Weapons burned inadequate holes in the wispy material as net, floaters, and Ashregan plunged toward the bottom of the canyon nearly a thousand feet below.

Firing wildly, one weapons operator struck a colleague's entangled vehicle. It exploded, destroying two more. By the time the mass of screaming soldiers and machines struck canyon bottom all were enveloped in flame.

Emerging from concealment, Humans strode to the edge to stare at the still burning bodies and vehicles far below. Those on the western ramparts waved to comrades opposite, men and women on both sides of the abyss acknowledging the success of the ambush.

Atop the eastern cliffs one man pushed up his cap and tucked his red-and-black flannel shirt back into his pants as he addressed a tiny communicator.

"Lukas, tell Denver we got another bunch." Far below something boomed dully. "No survivors. No, I don't think they had time to get a warning off." Camouflaged microdishes relayed his words through the mountains, shielded from orbiting scanners.

"One more thing. Get ahold of the Sorrell family back on Clover Ridge and see if you can talk 'em into spending some more time camping. They're pretty good at rustling up business."

★ XXV ★

Mature-absent-Leg did not mind the name. The limb had been lost in a juvenile accident, and it was a matter of confidence that upon regeneration as an adult the need for a change of identification was not felt. Besides, supreme Amplitur bioengineering had assured that the regenerated leg was indistinguishable from the original three.

Repeat-close-Looker stood nearby, contemplating the one-way security screen which separated them from the small chamber beyond even as last-minute checkouts were run on the activated recording equipment. Both Amplitur worked hard at controlling their thoughts, but it was impossible to mute their anticipation completely. After all, this was to be their first opportunity to confront one of the natives in person.

Some apprehension had been expressed by members of Mature-absent-Leg's staff at the Commander's decision to conduct the interview with only a single companion for support. Their concerns had been dealt with. They were safe now in Underspace and it was a task which could not elegantly be delegated. Mature-absent-Leg awaited the forthcoming confrontation eagerly. Repeat-close-Looker projected similar feelings.

Two Molitar entered the room with the specimen between them. It was a male, clad in the laundered but torn uniform of one of the many native armies. Observing that it walked with a pronounced limp, Mature-absent-Leg's sympathy was aroused. The native did not appear intimidated by its surroundings or its massive escort.

Repeat-close-Looker thought at the Molitar, who bowed slightly and left the room. The native evinced some confusion at their departure. Its puzzlement grew when a chair emerged from the floor near its feet together with a stand which held a basin of clear, cold water and samples of captured native food.

"Please sit down," said Mature-absent-Leg. A translator picked up the whispery voice and conveyed it to the room by means of concealed speakers.

The native's head jerked around. He pivoted slowly as he searched the room, his gaze finally coming to rest on the mildly reflective security screen that separated him from his interrogators.

"Why should I?"

A typically brusque and not unexpected native response, Mature-absent-Leg reflected. "Because there is no reason for you to stand. You must be tired."

"I'm not tired," the native snapped. When no response was forthcoming he sat down, clearly relieved to have the pressure off his damaged leg.

"I am going to let you see us now. Do not be shocked." Mature-absent-Leg hazed a thought, in response to which Repeat-close-Looker deopaqued the screen.

The native's reaction to the appearance of the Amplitur was guarded but calm.

"Do you know what we are?" the Commander asked, forming the sounds with its horny lips and soft interior mouthparts.

As it nodded affirmatively the native's eyes narrowed. Perhaps an instinctive defense posture, Mature-absent-Leg thought.

"You're Amplitur. Our friends have shown us pictures."

"Along with much additional inaccurate information." Mature-absent-Leg hoped that the translation was as reassuring and friendly as it had been programmed to be.

"You should feel honored. You are the first of your kind to meet us personally."

"For real? Well then, have a look." The native spread his arms and leaned back into the chair.

"We are already acquainted with your physiology, both external and internal."

"You are not frightened?" Repeat-close-Looker inquired.

"No, I'm not frightened." The native straightened slightly and both Amplitur could sense that it was lying. That, too, was expected. It was akin to the denial of reality the creatures exhibited in combat.

"You don't look like much." The native regarded them curiously. "Based on your reputations I thought you'd be a lot bigger."

"Physical size is not much of a determinant in the grand scheme of things," Repeat-close-Looker informed him.

"Maybe so, but I'd still rather wrassle one of you than a Molitar. Those are about the toughest guys you've got working for you."

"The Molitar do not work for us." Mature-absent-Leg shifted slightly on all four legs, the mottled orange skin rippling fluidly. "They are . . ."

"Yeah, I know, I know. They're part of the Purpose. Everyone is part of your Purpose." Lips parted to reveal white teeth. "Except the Massood, and the S'van, and a few of their friends. And us."

"You can be an important component of the Purpose." Mature-absent-Leg moved closer to the screen, the manipulative tips of the two tentacles on either side of its mouth spreading wide, flexing and contracting. "You can share fully in the beauty which has been revealed to us."

"We've got plenty beauty of our own, thanks. We don't want yours. Why don't you squids just take a hike back to wherever it is you come from?"

"We would be reneging on our destiny were we to do that," replied the Commander, ignoring the derogatory descriptive. "If there is any truth in what the S'van have told you, you realize we cannot."

"Yeah, that's what they said. But this is our solar system. If you insist on hanging around where you're not wanted, we're going to have to throw you out."

Such primitive, feeble attempts at humor were the native's way of maintaining its spirits, Mature-absent-Leg decided. Surely it must realize that it was imprisoned on an enemy warship somewhere in Underspace, possibly with no chance of ever seeing its own kind again. Once more the inherent denial of reality, which smacked of irrational mental focus. A trait which was useful nowhere except in combat, the Commander knew. Such contradictions would be eliminated once these creatures were brought into the Purpose. They would know a peace they had never known before.

The two Amplitur exchanged thoughts about procedure. This

particular specimen was not one Mature-absent-Leg would have chosen, but they had to begin somewhere and presently this single male was all that was available.

Repeat-close-Looker reached out mindwise, probing with the intelligence and care for which it was renowned. Since the Commander was not participating directly but was only conscious of a colleague's efforts, what happened next did not strike with its full force. When later asked to describe it in detail Mature-absent-Leg found it painful to contemplate, impossible to describe accurately.

Touching the native's thoughts was like tapping into an over-pressurized container bloated with blind anger and hatred. On contact it exploded in a fiery wave, sweeping logic and reason and sensitivity before it, submerging any proximate suggestion of intelligence in a flood of concentrated pain and angst. It stank of mindless destruction and anarchy, of raw emotion and animal instinct.

Immediately upon contact the native's eyes widened. It stared in shock at Repeat-close-Looker. That individual had already been rendered comatose. The prober lay on its right side where it had collapsed, tentacles curled tightly against its mouth, eyestalks completely retracted. Nearby, Mature-absent-Leg still stood on shaky limbs; head throbbing, vision blurred, acutely aware that the full force of the native's reaction had only brushed past.

The Commander stood as if paralyzed, thinking furiously as mind cleared and the initial pain lessened. Judging by the native's confusion it was clear that its defense had not been a conscious one. In a way that made what had happened even more terrifying. It meant that not only was the native dangerous, its response was unpredictable and uncontrolled.

It turned to stare bewilderedly at Mature-absent-Leg. The Commander shivered helplessly under that stare for a long moment, until it began to realize that the native could not willingly project whatever was in its mind in the manner of the Amplitur. The shivering faded.

The unfortunate Repeat-close-Looker had somehow tapped into an unsuspected component of the native's nervous system, something of a purely defensive and instinctive nature. It could not have been anticipated because nothing like it had ever been encountered before.

The native was standing now, gesturing at the motionless form of Repeat-close-Looker. "That son of a bitch was trying to get into my head. I felt it." He looked up at Mature-absent-Leg. "That's how you people work, right? You get inside people's brains and screw things around until they have no choice but to believe in your Purpose. That's what he was trying to do. Only he couldn't. Something hurt him." Realization dawned slowly. "*I* hurt him."

The man's confusion gave way to excitement. "It means you can't get to us, you can't twist us. And when you try to, something inside us fights back. Something you can't handle."

The native advanced until it was hammering both hands against the security screen. Though it knew the creature could not break through, Mature-absent-Leg unconsciously found itself retreating from the hairless, contorted visage. It sent out a quick, anxious projection. The door at the rear of the room opened to admit the two Molitar who had brought the native. Both had their weapons out.

The native spun to face them. What it did next was quite unexpected. It began to laugh, tears running down its scarred cheeks.

"You poor, dumb, backboneless SOBs, you can't do it to us. You can't do what you've been doing to everybody else. Wait till this gets out!"

Without warning it charged the two Molitar, heedless of the weapons they were carrying. For a horrible instant Mature-absent-Leg thought it had been reading his mind, quickly realized that could not be so. The natives had demonstrated nothing in the way of telepathic abilities.

As the nearest Molitar fired, the native threw itself forward. The shot passed above it to strike the security screen directly in front of the Commander, who flinched, eyestalks retracting instinctively. The blast did not touch him, the screen having been designed to dissipate far more intense energies.

The native's foot struck his massive assailant square on one joint. The Molitar let out a penetrating howl and collapsed heavily. Meanwhile his companion grabbed the native by its right arm, wrenching hard, striking with the other. The native ducked the blow, curled impossibly tight in on itself, and uncoiled with a lightning strike to its captor's eye. Blood fountained and the injured Molitar released its grasp.

In response to the Commander's alarmed thoughts, armed Crigolit and Ashregan began pouring into the room.

"Kill the thing!" Mature-absent-Leg projected anxiously. "Kill it!"

Uncivilized, unworthy, embarrassing thoughts. But the Commander was still glad when the thing finally died, unable at the end to deflect energy beams with its bare hands. It lay motionless on the floor, smoke slowly rising from the multiple wounds that had been necessary to bring it down, a lump of dead protoplasm no more or less threatening than any other sack of bone and fluid from which the motivating force had been removed.

Fleeing the observation chamber as fast as he was able, Mature-absent-Leg made his way toward Command Central, using the time to ponder possible courses of action.

They could muster every available vessel and soldier in an attempt to overwhelm this world before its defenses could be made even more secure, but that would leave vulnerable worlds on which the Purpose presently held sway. Worse still, an assault formulated out of panic and in haste might well fail. The Amplitur had achieved all that they had through patience and careful planning.

Before launching an attack one must first come to understand the enemy. An in-depth study of the natives' nervous system was an absolute prerequisite to any further combat. It was of paramount importance to secure additional live specimens.

The rest would be up to the Amplitur's unsurpassed bioengineers. The nature of the creatures' defense mechanism could be isolated, then analyzed and overcome or otherwise rendered harmless. Only then could these beings provide fertile ground for propagation of the Purpose. First it was vital to remove their lingering primitive characteristics, both mental and physical. The result would be a happy and content population.

To call the fleet staff's initial reaction skeptical was to severely understate, but the recordings that had been made of the confrontational session ultimately convinced them. There was also the disquieting reality provided by the still comatose Repeat-close-Looker, whom physicians had as yet been unable to revive.

One of the fleet group commanders was tracing a diagrammatic cube of the recordings with a tentacle tip. "Look at this burst of cerebral activity here. What does it mean?"

"I cannot intuit these imports," added another, its mastery of biologic theory notwithstanding.

The senior fleet specialist in alien neurology chose to venture an observation. "As Mature-absent-Leg has surmised, the native was as surprised by the presence of a defense mechanism as were its interrogators. I have reviewed the recordings and this seems inarguable. When Repeat-close-Looker was injured, Mature-absent-Leg and the native expressed equal astonishment."

"Why evolve a mechanism to defend against something that does not exist on your homeworld?" wondered another member of the staff.

"Nature is sometimes capricious, but never wasteful." The specialist unfurled its right tentacle. "The trait may have developed in response to other local conditions of which we as yet know nothing. I submit that this development is no more incredible than many other aspects of the bizarre world on which it has evolved." Thoughts swirled and melded.

"In light of what we have learned during our brief confrontation here it is clear that we attacked without first securing adequate information about our opponent. Is it therefore surprising that we have subsequently had to endure the losses of the overconfident?"

"While currently stable, the longer the situation on the surface is stalemated, the stronger the enemy's position becomes," said a tactical specialist. "What we have encountered here is unprecedented. Therefore we must evolve a precedent.

"Rendering uninhabitable the surface of the planet is not an option. These creatures can be the greatest force for the advancement of the Purpose since it was revealed to the Amplitur. I submit that we must withdraw until we have devised a more effective means for dealing with the particular difficulties they pose, while we are still in a strategic position to bring out the majority of our surviving forces."

"To do so now," disagreed another, "will greatly boost the determination and morale of the Weave."

"Morale is a transitory intangible." With that comment Mature-absent-Leg reasserted commander's prerogative. "What is happening here is reality. Let us plan to deal foremost with the reality.

"We have not encountered anything like these beings before.

That does not mean we are incapable of coping with any special difficulties they present. It requires only the application of time and study, as do all complex problems.'' Mature-absent-Leg directed a thought to the fleet specialist in alien neurology.

''You are convinced from your examination of the recordings executed during the interrogation procedure that the native had no understanding of what occurred when Repeat-close-Looker's mind touched his?''

''There is nothing to indicate awareness. As you observed, it realized what Repeat-close-Looker was attempting, but it in no way indicated it had consciousness of a method of resistance.

''Something lies buried within the native nervous system; something they themselves are unaware of. A cerebral twist, a specific gene: it is only a matter of isolating and identifying it. Given time we may even bend it to our advantage. It is nothing more than a chemical puzzle to be solved.''

''It will make things difficult,'' the military specialist commented, ''if it becomes known among the peoples of the Weave that they have among them a new ally who happens to be immune to our particular kind of gentle persuasion.''

''We will deal with any awkwardness if and when it arises,'' Mature-absent-Leg projected firmly.

The neurospecialist thought expansively. ''I am not so certain that 'immunity' is the correct term. There is something in their system that reacts violently to mental probing. If they are not probed, the defense mechanism is not activated. Therefore there is no reason for panic. It requires only time and the application of suitable intelligence to solve this new problem.''

''It cannot be done in a combat situation,'' another pointed out.

The inevitable question did not have to be formulated. Nor was there need for a vote. Decision unanimously followed understanding.

''We shall withdraw from this system.'' Mature-absent-Leg's eyestalks were fully extended. ''Preferably after securing additional specimens for study. Should we fail to obtain the necessary sampling here, we shall obtain them elsewhere, at another time. Since we will be departing without having suffered defeat, the intangible effects of our withdrawal should be minimized.'' This astute observation served to mollify the concerns of the military specialist.

"Upon full recovery, Repeat-close-Looker will be able to add to our knowledge of this matter and assist in future research."

"That is assuming," said the neurospecialist, "that the mind damage is not permanent." The observation provoked uneasy thoughts mixed with sorrowful reflection.

"I experience regrets for having had the specimen terminated," thought the Commander.

"You reacted defensively," said a group leader. "You did not know what had taken place nor what might follow. Given such circumstances a relapse into instinctive self-preservation is not to be faulted.

"Our consolation is that this dangerous reactive mechanism is involuntary in nature. It cannot be directed or you would have suffered the same fate as Repeat-close-Looker."

"That is so," agreed the Commander as the meeting dissolved. But despite that reassuring thought and the press of work ahead, Mature-absent-Leg was unable to expunge the pain of the disastrous interrogation session completely from his mind.

★ XXVI ★

"It's over."

Will glanced up from his workdesk, ignoring the view out over the lagoon. While the Belizean reef was no longer the center of Weave activity on Earth, such activities having long since been usurped by several national capitals, it was still an important research center. As there was no longer any reason for concealment, the submerged complex had begun to build upward: slim, elegant towers rising into the tropical sky.

"What do you mean it's over?"

"The battle for your world." T'var might have been smiling behind his dense growth of facial hair. "We've won."

Will knew he should have shouted, thrown his hands in the air, or otherwise reacted as billions of his fellow Humans no doubt already were. Instead he felt oddly calm.

"When did you get the news?"

"Just a few minutes ago. It arrived via closed transponder from a place called London." His English had gotten quite good, Will thought. "They're pulling out; the Crigolit, Ashregan, Molitar, Acaria, the Amplitur themselves. All of them, everywhere. Your Gobi and Great Plains, the Ukraine and Matto Grosso, even those bases they had managed to secure. Shuttles have been coming and going all morning. Our forces took several of them out before they could escape, and at least one warship that didn't slip back into Underspace quickly enough."

"I don't understand," Will said quietly. "I'd heard that we were pushing them back, but nothing to suggest total victory was imminent. What happened to make them suddenly pull up and leave?"

"No one knows." T'var hunted for and found a bench built to his height. "The word is that by this evening there won't be an enemy soldier left on your world or a hostile warship in your system. The Hivistahm are concerned that it may be some kind of trick, but the Hivistahm would worry if the Amplitur sued for peace tomorrow. The consensus among the Massood is that the pullout is genuine."

"There'll be a lot of celebrating."

"It's already begun," T'var told him. "Here at the base as well as across your world. This is a great moment for your people as well as for the Weave. Not that the Amplitur haven't been driven from other worlds, but it was accomplished far more quickly here than anyone thought likely or possible."

"They must not have cared for what they found," Will murmured thoughtfully.

"They encountered what they first found on Vasarih and later on Aurun, only much more of it." T'var was bursting with excitement. "We'll give them more of what they don't like until we finally push them back to their homeworld, wherever that may be and however long it may take."

"Perhaps," said Will slowly.

T'var gave him a funny look. "I don't understand your implication."

"You and your councils better not expect Humans to fulfill preconceived expectations. Now that the Amplitur have been driven out, mankind may not react to your liking. People united in the face of a common foe. Now that that foe has fled, don't be surprised if everyone decides they want to go back to the way things were before all this happened. I've been warning you and Caldaq about that possibility all along."

"Impossible," said T'var. "A species cannot demature."

Will snorted derisively. "Don't underestimate the determination of a world filled with fractious fools."

Despite the best efforts of the enemy to preserve the secret, Humanity and the Weave learned of mankind's resistance to Amplitur probing when a brace of Human soldiers were exposed to a captured Amplitur officer. Seeking to free himself, the officer struck out, with the result that he lapsed into convulsions. Astonished Massood who came upon the scene listened intently as the puzzled Humans reported the sequence of events.

The inferences which were drawn led to a series of delicate experiments which confirmed what the Amplitur already knew and feared, though an understanding of the Human body's actual defense mechanism awaited considerable further study.

The Massood troops in the field were not interested in reasons. Delighted and not a little awed by the news, they regarded their hairless colleagues with ever greater respect.

So it came as quite a shock when the population of Earth declined to leap wholeheartedly into the battle against the Purpose, exactly as Will Dulac had told the S'van it might.

The representatives of the Weave were taken aback. Not only had Humans proven themselves superbly in combat, but they alone among sentients were immune to the enemy's mental trickery and manipulation. Therefore the decision not to participate did not arise from fear.

S'van and Massood attempted to remonstrate with mankind. Their reward was bewilderment. Once it was assured that the Amplitur had fled, the temporary military political council which had been formed to coordinate planetary defense promptly dissolved, once more leaving the Weave with dozens of tribal governments to contend with. Each tribe had its own priorities, its own agenda. Regardless of which system of government its people professed, no two were exactly alike. Nor was there even agreement within tribal borders. Often local consensus was dominated by whichever faction could yell the loudest.

The Wais took pleasure in the byplay of complex mannerisms, the Massood in running. Humans seemed to prefer argument and disagreement. It made them impossible to deal with.

Will felt vindicated as the temporary anti-Amplitur alliance splintered and mankind returned to its old ways. He missed no opportunity to mention it to Jaruselka and Soliwik, T'var and Z'mam and all the rest.

"I warned you," he was telling Caldaq. "I told you we couldn't be depended on to fight a war beyond our own world. When the invaders fled so did the desire to fight.

"I expect you'll be able to recruit a few thousand more soldiers here, but you'll never get entire governments to participate."

"Nevertheless we must continue to try," the Massood responded.

The media reported daily on the ongoing debate, the learned

opinion of numerous experts serving, as always, to muddle the facts further. All governments participated lest one gain some unimaginable advantage over its neighbor.

Weave representatives pleaded and argued, elucidated and cajoled, all to no effect. It was true that the Amplitur had been driven off, but there was no permanence in such a victory. Unless they were utterly defeated they would return someday, stronger and more determined than before. If mankind declined to fight now, it would have to defend itself again in the future. All such admonitions and dire warnings aside, governments continued to refuse to commit resources to what remained for most people an obscure, impossibly distant conflict.

The planet prospered as regional conflicts faded under the glare of knowledge. Foolish to brandish weapons against another country when one day all might have to unite to teach an inimical alien species another lesson. Armies were maintained in the event of such an eventuality, but now their soldiers mingled freely with one another, discussing tactics and trading ideas. Those corporations which specialized in military research and development found themselves as busy as ever, modifying and improving weaponry for a conflict which might never come.

"You'll never get the kind of participation you want," Will kept telling T'var. "Mankind can't agree on small things. There's no way we'd ever get together on something like this. You're going to have to be satisfied with a few recruits here and there. No matter what arguments you use, the majority of the population will always opt for peace and isolation."

"As always, you seem pleased by the course of events, Will Dulac."

"Me? Hell, I'm delighted. This is the next best thing to having been ignored. Earth's a much nicer place now that peace has broken out. Also you've provided an outlet for people with warlike inclinations, not to mention the average malcontent. They can join your forces and work out their frustrations and anger light-years away from their peaceable neighbors. Those who make it back have usually been pretty tamed by what they've encountered.

"Meanwhile the rest of us can relax and get on with the business of finally advancing our culture and repairing the environment."

"Can you come with me?" T'var slid off his bench. "There's someone I'd like you to meet."

"All right. Just give me a second to shut this down." He made sure his work in progress was saved before cutting power to the electronic composer.

T'var took him to a new section of the ever-expanding research complex. Unlike most of the new buildings, which towered above the pristine lagoon, this one was grafted inconspicuously to the side of the reef.

A large circular doorway admitted them to a room unlike anything Will had previously encountered. He blinked as his eyes adjusted to a level of illumination well below the Human norm.

The far wall consisted of a gigantic transparent bubble which protruded into the sea. As he watched, a school of hundreds of mahogany snappers and yellow jacks swam past. Giant elephant-ear sponges framed the seascape.

Movement drew his attention from the breathtaking underwater ballet. Something large and bulky was moving in the shadows. Only when it passed in front of the bubble was he able, based on what he had been told, to identify the shape.

A Turlog.

He caught his breath. Turlog analysis had contributed to many of the victories on Vasarih and Aurun. Even the S'van admitted that without Turlog assistance and perceptiveness the Amplitur might well have overrun the Weave centuries ago. To the best of Will's knowledge no Human had yet set eyes upon a member of that shy and reclusive species.

Their importance to the war against the Purpose was inversely proportional to their limited numbers. They disdained, nay, they actively disliked the company of others, even individuals of their own kind.

Will knew a Turlog had been present on the ship which had first brought Caldaq and his companions to Earth, but he had not heard that any had participated in the planet's defense. He could not keep himself from staring.

The vast chitonous shape scuttled further into the diffuse blue light supplied by the bubble, advancing on half a dozen short, inflexible legs. About the size of a full-grown steer, it seemed to belong more to the underwater world outside than to the darkened room with its dim telltales and readouts.

It had both a hard exterior and an internal skeleton, a combination which resulted in an extremely slow-moving, awkward being. Two pale silvery eyes regarded him emotionlessly. Each stiff, hard-shelled arm ended in four-pronged pincers, which looked sharp and clumsy.

T'var kept his voice low, though whether out of habit or politeness Will didn't know.

"This is Pasiiakilion."

Automatically Will started to extend a hand, then hesitated. Not out of fear. Nothing so bulky and slow could be threatening. But he sensed no need here for extraneous movement, unnecessary gestures. He had been admitted; therefore his presence was accepted.

The pale eyes and inflexible face revealed nothing. Turlog and man stared silently at one another. Will felt that this creature would devote its entire being to whatever subject was at hand, be it a discussion of the nature of subatomic particles, galactic war, or the petals of a flower.

The silence was broken by a coarse, gravelly noise that reminded Will of raw rock spinning inside a gem tumbler. There must have been a translator nearby, because the rasping was transformed into barely intelligible English.

"Will Dulac. I know of you."

"And I think I've heard of you. Aren't you one of Caldaq's original crew?"

Waves washing gravel on a deserted beach. "It is quiet down here. I like your world. It interests me."

Will tried to see more of the room, which was filled with *things* and grotesque alien shapes. A heap of glowing mucus glistened damply in a far corner. Seeking a better look, he took a step forward.

"Please go no farther." The voice was as emotionless as it was raspy. "My egg cluster. Perhaps you may know that we are hermaphroditic."

Like the Amplitur, Will realized with a start. "No. I didn't know that."

"We wonder often about sex," murmured Pasiiakilion. "So much energy, so much drive and concentration spent merely to promote reproduction. But as our own efforts at reproduction seem inadequate, we make no value judgments."

Will whispered to the unnaturally subdued T'var. "Why did you bring me down here?"

"Something I thought you of all people should know," the S'van replied softly. "I could be reprimanded for doing this. Pasiiakilion can explain better than I." His attitude was very serious, very un-S'van. In the dim light his stocky form seemed less diminutive.

"Your people are contentious and confused," rumbled the Turlog, "but wonderful fighters. The best we have yet found."

"So I've been told." That was no revelation. Will waited.

"As your social development has lagged remarkably behind your technological accomplishments, you have yet to achieve a planetary government. Your geology has also worked against you. Thus you have no means of formally representing yourselves to the Weave."

"We don't want to join anyway," Will responded. "It's been agreed that if individuals want to fight for the Weave they should be allowed to do so, but there's no broad base of support for any kind of formal alliance."

"I know that. It is a good thing."

Will was taken aback, unsure he'd heard correctly. "I thought you wanted us in the Weave. I know that's how the Hivistahm and Lepar and Massood and all the others feel. If it was up to them right now every adult on Earth would be undergoing combat training."

"We want you for soldiers because that is what you do best," said the Turlog.

"No. It's not what we 'do best.' I can't deny that we seem to do it well, but . . ."

"Please let me continue," said Pasiiakilion, interrupting. "I am not used to talking and so am not very good at it." Will restrained himself.

"I give you truth. You are the best fighters. You may be more than that: you may represent a turning point, though it is far, far too soon to hazard such a prediction. Despite that, those of us who think hard about such matters do not want your people to join the Weave."

"Caldaq would say differently."

"As would many. But it would not be in the best interests of the Weave, or of your own kind."

Will knew he should have been delighted to find another philosophical ally among the aliens. Instead he was wary.

"That's what I've been saying for years. So you think we should stay out of formal alliances, too? That's great. If we're left alone we can be just as peaceable as the O'o'yan or Wais."

"No, you cannot. We want you to fight on, but we do not want you to join. We want your help, but not your companionship. You are dangerous. To the Amplitur, to every civilized species you encounter, to yourselves."

"With time that may change. No matter how much assistance your kind renders, the Amplitur will not be defeated tomorrow, or the next day, or any time in the foreseeable future. They are patient and resourceful because they are dedicated, however wrongly. Your people do not know patience. Today they find ready success in battle. That will change, or the Amplitur are much less than we have thought them to be.

"We do not want you in the Weave. The Hivistahm do not want you, the O'o'yan do not want you, the Wais and Lepar do not want you. Even the S'van do not want you."

Will looked sharply at T'var. Small dark eyes stared back at him.

"I see. You want us to be your mercenaries but not your friends."

"You are not sufficiently evolved to be friends," said Pasi-iakilion mercilessly. "It is thought that with help and teaching you might mature. But if we change you, then you will not be the fighters you are now. You are more valuable to the Weave as fighters than as friends." Will said nothing, waiting silently. Outside the bubble an eagle ray flew by on silent wings.

"If you could somehow," the Turlog continued relentlessly, "cobble together a rudimentary planetary government, if this United Nations of yours could acquire enough strength to be regarded as truly representative of your people, you would still not be offered membership in the Weave. Your presence would be disruptive, a characteristic already present in sufficient quantity among the civilized races. The introduction of an uncivilized one such as your own would be counterproductive, possibly explosive."

"You don't know that. I think you're wrong about my kind. I think you've been wrong from the beginning."

"I would like nothing more than to be able to believe that. It may be so. Hence the caution with which we proceed." A pincer waved, silhouetted by the blue light from the bubble. "But for now you understand why we are pleased that you do not wish membership in the Weave, a membership the Weave does not wish you to have but would be embarrassed to deny. This way both sides get what they want."

"You might explain that," Will murmured.

"It has been my lot to conduct an extensive study of your racial psychology. You cannot be trusted to respond rationally to a disclosure of the results, to recognize your own weaknesses. You would respond as you respond to everything contrary to what you want to believe: with violence.

"The Weave overflows with artists and philosophers, musicians and technicians. Fighters are in very short supply. Given a choice even the Massood would prefer not to fight. Now we have found you. We need you."

"What happens," Will wondered after a long pause, "when we've defeated the Amplitur, when we've beaten this Purpose of theirs? What happens to us then?"

"That is far in the future," said T'var quickly. "All that matters now is defeating them."

Silvery eyes had not strayed from Will's face. "Myself, I wonder at the ramifications of the mechanism which shields the Human mind from Amplitur manipulation. No others have this quality."

"Not even the Turlog?" Will asked challengingly.

"Not even the Turlog." Pasiiakilion shifted all six legs.

"Are you afraid of us?"

"Not of you. Of the enigma you present."

"Disruption," said T'var. "We don't need any more disruptions. The Weave has been in danger of falling apart since the day it was founded. Defeating the Amplitur may take another hundred years, a thousand. In any event none of us in this room will be around for the outcome. So we have to concern ourselves now about what we're leaving to our unknowing descendants. Besides," he added in as aggressive a tone as Will had ever heard from a S'van, "isn't this what you wanted all along? To keep your world as uninvolved as possible?"

"Yes, sure," Will replied. "I wanted us to be left alone. But not disliked."

"No one dislikes you," said Pasiiakilion somberly. "Because

of your accomplishments your people are admired, even venerated throughout the Weave.''

"Sure. Because it means someone else doesn't have to fight. It's not affection. You can admire a cobra but that doesn't mean you want to snuggle up to one.''

"It's what you would call a 'love-hate relationship,' '' said T'var as his sense of humor returned.

"Does it matter to you so much then, William Dulac,'' the Turlog inquired, ''why you have achieved that which you fought so long to gain?''

"I don't know,'' Will muttered. "I thought it did, but now you've confused me.''

"Do you have such a deep longing to be liked? Is it not sufficient for now to be respected?''

"If you're being respected for the right reasons, yes. For contributions to the advancement of civilization, or culture. Not for the ability to slaughter Crigolit.''

The Turlog pivoted to study the seascape outside the bubble. "I am sorry. The S'van and I thought you had the right to know what is the truth of things. For now.''

"Time to go.'' T'var tugged on Will's sleeve. "You've heard what I wanted you to hear.''

"But I'm not through. There are questions . . .''

"Another time,'' rasped the Turlog without rancor. "I have eggs to attend to.''

"You ought to be flattered,'' T'var told him once they were back in a properly lit corridor. He looked back over his shoulder. "Pasiiakilion gave you more time than I've ever seen him allot to anyone else, Caldaq included. Not only that, he responded to your own inquiries instead of just delivering himself of information. He very badly wanted you to understand.''

Will slowed his pace to that of the shorter S'van. "I don't think he liked me very much.''

"The Turlog don't 'like' anyone, not even other Turlog.'' T'var led the way into the lift that would carry them surfaceward. "They only help at all because they hate the thought of being subsumed into the Amplitur Purpose worse than they do the strain of cooperating with the Weave.''

"Everything he said was true?''

"I've never known a Turlog to lie.''

"Nobody wants us in the Weave?''

They exited at sea level. Will was relieved to find himself back among daylight and conversation, away from the gruff alien and its primal, disquieting habitat.

"Consider the Turlog," T'var urged his Human companion. "They are not liked, but they're admired and accepted for what they can contribute. We S'van are often more envied than liked, and no one is especially fond of the Lepar. Why then should you and your kind worry so much on this? You're in good company."

"It's more than not being liked," Will muttered. "The Lepar, the S'van, the Turlog are all considered civilized. We're not. We'll never be fully accepted until we've been invited into the Weave."

"It will happen."

Will looked down at the second captain. "When?"

"In time. When you are no longer what you are."

"Meaning the mindless killing machines depicted in some Weave propaganda? Oh, yes, I've been exposed to that. I've done plenty of research of my own these past few years."

"It will not happen in our lifetime, but it will happen."

"You're certain of that?"

"Of course. I've never been more certain of anything in my life." The S'van smiled ingenuously.

★ XXVII ★

Following the invasion it was much easier for the Weave to recruit Human soldiers. Many of those who had turned back the Amplitur attack were anxious, even eager to sign up for training on Motar. Then there were others who hadn't had the chance to participate, who saw in the offer the chance to fulfill their dreams of travel, or glory, or simply a chance to fight back.

There were the soldiers and officers of all the world's major armies, whom peace and rapprochement between the great powers had left idle, with no chance to utilize their own training. Poverty also provided a fertile recruiting ground for Weave recruiters. They made use of the testimonials of early recruits, including some that Will remembered from the early days in Belize.

Weave medical technology was far advanced beyond Earth's. Even serious injuries could be successfully treated. If a soldier wasn't killed outright there was a good chance he would make it back home healed, healthy, and well-off. The Weave was generous to its friends.

But there were many who felt as Will did, that mankind had no place in the millennia-long alien conflict. It was no longer a matter of patriotism, of fighting off another invasion attempt, but of free choice. Those who went, went of their own free will. Those who remained suffered no opprobrium for doing so.

While inferior to Weave science in many respects, there was the one area where Human achievement had leaped ahead. Advances in military technology no longer surprised Weave sociologists, however, ever since it had been determined that that was what the species had devoted its greatest efforts to since it had first acquired sentience.

Human scientists and laboratories, given access to Weave technology, soon set to work modifying and improving with a vengeance, turning out improved versions of standard weaponry at a rate that astonished even the S'van. They did so without the reluctance or moral qualms that often plagued Weave scientists. Facilities scattered across the face of the planet competed gleefully to see which could make the deadliest improvement or the most lethal modifications.

They did so without second thoughts. After all, none of their output was intended for use against fellow Humans. Here at last was the conflict mankind had secretly wished for but had never been able to enjoy. No more brother against brother, cousin against cousin, color against color or religion against religion. It was man and his allies and friends against the horrid, cephalopodian Amplitur and their brain-damaged slave races. Humans had always excelled when presented with uncomplicated, easy-to-comprehend options. Us against Them eliminated the need for irritating introspection.

There were a few who called into question the advisability of warring against sentients there had been no dialogue with. Against these arguments were arrayed the tales of returning Human soldiers who had actually fought against the enemy. They had no trouble with moral gray areas. The Amplitur were bent on sucking all other species into their Purpose. They knew not the meaning of neutrality. You were for them or against them.

If you were for them they promised you full participation in their Purpose . . . under their guidance, of course. Doing what they thought was the proper thing to do, acting the way they thought you should act. Only through resistance did a species retain its independence, its individuality.

There was no need to whip up pro-war hysteria on Earth. No need to spread the propaganda Will feared. The Amplitur and their code of the Purpose was enough to draw adequate numbers to the recruiting stations.

So people went off to fight alongside the Massood, supported by the S'van and the Hivistahm and Yula and the other peoples of the Weave. They returned admired, content, wealthy, inspiring more of their kind to do likewise. The bulk of Humanity was not involved. Will was pleased.

Caldaq was strolling through the upper levels of the base that by now had spread itself across much of the reef. Towers rose high above the still unspoiled waters, dominating the palms and coral islets.

Beyond the reef scheduled shuttles touched down and lifted off, carrying recruits and technicians and supplies to ships recently emerged from Underspace.

. The sentry system which had been placed in orbit at the limit of the sun's magnetosphere was as modern and efficient as the one that circled his own homeworld. Weave warships patrolled the water planet's outer atmosphere. Mankind felt secure, shielded by its friends even as it declined to participate in their organization. It was a great relief as time passed and no formal invitation to join was extended. It spared Humanity the embarrassment of declining. Mankind had no desire to hurt the feelings of its good friends.

Unbeknown to everyone except the composer Will Dulac, the General Council of the Weave was more than content to maintain the status quo.

A group of decorated Human soldiers were coming down the hall. They wore the yellow-slashed jumpsuits designed by the first recruits, and they talked animatedly among themselves as they advanced.

Spotting Caldaq they executed the peculiar hand and arm gesture which among them was considered a sign of respect to a superior. It was called a salute, Caldaq knew, a gesture unknown to Weave forces. Leave it to mankind to invent a purely military salutation. It struck him as unnatural and unnecessary. Why not simply greet another individual as you would otherwise? Why should a uniform make a difference? It was yet another example of the unique militaristic culture which had evolved among Humankind, apparent even in those who chose not to participate.

He waved, well aware that his response was not nearly as crisp and sharp as their own gestures, which they performed without breaking stride or conversation. It was as if they executed it unconsciously. Like breathing.

He turned as they passed, noted a pair of strolling Hivistahm technicians talking with an O'o'yan attendant. One of the Hivistahm saw the approaching Humans and whispered to its companion. Surreptitiously they got out of the way, sidling over to the wall without pausing in their conversation. The Humans noticed nothing. They were not sensitive to the reactions of their allies and hosts, wholly engaged as they were in their own conversation.

Caldeq observed the Hivistahms' posture, the way their necks retracted slightly, the way their eyelids half closed beneath the gaudy shields. The smaller O'o'yan kept his larger companions between himself and the Humans. They were expressing contempt if not outright fear of those who had just walked past them. It was not an uncommon reaction.

It was known what Humans did. They fought, magnificently. The sentients who did not, could not fight, like the Wais and Hivistahm and Lepar and others, were extraordinarily grateful for this. They admired what Humans did, but they did not like them for it.

Even among his own kind, Caldaq knew as he turned a corner, there were many who disliked Humans. Even those who subscribed to the mythology which was growing up around them. For example, there was no one better to fight alongside in the field than a Human, but outside of combat the Massood preferred not to socialize with them. They did not know how to behave in civilized company.

They were . . . clumsy.

Jaruselka was calling to him and he lengthened his stride to meet her. It was always a pleasure to be in her company. Her mere presence helped to banish discomfiting thoughts from his overburdened mind.

He had anticipated meeting her in the dining complex, but this was preferable. They could walk the rest of the way together. A Human would have sprinted to join him. Remarkable how they could outrun most anything over a short distance, he reflected. Another characteristic of their peculiar physiology. But over distance nothing could keep up with a Massood.

They exchanged greetings contentedly, nuzzling one another's necks and murmuring the secret mate-words. Only after she drew back did she express concern.

"You look troubled."

"No. Just thoughtful." He straightened.

"That has always been your problem." She chided him affectionately. "You worry like a Hivistahm."

"Do not say *that*," he replied, amused. "You wished to dine together?" He matched her stride.

"Yes. There is news for you, lifemate."

"Of the fighting on Kantaria?"

"No. You have been promoted." Her great eyes were shining.

He slowed, stared at her. He'd been so busy these past years he'd forgotten about such minor matters as promotion. The Massood did not seek personal advancement with, for example, the same avidity as Human beings. It was something that came, if it came at all, naturally and for good reason, like aging.

"I also have been honored."

"Then the news is all good."

"Perhaps. You are to be given a battlefield commission."

He frowned inwardly at that, his eyes closing halfway. "What of my work here?"

"Command feels you can be spared. Others have taken on much of the burden. The S'van interact far better with Humans than do we. It is felt there is no longer a need for a Massood presence in what has become an administrative facility, and as always our combat abilities are desperately needed where worlds are being contested. Kantaria, for example."

Ironic, he mused. He had anticipated utilizing recordings of the combat on that world to boost local recruiting. Now he would have the opportunity to see what progress was being made there in person.

Kantaria was populated by an immature developing race; mammalian, short and slim as the O'o'yan but without O'o'yan skills. Intelligent but only slightly civilized. They had nearly been conquered by the Amplitur only to have the Weave discover what was happening and intervene at the last moment. And he was to be a part of that vital effort, a part of something the Massood had grimly prided themselves on for hundreds of years.

He was not very familiar with the situation on Kantaria since the Weave presence there was a recent one. He knew only that the Amplitur and their allies were firmly established on much of the planet and would have to be driven off section by section.

"How do you feel, my warm one?" he asked Jaruselka as they walked.

"Pleased to be departing this world. We have been too many years here. We are to be given leave to visit home for a while in recognition of our achievements and the important work you have done. Your ancestors are much honored. As for joining the conflict on Kantaria, that too is an honor given the difficulties our forces face there.''

''What do they consist of?''

''Mostly Crigolit under the usual Amplitur supervision, though there are others. They include a new convert to the Purpose, the Mazvec. It is rumored that the Amplitur are trying them out on a world they have already largely secured in order to assess their abilities as fighters.

''Kantaria is not a great prize; not a developed world or advanced people. But there is potential, if it can be wrested back from the Amplitur.''

''Fodder for the Purpose,'' Caldaq muttered darkly.

''Exactly.'' Her gaze roved the wide corridor, so unlike the cramped quarters of the original base. ''I like some of the Humans we have met here, but I confess I can only make myself warm to them as individuals and not as a species. When they are brought together in numbers something happens to them. They change.''

''Research continues,'' he told her. ''Some scientists believe it may have something to do with pheromones. Others delve among the esoteric and the outrageous in search of explanations. It is not something to trouble the Massood. I gladly leave it to curse the sleepings of S'van and Hivistahm. It is easier simply to go where we are told and fight until we have won or lost. There is no ambivalence in combat.''

''Surely there are some here you will miss,'' she said. ''Will Dulac, for example.''

''Not at all.''

Her surprise was evident. ''You have shared a long relationship.''

''What you say is so. I have been cordial to Will Dulac. He was the first Human we encountered and in many ways remains the most admirable, I might even say civilized, example of his kind that I have met, together with a few exceptional tribal leaders. But he is Human, and I am still less than comfortable in his presence.''

They passed a large viewport. Past the towers and palms and burgeoning structures of Lighthouse Reef he could see the distant green mountains of the interior. Beyond, to the north, lay vast Human cities teeming with potential recruits. They were far outnumbered by the great mass of Humans who refused to help, each of whom considered him or herself to be the center of the universe, each of whom was concerned primarily with his or her own well-being and comfort. It was an attitude that made supreme good sense on the battlefield but went down poorly among the other citizens of the Weave.

"No, I will not be sorry to leave this place."

⋆ XXVIII ⋆

Caldaq was bitter and sorrowed. Fighting was not easy anywhere, but Kantaria itself seemed determined to make his life as miserable as possible.

It was an awkward, difficult place of rugged mountains cleft by deep valleys, of swift-flowing streams and constant cold rainfall. The landmass had been heavily glaciated in the recent past and as a result the topography was barbaric. It was matched by the weather, which was intolerable everywhere except a narrow band along the equator.

Worst of all there were no decent places to run.

The perpetual rain was as demoralizing to the sun-loving Massood as the snow which crowned many mountains. The tall fighters tolerated cool weather adequately, but not the constant precipitation. Fungi and mildew sprouted everywhere. Including, if one was not careful, on equipment and feet.

The short, bipedal natives resembled skinny, less hirsute versions of the S'van, but without their civilized graces. When confronted by an alien regardless of origin they fled to their stone huts and huddled fearfully inside around flickering fires. Incipient cities boasted a few larger structures of rock held together with crude cement.

It had taken Caldaq less than a year to realize why Kantaria would never be the site of a quick victory by either side. The terrain made ground combat extraordinarily difficult. While the Kantarians spoke the expected single tongue with local variants and dialects, there was no central seat of government; only local tribes and clans to organize. Their infant network of intertribal commercial contacts was growing but still fragile due to the lack of adequate infrastructure. It was easy to understand why their progress was slow.

The Weave might succeed in liberating an entire region only to be outflanked by Amplitur forces trickling through valleys and along mountain trails. Both sides could win and lose the same sector several times in a year. The enemy could heavily fortify captured towns against assault while battlefield communications remained primitive because relay satellites were shot down as rapidly as they could be deployed.

So the war went on, consisting largely of desultory forays by both sides against each other's fortified positions. A recent airborne assault on a major town had been a total disaster. Descending craft had come under fire not only from forces on the ground but from those dug into surrounding cliffs and mountainsides. The survivors had likened it to trying to land in a cauldron.

Unlike elsewhere it proved impossible to spare the natives, since they invariably occupied the contested valleys and mountain passes. No wonder they fled to their pitiable abodes at the first sight of either side's soldiers.

The only consolation Kantaria offered was the knowledge that the place was as hard on the Amplitur and their allies as it was on the Massood. But they had been there longer and held far more territory. With the greater mobility this afforded them they were winning, slowly but inexorably driving the Weave forces back.

It was not that the Crigolit were better suited to combat on Kantaria than the Massood, Caldaq knew, although the Amplitur's new allies the Mazvec seemed to tolerate the adverse conditions better than anyone else. It was that in such execrable circumstances fanaticism had an advantage over mere dedication. Blindly driven as they were by the Purpose, the Amplitur's soldiers were better able than the more contemplative Massood to ignore the festering circumstances in which they found themselves.

Furthermore, every time the Crigolit-Mazvec forces gained a valley or a ridgeline, they tended better to hold onto it, whereas the forces of the Weave could often be driven out. Sitting for months in the dreary, pouring rain sapped the resolve of the finest, most dedicated Massood soldiers, weakening their fighting resolve. They tended to grow lax and tired, having too much time to wonder what they were doing in such a miserable place.

Meanwhile the poor Kantarians were forced to listen to the blandishments of both sides, uncertain which way to lean, who to ally themselves with. They were hardly civilized enough to comprehend the issues at stake, let alone the concept of racial unification.

In such circumstances the Amplitur had another inherent advantage. They could take a village chieftain aside and artfully adjust his way of thinking until he saw only their point of view, then leave it to him to persuade his people.

In the first part of his second year on Kantaria, Caldaq lost Jaruselka.

⋆ XXIX ⋆

He had been supervising an assault on a Mazvec-held ridgeline which guarded the way to an important Kantarian city. He was in an aircar, the only sensible way to cover any distance on this impossible world, when a brace of floater-mounted Crigolit had slipped in behind while patrolling vehicles dueled overhead.

It wasn't even a planned attack which had caught them. Jaruselka had been riding in another aircar, supervising forward fire and safe from direct interdiction as her craft hugged a protective mountainside. The Crigolit floaters were as surprised as anyone when they stumbled unchallenged into the main part of the attacking force. They fired only to cover their retreat as they fled hastily toward the canyon from which they had emerged.

An explosive projectile, fired wildly by a fleeing floater pilot who probably never sighted on his target, had struck the granite wall above Jaruselka's aircar, blasting a huge gouge in the sheer cliff face. The car's pilot didn't have a chance to react and probably never knew what had happened. Countermeasures designed to defeat incoming projectiles and energy beams did not even react to the tons of falling rock which struck the vehicle and overwhelmed its stabilizers, sending it tumbling and crashing into the canyon below.

Caldaq saw it over and over in his mind: the metal and plastic shredding, mixing with the disintegrating granite, until stone and ship together came to rest at the bottom of the contested gorge. Little remained intact of the vehicle or its inhabitants. For that he was inordinately grateful. It allowed him to remember his lifemate as she had been, not as this world had rendered her.

Since then he had carried out his duties numbly, mechanically, fighting and watching others die amidst the unforgiving terrain and remorseless climate as they fought for a world whose inhabitants did not even understand why control of their modest culture should be so fiercely contested.

As often as was permissible he requested transfer offworld. Cognizant of his combat skills, his superiors turned him down as regularly as he applied. It turned into a personal ritual, each application confirming his own unhappiness and the pain of his loss.

There was nothing in this forlorn place worth Jaruselka's death, he knew. Nothing worth the depression his soldiers suffered as a consequence of the rain and cold. It was reflected in their performance, as the Weave lost mountain after mountain, valley after valley including the one in which his lifemate had died. They were being pushed back toward the western shore, to the cliffs and fjords of the frigid Kantarian ocean.

It was an agonizingly slow process, because for every several Amplitur successes the Weave might gain ground elsewhere. It sapped what remained of Caldaq's determination and came dangerously near affecting his professionalism.

We may have to concede them this world. It was a painful thought for a Massood officer to have to contemplate.

But that was the nature of the ancient conflict. Advance and retreat, surrender and acquire: the tides of combat. They might lose Kantaria and gain a world elsewhere.

He had come to realize that because of the nature of this world the Weave could not win here. Not only the odds but the planet itself was arrayed against them. Sooner or later he and the other senior field officers would find themselves recommending a complete pullout, thereby abandoning the unfortunate Kantarians to the inevitable genetic manipulations of the Amplitur. The poor natives were not mature enough to understand what was going to happen to them. A gentle, bewildered people would be forever transformed.

Some things a soldier should not dwell upon, he thought emotionlessly. In any event, he would not be alive to witness it.

Some day, some time in the future, the Weave would come back to Kantaria and liberate its people, in that far distant time when the Amplitur had been forcefully expelled from this portion of the galaxy. It was inevitable. But for now the burden of retreat would have to be entered into his family history, even though the loss was due to forces beyond the control of him or his colleagues.

They could continue the fight for a long time, could hold out for perhaps another hundred years or so before they were pushed back to the western sea. But it wasn't worth the sacrifice of energies best utilized elsewhere. Better to absorb a small defeat in hopes of gaining a greater victory on another world. He would accept that as he had accepted Jaruselka's death.

Except he had not yet succeeded in accepting that.

Enough time had passed for it to be allowable for him to mate again. He had no interest even though he knew she would have wished it for him, even as he would have wished it for her had the circumstances been reversed. And he prayed he could make that reversal occur. But he could not undo what had happened. He could only concentrate on his command, which today seemed to be going the way of the rest of his life.

It was raining hard; a steady, unrelenting downpour. As usual it would affect the enemy less than his own people. His command vehicle hovered at the south entrance to the valley, just beyond range of the battle raging ahead. He could see that a general pullback had already commenced as the Crigolit gunners poured heavy fire on his troops, even as they did their best to spare the village and fields which occupied the valley.

The Massood fought back, once even regaining a portion of the valley's eastern reaches. The valiant effort ended in disaster when a horde of Mazvec fell on the attackers and annihilated an entire squad. The subofficer in charge ordered the survivors to commence as orderly a retreat as possible.

Another miserable plot of land surrendered, Caldaq thought tiredly. They were going to have to abandon this valley, these mountains, these people, to the Amplitur. It was not the first time circumstances had required him to oversee such an action. Repetition had numbed his sensibilities. Emotionless orders issued from the damned machine of his soul as he carried out his assignment by rote.

Reinforcements were not an option. He'd known that before the fight had been joined. Several major battles were under way elsewhere and troops could not be spared from those sectors to bolster his efforts in this valley.

Presently I must leave this world, he thought. His grief had kept him longer than any sense of duty, to the credit of his family if not his spirit. It was time to go. Another year here would not bring Jaruselka back any more than it would turn the tide against the Amplitur. It was past time.

He studied the tridimensional projection which represented the immediate theater of conflict. Time to pull back; to another valley, another ridge. The geography of Kantaria was as bereft of hope as its people.

Eventually there would be no more valleys to pull back to. Then they would have to flee in transport shuttles, running the dangerous gauntlet to an evacuation fleet darting in and out of Underspace, hoping to avoid the Amplitur attacks which would surely follow their flight. They would leave behind a miserable world populated by an abandoned, confused people. The Amplitur would at least resolve their confusion.

Preparations for withdrawal were nearly complete when the subofficer came running into the command center. He was breathing hard and his body armor was scored from several near hits. His left ear was missing. Field hospitals on Kantaria were not equipped with such luxuries as regeneration facilities.

"Honored Commander."

"What is it, soldier?" A transmitter dangled from the long slim fingers of Caldaq's right hand.

"We cannot get away."

"Explain yourself." Caldaq's calm arose from the not unwelcome possibility that his spirit might soon be reunited with that of his beloved.

Jaruselka, Jaruselka; I am tired and I miss thee.

"Monitoring has located a hitherto unsuspected Crigolit strike force in a canyon behind us. They apparently have surface-to-air weaponry with guidance to match. Given our present situation I . . ."

"I am familiar with current conditions, soldier. Request a tactical strike from Support."

"Is there no other way, Honored Commander? The enemy is close upon us. I fear it may be impossible to hit them from long range without suffering damage ourselves."

"If what you say is true then we have no choice." Caldaq commented quietly, almost indifferently. "Without a strike they will pick us off one vehicle at a time. We cannot go forward because the enemy is advancing in strength and we cannot go anywhere else because our aircars will not surmount the peaks that surround this valley. It may be as you said that we cannot get out at all, but we can try. At least we will take many of the enemy with us.

"I would like to know how they slipped through our defensive perimeter."

"It has been suggested, Honored Commander, that they may have been dug in there all along, only waiting for us to retreat in order to spring their ambush. Or they may have only just arrived in this sector. Some of the new floaters they ride are so fast and travel so close to the surface that they are almost impossible to detect by traditional means."

"I have heard of them," said Caldaq tiredly.

The subofficer watched his commander uneasily. Caldaq looked exhausted, drained. Finally the younger Massood felt moved to prompt his elder.

"Sir? The strike?"

"Yes. Call for it. Tell Support not to sacrifice firepower for precision." He looked down to make sure his sidearm was in place. For years he'd worn it more for ceremony than anything else. Now he might actually have to use it.

A check showed that it was fully powered. One could not take that for granted ever since the Amplitur had introduced into some battles a genetically engineered bacterium which found Weave power cells the perfect place to breed.

"Inform all units, officer, to hold their positions for as long as they can. We will try to coordinate strike timing with Support. I will request a ten-minute pause at a time to be determined and communicated. During that time all units will attempt the downcanyon outrun. If we are lucky, the Crigolit will be concentrating on shielding themselves from the strike and some of us may be able to slip past before they have time to react."

The strike request was met with some hesitancy on the part of Support. Concurring in retreat was never easy. Caldaq loudly explained that the longer the strike was delayed, the less was the likelihood of any of the valley's defenders escaping.

The success of the enemy's tactics did not embarrass him. In this hellish terrain it was hard to tell what one's own troops were doing, let alone the enemy's. Someone had made a mistake, but there was no time for recriminations. There was time only for flight.

The command vehicle in which he rode was slower than most but more heavily armored. He did not care about himself, but he badly wanted to save those who had served under him. It would reflect well on the family.

His craft would make a large and tempting target as it trundled down the canyon. Normally it would be screened and defended by slider outriders, but he had lost so many soldiers in the failed attempt to take the valley that the craft would be forced to proceed without benefit of escorting fire.

It would be futile, he calmly decided, to try and disguise the command vehicle's progress, which would show up on even primitive monitors. He would order off all nonessential personnel. They could double up on attack sliders and transport cars. If the command vehicle made the run first and headed directly for the Crigolit positions, the move might confuse the enemy. At the very least it would draw their initial response. Heavily shielded, it could deflect fire that would down a slider instantly. If the diversion was successful, it ought to open a brief escape window for the rest of his command.

It might also be recognized for the ploy that it was. A thousand years of combat had given both sides a good idea of what tactics the other was likely to employ.

He was being too hard on himself. There were only so many strategic variations possible in a given situation. As field commander it was incumbent on him to analyze and direct. If the diversion resulted in the escape of only a few more of his people than otherwise, it would be well worth the effort.

Soon he would be with Jaruselka on the other plane of existence. Whatever that was. If it existed. It would not be a bad thing to die issuing orders intended to save others. At least he would not perish outside, in the unending rain.

His call for volunteers to crew the command craft was rapidly oversubscribed. They made what preparations they could in the limited time available. There was little time for farewells. Directives went out over those portions of the field communications system which had not yet been damaged by invasive Amplitur bacteria.

Support poured explosives on enemy positions ahead and to the rear. No words were spoken inside the command craft as the skeleton crew dwelt on final thoughts. Chronometers counted down.

Soon it was time to move.

The lumbering vehicle rose above the tops of the sheltering trees and pivoted westward, all shields and weaponry activated. The canyon was dark with swirling clouds of granite dust and the debris of pulverized vegetation. That would not be enough to shield them from enemy detectors, Caldaq knew. But the release of energy which would commence as soon as the command craft was engaged by Crigolit forces would help to screen the sliders carrying his surviving troops as they bolted for safety.

"Any reaction?" he inquired.

"No, sir." A single composed subofficer was doing her best to evaluate detection and surveillance reports that were normally monitored by three specialists.

Caldaq was not surprised. The report had said that the Crigolit force was well dug in. They would be in no hurry to emerge until they were certain the bombardment had ceased.

They never saw where the first missile came from.

It struck rear left, taking out a main thruster and cutting their maneuverability by nearly a third. Smoking and listing to one side, the command craft began to curve across the valley.

Caldaq hung onto his chair. "Adjust right rear thruster to compensate."

"Sir, that will slow us considerably," said the technician in charge.

"At maximum thrust this machine is already too slow. Do it!"

The subofficer gestured acknowledgment but said nothing as he struggled to comply.

We must look strange to the enemy, hovering here in plain sight, hardly moving, he thought. It might confuse them more effectively than the most exquisite maneuver. Indeed, the anticipated response was not forthcoming. Instead, a long pause was followed by a single, surgically placed missile which struck the command craft amidships.

It was sufficient to knock out all but a single remaining thruster. Deprived of support and forward motion the skid began a slow descent. Through the acrid smoke that filled the room he saw that they would probably land hard but intact, unless they took another hit on the way down. Habit rather than desire made him check to insure that his harness was tight. The ground was coming up fast.

Granted time to think, he realized that there must be Amplitur among the ambushing force. Crigolit or Mazvec would simply have obliterated the wounded command vehicle, whereas the Amplitur would try where possible to preserve life. Survivors could be evacuated from Kantaria for "education."

His fingers caressed the sidearm. He would not be a candidate for their schools. He knew about such places, where the Amplitur would work on you until you weren't sure what you were fighting for, or even who you were. Only that you were, had to be, must be, a servant of the Purpose. Caldaq held no illusions about his ability to resist that kind of persuasion. One did not resist lightning, earthquake, or Amplitur intrusion. Mentally, he was no stronger than anyone else.

Following successful "treatment" the Amplitur would slip the reeducated back onto their homeworlds, there to sow dissension and confusion. An altered Massood could do more damage to the war effort than the most powerful particle weapon.

Dimly he was aware that the subofficer for piloting was screaming at him through the flames and rush of air. "I apologize to my family, sir! I did the best I . . . !"

His voice was stilled by whatever also took away the light . . .

The ringing in his head remained when consciousness returned. A mocking, sadistic providence had left him bruised and battered but otherwise alive.

Coughing and fighting for air, he slapped three times at his harness release before it let him go. Without the straps to hold him in his seat he fell to the floor. There he rested a luxurious minute before struggling to his feet.

It was impossible to see anything through the boiling smoke. Better to make his way outside, if possible, and let his vision clear. Then he could think about helping others.

Memory guided him to an exterior door. Not surprisingly, the electronics did not respond and he had to cycle the lock manually. He fell through the resultant gap, sucking in huge lungfuls of moist, uncontaminated air.

No Crigolit or Mazvec troops saw him exit. Perhaps the command craft had come down in a relatively inaccessible area. More likely the enemy was on its way and simply had not yet reached the crash site.

Staggering toward the thickest stand of trees, he nearly tripped over the smoking body of his third-in-command. The subofficer was still alive, breathing shallowly. Caldaq dug up clumps of spongy moss and massaged the soldier with the saturated vegetation. Only when the jumpsuit had stopped smoldering did Caldaq heave the subofficer onto his shoulders and start for the woods.

As he did so a voice speaking perfect Massood ordered him to halt.

The woods were dense, dark, full of possible hiding places, and oh so near. He could not balance the moaning subofficer and draw his sidearm at the same time. As he took another step something like a sharp blade cut him in the side. Looking down he saw a tiny, steaming black hole in his uniform, just beneath the fifteenth rib. There would be a matching hole in his back.

As he stumbled onward he sought to analyze the wound with perfect objectivity. What vital organs, blood vessels, or nerves lay in the vicinity of the shot, and relationally, how long was he likely to be able to keep going? The problem was no less intriguing for the fact that it was of more than theoretical concern.

The shot did have one immediate consequence, he decided. It had stolen his feet. He felt rather than saw himself falling forward, the weight on his shoulders accelerating his descent. The subofficer let out a groan as they struck the ground together.

Having taken his feet they were now trying to steal his vision, he mused as he lay motionless on the macerated earth. He did not think he was bleeding. The weapon whose effects he had experienced was one that cauterized as it penetrated. That was not necessarily a good thing. It might mean he would die slowly.

His fingers were still functioning but not in tandem with his brain. They fumbled at his sidearm, taking an unconscionable amount of time to extract it from his belt. The hard plastic handle was comforting in his palm. Unfortunately, someone had increased the density of the compact device to that of a neutron star. No matter how hard he tried he found he could not lift it higher than his waist.

Voices reached him through the rain that was beating him to death. Sharp, clicking sounds characteristic of Crigolit. There was also a less audible nasal tone. Mazvec, perhaps. If he could only raise the damnable sidearm he might yet offer one final objection to the inexorable advance of the Purpose. But he could barely feel the weapon now, much less see it.

The voices came closer. The Crigolit tended to be excitable. If he was lucky, they might shoot him despite orders to the contrary.

They began to shout. I have been seen, he thought wearily as he fought to turn the sidearm just enough to aim the tip at his chest. I deny you a pupil if not the victory. But his traitorous fingers refused to obey. He swore at them as he passed out.

For the second time that day he awoke. It was dark and the stars of Kantaria only occasionally pierced the ever present clouds. It was raining again, a damp curtain of misery that added to his discomfort, soaking him beneath his body armor.

The subofficer he had carried into the woods was supporting him.

"Praise to the Lineage," said the soldier. "I found only the single beam wound, Honored Commander. It is good to see you alive. No, do not try to stand alone."

Caldaq felt strong arms beneath his own as the subofficer helped him to his feet. He swayed slightly as he studied their surroundings.

They were in a narrow side canyon. A crude shelter fashioned of branches and boughs had been erected alongside an overhanging boulder. Water ran swiftly down the middle of the narrow gorge.

"When I regained consciousness, sir, you were lying next to me. At first I thought you were dead, but your heart still beat. I brought you here."

"The others." Caldaq wished for better night vision.

"I do not know, sir. I heard firing when I came around and I could see flashes of light off to the west. It suggests that the enemy located the retreating column. How many of our people slipped past them I cannot guess. Perhaps that was what distracted them from searching for us."

"Some must have made it away," Caldaq muttered tightly. His side hurt badly, a continuous burning as if a knife had been lodged beneath his ribs and forgotten.

He did not dwell on the possible severity of his injuries. Yet another scrape with death had done nothing to alter his ambivalence toward life.

The subofficer he had rescued and who had in turn saved him harbored no such uncertainties. "The battle for this valley is over, sir. When the Crigolit have satisfied themselves of that they will move on. Then we can start toward base central. We have a chance.''

"Of course we do." Caldaq hid his own pessimism for the benefit of his companion. The trek would be arduous even for healthy Massood. Somehow they would have to cross rugged mountains and rain-swollen rivers. He wiped water from his face and damned this wretched, ungrateful world for the thousandth time.

"I still wonder how they managed to get behind us in strength, Honored Commander.''

"Perhaps an outlying detector failed.'' Much easier, Caldaq thought, to blame a military disaster on a failure of equipment rather than personnel.

Through falling rain and forest ramparts he saw motion. The subofficer would not have to worry about the difficult trek back to base central.

"They are coming,'' he whispered.

His service belt lay nearby, where the subofficer had placed it. He drew his sidearm and his companion did likewise. Together they waited beneath the leaking lean-to, grateful for what little concealment it offered. There was no thought of running. It would have taken all Caldaq's strength just to stand.

Shapes loomed in the murk; larger than a Crigolit, smaller than Molitar. Mazvec, perhaps. They advanced with tense grace, rain dripping from their field armor and opaqued visors. Their electronics were muted, so he was unable to tell how heavily armed they were.

One glanced in the direction of the lean-to. Caldaq raised his weapon and tried to aim. His vision was blurred and his arm shaky.

The armored figure turned and shouted through a voice membrane, disdaining the use of a communicator. That meant its companions must be close by. Sharp and loud, the exclamation rose above the noise of the downpour. Even in his dazed condition Caldaq recognized it immediately.

"Tyro, Ephram, get your butts over here! There's rats in the rain!''

Exhausted, Caldaq let his arm drop, sank back against the stone which formed the rear wall of the lean-to. He was unsure of the words which had been spoken but certain of their origin.

The armored figure vaulted a fallen log and bent toward the two Massood. There was a slight click as the soldier unsealed his visor and flipped it up. Caldaq squinted as bright light was played over his face.

"Glad to see you alive, Honored Commander." The soldier spoke in cracked Massood. Under the circumstances Caldaq forgave him his atrocious accent. The light swung up to the subofficer, back to Caldaq. "Just the two of you, sir?"

The subofficer explained. "We employed our field HQ as a decoy. The Crigolit were pleased to oblige."

"Yeah. The bugs love slow-moving targets."

They were soon joined by several other figures who formed an armored semicircle in the rain opposite the lean-to. Caldaq studied their faces beneath opened visors, flat and symmetrical within the helmets.

A red-striped medic knelt alongside. In an instant she'd set her field computer to Massood mode and was diagnosing. A Hivistahm would have made faster work of it but no Hivistahm could cope emotionally with front-line conditions. Caldaq felt something prick his side and the pain began to recede. He was immensely grateful for the relief, however temporary. A portion of his strength was returned to him.

"Sorry we got here so late, sir," said the soldier who'd found them. He was a young male, Caldaq noted, with naked pale skin and golden hair.

"The others," he heard himself mumbling. "The rest of the column . . ."

"You mean your people who were trying to get out? We showed up when they were halfway down the canyon, sir. The Amplitur and the Crigolit were waiting for them." Caldaq's heart sank. "But they weren't waiting for us." In the dim light Caldaq saw the white flash of the Human's incisors.

"We came down on 'em like trolls out of Tyrannia, sir. Scattered them to hell and gone. Damn but it was fine!"

Caldaq sensed the excitement in the Human's voice, knew it was the combat rush they alone among Weave fighters experienced. He could not criticize. Those racial deficiencies had saved his life, and those of who knew how many fellow Massood.

"Can you get us out of here?"

"No problem, Honored Commander. It's our valley now."

Caldaq heard but did not comprehend. "The Crigolit in front

of us . . . they were dug in, they had control of all critical positions . . .''

"The operative tense, sir, is past. After we came down on their intended ambush we just kept on going. Rolled 'em up like herring. Lost some good people, too," he added darkly. "The Crigolit, they're hard fighters, but they think instead of reacting, if you know what I mean. They never recovered from the initial surprise of our appearance." He stared into the darkness.

"Nice rain tonight. Reminds me of home."

The Human medic continued to work on his side, muttering as she did so. "Small-bore beam weapon." She glanced up at him. "You were lucky, sir. A little to the left and your spine would've been severed." She smiled reassuringly at him, and he wondered anew at the Human ability to feel warmth and pleasure in the most appalling conditions.

"No permanent damage, nothing that can't be fixed," she was saying. "Bet it hurt like hell, though. I'd go in myself but I'd rather let the Hivi surgeons back on the coast have a go. Wish I had their technique. Never will."

"I am grateful for your ministrations," Caldaq told her in her own language.

Behind him the subofficer stretched out a long arm. Another of the Human soldiers clasped the long Massood fingers, then slid his hand up the arm to the elbow as greetings were exchanged. As the soldiers chatted amiably the medic peered into Caldaq's face.

"I've given you something to make you sleep, sir. I'd rather you didn't try to walk. We'll have you out of here in a few minutes. I know how uncomfortable you must be in this rain."

Caldaq felt consciousness beginning to blur. Not from trauma this time but from the gentle chemistry of the sedative. Peace began to spread throughout his battered body, as if he were being massaged from the inside out.

A new voice, a face gazing into his. Vaguely he noted the officer's stripes that crisscrossed the right shoulder. "What've we got here?" the figure asked.

"Couple of half-drowned rats, sir," said the soldier who'd found them. "One's a field commander."

"Your pardon," mumbled a fast-fading Caldaq, "but I am not certain in this context of the use of the term 'rat.' "

"Nothing personal, sir," said the officer. "It's your faces.

Humans have a tendency to nickname everything and soldiers more so than civilians. I assure you it's in no way derogatory. Quite the contrary.''

"Since I do not know what a rat is I can hardly take offense at being compared to one." Caldaq's nose and whiskers twitched feebly in the rain.

The officer looked up. "It was a near thing here, a near thing. When the initial reports started coming through, my unit volunteered to take a crack at breaking your people out. Now it's the Crigolit and the Amplitur who are running for cover. My people are helping them along, picking them off in the darkness. The Crigolit don't do so well in the rain at night, their instrumentation notwithstanding.''

He paused and leaned close. Almost asleep, Caldaq ignored the rain that dripped off the man's upraised visor.

"Hey, don't I know you?''

"I do not believe so,'' Caldaq murmured sleepily as the sedative began to exert itself.

The Human began to whistle softly. It was a skill they were adept at. Through the haze which had enveloped his brain Caldaq thought he recognized the melody, though it had been a long time since the jarring tones had assaulted his ears.

"What do you think?'' the man asked gently. "Does it sound any better now?''

"I am glad to hear,'' Caldaq replied, angry at his inability to form the consonants correctly, "that you are still making your music, William Dulac.'' As he drifted into a sound, restful sleep he found himself struggling with the contradictory image his friend presented in field armor. Were the Humans commissioning composers now?

★ XXX ★

Thereafter he dreamed. He dreamed that their sled was attacked twice on the long flight back to the coast and Weave regional headquarters. He dreamed he saw Will Dulac storming among the other soldiers, raging and bellowing orders as they fought off repeated attacks. Each jolt and roar was an individual nightmare, muted only by suspension in the medical pallet. Like the eviscerated entrails of some glassine beast, transparent tubes recycled and replenished his bodily fluids as he dreamed.

In the distance and through the mist of medication he thought he heard himself speaking.

"I thought you despised all this. I thought participation in the resistance against the Amplitur was against everything you stood for. You said always that you wanted to be civilized like the other Weave races, that you wanted more than anything else to keep your people out of the war and the fighting."

"I did. I said all that. But I couldn't, and finally I gave up. Gave in, rather." Will smiled that strange Human smile. "Until I did it was tearing me apart, to the point where I couldn't work, couldn't compose, could hardly think."

"What happened?" asked the disembodied voice he thought he recognized as his own.

"I was asked by a S'van to compose some Human music to accompany images which had been recorded of the fighting on Vasarih. I replied that I didn't think I could do that, but that I would try." He paused.

"It turned out to be the easiest, least stressful composition of my life. The music came pouring out, fully orchestrated. Hardly required any revision. I sent it to my agent and it turned into a huge hit on Earth. People still hum the principal theme.

"I kept writing in the same vein. It was easy. I ended up with a six-movement symphony, over an hour's worth of music. There was talk of a Pulitzer, but I don't care about that anymore.

"I wanted to do more in the same vein, so I thought I should get out and experience what was happening and not just sit in a room watching recordings. Be true to the work, so to speak. Write about your experiences, paint what you see, compose what you feel. So I signed up. And they kept promoting me. I didn't ask for that. I didn't ask for any of this. But you know what? I'm good at it. When I was a kid my grandfather used to take me hunting in the bayous. Except for the technology this isn't as different as I thought it would be. Because the quarry's still not Human.

"Organizing an attack isn't so different from organizing a symphony. You orchestrate your forces and plan your strategy. I don't know. It just feels right. And all the internal conflicts, the uncertainties, are gone now. My body and mind may be at war, but my soul's at peace. Maybe that's what being Human is all about. The debate on that is unending, you know."

"No, I did not know," Caldaq whispered weakly.

"That's right. You've been stuck on Kantaria for quite a while, haven't you?

"I'm not confused anymore, old friend. I'm here to fight, and to interpret this conflict musically. The two are inseparable now. I know plenty of other artists who feel the same way. More and more are coming around to that way of thinking all the time. There's something natural about it, something easy. Maybe it's chemical. Something happens inside the Human system in a combat situation that makes you feel more alive, more aware, than at any other time. If you'll tell me where Jaruselka's stationed I'll be sure to . . ."

"Dead. More than a year ago."

Will was silent for a long time. "I'm sorry. I didn't know."

"Here, on this world," Caldaq was murmuring. "I could not save her. I could not do anything but watch."

It was quiet in the room for a long while before Will spoke again. "If you wouldn't object, I'd like to compose a little memorial piece for her. I'll utilize Massood tonalities so the result won't make you wince."

Humans spoke of their dead with an enthusiasm other races reserved exclusively for the living, Caldaq knew. They painted, wrote, composed music, and sculpted death. It was a morbid racial affectation no other Weave species shared. Why write about the dead when one could write about the living? Yet mankind seemed to glory in it.

Such Human peculiarities had saved his life.

The dream passed, was followed by another. Will again, talking reassuringly.

"We're out of danger now. Just crossed over the southwest massif. Soon we'll be at Base Central. They've got a bed with your name on it reserved at the hospital."

Caldaq saw that his friend was surrounded by smaller figures, heard him speaking in a strange language. The man looked back at him, switched his translator to Massood.

"Kantarians. Even though we secured their village some of them wanted to come with us. They want to help. I've been told that's something of a breakthrough. You know, Caldaq, if it wasn't for you we'd still be fighting among ourselves back on Earth instead of helping out people like these."

Caldaq found he was able to turn his head, saw the way the slim, diminutive natives hung close to the taller, bulkier shape of the Human. They were approximately the same size as Hivistahm or Lepar.

It was strange to see them crowding around Will Dulac, him smiling down at them even though they might not understand the expression, listening to them converse in elfin tones before the Human shooed them out. Their attitude had been almost worshipful.

But that was wrong, all wrong. Sentients needed to respect one another as equals.

"Nice folk, the Kantarians." Will shut the door and walked back to Caldaq's pallet. The battle sled lurched slightly and the Commander's eyes widened. Will hastened to reassure him.

"Just weather. You know what the weather's like hereabouts."

"Horrible," Caldaq muttered. "Rain all the time, dampness everywhere."

"Our people don't mind it. S'van researchers say it has to do with the variety of weather we get on our own world. Apparently it's considerably less stable than anywhere else. From what I've

heard I think we'd find the weather on the other Weave worlds
pretty boring. I guess we can make ourselves at home just about
anywhere.''

"How could any civilized being think of this awful place as
a home?''

"The Kantarians do.''

"They are not civilized.''

"Neither are we, remember? Maybe that's why we're getting
along so well with them.''

Caldaq thought about that when he awoke in his comfortable
bed in the main hospital at Base Central, his pain much subdued. The Hivistahm tech who happened to be checking on him
clicked its teeth in delight when the Commander opened his
eyes.

"How long?'' Caldaq asked immediately.

"Ten days almost, Commander.'' The tech was checking readouts on nearby monitors.

On command the bed raised him to a sitting position. He saw
that he was in a private cubicle as befitted his rank.

"Is there a Human officer, Will Dulac, on base? I realize you
would not know, but if you could initiate inquiries it would be
appreciated.''

"Truly there is for that no need, Commander.'' He handed
Caldaq a pill which the Massood obediently swallowed. "Everyone knows of the Human Dulac.''

"They do?''

"Naturally, since regional commander he is.''

" 'Regional commander.' '' To Caldaq the notion seemed as
alien as an Amplitur probe.

"Truly. Many battles have the Humans won since they arrived
here in force. They are in the process of pushing the Crigolit
main body back over the continental divide. It is rumored that
Human infiltration squads are already swift strikes conducting
on supply lines and depots in the foothills of the eastern slopes.''

"Do you know of my own group? Southern sector forces Two
and Three?''

"Those who survived the battle in which you wounded were
are alongside the Humans fighting. They to go back volunteered, I understand.'' The Hivistahm whistled. "Truly strange

are the ways of those who capable of combat are. Is it true your people fight better in the company of Humans?''

''Not that I have noticed.''

The technician hardly heard him. ''Time it is to wait expectantly. Some say that the Humans will push the Crigolit, Mazvec, and Amplitur off Kantaria by year end.''

''Not possible,'' Caldaq mumbled. ''The enemy is too firmly established on this world, too well entrenched. Their lines of supply are secure and . . .''

Extraordinarily, the technician interrupted him. It was unheard of for a Hivistahm to interrupt a Massood.

''None of that to these Humans matters. It is understandable, as they not civilized are. I have the recordings seen. Visualize the most ferocious, hostile land-dwelling creature imaginable and then intelligence give it. Truly there you have a Human. Although,'' the tech added after a moment's hesitation, ''some of their music nice is.'' Double eyelids blinked in the smooth flat light of the hospital room. The tech's cleansuit bristled with specialty insignia.

''Tell me something.''

''If I can, Commander.'' The tech checked his chronometer and Caldaq noted the length of his claws, which were extreme for a Hivistahm. Perhaps they served some practical function.

''What think you of Human beings?''

''I personally?''

''Truly,'' Caldaq said in Hivistahm.

The technician was forced to pause. Hivistahm much preferred to render opinions in a group. But after a moment's thought he said, ''I have for them little use myself. Of true culture or the higher civilized disciplines they know little, despite their protestations to the contrary. I admire their tenacity and their fighting abilities even as I personally abhorrent find them. But I am for their presence glad as it means I am to fight myself not required.'' He shuddered visibly. ''Humans fight and die for the Hivistahm and the Hivistahm worlds.''

''They fight for their own purposes,'' Caldaq corrected him.

''Their passion for odd sorts of remuneration well known is.'' The technician clicked its claws together. ''It only their uncivilized status confirms. It does not trouble me that they fight for such reasons. It matters only that in fighting they the rest of us shield and defend.''

"No, I meant how do you feel about them on a personal level."

"I have few Humans myself met," said the tech thoughtfully. "Those I have encountered are invariably grateful for any good treatment they receive, as though it were some sort of exceptional bonus instead of an inalienable right. They have of civilized behavior but a poor grasp and thus regard what is natural as unusual.

"Personally? I have to know them personally no desire. Were you to place me in a room with one I think that I should quickly start kicking the door in an effort to flee. But in this environment"—and he indicated the surrounding medical complex— "I am with my own kind most of the time. I have the support of the group or of S'van or O'o'yan. Even Yula and Massood. I am among Humans not isolated."

"Then it doesn't trouble you?"

"What does not trouble me?" said the technician.

"That the Humans are doing so much of the fighting and are having so much success at it. That fighting is the thing they do best."

Bulbous eyes peered querulously down at him. "Truly it pleases me, as it pleases all Hivistahm."

The door slid aside silently to admit an O'o'yan tech; a shorter, slimmer version of the Hivistahm. It differed from the one Caldaq had been conversing with primarily in coloring and skull structure as well as attitude.

"Truly I must to other work now attend, Commander. You should rest. If you will do that, then I believe I can recommend that you from this facility in a day or two be discharged."

"My thanks," Caldaq said in a passable Hivistahm. The technician's Massood had been quite good, but then a medical tech on Kantaria would spend most of its time working on wounded soldiers and would be expected to know the language of the injured. Despite that, he had yet to see a Hivistahm speaking English. When working on injured Humans they invariably utilized their translators. Because they had yet to master a new allied tongue, or because they saw it as a way to maintain a certain distance between themselves and their new patients?

This technician had already said he had admiration but no love for Humankind. The O'o'yan could be expected to express similar sentiments. From all Caldaq had heard and seen only the Massood were able to share certain feelings and emotions with their Human colleagues. The S'van pretended well, but in this they could not fool an experienced observer like Caldaq. They had no more love for Humanity than did the Hivistahm.

It gave him something to ponder as he lay on the pallet recovering his strength. He discussed his concerns, quietly and casually, with the many who came to attend to his needs. They included fellow Massood officers glad to learn of his survival as well as numerous Hivistahm, O'o'yan, and S'van technicians. He asked all of them the same questions, even the Lepar who cleaned his room.

One who did not come again was Will Dulac. He was among those directing the relentless assault on the central Crigolit positions in the eastern mountains. Caldaq contented himself with those who took the time to visit with him.

He was remonstrating with two unit commanders who had arrived to pay their respects to the hero of Takicohn Valley. To them had gone the pleasure of informing Caldaq of the honor that was to be bestowed on him. He protested as vigorously as he was able, insisting that he deserved no such recognition. He had lost the battle. To his way of thinking, a glorious retreat was unworthy of commendation.

They joked about it, pointing out that he was too weak to refuse, and read the text of the award that would be entered in his family records for all to venerate. Thus frustrated, he availed himself of the opportunity to unburden himself of the fears that had been festering in his mind as he lay in the hospital.

"We must stop using Human soldiers." He tried to employ the command accent to the fullest, to convey to these two fellow officers the depth of his feeling.

Clearly his words had an effect. His visitors exchanged a puzzled look before the one called Huswemak eyed him uncertainly.

"Why?" he inquired. "They are the best fighters we have ever had. Already they have turned many battles in our favor. Here they have saved a campaign we were losing. I myself have seen them throw themselves on heavily fortified positions heedless of their own safety in order to rescue Massood troops."

"That is not why they fight in what appears to us to be a reckless manner. There is nothing of the altruistic about them." Caldaq shifted on the bed.

"It took me a long while to realize this. I knew a Hivistahm third-of-study who tried to explain it to me but like you, I could not see. I was blinded by the prospect of Human aid.''

"Could not see what?'' inquired the other officer, struggling not to sound patronizing. Clearly the Honored Commander was still suffering the aftereffects of his life-threatening injuries.

"That Humankind is potentially as dangerous to us as to the Amplitur.''

"You must be very tired, Caldaq,'' said Huswemak soothingly. He started to rise.

"I am quite clearheaded,'' Caldaq replied tersely.

Thus admonished, the officer had no choice but to sit down again. "The Humans hit our enemies as hard as they can. If one is given access to their thoughts they make it clear that they despise the Amplitur and what they stand for. I fail to see how that makes them a threat to us.'' Huswemak wondered if the psytechs had cleared Caldaq for release. It was widely known that he had suffered severely from the loss of his mate a year earlier.

"Humans are dangerous,'' Caldaq was telling them.

"Dangerous to the Amplitur and Crigolit.'' Arenont's lips rippled with amusement. "I myself have seen an injured Human take on a Molitar in the field and defeat it. You would not believe such a thing possible if you did not witness it for yourself.'' She turned to her colleague. "Perhaps it would be advisable for us to call for a physician.''

"I tell you there is nothing wrong with my mind!'' Caldaq's nose and whiskers quivered.

"But you have been through a terrible time.'' Huswemak rose. "The mind as well as the body can suffer from trauma.''

Caldaq used the bed to straighten himself. "Listen to me! I was of the same mind as you. I once thought as you did.''

"You are famed among the people for your uniquely non-Massood ability to pause and ponder.'' Arenont gestured deferentially. "Is it not possible that you have recently had too much time to think? This is a problem which often afflicts the S'van.'' The two officers stood by the door, which parted silently to allow them egress.

"Out of respect we will pass along your comments.''

"To the medical staff?'' Caldaq shot back sardonically. Clearly his concerns had made no impression on them whatsoever.

"To relevant parties," replied Huswemak softly.

When they had gone Caldaq lowered the pallet and lay staring at the pale blue ceiling. Useless to share his worries with others. They would not believe. They *chose* not to believe.

He remembered something Arenont had said. Perhaps the S'van would be more open-minded. Having little presence on the battlefield they would be less likely to be overawed by Human achievements. Skeptical they might be, but they would listen. The S'van always listened. If he could at least set some among them to thinking . . .

On the day he was to be discharged he received a visit from a Hivistahm physician. This in itself was expected, but the physician's identity was not.

It was she who had been the interfacer on his ship: the one who had been devastated by Will Dulac's reaction to the artificial mind probe.

Though he was far from expert at judging Hivistahm health it was clear that the past years had not been kind to her. Too many prosthetic scales dotted her neck and the graceful, elongated head. Her eyeshades were thick and dark, unfashionably unadorned.

She was elegantly clad in the pale green uniform of a full physician. Insignia of rank gleamed on her shoulders. Before entering she sampled the air of the room, an instinctive Hivistahm reaction.

"Honored Commander Caldaq: Do you know me?"

"I do." He stood by the edge of the pallet which had nurtured him back to health. "I did not know you were on Kantaria."

"I have not here long been. Truly one does not have to be to of your exploits hear."

"It seems I am to be exalted for a grand failure. I am not pleased." His upper lip curled. "Have they sent one who knew me to decide whether I am sane enough to return to my work?"

"Sarcasm better suits the S'van," she commented. "I have heard of what you have been saying. I know quite sane you are."

"If anyone should, it ought to be you. And Third-of-Study, if you remember him."

"Well I recall. He spoke, I was silent. I needed to heal." She came close and stared up at him. "I know firsthand the truth of what you have been saying."

Caldaq looked down at her. "Because of what happened to you on the ship?"

"Truly that, and other things. I have had time to study, to observe."

He inhaled sharply. "Then perhaps between the two of us we may yet convince others of the danger. I intend to take this matter as far as possible. To the Military Council, if need be. The support of a non-Massood, and a physician at that, will be very welcome. You will help me?"

"I will do no such thing," she replied.

"But you agree with me." Caldaq was stunned. "It was you who once insisted we kill the man Will Dulac and flee his system. Or have you forgotten?"

"Truly I have not. But help you I will not. It would not matter anyway."

"I do not understand."

"Of course you do not. You are a soldier, a fighter. But for the very reasons you enumerate it is too late now things to change. Perhaps at the beginning, when first we these people on their homeworld encountered, a case might have been made for granting them the isolation they requested. But now they have integrated themselves too fully into our forces, have made themselves to the war effort invaluable. Your fellow Massood have told you that. The other species, my own people, will with Humankind have nothing to do, but they revere them for what they have accomplished on behalf of the Weave."

"Attitudes can be changed. Why won't you help me?"

"Because despite my personal fears and concerns, or yours, there is no avoiding the fact that the Humans a difference in the fighting have made. They have a status quo shattered which for hundreds of years existed. Truly they the new figure in the equation are."

"We fought well without the aid of Humans. It can be so again," Caldaq insisted.

"I have what you propose already tried. Quietly, in the manner of my kind. I have cultivated important contacts, have gained the interest of those who have the attention of Council members. I have shown them the records of my own personal experience, despite the fact that I relive that pain time and again. Truly a nuisance of myself I made.

"That was when I was of something not generally known

informed, something perhaps unknown even to members of the General Council.''

"Critical information would not be kept from the General Council,'' Caldaq protested.

The physician indicated humor. "You a fine soldier are, Caldaq of the Massood. Among your people you would qualify as a deep thinker. But you are not Hivistahm, not S'van. Innocence is a trait to be encouraged among fighters.

"The truth is that the war we were losing.''

"No,'' Caldaq objected. "Both sides won victories and sustained losses.''

"Truly, but in subtle ways it had been clear to the Military Council for some time that the Amplitur winning were. Defeat could greatly prolonged be, but not prevented. Tout a minor victory here, play down a major defeat elsewhere. In this manner was kept from the general population this knowledge.

"Understand that this was as much a revelation to me as it must be to you now. Only when I chose the matter of intimate Human involvement in the resistance to pursue was it decided that I should to a carefully masked reality be exposed.

"It was made clear to me in nonmilitary terms that during the last hundred years the Weave had begun to lose the war. With their singleness of purpose and ability to mentally manipulate their allies the Amplitur an advantage had which the acrimonious members of the Weave could not hope to counter. That advantage had at last begun to tell.

"And then the Humans. They do not like any other known race act. Though manifestly uncivilized they have an advanced technology managed to develop. They are unlike anything the Amplitur have encountered, the product of an abnormal evolution. Mediocre artists and technicians, they combine minimal intelligence with an extraordinary proclivity for violence. Their presence has the military revitalized and the Amplitur and their allies stunned. And then there is the as yet unexplained mechanism within their nervous system which enables them not merely to resist but fight off the Amplitur mind probe.

"Not only has the inevitable defeat been staved off, our forces are reversing losses and the offensive taking. I do not mean to minimize the danger I think Humans present to our civilization, but that civilization must first be preserved before we can deal with what is at present only a theoretical threat. Under the circumstances, you can see truly why the Military Council no choice has but to make maximum use of Human volunteers. Were anyone otherwise to suggest they would be instantly replaced.''

Caldaq was silent for a long moment. ''Do you understand the real danger they represent? It is not that they are good fighters, or independent of mind. It is that they *like* fighting. They revel in it, they luxuriate in it. They have spent millennia trying to deny this birthright because they were forced to fight each other. Now they have an opponent who is not Human. No longer do they have to strive to resist their natural instincts.'' He paused. ''I saw this happen to a friend of mine. One you would remember well.''

''It does not matter. Whatever the outcome of the war or Human-Weave relations, neither you nor I will be around to see them. The historians will judge. I am here to tell you there is nothing that can be done.''

''We could try,'' Caldaq insisted.

''Try what? The Humans aware of us now are. With every passing day they become more familiar with Weave technology, Weave tactics, Weave strategies, and Weave civilization. They cannot back to their homeworld be forced. There is no going back.

''Suppose you could the Council convince of your fears. What would you have them do? Forcibly all Human soldiers from Weave units expel? The Amplitur nothing better would like.''

''Nothing so extreme is required. It is only necessary to deny transportation facilities to Earth.''

''You think so? You have only lived among them, fought alongside them, known them as soldiers, whereas I have had the opportunity to continue to study them. You forget that their technological advancement was restricted by its emphasis on the military and by intertribal conflict. With the end of such conflicts they have been freed to normally develop for the first time in their history.

''They have for improvision and for improving upon existing technology a remarkable capacity which for the first time in their development they are putting to use.''

''What are you saying?'' Caldaq muttered.

''That their exposure to Weave technology has given them

knowledge enough to build their own ships. They the ability have. They no longer to their own world can be restricted.''

Caldaq sat down heavily. "Then all is lost.''

"Nothing is lost. Truly. You and I are not the only ones of the potential problem cognizant, although I am more intimately familiar with it than any other. Others alerted have been, or similar conclusions as the result of their own studies have reached. While it would be heretical to discuss it in public, I can assure you that certain select small study groups do so in private.

"As the war against the Amplitur is pursued, informed members of the nonmilitaristic species will decide how with the problem of Humankind to deal. As Humans learn from the Weave, so will the Weave learn from them. As we study them, we may even learn the secret of their biological defense against Amplitur intrusion. It would be worth retaining them as allies if for that only. Eventually they will be managed and integrated into Weave civilization.''

" 'Managed'?'' Caldaq murmured. "That sounds very much like the approach the Amplitur would take.''

The physician was undisturbed by the commander's accusation. "We will not change Humankind in that fashion. Their independence of thought will not be restricted. Were we to attempt to do so, we would indeed be like the Amplitur.'' Teeth clicked together. "Who knows but that they might react to us as they have to the Amplitur? No. This is more a matter of Human energy to useful channels turning.''

"If you and your friends believe you can do that, then you are unrepentant optimists.''

"Truly we can be nothing else. You fear Humans. I have more reason to do so, yet I have succeeded in coming to terms with their presence among us. I am of the potential difficulties they present aware but still wish to a basis for eventually dealing with them establish.''

Caldaq wished Jaruselka were there beside him. He missed her calming influence, her sound advice. Missed the partnership.

"We will never be able to manage them,'' he said quietly. "All sentients develop and mature through mutual cooperation. Humans are the only species to have done so as the result of continual conflict. Their genetic makeup as well as their society is warped.''

"Truly we can help to change that,'' said the physician. "Any people helped can be.''

"Are you so certain?'' Caldaq asked her.

"The S'van can manipulate us while we unaware of it remain. I have seen them do the same to Humans. S'van suggestion is not the same as Amplitur manipulation.

"Humankind is its destiny fulfilling, doing what it was designed to do. For that they are to be pitied more than feared. My people do not socialize with them. Nor do the S'van, or the Wais, or any other. They are at once brilliant and barbaric, but they are not hopeless. In time they can be civilized.''

"If not, it will be our fault,'' Caldaq pointed out. "We have asked them to fight, to give free rein to the very instincts they have been struggling throughout their history to suppress.''

"At least they cannot now themselves exterminate. By providing them with a common enemy we have given them unity as a species, something they might otherwise never have achieved. Did you know that they were their own planet destroying? They were dying in the grip of their own perverted instincts. They spoke contradictory nonsense like 'fighting for peace.' We have them the outlet they needed given. We have given them time. And in time we will give them civilization.

"But not now. For now we need them as they are, as they have been. Dangerous. Truly.''

"It is a terrible responsibility.'' Caldaq gazed into the distance. "I had the opportunity to observe Humans at peace, verging on true civilization.''

The physician dismissed the comment. "What you saw was the veneer Humans invented have to their sanity maintain. Inside they are all alike. It is something even they are beginning to admit to. As a physician I know that for a patient the first step in receiving successful treatment is to admit that one needs help. For the moment, however, we must convince them that they do not. Are you now changing your opinion of them?''

It was raining outside. From the hospital room Caldaq could see the western ocean, dark green glass beneath a troubled sky.

"No. I fear them as they are, and so it concerns me that we do not begin immediately to try to civilize them. The more we allow them to utilize their natural abilities on our behalf, the more difficult it will be to eventually change them.''

"Truly that is so. But we have no choice. We must continue upon the path we have chosen and hope that when we reach its end, Humans will continue to walk with us.'' The physician stared at the Massood's back.

"If it helps, you might an alternative future contemplate.''

Caldaq glanced tiredly back over his shoulder. "What?''

The physician spoke with all the somberness of which her kind was capable. "Consider the possibilities if the Amplitur had encountered Humankind first.''

ABOUT THE AUTHOR

Born in New York City in 1946, Alan Dean Foster was raised in Los Angeles, California. After receiving a bachelor's degree in political science and a Master of Fine Arts in motion pictures from UCLA in 1968–1969, he worked for two years as a public relations copywriter in a small Studio City, California, firm.

His writing career began in 1968 when August Derleth bought a long letter of Foster's and published it as a short story in his biannual *Arkham Collector Magazine*. Sales of short fiction to other magazines followed. His first try at a novel, *The Tar-Aiym Krang*, was published by Ballantine Books in 1972.

Foster has toured extensively around the world. Besides traveling, he enjoys classical and rock music, old films, basketball, body surfing, scuba diving, and weight lifting. He has taught screenwriting, literature, and film history at UCLA and Los Angeles City College.

Currently, he resides in Arizona.